David A. Gemmell's firs ... published in 1984 and went on to become a classic. His most recent Drenai and Rigante novels are available as Corgi paperbacks; all are *Sunday Times* bestsellers.

Lord of the Silver Bow and *Shield of Thunder* are the first two in a trilogy of novels encompassing the Trojan War. The final novel, *Fall of Kings*, will be available in hardcover in September 2007.

Widely regarded as the finest writer of heroic fantasy, David Gemmell lived in Sussex until his tragic death in July 2006.

DAVID GEMMELL
TROY

SHIELD OF THUNDER

CORGI BOOKS

TROY: SHIELD OF THUNDER
A CORGI BOOK: 9780552151122

Originally published in Great Britain by Bantam Press,
a division of Transworld Publishers

PRINTING HISTORY
Bantam Press edition published 2006
Corgi edition published 2007

1 3 5 7 9 10 8 6 4 2

Copyright © David A. Gemmell 2006

Set in 10/12pt Sabon by
Falcon Oast Graphic Art Ltd

Corgi Books are published by Transworld Publishers,
61–63 Uxbridge Road, London W5 5SA,
a division of The Random House Group Ltd,
in Australia by Random House Australia (Pty) Ltd,
20 Alfred Street, Milsons Point, Sydney, NSW 2061, Australia,
in New Zealand by Random House New Zealand Ltd,
18 Poland Road, Glenfield, Auckland 10, New Zealand,
in South Africa by Random House (Pty) Ltd,
Isle of Houghton, Corner of Boundary Road & Carse O'Gowrie,
Houghton 2198, South Africa,
and in India by Random House Publishers India Private Limited,
301 World Trade Tower, Hotel Intercontinental Grand Complex,
Barakhamba Lane, New Delhi 110 001, India.

Printed and bound in Great Britain by
Cox & Wyman Ltd, Reading, Berkshire.

Papers used by Transworld Publishers are natural, recyclable
products made from wood grown in sustainable forests. The
manufacturing processes conform to the environmental regulations
of the country of origin.

Shield of Thunder is dedicated with great love to Stella, for the journeys across the desert, for the waterfall at La Quinta, and for sailing the Great Green, through twenty priceless years of joy and friendship.

ACKNOWLEDGEMENTS

Grateful thanks to my editor Selina Walker, my copy-editor Nancy Webber, and to my test readers Tony Evans, Alan Fisher, Stella Gemmell, Oswald Hotz de Bar, Steve Hutt, Tim Lenton and Anne Nicholls. The description 'test readers' does not convey just how vital the role is. Throughout the creation of the *Troy* series narrative threads and characters have been developed and enhanced, and scenes cut or expanded, following comments from the 'team'. I am enormously grateful to them.

The Great Green

RHODOPE MOUNTAINS

R. Nestos • Kalliros

• Xantheia

THRAKI

• Ismaros

SAMOTHRAKI

Carpea•

IMBROS

Zeleia•

LEMNOS

Troy•

Dardanos

Mt. Olympos•

Mt. Ida▲

• Thebe under
Plakos

THESSALY

LESBOS

EUBOEA

KIOS

Thebes• Aulis•

ITHKA

• Athens

KARIA

KEPHALLENIA

Mykene•

Argos•

• Miletos

Pylos•

• Sparta

KOS

RHODOS

KYTHERA

THERA

KRETOS

• Knossos

Phaistos•

Beneath the Shield of Thunder waits
The Eagle Child, on shadow wings,
To soar above all city gates,
Till end of days, and fall of kings

The prophecy of Melite

PROLOGUE

A COLD WIND BLEW DOWN FROM THE SNOW-COVERED mountains, hissing through the narrow streets of Thebe Under Plakos. Snow was falling in icy flurries from the dark clouds massing over the city. Few citizens were on the streets that night, and even the guards at the palace huddled close to the gate, their heavy woollen cloaks drawn tightly around them.

Inside the palace there was an air of increasing panic as the pain-filled day drifted into a night of screams and anguish. People gathered, silent and fearful, in the cold corridors. Every now and again there came a flurry of activity, as servants ran from the queen's bedchamber to fetch bowls of water, or fresh cloths.

Close to midnight the hooting of an owl could be heard, and the waiting courtiers glanced at one another. Owls were birds of ill omen. All knew that.

The cries of pain began to fade to soft moans, the queen's strength all but gone. The end was close. There would be no joyous birth, only death and mourning.

The Trojan ambassador, Heraklitos, tried to maintain an air of heavy concern. It was not easy, for he had not met Queen Olektra and cared nothing if she lived or died. And despite his ambassador's robes of white wool, and the long sheepskin cloak, he was cold, his feet numb. He closed his eyes and tried to warm himself with thoughts of the riches he would earn from this journey.

His mission in Thebe Under Plakos had been twofold: to secure the trade routes, and to deliver gifts from Troy's young king, Priam, thus establishing a treaty of friendship between the neighbouring cities. Troy was growing fast under Priam's inspirational leadership, and Heraklitos – like many others – was growing wealthier by the day. However, many of the most valuable trade goods – perfumes, spices, and cloths embroidered with glittering gold thread – had to be carried through war-torn eastern lands, ravaged by roving bands of brigands or deserters. Outlaw chiefs held the high passes, and demanded taxes from caravans travelling through. Priam's soldiers had cleared many of the routes close to Troy, but to the south, in Thebe, beneath the shadow of mighty Mount Ida, it was King Ektion who ruled. Heraklitos had been sent to encourage the king to gather more troops and campaign against the brigands. The mission had been succesful. Even now Ektion was raiding deep into the mountains, destroying bandit towns and clearing the trade routes. All that remained was for Heraklitos to offer congratulations on the birth of the new babe, and then he could journey back to his palace in Troy. He had been away too long already, and there were many pressing matters awaiting him.

The queen had gone into labour late yesterday, and Heraklitos had ordered his servants to be ready to depart early this morning. Yet here he was, at midnight on the second day, standing in a draughty corridor. Not only had the promised babe failed to arrive, but Heraklitos could tell from the fearful looks on the faces of the people around him that a tragedy was looming. Priests of Asklepios, the god of healing, had been called for, and they had scurried into the royal apartments, to aid the three midwives already in attendance. A bull was being sacrificed in the courtyard below.

Heraklitos had no choice but to stand and wait. To leave would be seen as a sign of disrespect. It was most annoying, for when the unfortunate woman died the city would go into mourning, and Heraklitos would be obliged to wait days for the funeral.

He saw a hawk-faced old woman staring at him. 'A sad, sad day,' he said solemnly, trying to muster a tone of infinite sorrow. He had not seen her arrive, but she was standing now, leaning on a carved staff, her expression set, her eyes dark and fierce, her white hair uncombed and framing her head like a lion's mane. She was wearing a long grey robe, an owl embroidered upon the breast with silver thread. A priestess of Athene then, he thought.

'The child will not die,' she said, 'for she has been blessed by the goddess. Though the queen will, if these fools do not call upon me.'

A thin, round-shouldered priest left the queen's bed-chamber. He saw the hard-faced woman and dipped his head in greeting. 'I fear the end is close, Great Sister,' he said. 'The child is breeched.'

'Then bring me to her, idiot.'

Heraklitos saw the priest redden, but he stepped back, beckoning the woman forward, and they returned to the bedchamber. A tough old crow, thought Heraklitos. Then he recalled that the priestess had spoken of the babe as *she*. A seeress then – or believed she was. If she was right, then the wait was even more galling. Who cared if a girl child lived or died? Or even a boy, he thought glumly, since King Ektion already had two strong young sons.

The night wore on and Heraklitos, and some twenty others, waited for the inevitable sound of wailing that would herald the queen's death. But then, just as the dawn broke, there came the birth cry of a newborn. The sound, so full of life, brought to the jaded ambassador a sudden sense of joy, an uplift to the spirit he would not have thought possible.

A short while later the courtiers, Heraklitos among them, were led into the queen's apartments to greet the new arrival.

The babe had been laid in a crib at the bedside, and the queen, looking pale and exhausted, was resting against embroidered cushions, a blanket across her lower body. There was a great deal of blood upon the bed. Heraklitos and the others gathered around silently, holding their hands over their hearts in a gesture of respect. The queen did not speak, but the priestess of Athene, her hands caked with drying blood, lifted the infant from the crib. It gave a soft, gurgling cry.

Heraklitos saw what at first appeared to be a smear of blood upon the child's head, close to the crown. Then he realized it was a birthmark, almost perfectly round, like a shield, but with a jagged white line of skin running through it. 'As I prophesied, it is a girl,' said the priestess. 'She has been blessed by Athene. And here is the proof,' she added, tracing her fingers across the birthmark. 'Can you all see it? It is Athene's shield – the Shield of Thunder.'

'What will be her name, highness?' asked one of the courtiers.

The queen stirred. 'Paleste,' she whispered.

The following day Heraklitos left on the long journey back to Troy, bearing news of the birth of the Princess Paleste, and the more important tidings of a treaty between the two cities. He was not, therefore, present when King Ektion returned and went to his wife's bedside. The king, still in battle armour, leaned over the crib and reached inside. A tiny hand came up towards his. Extending a finger, the king laughed as the babe gripped it tightly. 'She has the strength of a man,' he said. 'We shall name her Andromache.'

'I have given her the name Paleste,' said his wife.

The king leaned down and kissed her. 'There will be more children, if the gods will it. The name Paleste can wait.'

For Heraklitos the next nineteen years proved rich and fulfilling. He journeyed south to Egypte, east to the centre of the Hittite empire, and northwest through Thraki and Thessaly and down to Sparta. All the while he grew richer. Two wives had borne him five sons and four daughters between them, and he had been blessed by the gods with good health. His wealth, like that of Troy, had grown steadily.

But now his luck had run out. It had begun with a steadily increasing pain in his lower back, and a hacking, dry cough that would not leave him, even in the warmth of the summer sun. His flesh had melted away, and he knew that the Dark Road was approaching. He struggled on, still seeking to serve his lord, and was called one night to the royal apartments, where King Priam and his wife Hekabe had been consulting a seer. Heraklitos did not know what the man had prophesied, but the queen, a fierce and ruthless woman, seemed in a high state of tension.

'Greetings, Heraklitos,' she said, without any reference to his weakness, or concern for his health. 'Some years back you were in Thebe Under Plakos. You talked of a child born there.'

'Yes, my queen.'

'Tell me again.'

So Heraklitos told the tale of the babe and the priestess. 'You saw the Shield of Thunder?' asked Hekabe.

'I did, my queen, red and round with a white streak of lightning through the centre.'

'And the child's name?'

The question took the dying man by surprise. He had not thought of that day in years. He rubbed at his eyes, and saw again that cold corridor, and the lion-haired priestess, and the pale, exhausted queen. Then it came to him.

'Paleste, highness.'

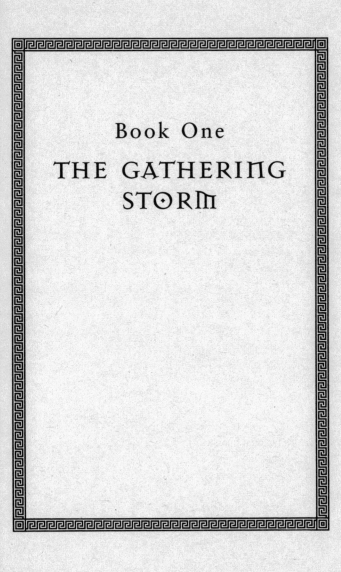

Book One

THE GATHERING STORM

I

A black wind rising

PENELOPE, QUEEN OF ITHAKA, UNDERSTOOD THE NATURE of dreams, and the portents and omens which dogged men's lives. So she sat on the beach, a gold-embroidered shawl round her slender shoulders, and glanced at the sky from time to time watching for passing birds, and hoping for a better omen. Five swallows would predict a safe journey for Odysseus, two swans good fortune; an eagle would indicate a victory – or, for Odysseus, a trading success. But the skies were clear. A light wind sprang from the north. The weather was perfect for sailing.

The old galley had been repaired, debarnacled and recaulked ready for spring, but new timbers and a coat of fresh paint could not conceal her age, which showed in every line as she lay half in and half out of the shallow water.

'Build a new ship, Ugly One,' she had told her husband countless times. 'This one is old and tired and will be your downfall.' They had argued about it for years. But in this she had no power to sway him. He was not by nature a sentimental man; his affable demeanour hid a core of bronze and horn, yet she knew he would never replace the old ship he had named after her.

Penelope sighed, a gentle sadness settling over her. I am that ship, she realized. I am getting old. There is grey in my hair, and the time is swift passing. But more significant than the fading of her chestnut hair, or the increasing lines upon her face, the monthly flows of blood that indicated youth and fecundity were becoming less frequent. Soon she would be past child-bearing age, and there would be no new sons for Odysseus. The sadness deepened into sorrow as she remembered pale Laertes, and the fever that had melted away his flesh.

On the beach Odysseus was striding angrily round the galley, his face red, arms gesturing, bellowing at his crew, who hurried to load the cargo. There was a sorrow among the men too; she could feel it as she watched them. A few days previously their comrade Portheos, whom they called Portheos the Pig, a fat, jovial and popular young man who had sailed with the *Penelope* for many summers, had died. His young wife, pregnant with their fourth child, had awoken at dawn to find Portheos dead on their pallet bed beside her.

On the *Penelope* two crewmen were hauling on a heavy bale of brushwood, used for packing cargo in the hold. Suddenly one lost his grip and stumbled, and the other was catapulted into the sea after the stack of wood. Odysseus swore colourfully and turned to his wife, raising his arms in a gesture of despair.

Penelope smiled, her spirits lifting as she watched him. He was always happiest when about to leave for foreign shores. Throughout the spring and summer he would roam the Great Green, buying and selling, telling his stories, meeting kings and pirates and beggars.

'I'll miss you, lady,' he had told her the previous night as she lay in his arms, her fingers gently curling into the red-grey hair of his chest. She made no reply. She knew when he would remember her – at each night's fall, when the dangers of the day had been passed, he would think of her and miss her, a little.

'I will think of you every day,' he added. Still she said nothing. 'The pain of your absence will be a constant dagger wound in my heart.'

She smiled against his chest and she knew he felt the smile.

'Don't mock me, woman,' he said fondly. 'You know me too well.'

On the beach in the dawn light she watched him as he stomped across the sand to speak to Nestor, king of Pylos and her kinsman. The contrast between the two men was remarkable. Odysseus, barrel-chested, loud and angry, attacked each day as if it were a mortal enemy. Nestor, slim, grey and stooped, was a small point of calm in the storm of activity on the beach. Although Nestor was only ten years older than her husband, he had the demeanour of an ancient; Odysseus was like an excited child. She loved him, and her eyes pricked with unaccustomed tears for the journeys and perils he faced.

He had only returned to her a few days before,

accompanied by Nestor, after a reluctant voyage to Sparta at the request of Agamemnon, king of Mykene.

'Agamemnon is intent on revenge,' old Nestor had said, sitting in the *megaron* late in the evening, a cup of wine comfortably full in his grip, one of his hounds at his feet. 'The meeting at Sparta was a failure for him, yet he will not be diverted from his path.'

'The man is obsessed,' said Odysseus. 'He summoned the kings of the west and talked of alliance and peace. Yet all the while he dreams of a war with Troy – a war he can only fight if we all join with him.' Penelope heard the anger in his voice.

'Why would any join him?' she asked. 'His hatred for Troy is a private matter.'

Nestor shook his head. 'There are no private matters for the Mykene king. His ego is colossal. What touches Agamemnon touches the world.' He leaned forward. 'Everyone knows he is angry at being thwarted by Helikaon and the traitor Argurios.'

'The *traitor* Argurios, is it?' snapped Odysseus. 'Interesting what makes a man a traitor, is it not? A fine warrior, a man who had faithfully served Mykene all his life, was declared outlaw and stripped of his land, possessions and good name. Then his king tried to have him killed. *Treacherously*, he fought for his life and that of the woman he loved.'

Nestor nodded. 'Yes, yes, kinsman. He was a fine warrior. Did you ever meet him?' Penelope knew he was seeking to defuse Odysseus' anger. She masked a smile. No-one with any sense wanted to see Odysseus in a fury.

'Aye, he sailed with me to Troy,' replied Odysseus.

'An unpleasant man. But every one of those Mykene would have been slaughtered at Priam's palace had it not been for Argurios.'

'As it was they were slaughtered when they returned home,' Penelope added quietly.

'It was called the Night of the Lion's Justice,' said Nestor. 'Just two escaped, and they were declared outlaw.'

'And this is the king you wish to support in a war?' asked Odysseus, swigging mightily on his wine cup. 'A man who sends valiant warriors to fight his battles, and then murders them when they fail?'

'I have not yet offered ships or men to Agamemnon.' The old man stared into his wine cup. Penelope knew that Nestor had not argued against a war, but had kept his own counsel among the kings gathered at Sparta. 'However, Agamemnon's ambitions affect everyone,' he said at last. 'With him you are either friend or foe. Which are you, Odysseus?'

'Neither. All men know I am neutral.'

'Easy to be neutral when you have secret supplies of wealth,' said Nestor. 'But Pylos depends on trading its flax up into Argos and the north. Agamemnon controls the trade routes. To go against him would be ruinous.' He glanced at Odysseus, and his eyes narrowed. 'So tell me, Odysseus, where are these Seven Hills that are making you rich?'

Penelope felt the tension in the room rise, and she glanced at Odysseus.

'On the edge of the world,' Odysseus replied, 'and guarded by one-eyed giants.'

Had Nestor not been drinking heavily he would have noticed the harsh edge in Odysseus' reply. Penelope took a deep breath, preparing herself to intervene.

'I would have thought, *kinsman*, that you might have shared your good fortune with others of your blood, rather than a foreigner,' said Nestor.

'And I would have,' said Odysseus, 'save that the foreigner you speak of discovered the Seven Hills, and opened up the trade route. It is not for me to share his secrets.'

'Only his gold,' snapped Nestor.

Odysseus hurled his wine cup across the room. 'You insult me in my own palace?' he roared. 'We had to fight for the Seven Hills, against brigands and pirates, and painted tribesmen. That gold was hard won.'

The angry atmosphere lay thick in the *megaron*, and Penelope forced a smile. 'Come, kinsmen. You sail for Troy tomorrow for the wedding feast and Games. Do not let this night end with harsh words.'

The two men looked at each other. Then Nestor sighed. 'Forgive me, old friend. My words were ill advised.'

'It is forgotten,' said Odysseus, gesturing at a servant to bring him another cup of wine.

Penelope heard the lie in the words and knew that Odysseus was still angry. 'At least in Troy you will be able to forget Agamemnon for a while,' she said, seeking to change the subject.

'The western kings are *all* invited to see Hektor wed to Andromache,' said Odysseus glumly.

'But Agamemnon will not be there, surely?'

'I think he will, my love. Sly Priam will use the opportunity to bend some of the kings to his will. He will offer them gold and friendship. Agamemnon cannot afford *not* to go. He will be there.'

'Is he invited? After the Mykene attack on Troy?'

Odysseus grinned, and imitated the pompous tones of the Mykene king. 'I am saddened' – he spread his hands regretfully – 'by the treacherous attack by rogue elements of the Mykene forces on our brother King Priam. The king's justice has been meted out to the outlaws.'

'The man is a serpent,' Nestor admitted.

'Will your sons compete in the Games?' Penelope asked him.

'Yes, they are both fine athletes. Antilochos will do well in the javelin, and Thrasymedes will beat any man in the archery tourney,' he added, with a wink.

'There'll be a green moon in the sky that day,' muttered Odysseus. 'On my worst day I could spit an arrow further than he could shoot one.'

Nestor laughed. 'How coy you are with your wife in the room. The last time I heard you brag about your skills you said you could fart an arrow further.'

'That too,' said Odysseus, reddening. Penelope had been relieved to see good humour restored.

On the beach the *Penelope* was finally fully loaded, and the crew were straining on ropes in the effort to get the old ship refloated. The two sons of Nestor were there, both waist-deep, their backs against the timbers of the hull, pushing her out into deeper water.

The queen of Ithaka stood and brushed pebbles from

her dress of yellow linen, and advanced down the beach to say farewell to her king. He stood with his first mate Bias the Black, dark-skinned and grizzled, the son of a Nubian mother and an Ithakan sire. Beside him was a massively muscled, blond sailor named Leukon, who was becoming a fistfighter of some renown. Leukon and Bias bowed as she approached, then moved off.

Penelope sighed. 'And here we are again, my love, as always,' she said, 'making our farewells.'

'We are like the seasons,' he replied. 'Ever constant in our actions.'

Reaching out, she took his hand. 'And yet this time is different, my king. You know it too. I fear you will have hard choices to make. Do not make bull-headed decisions you will regret afterwards and cannot change. Do not take these men into a war, Odysseus.'

'I have no wish for war, my love.' He smiled, and she knew he meant it, but her heart was heavy with foreboding. For all his strength, his courage, and his wisdom, the man she loved had one great weakness. He was like an old warhorse, canny and cautious, but at the touch of the whip he would ride into fire. For Odysseus that whip was pride.

He kissed both her hands then turned and stomped down the beach and into the sea. The water was chest-high before he grabbed a rope and hauled himself up on board. Instantly the rowers took up a beat and the old ship started to glide away. She saw him wave his arm, silhouetted against the rising sun.

She had not told him of the gulls. He would only

scoff. Seagulls were stupid birds, he would say, they have no place in prophecy.

But she had dreamed of a colossal flock of gulls that blotted out the sun, like a black wind rising, turning the midday sky to night.

And that wind brought death and the end of worlds.

The young warrior Kalliades sat in the mouth of the cave, a dark cloak wrapped round his slim frame, his sword heavy in his hand. He scanned the arid hillside and the fields beyond. There was no-one in sight. Glancing back into the gloom of the cave he saw the injured woman lying on her side, her knees drawn up, the red cloak of Banokles covering her. She seemed to be sleeping.

Bright moonlight speared through a break in the clouds. Kalliades could see her more clearly now. Her yellow hair was long, and her pale face was bruised and swollen, smeared with drying blood.

The night breeze was cold and Kalliades shivered. From the high cave he could see the distant sea, reflected stars glittering on the water. So far from home, he thought.

The vivid red scar on his right cheek was itching and he idly scratched it. The last of many wounds. In the quiet of the night he remembered the battles and the skirmishes that had seen sword and dagger blades pierce his flesh. Arrows and spears had cut him. Stones shot from slings had dazed him. A blow to the left shoulder from a club had left him with a joint that ached in the winter rains. At twenty-five he was a ten-year veteran, and carried the scars to prove it.

'I'm going to light a fire,' his huge comrade said, moving out of the shadows. In the moonlight Banokles' blond hair and full beard shone like silver. Blood had spattered over his breastplate, dark spots on the bright bronze discs fastened to the heavy leather undershirt.

Kalliades turned towards the powerful warrior. 'A fire will be seen,' he said quietly. 'They will come for us.'

'They will come for us anyway. Might as well be now, while I'm still angry.'

'You have no reason to be angry at them,' Kalliades pointed out wearily.

'I'm not. I'm angry with *you*. The woman meant nothing to us.'

'I know.'

'And it's not as if we saved her for long. There's no way off this island. We'll likely be dead by noon tomorrow.'

'I know that too.'

Banokles said nothing more for a while. He moved alongside Kalliades and glared out at the night. 'I thought you were going to light a fire,' said Kalliades.

'Don't have the patience,' grumbled Banokles, scratching at his thick beard. 'Always end up cutting my fingers on the flints.' He shivered. 'Cold for this time of year,' he added.

'You wouldn't be so cold if you hadn't covered the woman who means nothing to us with your cloak. Go and gather some dead wood. I'll start the fire.' Kalliades moved away from the cave mouth, took some dried bark from the pouch at his side, and shredded it. Then with smooth strokes he struck flint stones together, sending showers of sparks into the bark. It took some time, but finally a tiny plume of smoke showed. Dropping to his belly Kalliades blew gentle breaths over the tinder. A flame sprang up. Banokles returned, dropping a pile of sticks and branches to the ground.

'See anything?' Kalliades asked him.

'No. They'll come after sunrise, I expect.'

The two young men sat in silence for a while, enjoying the warmth from the small fire.

'So,' said Banokles at last, 'are you going to tell me why we killed four of our comrades?'

'They weren't our comrades. We were just sailing with them.'

'You know what I mean.'

'They were going to kill her, Banokles.'

'I know that too. I was there. What did that have to do with us?'

Kalliades did not reply, but he glanced once more at the sleeping woman.

He had first seen her only yesterday piloting a small sailboat, her fair hair gold in the sunlight, and tied back from her face. She was dressed in a white, knee-length tunic, with a belt embroidered with gold wire. The sun had been low in the sky, a light breeze propelling her craft towards the islands. She had seemed oblivious of her danger as the two pirate ships closed on her. Then the first of the ships had cut across her bow. Too late she tried to avoid capture, tugging at the sail rope, seeking to alter course and make a run for the beach. Kalliades had watched her from the deck of the second ship. There was no panic in her. But the little boat could not outrun galleys manned by skilled oarsmen. The first ship had closed in, grappling lines hurled over the side, the bronze hooks biting into the timbers of her sailboat. Several pirates clambered over the side of the ship and jumped down into her craft. The woman tried to fight them, but they overpowered her, blows raining down on her body.

'Probably a runaway,' Banokles had remarked, as the two of them watched the semi-conscious woman being hauled to the deck of the first ship. From where they stood, on the deck of the second vessel, both men could see what followed. The crew gathered around her, tearing off her white tunic, and ripping away the expensive belt. Kalliades had turned away in disgust.

The ships had beached that night on Lion's Head Isle, on the sea route to Kios. The woman had been dragged across the beach and into a small stand of trees by the captain of the second ship, a burly Kretan with a shaved head. She had seemed docile then, her spirit apparently broken. It had been a ruse. As the captain raped her, she had somehow managed to pull his dagger from its sheath, and rip the blade across his throat. No-one saw it, and it was some time before his body was found.

The furious crew had set off to search for her. Kalliades and Banokles had wandered away with a jug of wine. They had found a grove of olive trees, and had sat quietly drinking.

'Arelos was not a happy man,' Banokles had

observed. Kalliades had said nothing. Arelos was the captain of the first ship, and kinsman to the man slain by the runaway. He had built a reputation for savagery and swordcraft, and was feared along the southern coasts. Given any other choice Kalliades would never have sailed with him, but he and Banokles were hunted men. To stay in Mykene would have meant torture and death. The ships of Arelos had offered them a means of escape.

'You are very quiet tonight. What is bothering you?' Banokles had continued, as they sat in the quiet of the grove.

'We need to quit this crew,' said Kalliades. 'Apart from Sekundos, and maybe a couple of others, they are scum. It offends me to be in their company.'

'You want to wait until we are further east?'

'No. We'll leave tomorrow. Other ships will beach here. We'll find a captain who will take us on. Then we'll make our way to Lykia. Plenty of mercenary posts there, protecting trade caravans from bandits, escorting rich merchants.'

'I'd like to be rich,' said Banokles. 'I could buy a slave girl.'

'If you were rich you could buy a hundred slave girls.'

'Not sure I could handle a hundred. Five maybe.' He chuckled. 'Yes, five would be good. Five plump, dark-haired girls. With big eyes.' Banokles drank some more, then belched. 'Ah, I can feel the spirit of Dionysus seeping into my bones. I wish one of those plump girls was here now.'

Kalliades had laughed. 'Your mind is always occupied by either drink or sex. Does nothing else interest you?'

'Food. A good meal, a jug of wine, followed by a plump woman squealing beneath me.'

'With your weight on her no wonder she'd be squealing.'

Banokles had laughed. 'That's not why they squeal. Women adore me because I am handsome and strong and hung like a horse.'

'You neglect to mention that you always pay them.'

'Of course I pay them. Just as I pay for my wine and my food. What point are you trying to make?'

'Obviously a poor one.'

Around midnight, as they were preparing to sleep, they heard shouts. Then the woman had staggered into the grove, chased by five crewmen. Already weak from the ugly events of the day, she had stumbled, falling to the ground close to where Kalliades was sitting. Her white tunic was ripped and filthy, and stained with blood. A crewman named Baros ran in, a wickedly curved knife in his hand. He was lean and tall, with close-set dark eyes. He liked to be called Baros the Killer. 'I'm going to gut you like a fish,' he snarled.

She had looked up at Kalliades then, her face pale in the moonlight, her expression one of exhausted desperation and fear. It was an expression he had seen before, one which had haunted him since childhood. The memory speared through him, and he saw again the flames, and heard the pitiful screams.

Surging to his feet, he stood between the man and his victim. 'Put the knife away,' he ordered.

The move surprised the crewman. 'She's for death,' he said. 'Arelos ordered it.' He stepped towards Kalliades. 'Do not seek to come between me and my prey. I have slain men from every land round the Great Green. You want your blood spilled here, your guts laid out on the grass?'

Kalliades' short sword hissed from its scabbard. 'There is no need for anyone to die,' he said softly. 'But I'll not allow the woman to be hurt further.'

Baros shook his head. 'I told Arelos he should have cut your throats and taken your armour. You just can't trust a Mykene.' He sheathed his knife, and stepped back, drawing his own sword. 'Now you are in for a lesson. I have fought more duels than any man of the crew.'

'It is not a large crew,' Kalliades had pointed out.

Baros leapt forward with surprising speed. Kalliades parried the thrust, then stepped in, hammering his elbow into the man's face. Baros fell back. 'Kill him!' he screamed. The other four surged forward. Kalliades killed the first, and drunken Banokles hurled himself at the others. Baros darted in again, but this time Kalliades was ready. He blocked the thrust, rolled his wrist, and sent a riposte that opened Baros' throat. Banokles had killed one man, and was grappling with another. Kalliades ran to his aid, just as the fifth man slashed his sword towards Banokles' face. Banokles saw the blow coming, and swung the man he was fighting to meet it. The blade clove into his assailant's neck.

As Kalliades charged in, the surviving crewman turned and ran away into the night.

Sitting now beside the crackling fire in the cave, he glanced at Banokles. 'I am sorry to have brought you to this, my friend. You deserved better.'

Banokles took a deep breath, then let it out slowly. 'You are a strange one, Kalliades,' he said, shaking his head. 'But life with you is never dull.' He yawned. 'If I am going to kill sixty men tomorrow I'll need some rest.'

'They won't all come. Some will be left with the ships. Others will be whoring. Probably no more than ten or fifteen.'

'Oh, I'll rest easier knowing that.' Loosening the straps of his battered breastplate Banokles lifted it clear and dropped it to the ground. 'Never could sleep properly in armour,' he said, then stretched himself out beside the fire. Within moments his breathing had deepened.

Kalliades added wood to the fire, then returned to the cave mouth. A cool breeze was blowing, and the sky was now ablaze with stars. Banokles was right. There was no way off this island, and tomorrow the pirate crew would come hunting them. He sat lost in thought for some time, then heard a stealthy movement behind him. Rising swiftly he turned – to see the blood-smeared woman advancing on him, a fist-sized stone in her hand. Her bright blue eyes shone with hatred.

'You won't need that,' he said, backing away. 'You are in no danger tonight.'

'You lie!' she said, her voice harsh, and trembling with anger. Kalliades drew his dagger and saw her tense. Casually he tossed the blade to the floor at her feet.

'I do not lie. Take the weapon. Tomorrow you will need it, for they will be coming for us.'

The woman crouched down and tried to pick up the fallen dagger. But she lost her balance and half fell. Kalliades remained where he was. 'You need to rest,' he said.

'I remember you now,' she told him. 'You and your friend fought the men who were attacking me. Why?'

'Oh, Great Zeus, let him answer that question,' said Banokles sleepily, from his place by the fire. Sweeping up the dagger the woman tried to turn to face him, but stumbled again.

'Blows to the head can do that,' said Banokles, getting up and wandering over to join them. 'You should sit down.'

She stared hard at Kalliades. 'I saw you from my boat,' she said. 'You were on the second ship. You saw them cut across my bows and throw grappling lines. You watched as they dragged me aboard.'

'Yes. We were sailing with them.'

'You are pirates.'

'We are what we are,' conceded Kalliades.

'I was to be passed to your ship tomorrow. They told me that while they were raping me.'

'It is not *my* ship. I did not give the order to attack you. Nor did I or my comrade take part in what followed. No man could blame you for your anger, but do not direct it at the men who saved you.'

'Now let us hope someone saves *us*,' added Banokles.

'What do you mean?' the woman demanded.

'We are on a small island,' replied Banokles. 'We

have no gold, and no ship. Angry men will come looking for us tomorrow. Now, we are great warriors,
Kalliades and I. None better. Well . . . not now Argurios
is dead. Between us I reckon we could survive against
seven or eight warriors. There are around sixty fighting
men in the pirate crews. And not one soft-bellied puker
among them.'

'You have no plan of escape?'

'Oh, I do not make plans, woman. I drink, I whore,
I fight. Kalliades makes plans.'

'Then you are both fools,' she said. 'You have
brought about your doom.'

'Where I come from slaves are respectful,' said
Banokles, an edge of anger in his voice.

'I am no man's slave!'

'Have the blows to your head knocked all sense from
you? Your craft was taken at sea. It carried no banner,
and no safe conduct. You were captured and now the
pirates own you. Therefore, you are a slave according
to the laws of gods and men.'

'Then I piss on the laws of gods and men!'

'Be calm, both of you!' ordered Kalliades. 'Where
were you sailing to?' he asked her.

'I was heading for Kios.'

'You have family there?'

'No. I had some wealth on the boat, gems and
trinkets of gold. I was hoping to find passage on a ship
to Troy. The pirates took everything. And more.' She
rubbed at her face, scrubbing away at the dried blood.

'There is a stream over there,' said Kalliades. 'You
could wash your face.'

40

The woman hesitated. 'Then I am not your prisoner?' she asked, at last.

'No. You are free to do as you please.'

She stared hard at Kalliades, then at Banokles. 'And you did not help me in order to make me your slave, or to sell me to others?'

'No,' Kalliades told her.

She seemed to relax then, but continued to hold the dagger in a tight fist. 'If what you say is true I should . . . thank you both,' she said, struggling with the words.

'Oh, don't thank me,' said Banokles. 'I would have let you die.'

II

The Sword of Argurios

KALLIADES DOZED FOR A WHILE IN THE CAVE MOUTH, HIS head resting against the rock wall. Banokles was snoring loudly, and occasionally muttering in his sleep.

In the pre-dawn Kalliades left the cave and walked to the stream. Kneeling by the bank he splashed his face, then ran his wet fingers through his close-cropped black hair.

He saw the woman leave the cave. She too wandered down to the stream. Tall and slender, she walked with her head high, her movements graceful, like a Kretan dancer. She was not a runaway slave, Kalliades knew. Slaves learned to walk with their heads down, their posture submissive. He did not speak, but watched her as she washed the dried blood from her face and arms. Her face was still swollen, and there were bruises round her eyes. Even without the swelling she would not be pretty, he thought. Her face was strong and angular, her brows thick, her nose too prominent. It was a stern face and one which he guessed was a stranger to laughter, even in better times.

When she had cleaned herself she lifted the dagger. For a heartbeat Kalliades thought she was going to cut her own throat. Then she grabbed a length of her blond hair and sawed the dagger through it. The warrior sat silently as she continued to hack at her hair, tossing handfuls to the rocks. Kalliades was mystified. There was no expression on her face, no anger showing. When she had finished she leaned forward and rubbed her hands across her scalp, shaking loose hairs from her head.

Finally she stepped from the stream and sat down a little way from him. 'Aiding me was not wise,' she said.

'I am not a wise man.'

The sky began to lighten, and from where they sat they could see fields covered with thousands of blue flowers. The woman stared at them, and Kalliades saw her expression soften. 'It is as if the colour of the sky has leached to the earth,' she said softly. 'Who would have thought that such beautiful plants could grow in such an arid place? Do you know what they are?'

'They are flax,' he said. 'The linen of your tunic came from such plants.'

'How is it turned to cloth?' she asked. Kalliades stared out over the flax fields, remembering the days of his childhood, when he and his little sisters worked the fields of King Nestor, tearing the plants up by the roots, removing the seeds that would be used for medicinal oils or the sealing of timbers, placing the stems in the running water of the stream to ret. 'Do you know?' she prompted him.

'Yes, I know.' And he told her of the back-breaking labour of children and women gathering the plants, retting the stems, then, once retted and left to dry, beating them with wooden hammers. Then the children would sit in the hot sunshine, scraping the stems, removing the last of the wood. After that came the hackling, the exposed fibres being drawn again and again through ever finer combs. Even as he told her of the process Kalliades found himself wondering at the resilience of women. Despite all she had been through, and what would probably lie ahead, she seemed fascinated by this ancient skill. Then he looked into her pale eyes, and saw that the interest was merely superficial. Beneath it there was tension and fear. They sat in silence for a while. Then he glanced at her and their eyes met. 'We will stand to the death to prevent them from taking you again. On this you have my oath.'

The woman did not reply, and Kalliades knew she did not believe him. Why should she, he wondered?

As he spoke Banokles came strolling from the cave, halted at a nearby tree and raised his tunic. Then he began to urinate with rare gusto, stepping back and aiming the jet of water as high up the trunk as possible. 'What is he doing?' asked the woman.

'He is very proud of the fact that not a man he ever met could piss as high as he can.'

'Why would they want to?'

Kalliades laughed. 'You have obviously not spent long in the company of men.' He cursed inwardly as her expression hardened. 'A stupid remark,' he said swiftly. 'I apologize for it.'

'No need,' she said, forcing a smile. 'And I will not be broken by what happened. It is not the first time I have been raped. I tell you this, though: to be raped by strangers is less vile than to be abused by those you have trusted and loved.' Taking a deep breath, she transferred her gaze back to the fields of blue flowers.

'What is your name?'

'When I was a child, they called me Piria. That is what I will use today.'

Banokles walked over to where they sat and slumped down beside Kalliades. He looked at the woman. 'That's an ugly haircut,' he said. 'Did you have lice?' Piria ignored him and looked away. Banokles turned his attention to Kalliades. 'I'm hungry enough to chew bark off a tree. What say we walk down into the settlement, kill every cowson who comes against us, and find something to eat?'

'I can see why you are not the one who makes plans,' said Piria.

Banokles scowled at her. 'With a tongue like that you'll never find a husband,' he said.

'May those words float to the ears of the Great Goddess,' she said bitterly. 'Let Hera make them true!'

Kalliades walked away from them, and stood by a twisted tree. From here he could see down over the flax fields to the distant settlement. People were already moving, women and youngsters preparing to work the fields. There was no sign yet of the pirate crew. Behind him he could hear Banokles and the woman bickering.

Troy was where it all went wrong, he decided. Before that doomed enterprise he had been considered a fine warrior and a future captain of men. And he had been proud to be selected for the raid on the city. Only the elite had been considered.

It should have been a resounding success, with plunder for all. Hektor, the great Trojan warrior, had been slain in battle, and a rebellious Trojan force would attack the palace, killing King Priam and his other sons. Mykene warriors would follow them in, finishing off any loyal soldiers. The new ruler, his allegiance pledged to the Mykene king, Agamemnon, would reward them royally.

The plan was perfect. Save for three vital elements.

First, the general Agamemnon placed in charge of the raid was a coward named Kolanos, a cruel, malevolent man who had used lies and deceit to bring about the downfall of a legendary Mykene hero. Second, that hero – the great Argurios – was, at the time of the raid, in Priam's palace, and had fought to the death to hold the last stairway. And, third, Hektor was not dead, and had returned in time to lead a force against the Mykene rear. The prospect of victory and riches had vanished. Only the certainty of defeat and death had remained.

The gutless Kolanos had tried to bargain with King Priam, offering to give all Mykene plans to the Trojan king in return for his life. Amazingly Priam had refused. To honour Argurios, who had died defending him, Priam freed the surviving Mykene, allowing them to return to their ships, along with Kolanos. He had asked only one thing in return: that he might hear Kolanos scream as the ships sailed away.

And he had screamed. The furious survivors had

hacked him to pieces even before the galleys cleared the entrance to the bay.

The journey home had been without incident, and the men, though demoralized by defeat, had been happy to be alive. Back in Mykene they were greeted with scorn, for they had failed in what they set out to achieve. Worse was to follow.

Kalliades shivered as he recalled how three of the king's men had burst into his house and sprung upon him, pinning his arms. One had yanked his head back, and then Kleitos, aide to Agamemnon and kinsman to the dead Kolanos, had stepped forward, a thin-bladed dagger in his hand.

'Did you think you were beyond the king's justice?' Kleitos had said. 'Did you think you would be forgiven for killing my brother?'

'Kolanos was a traitor who tried to sell us all. He was just like you. Brave when surrounded by soldiers and gutless when faced with battle and death. Go on, kill me. Anything would be better than smelling your stinking breath.'

Kleitos laughed then, and a cold fear had seeped into Kalliades' bones.

'Kill you? No, Kalliades. Agamemnon King has ordered you to be punished, not killed immediately. No warrior's death for you. No. I am to put out your eyes, then cut off your fingers. I will leave you your thumbs, so that you can gather a little food from beneath the tables of better men.'

Even now the memory was enough to make Kalliades sick with fear.

The thin-bladed knife had been slowly raised, the point creeping towards his left eye.

Then the door had crashed in, and Banokles had surged into the room. A huge fist had hammered into Kleitos' face, hurling him from his feet. Kalliades had torn himself clear of the startled men holding him. The fight that followed was brutal and short. Banokles broke the neck of one soldier. Kalliades had struck the second, forcing him back, giving himself time to draw his dagger and slash it across the soldier's throat.

Then Kalliades and Banokles had run from the house to the nearby paddock meadow, stolen two horses and ridden from the settlement.

Agamemnon later called it the Night of the Lion's Justice. Forty of the men who survived the attack on Troy were murdered that night; others had their right hands cut off. Kalliades and Banokles were declared fugitives, and golden gifts were offered to any who captured or slew them.

Kalliades gave a rueful smile. Now, having escaped skilled assassins, highly trained soldiers and doughty warriors seeking bounty, here they were, waiting to be killed by the scum of the sea.

Piria sat with the huge warrior, her manner outwardly calm, her heart beating wildly. It seemed to her that a frightened sparrow was caged within her breast, fluttering madly, seeking escape. She had known fear before, yet always she had conquered it with a surge of anger. Not so now.

The day before had been brutal, but she had been

filled with fury, and then desperation as the pirate crew overwhelmed her. The savage blows and the piercing pain had somehow rendered her fearless. Piria had ceased to struggle, endured the torment, and waited her moment. When it came she had felt a surging sense of triumph as she watched the pirate's blood spraying from his severed jugular, his open, astonished eyes above her. He had struggled briefly, but she had held him close, feeling his heart beat against her chest. Then the beating slowed and stopped. Finally she had pushed his body from her and slipped away into the shadows.

Only then did the real terror strike her. Lost and alone on a bleak island, she felt her courage melting away. She had run to a rocky hillside, and crouched down behind an outcrop of stone. At some point, though she had no inkling of when it started, she found she was sobbing. Her limbs trembled, and she lay down on the hard ground, her knees drawn up, her arms shielding her face, as if expecting a fresh attack. In the bleakness of her despair she heard the words of the First Priestess lashing her. 'Arrogant girl! You boast of your strength when it has never been tested. You sneer at the weakness of the women of the countryside when you have never suffered their distress. You are the daughter of a king, under whose shield you have lived protected. You are sister to a great warrior, whose sword would cut the heads from those who offended you. How dare you criticize the women of the fields, whose lives depend on the whims of violent men?'

'I am sorry,' she had whispered, her face pressed to the rock, though it was not the answer she had given when the First Priestess railed at her. She couldn't remember now exactly what she had said, but it was defiant and proud. As she lay among the rocks, all pride had fled from her.

At last, exhausted, she had slept for a little, but the pain in her abused body woke her. Just in time, for she could hear footsteps on the hillside.

And she had run for her life, coming at last, her strength gone, to a small grove of trees. There she had expected to die. Instead two men had fought for her, then helped her to a cave high in the hills.

They had not raped her, nor offered any threat, and yet her terror would not subside. She glanced at the man called Banokles. He was heavily muscled, his face brutish and coarse, his blue eyes unable to disguise the lust he felt as he stared at her. There was no defence against him, save for the wall of contempt she had created. The small dagger Kalliades had given her would be useless against such a man. He would knock it from her grip, and bear her down like the pirates on the ship.

She swallowed hard, pushing the awful memories away, though it was beyond her skill to shut out the pain of her injuries, the bruising and cuts from punches and slaps, and the piercing of her body.

The big warrior was not looking at her, but staring at the tall, slim young man standing some distance away by a twisted tree. She recalled his promise to stand by her, then anger flowed once more.

He is a *pirate*. He will betray you. All men are betrayers. Vile, lustful and devoid of pity.

Yet he had vowed to protect her.

A man's promises are like the whispers of a running stream. You can hear them, but they are meaningless sounds. That's what the First Priestess had said.

The large warrior moved to the stream, leaning forward to cup his hands in the water and drink. His movements were not graceful, like his companion's, but then, she reasoned, it must be difficult to bend in such heavy armour. The breastplate was well made, scores of bronze discs held in place by copper wire. Banokles splashed his face with water, then pushed his thick fingers through his long blond hair. Only then did Piria see that the upper part of his right ear was missing, and a long white scar extended from the remains of the lobe and down into his bearded chin. Banokles sat back and massaged his right bicep. Piria saw another scar there, vivid, red and no more than a few months old.

He saw her looking at him, and his cold blue gaze met her own. Anxious to hold him at bay with words she said: 'Spear wound?'

'No. Sword. Straight through,' he told her, swinging his body and showing her the back of his upper arm. 'Thought it had crippled me for sure, but it has healed well.'

'Must have been a powerful man, to drive a sword that deep.'

'It was,' said Banokles, pride in his voice. 'None other than Argurios. The greatest Mykene warrior of all. Sword would have gone through my throat if I hadn't slipped. As it was it got stuck in my arm.' He turned and pointed to Kalliades. 'That's it there,' he said, pointing to the bronze weapon at Kalliades' side. 'The same sword made that big scar on Kalliades' face. Very proud of that sword, Kalliades is.'

'Argurios? The man who held the bridge at Partha?'

'The very same. Great man.'

'And you were trying to kill him?'

'Of course I was trying to kill him. He was with the enemy. By the gods, I'd love to be known as the man who killed Argurios. I didn't, though. Kolanos shot him with an arrow. An arrow! Bows are the weapons of cowards. Makes my stomach churn to think of it. Argurios was the reason they won. No doubt of it. We had the stench of defeat in our nostrils, but it was a Mykene who won the battle.'

'What battle was this?'

'In Troy. Would have made me rich. All that Trojan gold. Ah, well. Always another day.' Leaning back, he scratched his groin. 'My stomach is beginning to think my throat's been cut. I hope Kalliades comes up with a plan soon.'

'A plan to defeat two pirate crews?'

'He'll think of something. He thinks a lot, does Kalliades. He's really good at it. He got us out of Mykene lands, even though they had hundreds of men searching for us. Outwitted them all. Well . . . had to kill a few too. But mostly it was Kalliades' planning.'

'Why were you being hunted?' she asked, not really caring about the answer, but anxious to keep a conversation going until Kalliades returned.

'Mostly because we lost in Troy. Agamemnon King has no love for losers. Added to which we killed his general, Kolanos. Useless goat-shagging lump of cow turd he was. Ask me, we did Agamemnon a great favour. Anyway, killing Kolanos, which seemed a good idea at the time – and enjoyable, I must say – wasn't greeted with acclaim back home. As far as they were concerned we'd gone to war, lost, and then killed our general. Which, of course, was completely true. The fact that he was a gutless goat-shagging lump of cow turd got overlooked somehow. Three days after we got back Agamemnon King ordered the killers out. A lot of good men died that night. Still, we got away.'

'Kalliades told me you saved him.'

He nodded. 'Done a lot of stupid things in my life.'

'You regret it?'

Banokles laughed. 'Sitting here on a mountain waiting to be attacked by pirates? Oh yes, I regret it. Could have had Eruthros for a sword brother. Man knew how to laugh and tell funny tales. Good companion he was. Kalliades isn't much for laughter these days. Never was, come to think of it. I reckon it's all the thinking. It's not natural to think all the time. Best to leave that to old men. They need to think. It's all they have left.'

'You said you were about to die in Troy. How did you escape?'

Banokles shrugged. 'I don't know. That's the truth of it. The Trojan king started talking, but I wasn't really listening. The arm wound was burning like fire and I was preparing myself for a fight. Then we were all being escorted from the *megaron* and back to the ships. It was something to do with Argurios being a great hero. Lost on me. Ask Kalliades. Here he comes.'

Piria was relieved to see the young warrior striding back towards them.

'Thought of a plan?' asked Banokles.

Kalliades nodded grimly. 'We'll make our way back to the settlement, kill every cowson who comes against us, and find something to eat.'

'There,' said Banokles, triumphantly. 'I told you he'd think of something.'

For Piria the short journey into the settlement was terrifying. The dark voice of her fears whispered to her that Kalliades had lied, that he would seek some truce with Arelos, the pirate chief. Why else would he be heading towards the settlement? She wanted to run, to flee once more into the hills, but her body was racked with pain, her limbs too tired, her strength all but gone. If she attempted flight either Kalliades or Banokles would catch her, and bring her down.

All that remained was to choose the manner of her death. Piria held tight to the dagger Kalliades had given her. She had seen how sharp it was, as she hacked away her hair. It would slice swiftly through her throat as the pirates advanced on her.

Neither of the men spoke to her as they approached the squalid little settlement. What a place to die, she thought. A few filthy buildings erected round a well, and farther off some twenty hastily built shacks to house the workers in the flax fields. An old dog stirred on the street as they approached, watching them warily. No-one else was in sight.

Kalliades walked to the well and sat down on the low

wall at its rim. 'I can smell fresh bread,' said Banokles, heading off towards one of the larger buildings. Piria thought about running, then saw a group of six pirates walking up from the beach. Banokles saw them too, and, with a curse, returned to Kalliades' side. The pirates glanced at one another, uncertain. Then they slowly approached, fanning out to form a semicircle round the well.

'Where is Arelos?' Kalliades asked. One of the men, round-shouldered and thin, shrugged, but did not reply. His hand was on his sword hilt. Piria saw that the others were watching him, waiting for an order to attack. Then Kalliades spoke to him again, his voice harsh and challenging. 'Then go and find him, goat face. Tell him Kalliades has issued the Challenge and will await him here.' The power and the contempt in his tone stunned them.

'He'll slice you into pieces,' said the thin man, more wary now.

Kalliades ignored him. 'I thought you were going to find bread,' he said to Banokles.

'Bread? What about these sheepshaggers?' Banokles gestured towards the waiting pirates.

'Let them find their own bread. Oh, and on your way, kill that goat-faced whoreson I told to fetch Arelos.'

Banokles grinned, and drew his sword.

'Wait! Wait!' cried the pirate, stepping back several paces. 'I am on my way.'

'Be quick,' ordered Kalliades. 'I am tired, I'm hungry and I'm irritable.'

The man sped away, back down towards the beach.

Banokles pushed his way through the other pirates and walked off in search of the bakery.

Piria stood very quietly, trying not to look at the remaining five men. But she could not avoid it, and saw they were staring at her.

'You cut her hair off?' one of the men asked Kalliades. He was short, with a round face and a flattened nose. 'By the gods, she was plain as a rock before. Now she's just plain ugly.'

'I think she has great beauty,' responded Kalliades. 'And a man with a face like a pig's arse should think twice before talking of ugliness.' Several of the pirates chuckled. Even the insulted man grinned.

'Well, ugly or not, I missed out on her yesterday,' he said. 'You won't object if we have a little fun before Arelos gets here?'

'Oh, I object,' said Kalliades.

'Why? She's not yours.'

Kalliades smiled. 'We are walking the same road, she and I. You understand the Law of the Road?' The man shook his head. 'It is a Mykene custom. Travellers in a hostile land agree to become brothers in arms for the duration of the journey. So an attack on her becomes an attack on me. Are you as skilful as Baros?'

'No.'

'Are any of you?'

'Baros was a great fighter.'

Kalliades shook his head. 'No, he wasn't. Not even average.'

'Well, Arelos *is* a great swordsman,' said the man. 'You'll find that out soon enough.'

'You think you can beat him?' asked another man. He was older than the others, and his thick arms showed the scars of many fights.

'When I do I might make you captain, Horakos,' Kalliades told him.

Horakos laughed. 'Not me. I don't like giving orders. You might ask Sekundos. He's a good man, knows the sea. You realize Arelos might not accept the challenge? He might just tell us to cut you down.'

Kalliades said nothing. Banokles appeared, his arms laden with loaves. 'Brought some extras, lads,' he said, passing out the food. The pirates sat down on the ground, Banokles among them. 'Will you want my cuirass, Kalliades?'

'No.'

'Arelos will probably wear armour.'

'No he won't,' said Kalliades, pointing back down towards the beach. Some thirty men were marching up the dusty road. At the centre strode the powerful figure of Arelos.

Piria watched them come, and lifted her dagger. Arelos was almost as large as Banokles, his arms heavily muscled. He had a broad, flat face, flame-red hair and deep-set green eyes, which just now were blazing with anger. He wore no armour, but a sword belt was strapped to his waist.

He halted a little way from Kalliades, who stood and spoke. 'I challenge you, Arelos, for the right to lead the crew. As custom dictates, you may fight or you may accept my leadership.'

'Kill him!' said Arelos, drawing his sword.

Kalliades' laughter rang out, the sound rich and merry, and so inappropriate to the moment that it stopped them in their tracks. Then he spoke. 'Your men predicted you'd be too gutless to fight me. They obviously know you better than I. Of course, now that we stand here, facing one another, I can feel your fear. Tell me, how did a sheep-shagging coward become a captain of pirates?' As he spoke Kalliades took a swift step towards Arelos. The pirate leader backed away.

'I said kill him!' he screamed.

'Wait! No-one move!' shouted Horakos. Rising to his feet, he stared at Arelos. 'You know the Law of the Sea. You cannot refuse a challenge from a crewman. If you do you are leader no longer and we vote for a new captain.'

'So,' said Arelos, staring hard at the man, 'you have chosen to go against me, Horakos. When I have cut the heart from this Mykene I will strangle you with your own entrails.' Swinging back towards Kalliades, he forced a laugh. 'I hope the shag the whore gave you was worth it. Because now there is only pain. And when I've finished with you I'll cut her apart a joint at a time.'

'No, you will not,' said Kalliades, his voice soft. 'You know it in your heart, Arelos. You are about to walk the Dark Road, and your guts are turning to water.'

With a roar of rage Arelos leapt to the attack.

And Kalliades stepped in to meet him.

III

The Sacker of Cities

A SHORT WHILE EARLIER SEKUNDOS THE KRETAN HAD
watched Arelos stalk from the beach, almost half the
men following him. He had not even been tempted to
join them. Obviously they had located the runaways
and were out for blood.

Sekundos sat by the ashes of last night's fire, his
thoughts sombre. He had been a pirate for more than a
lifetime. He had outlived all five of his sons and one of
his grandsons. Yet still, though his hair was now iron
grey and his limbs ached in the wet winter months, he
had lost none of his love for the Great Green, the feel
of the trade winds on his leathered features, the salt
spray on his skin.

He no longer fooled himself, as some of the younger
men did, that piracy was a noble venture conducted by
heroes. It was merely a way of ensuring food and
clothing for his family, and a little wealth to pass on to
his heirs.

Sekundos had once commanded three ships of his own, but ill weather saw him lose two, and the third was sunk last summer by the madman Helikaon – may the gods curse him! Sekundos' last surviving son had been commanding the vessel at the time and now his bones lay mouldering below the Great Green. No man should outlive his children, thought Sekundos.

Now, far in excess of sixty years of age, Sekundos had joined the crews of the loathsome Arelos. The man was lucky, which was why he had risen to command two ships, but, as far as Sekundos was concerned, he was an idiot. True, he was a good swordsman, but he also revelled in murder and slaughter, which was not profitable. Captured men or women could be sold in the slave markets of Kretos, or the cities of the eastern coast. Dead men were worth nothing.

And Arelos had gathered round him too many like-minded men, which led inevitably to scenes like the one yesterday when they had captured a young woman who would have fetched as much as sixty silver rings in Kretos. First they had swarmed over her like wild animals, and now she was marked for death.

Sekundos hated such stupidity.

He had been cheered when the Mykene pair had joined the crew. Kalliades was a quiet man, but he had a brain, and the lout with him was strong and, Sekundos guessed, loyal. They were like the men he used to sail with. Stalwart and steady. Now they too were to be killed.

Thirty years ago Sekundos would have waited his moment and challenged Arelos to a duel for the right to captain the ships. Now he merely accepted his orders, hoping their luck would hold and he would return home for the winter laden with booty. Somehow he doubted it. Slave raids were always profitable, even though they did not yield the treasure gained by plundering ships carrying gold ingots or silver bars. Still, how many of those could Arelos guarantee in any season? Most of them sailed from the high eastern coasts, usually accompanied by a war galley for protection. And then there was Helikaon the Burner. Sekundos shivered at the thought of him.

Last year Helikaon had captured a pirate ship and burned it with the crew still on board, their hands lashed to the rails. Only an idiot like Arelos would consider sailing into Dardanian waters, haunt of Helikaon's dread ship, the *Xanthos*.

Idly Sekundos stirred the ashes of the fire with a stick, seeking glowing embers to feed a new blaze. When at last he had the fire going again he sat beside it, the cold of the night still in his bones.

Several of the older crewmen joined him by the fire. 'Going to be a fine day,' said Molon, a stocky man of middle years. He handed Sekundos a chunk of stale black bread. 'I would guess they found the Mykene pair. I hope they don't drag them back here for torture.'

'They won't drag them anywhere,' said Sekundos. 'You don't take men like that alive.'

Molon stared out over the hills. 'They'll kill the woman too,' he said. 'Waste of a good slave. A hundred silver rings, I reckon.'

'More like sixty,' said Sekundos. 'Wasn't pretty

enough to make more, even with the golden hair. And too tall. Kretans don't like tall women.'

'I'll wager they don't like throatcutters much either,' remarked a thin, round-shouldered man with a wispy beard. He was young, and new to the sea. Sekundos did not like him much.

'Well, we wouldn't tell them that, would we, Lochos?' replied Molon.

'Surprising how word gets out,' said the thin man. 'The whisper would go round the slave market even before the bidding started.'

'Why do you think Kalliades did it?' asked Molon.

Sekundos shrugged. 'Maybe he just didn't like Baros. For a copper ring I'd have gutted him myself.'

Lochos laughed. 'A copper ring – and the gods giving you forty years back, old man. Baros was a fine fighter.'

'Not fine enough,' put in Molon. 'They say Kalliades killed him in a heartbeat. Say what you like about Mykene warriors, you wouldn't want to get in a scrap with one.'

Another ship had beached the night before, its crew setting a cookfire some hundred paces farther along the rocky shoreline. It was an old vessel with a high curved prow, similar to the first ship Sekundos had ever owned. He gazed at it fondly, noting how well it had been cared for. Not a sign of barnacles, and there was fresh linseed oil on the timbers.

'Arelos is thinking of taking her,' said Lochos. 'Only about thirty in the crew.'

Sekundos sighed. 'You note the crimson eyes painted on the bow?'

'Yes. What of it?'

'It is the *Penelope*, out of Ithaka. You recall the stocky man with the wide golden belt, and the red-gold beard? The first ashore late yesterday? That is Odysseus. They call him the man without enemies. A lot of young sailors think that's because he is such an amusing storyteller. It is not. It is because when he was a young warrior Odysseus killed all his enemies. Back in the days when he was known as the Sacker of Cities. Take a look at the big black man sitting sharpening knives. That is Bias. He can hurl a javelin with such power that it could damn near go right through a bony man like you, Lochos. And you see the blond giant by the fire? That is Leukon. Last summer he fought in the Games at Pylos. He's a fighter, and one blow from his fist would cave in your skull. There's not one man in Odysseus' crew who can't be counted on when the thunder rolls. Take the *Penelope*? We'd lose more than half our men – and the rest would carry wounds.'

'You say,' sneered Lochos. 'But all I saw yesterday was a fat old man in a golden belt, and most of his crew look ancient and worn out – just like you. I could take him.'

'I'll enjoy watching you try,' said Sekundos, stretching and climbing slowly to his feet. 'Of course you need to remember something.'

'What's that?' asked Lochos.

Sekundos' foot slammed into the seated man's face, knocking him backwards, blood spraying from his broken nose. He struggled to rise but Sekundos leapt on him, hammering his fist twice more into the injured nose. Then Sekundos grabbed him by the throat and hauled him upright. 'You need to remember that us old ones are sneaky bastards. Take Odysseus? He'd pin your ears back and swallow you whole. And what he shat out would be worth more than you are.' Sekundos threw the dazed man to the ground, then returned to his seat.

'You are in a foul mood,' said Molon amiably.

'No, I am in a good mood. If it was foul I'd have cut his damned throat.'

Just then one of the men pointed towards the settlement. 'By the gods, isn't that Kalliades?' he said.

Sekundos lifted his hand to shield his eyes from the bright sunshine. Then he saw them. Kalliades, Banokles and the girl, walking down towards them. The girl's hair had been shorn away. Sekundos swore. 'That's another thirty silver rings off the price,' he said.

'What is that he's carrying?' asked Molon, pushing himself to his feet.

Sekundos chuckled. 'Clever lad. Should be interesting to see what happens next.'

The three newcomers were followed onto the beach by a large number of the pirate crew – all keeping their distance. Sekundos waited. Kalliades walked up to the fire – and tossed the severed head of Arelos to the sand.

'We fought the duel,' said Kalliades.

'So you are the captain now?' asked Sekundos.

'I have no wish to be captain, Sekundos. Piracy does not suit me. Horakos nominated you.'

'A great honour, I am sure, lad.' He stared hard at Kalliades. The man had a cut on his cheek that was dripping blood to his tunic. 'You'll need some stitches in that.'

'In a while.'

'And we get the woman back?'

'No. I keep her. You get the ships.' He glanced down at Lochos, who was lying on his back, holding a cloth to his bleeding nose. 'What happened to him?'

'He attacked my boot with his nose. You've got nerve, Kalliades. I'll say that for you. What makes you think I won't order the men to hack you to pieces and take the woman?'

Kalliades shook his head. 'You'd have to challenge me, Sekundos. The Law of the Sea. You want to challenge me?'

Sekundos laughed. 'No, lad. You can keep the woman. With her hair slashed like that she's hardly worth the cost of feeding her.'

'Whose ship is that?' asked Kalliades, pointing towards the *Penelope*.

'Odysseus'.'

'The storyteller. Always wanted to meet him.'

'He tells a fine yarn,' agreed Sekundos. 'But he doesn't carry passengers for free.'

'Then it's as well that I robbed Arelos after killing him,' said Kalliades, tapping the heavy pouch hanging from his belt. 'And now it is decision time for you, my friend. Do we wish each other well and walk away, or did you have other plans?'

Sekundos considered the question. In reality he had no choice. He was too old to challenge Kalliades. Then the thought struck him that he was too old to face any challenge. He swung towards the waiting pirates.

'Do you lads wish to serve under me, or does any other man here want the command?'

'We'll serve you, Sekundos,' answered the thickset Horakos. 'What are your orders?'

'Make ready the ships,' he told them. 'The wind is fair and I smell plunder on the sea!' The pirates sent up a cheer, and then moved off towards their ships. Sekundos gestured to Kalliades and led him away from the rest. 'I do wish you well, lad,' he said, 'but be wary of Odysseus. I happen to like the man, but he is – shall we say? – unpredictable. If he learns you are Mykene outlaws he might just laugh and welcome you like brothers, or turn you over to the first Mykene garrison he finds. He has a contradictory nature.'

'I'll remember that,' Kalliades told him.

'Then remember this also: when you meet him you'll be reminded of a big old dog, friendly and excitable. Look into his eyes. You'll see there is also a wolf there.'

The dreams of Odysseus were troubled. A child was calling to him from beneath the waves, but Odysseus was unable to move. He realized he was tied to the mast of the *Penelope*. There was no-one else on board, and yet the oars lifted in unseen hands and clove the water in perfect unison. 'I cannot reach you,' he shouted to the lost child.

He awoke with a start to see the blond giant, Leukon, kneeling by his side. 'Something you should see, Odysseus,' he said. Odysseus sucked in a great breath. His heart was still hammering, and his head ached from the surfeit of wine the night before. Pushing himself to his feet he rubbed at his eyes, then glanced upwards. The wind was fresh and gentle, the sky serenely blue. He looked along the beach. A group of pirates had gathered round a large campfire. Odysseus blinked, and squinted.

'That's a head he's just tossed beside the fire,' said Leukon. 'By the colour of the hair I'd say it might be Arelos.'

'I thought Arelos was taller,' muttered Odysseus. Bias, who had moved alongside, laughed at the comment, but Leukon merely shook his head.

'Hard to tell when it's just a head,' he pointed out. Odysseus sighed. Leukon looked for the literal meaning in every comment. Irony was largely wasted on him. When Portheus the Pig had sailed with them he always made Leukon the butt of his jokes. Thoughts of the dead Portheus dampened Odysseus' spirits still further. Every crew needed a joker, someone to lift morale when times were hard or the weather cruel. Pushing thoughts of Portheus away, Odysseus turned to Leukon.

'Recognize anyone else?' he asked.

'I think the grey-haired man is Sekundos. Don't know the others.'

Odysseus saw a woman in a torn tunic standing alongside a huge, blond-bearded warrior. The savage haircut suggested she had lice. The group round the fire split up, the pirates moving towards their galleys. Then the two warriors and the woman began to walk towards the campfire of the *Penelope*'s crew. 'What do you make of them?' Odysseus asked Bias.

'Tough men. There's been a fight. The tall one has a wound on his face.'

'A fight? Of course there's been a fight. There's a severed head on the beach,' grunted Odysseus, stepping away from them and gazing at the approaching trio. The tall man, with the cut on his face, was a stranger, but the powerfully built blond warrior, wearing the bronze-reinforced breastplate, was familiar to him. Odysseus seemed to recall the man was a Mykene soldier.

As they came closer Odysseus saw that the wound on the tall warrior's face had slashed across an older scar. Blood was still flowing to his dark tunic. 'I am Kalliades,' said the man. 'My friends and I seek passage, Odysseus King.'

'Kalliades . . . hmm. Seems I have heard that name before. A Mykene warrior who fought alongside Argurios.'

'Yes. And against him. Great man.'

'And you are Banokles One Ear,' said Odysseus, turning to the huge warrior. 'I remember you now. You picked a fight with five of my crew two summers ago.'

'Thrashed them all,' said Banokles happily.

'You lie like a hairy egg,' responded Odysseus with a chuckle. 'When I dragged them back you were down on the street with your hands over your head and blows raining in from all sides.'

'Just taking a small rest to recoup my strength,' said Banokles. 'By Hephaistos, once on my feet I'd have ripped their heads off.'

'No doubt,' said Odysseus. 'And what is your tale?' he asked the cropped-headed whore.

'I am travelling to Troy,' she answered him. That voice! Odysseus fell silent, his eyes narrowing as he scanned her face. There was no doubt as to her identity, and Odysseus knew now that she had slashed away her hair for reasons other than lice. The last time he had seen her, as a child of around twelve, she had taken scissors to her golden locks, cutting the hair back to the scalp, nicking the skin in several places. It had been a sad sight.

He saw from her expression that she knew he recognized her. 'My name is Piria,' she lied, her pale gaze holding to his own.

'Welcome to my camp, Piria,' he said, and saw the relief in her eyes.

Turning away from them, he watched the pirate galleys being launched. It gave him time to think. He was in a quandary now. She was travelling using a false name. That probably meant that she had left the Temple Isle without permission. Women sent to serve on Thera generally remained there all the days of their lives. In fact he knew of only two women who had been released from the isle in more than thirty years.

There was a story, though, of another runaway, many years ago. She had been returned to the isle, and buried alive to serve the god below the mountain.

He pondered the problem. If this girl was a runaway, and he was discovered to have knowingly assisted her flight, he could be cursed by the High Priestess. The old woman was a princess of the Mykene royal family, and worse than her words would be the fact that her hatred could cost Odysseus dearly in his trade with the mainland. And perhaps earn the enmity of her kinsman, Agamemnon.

The pirate galleys rowed out onto the clear blue water, and Odysseus watched as they raised sail. Another problem struck him. Why had two Mykene soldiers been travelling with pirates, and why were they now seeking passage on a ship whose destination they could not know?

The words of Kalliades echoed in his mind. Odysseus had asked about Argurios, and Kalliades had said he had fought with him and against him. The only time Mykene soldiers had fought against Argurios was in Troy last autumn. Agamemnon had ordered the murders of all involved. What was it Nestor had said? Two escaped and were declared outlaw.

Sweet Hera! He was standing with a runaway priestess and two Mykene renegades.

'The *Penelope* is a small ship,' he said at last, 'and when our cargo arrives there will be little room left. We are travelling to Troy for the wedding of the king's son, Hektor. However, we will be stopping at a number of islands on the way. Did you have a destination in mind?'

Kalliades gave a rueful smile. 'Wherever fair winds take us,' he said.

'No wind is favourable if a man does not know where he is going,' Odysseus told him.

'All winds are favourable to a man who does not care,' responded Kalliades.

'I need to think on this a while longer,' said Odysseus. 'Come and join us for breakfast. Bias will stitch that cut on your face, and you can tell me how you came to be collecting heads.'

Kalliades sat beside the breakfast fire, his irritation growing. The black sailor, Bias, was kneeling alongside him, one hand pinching the skin of his face, the other pushing a curved bronze needle threaded with black twine through the flaps of the wound, drawing them together. Close by, Banokles was regaling Odysseus and the crew of the *Penelope* with a ludicrously distorted version of the rescue of Piria, and the fight with Arelos. He made it sound as if Arelos was a demigod of battle. The truth was more prosaic. The man had been merely skilful, lacking true speed of hand. The fight had been brief and bloody. Kalliades had stepped in swiftly to deliver the death wound. As he did so, Arelos had slumped forward, butting Kalliades' cheek and splitting the skin.

Kalliades looked into the dark eyes of Bias. The man was smiling as he listened to Banokles spinning his tale.

'A good tale,' they heard Odysseus say, as Banokles concluded the overblown story. 'Though it lacks a truly powerful ending.'

'But he won and survived,' argued Banokles.

'Indeed he did, but for the story to make men shiver there needs to be a mystical element. How about this . . . the moment the head of Arelos was cut from the body a plume of black smoke rose from the severed neck, forming the figure of a man wearing a high, plumed helm.'

'I like that,' said Banokles. 'So what is the figure of smoke?'

'I don't know. It is your story. Perhaps it was a demon who had possessed Arelos. You sure you didn't see a little smoke?'

'Now you mention it I think I did,' Banokles told him, to the laughter of the crew.

Kalliades closed his eyes. Bias chuckled. 'Welcome to the *Penelope*,' he whispered, 'where the truth always gives way to the Golden Lie. There, the wound is sealed. I'll cut and draw the stitches in a few days.'

'My thanks to you, Bias. So, what brought the *Penelope* to this island? The flax plants are still in flower and I have seen no sign of other industry.'

'You'll see soon enough,' Bias told him. 'It should be an amusing day. Well, for passengers anyway. I doubt there'll be much laughter among the crew.' Sitting back, he scooped up a handful of sand and scrubbed the blood from his fingers. 'A fine bruise is going to form round that cut,' he said.

'Where is the *Penelope* heading next?'

'We are making for an island a day's sail to the east, then, if the gods bless us, we'll head northeast for Kios, then the eastern coast and Troy.'

Banokles joined them, handing Kalliades a dark loaf and a round of cheese. 'Did you hear that about the plume of smoke?' he asked.

'Yes.'

'What could it be, do you think?'

'I don't know, Banokles. There was no plume of smoke.'

'I know that. Intriguing, though.'

Bias chuckled. 'It was the spirit of an evil warrior from long ago, who was cursed never to see the Elysian Fields. His soul was trapped in an ancient dagger, which the pirate leader found in a grave he desecrated. When Arelos stole the dagger the evil spirit overcame him, filling him with hate for all living things.'

'Now *that* is storytelling,' said Banokles admiringly.

Bias shook his head. 'No, lad, *that* is stolen from a tale Odysseus tells. With luck you'll hear the full story at some time on the voyage. We'll beach somewhere, alongside other ships, and sailors will beg Odysseus to tell a tale or two. You might hear that one, though he will certainly have devised new stories over the winter. When last we spoke he was preparing something about a witch with snakes for hair. I'm looking forward to that.' Bias glanced along the beach. 'Now the fun begins,' he said.

Kalliades turned. Some two hundred paces away a fat old woman, wearing a shapeless gown of faded yellow linen, was leading a herd of black pigs onto the beach. Every now and again she would tap her staff against the side of an animal seeking to leave the herd, and it would obediently trot back into the pack.

'*That* is your cargo?' asked Kalliades.

'Yes.'

'You need help slaughtering them?' asked Banokles.

'They are not going to be slaughtered,' said Bias.

'We're shipping them live to another island. Swine fever killed all the pigs, and there is a merchant there who will pay dearly for another breeding herd.'

'Shipping live pigs?' Banokles was astonished. 'How will you contain them?'

Bias sighed. 'We're using the mast and the spare mast to create an enclosure at the centre of the deck.'

'Why would anyone want to ship live pigs?' asked Banokles. 'They'll cover the deck with shit. I was raised on a pig farm. Believe me when I tell you that pigs can *really* shit.'

Kalliades pushed himself to his feet and wandered away from the two men. He had no interest in pigs or their excrement. Even so, he watched the fat old woman walking with the beasts. They were trotting along quite happily behind her, making small squeaking, grunting sounds. Odysseus strode to meet her. As he approached, three of the pigs darted away from him, but the woman made a whistling sound and they stopped and turned.

'Welcome to my campfire, Circe,' said Odysseus. 'Always a pleasure to see you.'

'Save the flattery, king of Ithaka.' She gazed at the *Penelope* with baleful eyes, then gave a harsh laugh. 'I hope you are getting a sack of gold for your troubles,' she said. 'You will earn it. My little ones will not be happy at sea.'

'They seem docile enough to me.'

'Because I am with them. When Portheos first approached me with this idea I thought him simple in the head. When you rejected his plan I assumed it was because of your greater intelligence.' She gazed round the beach. 'Where is he, by the way?'

'Died in his sleep back home.'

Kalliades heard the old woman make a clucking sound. She shook her head. 'So young. A man of such laughter should live to a great age.' She looked at Odysseus and remained silent for a while. 'So,' she said, at last, 'why did you change your mind about the plan?'

'It is merely trade. Oristhenes no longer has pigs. A pig breeder without pigs has no purpose in life.'

'Have you considered *why* no-one else is bringing him live pigs?'

'What others do or don't do is not my concern.' A large, black boar began snuffling at Odysseus' feet, nudging its snout against his bare leg. Odysseus tried to push it away with his foot.

'He likes you,' said Circe.

'I like him too. I am sure we will be fast friends. You have any advice for me?'

'Carry plenty of water to swill down the decks. And a few splints for the broken bones your crew will suffer if the pigs panic and break through your enclosure. If you reach Oristhenes' island without mishap, ensure that Ganny here' – she tapped the big black boar with her staff – 'is the first one you lower to the beach. The others will gather round him. If Ganny is content you will have little trouble. If he is not, there will be mayhem.'

Kalliades saw that Piria had also moved away from the campfire, and was sitting alone on a boulder. He walked across to her. She looked up, but did not offer a greeting.

'Why are there pigs on the beach?' she asked.

'Odysseus is taking them to another island.'

'We are to travel with pigs?'

'It would seem so.' The silence between them grew, then Kalliades asked, 'You wish to be alone?'

'You can have no idea of how much I wish to be alone, Kalliades. But I am not alone. I am surrounded by men – and pigs. Not a great deal of difference there,' she added scornfully.

He turned away, but she called after him. 'Wait! I am sorry, Kalliades. I was not referring to you. You have been kind to me, and – so far – true to your word.'

'Many men are,' he said, seating himself on a rock close by. 'I have seen cruelty. I have seen kindness. Sometimes I have seen cruel men being kind, and kind men cruel. I do not understand it. I do know, though, that all men are not as the pirates who took you. You see that old man there?' He pointed to a white-haired figure standing back from the crew and watching the pigs being herded towards the *Penelope*. He was tall and stooped, and wore a cloak of blue over a dark, gold-embroidered tunic.

'What of him?'

'That is Nestor of Pylos. When I was a child I worked in his flax fields. I was a slave and the son of a slave. The king has many sons. Every one of them was sent to work among the slaves in the fields for a full season. Their hands bled, their backs ached. My mother told me the king did this so that his sons would understand the harshness of life beyond the palace, and not be scornful of those who worked in the fields. Nestor himself journeyed through his lands, talking to those who laboured for him, seeing that they were well fed and clothed. He is a good man.'

'Who still owns slaves,' she said.

Kalliades was bemused by the comment. 'Of course he owns slaves. He is a king.'

'Was your mother born a slave?'

'No. She was taken from a village on the Lykian coast.'

'As I was – by pirates?'

'I suppose so.'

'Then Nestor is just like them. What he wants he takes. But he is called a good man because he feeds and clothes the people he has torn from their loved ones and their families. The evil of it all sickens me.'

Kalliades fell silent. There had always been slaves, as there had always been kings. There always would be. How else would civilization flourish? He glanced towards the *Penelope*.

Several crewmen had harnessed a canvas sling to two ropes. They had lowered the ropes from the deck of the beached ship, and men on the shore were trying to lift a pig into the sling. The beast began to squeal and thrash its legs. The sound panicked the other pigs. Four of them began to run along the beach, chased by sailors. The old crone with the staff shook her head, and walked back away from the mayhem. Kalliades saw Banokles hurl himself at a large pig, which swerved as Banokles was in the air. The warrior sprawled into the sand and slid head first into the water. Within moments the scene on the beach was chaotic. Odysseus began bellowing orders.

The pig in the sling had been hauled halfway to the deck, but was thrashing so wildly that the ropes were swinging from side to side. Suddenly the beast began to urinate, showering the men below. The remaining pigs, some fifteen in all, bunched together and charged down the beach directly towards Odysseus. There was nothing for him to do but run. The sight of the stocky king, in his wide golden belt, being chased by a herd of squealing pigs was too much for the crew. Laughter broke out.

'It is going to be a long day,' said Kalliades. He glanced at Piria. She was laughing too.

It was good to see.

At that moment Odysseus halted in his run, swinging round to face the herd. 'Enough!' he bellowed, his voice booming like thunder. The animals, startled by the noise, swerved away from him. One huge black pig trotted up to the king and began to nuzzle his leg. Odysseus leaned down and patted its broad back. Then he strode back towards the *Penelope*, the black pig ambling along beside him. The other animals began to made soft squealing sounds and fell in behind the king.

'Laugh at me, would you, you misbegotten cowsons,' stormed Odysseus as he approached his crew. 'By the balls of Ares, if I could teach these pigs to row I'd get rid of you all.'

'An unusual man,' Kalliades observed. 'Can he be trusted?'

'Why are you asking me?' Piria said.

'Because you know him. I saw it in his eyes when you spoke.'

Piria remained silent for a while. Then she nodded. 'I knew him. He visited my father's . . . home . . . many times. I cannot answer your question, Kalliades. Odysseus was once a slave trader. Years ago he was known as the Sacker of Cities. I would not willingly put my trust in any man who earned such a title. As it is I have no choice.'

IV

Voyage of the pigs

BIAS THE BLACK WAS SITTING QUIETLY AMONG THE ROCKS, an old cloak round his broad shoulders. The crew were still struggling to load the pigs. Bias was not tempted to help them. Close to fifty, he needed to protect his javelin arm if he was to have any chance in the Games at Troy. So he sat quietly, honing his bone-handled fighting knives. Odysseus claimed his liking for knives was part of his heritage as a Nubian, but this seemed unlikely to Bias, who had been born on Ithaka, and had known no other Nubians as a youngster. His mother had certainly never spoken about knife fighting.

'You could be the grandson of the king of Nubia,' Odysseus had said once. 'You could be heir to a vast kingdom, with golden palaces and a thousand concubines.'

'And if my prick had fingers it could scratch my arse,' Bias had replied.

'That's the problem with you, Bias. You have no imagination,' Odysseus had chided him.

Bias had laughed then. 'Why would a man need imagination who travels with you, King of Storytellers? Why, with you I have journeyed through the sky on a flying ship, fought demons, hurled my javelin into the moon, and strung a necklace of stars for a jungle empress. I have had sailors ask me when I am returning to my homeland to take up my crown. Why is it that so many people believe your stories?'

'They like to believe,' Odysseus told him. 'Most men work from dawn to dusk. They live hard, they die young. They want to think that the gods smile down on them, that their lives have more meaning than in fact they do. The world would be a sadder place without stories, Bias.'

Bias smiled at the memory, then sheathed his fighting knives and stood. Odysseus was walking towards him.

'You idle cowson,' said the Ugly King. 'What's the point of being built like a bull if you don't use your strength when it's needed?'

'I use it,' said Bias. 'Not for pigs, though. And I don't see you hauling them up to the deck.'

'That's because I'm the king,' replied Odysseus, grinning. He sat himself down, gesturing Bias to join him. 'So, what do you make of our passengers?'

'I like them.'

'You don't even know them.'

'Then why ask me?'

Odysseus sighed. 'The men are Mykene outlaws. I'm thinking of handing them over in Kios. There'll be gold for them.' Bias laughed then. 'What is amusing you?'

Bias looked at his king. 'I have served you for nigh on

twenty-five years. I've seen you drunk, sober, angry and sad. I've seen you mean, bitter and vengeful, and I've seen you generous and forgiving. By the gods, Odysseus, there's nothing about you I don't know.'

At that moment the last of the pigs broke away from the men trying to load it into the canvas sling. It ran along the beach, squealing. Several crew members raced after it. Bias fell silent, watching the chase. It was Leukon who caught the beast, hoisting it up in his huge arms and striding back towards the *Penelope*.

'It is like this pig venture,' continued Bias. 'You say it is about profit. It is not. It is about dead Portheos. His stupid plan, a plan that meant so much to him. You laughed at him for it. Now you grieve for him, and this is your tribute to his memory.'

'I can only suppose there is a point to this?' snapped Odysseus.

'Yes, and you already know what it is. You can talk all you like about selling Kalliades and the big man for gold. It is not in you, Odysseus. Two brave men rescued a young woman on this island, and they have come to you for help. You want me to believe you are minded to betray them? I think not. If all the gods of Olympos descended on us and *demanded* you give them up you'd refuse. And I'll tell you something else: every man in the crew would stand alongside you when you did.'

'Why would they do anything so foolish?' asked Odysseus softly, his spurt of anger fading.

'Because they listen to your stories of heroes, Ugly One, and they know the truth of them.'

* * *

The day was calm, the breeze light as the *Penelope* put to sea. Kalliades, Banokles and Piria stood on the left of the small aft deck. Upon the right Odysseus manned the long steering oar, while Bias called out the beat for the rowers. Nestor, and his two sons, were on the foredeck, some twenty paces forward.

Kalliades stood silently, marvelling at the beauty of the old ship. Drawn up on the beach she had looked blocky and coarse, her timbers worn. But she glided upon the Great Green like a dancer. The pirate ship had wallowed and struggled through the waves, but then her keel had been encrusted with barnacles, her crew careless and lacking in skill. The thirty men of the *Penelope* were highly trained, the oars rising and dipping in perfect unison.

The small herd of pigs was clustered in a rectangular enclosure on the main deck. It had been cunningly crafted, two masts on raised wooden blocks, with a fence of knotted rope between them. The animals seemed calm enough as the voyage began.

Kalliades glanced at Piria. In the bright sunshine her face was tired and pale, the heavy bruises standing out. There was swelling beneath her right eye and Kalliades saw deep, angry scratches on the skin of her neck. Who are you, he wondered? How is it you know Odysseus?

He had noted her hesitation when speaking of the visits Odysseus had paid to her father. The word *home* had been used in place of something else. What? Farm? Palace? Estate? There was little doubt in Kalliades' mind that Piria was from a wealthy family. She was staring out to sea, lost in thought, and oblivious of his gaze. Kalliades had told the pirate he considered her beautiful. He had said it to deflect the casual insult the man had offered her. Now he realized there was truth in the compliment. How strange, he thought, that the slashing away of her hair should have revealed such beauty. Her neck was long and slender, her profile exquisite. She saw him looking at her, and her gaze hardened, her mouth tightening. Then she turned away from him.

He thought about speaking to her, offering soft words, but decided against it. You have other concerns, he chided himself. Odysseus knew your name. That had been a surprise. Kalliades did not consider himself famous, and had no reason to believe his name was known outside areas of Mykene influence. The fact that it was meant the king of Ithaka might also know of the bounty Agamemnon King had placed upon his head.

He looked across at Banokles. The man was completely untroubled by thoughts of betrayal or capture. He had wandered down the narrow gap between the enclosure and the rowers, and was chatting amiably to the blond sailor, Leukon. Banokles had a gift for making friends.

Odysseus called Bias to him, instructing him to take the steering oar. Then the stocky king eased past Piria and moved towards the foredeck. As he came abreast of the enclosure the largest of the black pigs gave a little grunt and leaned towards him. Odysseus halted and scratched at the beast's ear. The pig tilted its head up. Odysseus patted it then moved on to stand beside Nestor. The black pig watched him.

'Always had a way with animals,' said Bias. 'Except horses. Worst rider you'll ever see.'

As the morning wore on the sun grew warmer, and the breeze faded away. Banokles' warning about the pigs proved false. In fact they were fastidious animals. The floor of their enclosure had been covered with dry grass to soak up any urine, but the animals used only the forward end of their pen to defecate. This was fortunate for those on the aft deck – not so lucky, though, for Nestor and his sons. The elderly ruler was holding a cloth over his nose. Unluckiest of all, however, were the lead oarsmen, whose rowing seats were immediately left and right of a growing pile of ordure.

By mid-afternoon, as the *Penelope* sailed serenely past a cluster of islands, heavy clouds began to form above the ship. The wind picked up. Kalliades glanced at the darkening sky. 'Storm brewing?' he asked Bias.

The black man shook his head. 'Going to be brisk, though. Not a problem for us. The island yonder is where we are headed.' He pointed to a distant, golden mound close to the horizon. 'We'll beach on Titan's Rock before sunset.'

The *Penelope* was sailing now past a group of islands, with high cliffs and narrow beaches. In the distance Kalliades saw what appeared to be a fast-moving dark cloud, travelling against the wind. He pointed it out to Bias. It was a colossal flock of birds heading out to sea. Just then a school of some twenty or more dolphins burst into sight, leaping and twisting then swimming at speed past the ship, heading in the same southerly direction as the birds.

'Something has alarmed both fish and fowl,' said Bias.

Someone groaned loudly. The lead rower, Leukon, overcome by the stench of the manure, let go his oar and leaned over the side, emptying his belly to the sea. Banokles ran down the narrow gap between the pig pen and the rowers.

'I can take his place for a while,' he shouted.

'Do it, lad,' Bias called out.

Odysseus moved down from the foredeck as Leukon made his way towards the rear of the ship, away from the stench. Kalliades saw the largest of the pigs pushing through the herd towards Odysseus. Rearing up, it placed its front legs on the horizontal mast and squealed loudly. Leukon was passing by. Angrily he lashed out, his huge hand cracking against the pig's snout. The animal gave a mighty scream and scrambled over the makeshift fence, launching itself at Leukon. All the pigs began to snort and squeal. Leukon was hurled from his feet, but he kicked out at the lunging pig, desperate to keep it away from him. The rower immediately to the left rose from his seat to aid his comrade. The pig lunged at him, then scrambled up onto the low rowing bench. Its trotters slid helplessly on the sleek wood, and, before anyone could reach it, the beast plunged squealing into the sea.

Odysseus, furious now, ran at Leukon. 'Why did you hit the pig?' he shouted.

'It annoyed me!' responded Leukon angrily.

'Ah,' said Odysseus. 'Well, that's fine then. Something annoys you and you hit it. Did it make you feel better?'

'Yes.'

Without another word Odysseus threw a straight left that hammered into Leukon's face, hurling the man from his feet once more. He hit the deck hard, and lay there blinking in shock. 'Well, you were right this time, dung brain,' said Odysseus. 'I *do* feel better.' Swinging to the crew, he said: 'Now let's get Ganny back on board.'

At the beginning the task seemed simple. Several of the crew dived into the water and looped ropes were lowered, ready to be tied round the errant pig. But every time the crewmen swam towards him he attacked them, butting and biting. Finally Odysseus took off his golden belt and leapt into the sea himself.

Another huge flock of dark birds soared above the *Penelope*. Then the ship began to tremble. Kalliades grabbed for the rail. The wind died down, and yet the sea, so calm only moments before, was now choppy and uneven. Kalliades heard a distant rumble, and saw boulders tumbling down a hillside on the nearest island.

Piria was staring at the distant avalanche. She looked at him. 'Someone the gods loved just died,' she said. 'Now they stamp upon the earth in their anguish.'

The men in the sea had forgotten the pig now, and were swimming swiftly back to the *Penelope*. Odysseus was hauled back to the deck and stood there glowering down at the pig.

'It's only one beast. It is not worth risking the ship for,' said Bias. 'That earthquake will bring some ship-cracking waves in its wake.'

Odysseus swung towards Leukon. 'The cost of that pig comes from your share,' he said. 'Any complaints?'

'No, my king.'

'Good! Oarsmen, to your places.'

Heavy clouds were massing above the *Penelope*, but there was no rain. The wind was stronger, the sea less calm. The ship began to sway with the swell and the rowers were forced to work hard to head for a narrow bay on the headland of Titan's Rock. Odysseus had returned to the steering oar, while Bias walked along the deck calling out the beat.

'Lift . . . set . . . pull.'

Kalliades saw Piria looking back over the sea. 'Can you still see it?' he asked.

'Yes. A long way back.'

Kalliades scanned the surging sea. Every now and again he saw a dark shape appear, and then be hidden by the waves.

'You think it might make it to the shore?' asked Piria.

'No. It will die out there.'

'How sad.'

'No sadder than being slaughtered to feed a family. All living creatures must die. This is his time.' He smiled then. 'You are concerned for a pig?'

Piria shrugged. 'He has a name. Ganny. So he is not just a pig any more.'

Odysseus was also glancing back. He saw Kalliades watching him. 'Too far for a pig to swim,' said the Ugly King.

'By a long way,' agreed Kalliades. 'A shame, though,' he added.

'I hate losing cargo,' said Odysseus, turning his gaze towards the beach. Then he bellowed at the crew: 'Put your backs into it, you cowsons! You think I want to spend the night out here?'

The light of the full moon was so bright it cast shadows on the beach of Titan's Rock. The crew had set two cookfires and a larger campfire, on higher ground sheltered by rocks, round which most of the crew sat in a ragged circle. From her vantage point on a stony outcrop Piria watched the men playing knucklebones, gossiping and arguing. The smell of cooking fish reached her, and her empty stomach spasmed. She was reluctant to leave her seat and walk across to the crew. They had forgotten about her as they went about their evening tasks, and she was unwilling to remind them, to see their eyes crawling over her, speculation in their faces. For the first time in days she felt a measure of peace, and she guarded it jealously, wrapping the borrowed red cloak of Banokles round her.

Her tension eased a little as she gazed at the brushwood enclosure where the pigs were settling for the night. The old woman, Circe, had been mischievous in her predictions. There had been no broken bones among the crewmen, only some scrapes and bruises as they manhandled the pigs off the *Penelope*.

Now, in the moonlight, she could see the herd had settled to sleep, their fat bodies pressed together, faint grunting sounds coming from the enclosure. Every now and then one beast would shift about, making his comrades squeal softly, before going back to sleep.

Piria was grateful to the pigs. They had distracted everyone's attention from her during the voyage. Pain from her injuries flowed over her in nauseating waves. Her head ached constantly and her neck moved uncomfortably on her shoulders, as if it had been wrenched off then replaced by an unskilled craftsman.

She saw the black crewman, Bias, walking towards her, a bowl in one hand, a round section of corn bread in the other. Fear rose in her and her hands began to tremble. She imagined him offering her the food and then making some crude approach. He came closer and handed her the bowl and the bread. She could smell fish and onions, but her fear had stripped away her hunger.

'You should come down to the fire,' he said. 'It is a cold night.'

'I will sleep here,' she replied.

Bias looked doubtfully at the rocky ledge. 'It looks uncomfortable.'

'I am used to discomfort.'

He nodded and turned back to the warmth of the fire. Piria nibbled on the corn bread and dipped it in the fish juices. She felt the warmth reach down to her stomach, and realized her skin was like ice. She pulled her cloak more closely round her. A wave of despair and loneliness suddenly overcame her and she felt the prick of tears under her eyelids.

'What have you done?' she whispered.

She remembered that summer night by the prophecy flame in the great temple. She and Andromache had been giggling, soused in wine, drunk on love. The two young women had asked old Melite to prophesy their future together. It was more in drunken jest than with any serious intent. All the priestesses knew that Melite had once been a seeress, but now, half blind and touched in the head, her words were often meaningless. And so it had seemed at the time.

'No future here, young Kalliope,' Melite had said. 'Before the days shorten Andromache will be lost to the Blessed Isle, returned to the world of men and war.'

Despite their disbelief the two women were dismayed by the prophecy, which cut through the wine, dashing their carefree mood.

Eighteen days later came the ship, bearing the message from Hekabe, queen of Troy. Andromache was summoned before the First Priestess and told she had been given leave to quit the Temple Isle in order to be wed to Hekabe's son, the warrior Hektor. Piria had been with her in the council chamber.

'My sister, Paleste, is betrothed to Hektor,' Andromache had argued.

The High Priestess had looked uncomfortable. 'Paleste died in Troy. A sudden illness. Your father and King Priam have agreed that you will honour the pact they made.'

Piria knew that Paleste had been dear to Andromache, and saw the shock register on her face. Her head dropped and she was silent for a while, then her expression hardened, and she looked up at the High Priestess, her green eyes glinting with anger. 'Even so I will not go. No man has the right to demand a priestess quits her sacred duty.'

'These are special circumstances,' said the High Priestess, her tone uncomfortable.

'Special? You are selling me for Priam's gold. What is *special* about that? Women have been sold since the gods were young. Always by men, though. It is what we have come to expect from them. But from *you*!' Andromache's contempt filled the room like a seething mist, and Piria saw the High Priestess blanch. She expected an angry response. Instead the older woman merely sighed.

'It is not just for Priam's gold, Andromache, but for all that gold represents. Without it there would be no temple on Thera, no princesses to placate the beast below. Yes, it would be wonderful if we could ignore the wishes of powerful men like Priam, and do our duty here unmolested. Such freedom, however, is a dream. You are a priestess of Thera no longer. You will leave tomorrow.'

That night, as they lay together for the last time, listening to the breeze whispering through the leaves of the tamarisk trees, Piria had begged Andromache to flee with her. 'There are small boats on the far side of the isle. We could steal one and sail away.'

'No,' said Andromache, leaning down and kissing her tenderly. 'There would be nowhere to run, my love – except into the world of men. You are happy here, Kalliope.'

'There can be no happiness without you.'

They had talked long then, but finally Andromache had said: 'You must stay, Kalliope. Wherever I am I will know you are safe, and this will strengthen me. I will be able to close my eyes, and see the isle. I will see you run and laugh. I will picture you in our bed, and it will comfort me.'

And so, her heart seared, the woman now called Piria had watched the ship sail east in the morning sunlight.

Despite her sorrow she had tried to immerse herself in her duties, in the prayer chants and the offerings to the Minotaur, rumbling beneath the mountain. The days had ground on, bleak and empty, through the winter. Then, in the spring, old Melite collapsed while gathering crocuses and white lilies for the midday ritual. They had carried her to her room, but her breath was rasping, and all knew that death was not far off.

Piria had been watching beside her, late in the night, when the old woman had sat upright in her bed, her voice suddenly rich and strong. 'Why are you here, child?' she asked.

'To be with you, sister,' Piria replied, putting her arms round the old woman and easing her back on the pillows.

'Ah yes. On Thera. Where is Andromache?'

'She has gone. You remember? To Troy?'

'Troy,' whispered the old woman, closing her eyes. She was silent for a while, then she cried out, 'Fire and death. I see Andromache now. She is running through the flames. There are savage men pursuing her.' The old woman began waving her arms. 'Run!' she screamed.

Piria grabbed at a flailing hand. 'Be calm, Melite,' she said. 'You are safe.'

The dying priestess opened her eyes, her body tense. Tears began to flow. 'Wicked, wicked men! Doom will find you. The Minotaur will devour you. He will come with great thunder, and the sky will darken and the sun vanish.'

'What of Andromache?' whispered Piria. 'Can you still see her? Speak!'

The old woman relaxed and smiled. 'I see you, brave Kalliope. I see you, and all is well.'

'You see me with Andromache in the flames?'

Melite spoke no more. Piria had looked into the old woman's eyes. She was dead.

Alone on the beach Piria blinked away the tears and shook her head. Was it a true vision, she wondered now? Did it mean she was destined to rescue Andromache from evil men? Or had the dying old woman merely meant she could see her sitting by the bedside?

She sighed. Too late now to question it, or the reckless decision she had made as a result of it. The night of Melite's death she had gathered a few golden trinkets and some food and set off for the north of the island, where she had stolen the small sailboat.

Piria saw the portly figure of Odysseus walking along the strand, angling away from the ship and from the crew, his head averted from her. She knew he had been avoiding her, and on an impulse she stood carefully then climbed down to the beach. By the time she reached him Odysseus was kneeling, intently carving a face in the sand with his knife. He looked up, saying nothing, his face unwelcoming.

For a moment she was silent. Then: 'Why did you try to rescue the pig?' she asked.

He raised his eyebrows as if he had expected a different question. 'Circe told me the other pigs would follow Ganny. We needed him to control them.' He stood up and, after cleaning it on his grubby tunic, replaced the blade in his belt. Then he scuffed the sand with his foot, brushing away the carved face.

'Yet you got them off the ship and into their enclosure without him.'

There was silence between them again. Odysseus seemed tense, his normally bluff demeanour now still and watchful. Piria feared he had already decided to betray her and was feeling guilty.

'I wanted to thank you,' she said, forcing a smile, 'for accepting me as Piria. And for giving me passage on your ship to Troy.'

He grunted non-committally.

'You knew of Kalliades before you met?' she asked him.

He looked at her then. 'Yes, I knew of him. He has a reputation as a fine soldier.'

'He and his friend rescued me from pirates, from certain torment and death, for no thought of reward.' The dark fears within did not believe her words, but she pushed on, anxious to sway the Ugly King. 'He is a man of courage and one to be trusted.' She looked into the king's eyes. 'There are few enough like him here on the Great Green – this sea of scum.'

He said nothing, so she nodded and started to walk away. Then she turned.

'Are you such a man, Odysseus?'

He was saved from answering by a sudden

commotion in the pig pen. Piria turned to look. The pigs were squealing and grunting anxiously, and many of them had raced to the seaward end of the enclosure, where they were tearing with their trotters at the dry brushwood.

Then the ground began to shake. Piria was pitched sideways. Odysseus caught her, and held tight to her as rocks rumbled down the hillsides. The sea began to roil, then drew back from the beach in a sudden rush, building into a huge breaker, which swept forward, surging round Odysseus and Piria and up the beach. The cook-fires were washed away, but the main blaze, on higher ground, escaped the flood, as did the pig pen. The *Penelope* had been lifted on the first wave and carried deep onto the beach.

Large waves pounded the shore, but the ground ceased to shake. The pigs were squealing in panic now. Cursing, Odysseus strode over to them, Piria beside him.

'Be quiet, you pox-ridden cowsons!' he bellowed, and the pigs fell silent, shocked by the sudden sound.

In the stillness a distant squealing could be heard, borne faintly from the sea on the night wind.

'There!' One of the men pointed out across the water and, straining her eyes, Piria could just make out a small black dot as it crested a distant white breaker in the moonlight.

'Ganny,' breathed Odysseus. 'By all the bastard gods . . .'

He flung off his jewelled belt and sandals and raced into the waves. With a curse, Bias ran after him and grabbed him by the shoulder.

'My king, don't do this!' he shouted, his voice diminished by the sound of the breakers. 'The waves will throw you against the rocks. You'll be killed.'

Odysseus shrugged him off without a word and waded into the surf. Cursing loudly, Bias followed him. After a moment's hesitation two more crewmen went after them.

The pig was being swept in fast, and, as it came closer, Piria could see it was exhausted, its legs flailing weakly as it was flung up then spun round on the spume. There was a line of black rocks far out from the shoreline and Ganny was being hurtled towards them. The pig's cries were weakening and Piria feared it was dying.

To have swum all that distance, following the ship with hope in its heart . . .

Odysseus had half waded, half swum to the jagged line of rocks and was clambering over them, battered by the waves. The other men joined him, struggling, and Piria could see that their strength was being tested by the force of the sea. They moved along the rocks, hoping to cut Ganny off as he was swept towards them.

A great wave hid the black pig, then Piria spotted it again being borne towards the edge of the rock on which Odysseus stood. As the next wave lifted the beast Odysseus hurled himself headlong into the sea, his body striking Ganny and deflecting his course. A second wave crashed over them both and man and pig disappeared into the spume. When they reappeared they were beyond the line of deadly rocks.

Bias and the other two crewmen dived in after them

and for a while Piria could make out nothing. Then she saw the two crewmen carrying the exhausted pig to shore, Bias and Odysseus wading through the surf behind them.

The animal was laid down on the sand near its fellows, which fidgeted, grunting, in their pen, craning anxiously for a look at their friend. Seawater was dribbling from Ganny's mouth and he was breathing shallowly. His trotters moved weakly, and the crewmen were uncertain what to do.

Odysseus was visibly weary, water sluicing off him onto the sand. He was cut and bruised and there was a long abrasion on his forearm where he must have fended himself off the rocks. He stood over the pig and sighed.

'He needs rest and warmth,' he said. 'Place him near the fire.' He pointed at Leukon and growled, 'Give him your cloak. This is all your fault, you moron.'

The blond crewman quickly doffed his yellow cloak and knelt to wrap it awkwardly round the stricken beast. Odysseus turned away, and limped towards the *Penelope*. As he passed her Piria heard him mutter, 'Stupid pig.'

V

The royal priestess

KALLIADES WAS SITTING ALONE, AWAY FROM THE FIRE. THE sea was calm again, but the night was cool, a chill breeze whispering over the rocks. Most of the crew were asleep. He glanced up to where Piria was sitting, huddled against a rock which shielded her from the wind. He was about to walk over to her when he saw the big black man, Bias, carrying firewood to where she sat, and lighting it with a brand from the main campfire. Then he brought her a blanket. Kalliades wished he had thought of that.

Closing his eyes he leaned back against a rock, his thoughts sombre. Then he heard movement behind him, and his heart leapt, for he thought it might be Piria come to sit with him. Opening his eyes he saw the stocky figure of Odysseus. The Ugly King sat down beside him.

'There is something about the sea at night that makes a man feel small,' he said.

'I feel like that when I gaze upon mountains,' Kalliades told him.

'Ah, that's because you are a landsman. You are right, though. The seas and the mountains are eternal and unchanging. We are just here for a little while and then we fade into the dust of history.' He fell silent for a moment, then said, 'So, tell me, what happened that night in Troy?'

It was innocently asked, but Kalliades felt his stomach tighten. Odysseus knew, then. Kalliades felt suddenly foolish. Yesterday on the beach he had spoken of fighting *against* Argurios. That had been a stupid slip of the tongue. What now, he wondered? There was a Mykene garrison on Kios. Would that be Odysseus' plan? Sell them for Agamemnon's gold? He saw Odysseus looking at him intently, and realized he hadn't answered the man's question.

'We lost,' said Kalliades curtly. 'Shouldn't have. We were led by a fool.'

'How was he foolish?'

'I have no wish to talk about it,' said Kalliades. 'What do you intend to do with us?'

'Oh, stay calm, lad. I don't intend to *do* anything. As far as I am concerned you are merely passengers.'

'You are not interested in Agamemnon's bounty? I find that hard to believe.'

Odysseus chuckled. 'To be honest it crossed my mind. Unfortunately I have a gullible crew. So you are free to do as you please.'

Kalliades was intrigued. 'How does their gullibility affect your decisions?'

'It was pointed out to me that you and your friend are two fine heroes, who risked their lives for a woman they didn't know. In short, the kind of men I tell stories about. So, much as Agamemnon's gold would have been welcome, I must forsake it.'

Kalliades said nothing. He doubted that the wishes of the crew would have any real effect on Odysseus' decisions, and recalled the words of Sekundos about the contradictory nature of the man. Then Odysseus spoke again. 'Are you ready now to tell me why your general was foolish?'

Kalliades' mind drifted back to that blood-filled night, and he heard again the cries of the wounded, the clash of swords, and the grinding of shields. He saw once more the mighty Argurios holding the stairs, the dread Helikaon beside him. 'Why foolish?' he said. 'He let the enemy dictate the strategy. Once we'd stormed the walls of the palace and were fighting in the *megaron* Argurios pulled his men back to the great staircase. Then he and Helikaon stood there, as if daring us to attack them. We had greater numbers. We should have taken ladders and scaled the gallery above the stairs. Then we could have hit them from two sides. But we didn't. We just kept trying to defeat the two heroes. On the stairs our greater numbers counted for nothing. Then Hektor came, and it was we who were surrounded.' He talked then of how Kolanos had tried to bargain for his life by offering to betray Agamemnon, and how King Priam had refused him. 'I still don't understand it,' said Kalliades. 'The king we sought to kill allowed us to live, and the king we sought

101

to serve ordered us murdered. Perhaps you can make a story out of that, Odysseus.'

'I expect that I will one day.'

'And what of Piria?' asked Kalliades. 'Is she also free to do as she pleases?'

'You care for her?'

'Is that so strange?'

'Not at all. Merely a question. But to answer yours, yes, she is free to do as she wants. She will not stay with you, though. You realize that?'

'You don't know that, Odysseus.'

'There are many things I do not know. I do not know where the wind begins, or the sky ends. I do not know where the stars go in the daytime. But I know women, Kalliades, and Piria is not a woman who desires men. She never was.'

'Where do you know her from?'

Odysseus shook his head. 'If she has not told you, lad, then it is not for me to say. But to be close to her is to court danger.'

'She has suffered enormously these last few days,' said Kalliades. 'Her hatred of men is understandable. Yet I think she likes me.'

'I am sure that she does. Like a brother,' Odysseus added. 'I shall see her safely to Troy. Once there, however, she will be in great peril.'

'Why?'

'Like you she has a price on her head – many, many times greater than yours.'

'Why tell me this?'

'I like her,' said Odysseus, 'and I think she will

need friends in the days to come. Loyal friends.'

'Do you know why she is heading for Troy?'

'I believe I do. There is someone there she loves – and loves deeply enough to risk her life for.'

'But not a man,' said Kalliades softly.

'No, lad. Not a man.'

Odysseus rose and walked away from Kalliades, to the brushwood pig pen. The beasts were sleeping, huddled together on the landward side of the enclosure. He glanced back to the main fire, and saw Ganny, the yellow cloak stretched over him. The pig's head came up, and he looked at Odysseus. The king strolled over to him. 'You're a lucky fellow,' he said softly. 'The waves from that quake were what brought you in. Perhaps the gods love you.' Ganny gave a soft grunt, then fell asleep again. Odysseus smiled. 'Stupid pig,' he said fondly. 'I shall speak to Oristhenes and ensure you end up on no man's table.'

And now you are having moonlight conversations with pigs, he chided himself.

Adding wood to the fire he stretched himself out on the sand, hoping to sleep. Random thoughts fluttered across his mind like irritating bats. The woman Piria, whom he had known as the Princess Kalliope, was a danger to all who came into contact with her. Then there was the Mykene warrior and his lout of a companion. Agamemnon had declared them outlaws – renegades. To help them would undoubtedly earn the enmity of the Mykene king. Odysseus rolled over and sat up, brushing sand from his tunic.

The enmity of Agamemnon. There was a chilling thought.

And yet, was there anyone Agamemnon did not hate? Even his friends were only enemies in waiting. Moving to a water sack Odysseus drank deeply. Bias was sleeping close by. Odysseus prodded him with his foot. 'Are you awake?' he said, digging his toe harder into Bias's ribs. The black man grunted.

'What is it?'

'Well, as long as you are awake I thought we'd sit and talk of old times.'

Bias yawned, and cast a baleful glance at his king. 'Why do you never wake anyone else when you can't sleep?'

'They don't get as irritated as you do. It is less entertaining.'

'They get just as irritated, Ugly One – they simply don't show it.'

'I was thinking of keeping Ganny and selling the others. A mascot for the *Penelope*.'

Bias sighed. 'No you weren't. You're just saying that to rile me.'

'It's not a bad idea, though.'

'What? To rile me – or keep the pig?'

'Both have merit – but I meant the pig.'

Bias chuckled. 'I can see that it would be amusing. Yes,' he said, after some more thought, 'I like the idea.'

'It is a stupid idea,' snapped Odysseus. 'Pigs are sociable creatures. He would be lonely. He'd also stink the ship out.' He glanced at Bias, and read the knowing look on his face. 'Oh, all right, there is no tricking you tonight. I do like that pig, though!'

'I know. I heard you talking to it. Getting thick out there,' he added, pointing out to sea, where a white wall of mist was slowly seeping over the rocks.

'A good bright morning will clear it.' Odysseus rubbed at his eyes. They were gritty and tired.

'Have you considered what you'll do with our passengers?' asked Bias, reaching for the water sack and taking a swig.

'Take them wherever they want to go.'

'That's good.'

'The woman too.'

Bias looked at him. 'I didn't think there was any doubt about the woman.'

'Ah, did I not mention her?' said Odysseus, dropping his voice. 'She's a runaway priestess from Thera. It will mean death for anyone known to have helped her.'

'A runaway . . . Pah! You are still trying to trick me.'

'No, I am not.'

'Stop this now, Odysseus,' said Bias. 'I am in no mood for such jests.'

Odysseus sighed. 'You say you know me, Bias, my friend. Then look into my eyes and see if I am jesting. She is who I say.'

Bias stared at him, then took another drink. 'I am beginning to wish this was wine,' he said. 'Now speak truly, my king. Is she a runaway from Thera?'

'Yes.'

Bias swore. 'Did they not burn the last runaway?' he whispered, looking round nervously to see if any of the crew were awake.

'Buried her alive. They burned the family who took her in, and the captain of the ship she escaped on. Oh yes, and cut the head from the man she fled to be with.'

'Yes, I recall it now,' said Bias. 'So who is Piria? Please tell me she is the daughter of some tribal chieftain far from the sea.'

'Her father is Peleus, king of Thessaly.'

'Triton's teeth! She is the sister of Achilles?'

'Indeed she is.'

'We could hand her over in Kios,' said Bias. 'There is a temple of Athene there, and the priests could hold her until her family were notified.'

'Hand her over? Bias, my lad, was it not you who pointed out that two brave men rescued this maiden? And that my stories are all of heroes? Where is the difference?'

'You know very well what the difference is,' hissed Bias. 'The two Mykene will vanish away, join some foreign garrison and no-one will be the wiser. The girl is the sister of Achilles. Achilles the Slayer, the Blood Drinker, the Disemboweller. When she is captured – and she will be captured, Odysseus – the word will go out that the *Penelope* was involved in her escape. You want Achilles hunting you? There is no more famous killer in the lands of the west.'

Odysseus laughed softly. 'So, your argument is that we can be heroic when there is little chance of discovery, but if there is real risk we should be craven?'

Now it was Bias who sighed. 'It doesn't matter what I say. Your mind is set.'

'Yes, it is. Understand this, though, my friend. I agree with everything you've said.'

'Then why risk it?'

Odysseus fell silent for a moment. 'Perhaps because there is a story here, Bias. And I do not mean some tale to be told on a moonlit beach. This is a thread in a great tapestry. Perhaps I want to see the weave complete. Think of it. A royal priestess flees the Temple of the Horse, and is captured by pirates. Two of those pirates turn on their companions and risk their lives to save her. Then we happen along. Now, the Great Green is massive. What are the odds that she would end up on a ship captained by a king who recognizes her? And where is she heading? To the Golden City, where all the kings of west and east are gathering. Into a city seething with schemes, plots and dreams of plunder.'

'And Achilles will be there,' Bias pointed out.

'Oh, yes. How could he stay away? Hektor and Achilles, two giants of battle, two legends, two heroes. Pride and vanity will drive Achilles to Troy. He will hope that Hektor chooses to take part in his own Wedding Games. He will dream of bringing him low, so that men will talk of only one great hero.'

'So we are to sail into Troy bearing the renegade sister of Achilles? And what will she do there? Wander the streets until someone recognizes her?'

Odysseus shook his head. 'I believe she will seek out another former priestess of Thera – a friend.'

Realization dawned on Bias. 'You are talking of Andromache?'

'Yes.'

'Achilles' runaway sister will go to Hektor's betrothed?'

'Yes. Now can you see what I mean about the thread and the tapestry?'

'I don't care about threads,' said Bias, with feeling. 'However, the crew must not learn her identity.'

'She will not tell them. And the less they know the more content they will be.'

'*I* would have been more content not knowing,' said Bias angrily.

Odysseus grinned. 'Still think you know me better than I know myself?'

Bias was silent for a while, and when he spoke Odysseus heard the sadness in his voice. 'Oh, there is nothing in this that does not match what I know of you, Odysseus. The man I truly did not know was myself.'

'I think we never really know ourselves,' said Odysseus, with a deep sigh. 'I used to be the Sacker of Cities, a slave trader and a reaver. I thought I was content. Then I became the trader, the man with no enemies. And I *think* I am content. I was wrong then; am I wrong now?' He looked at Bias. 'Sometimes I think that the more I learn the less I know.'

'Well, *I* am more content serving the man with no enemies,' said Bias.

They sat in silence for a while. Finally Odysseus rose. 'I still dream of him, you know,' he said. 'I still hear his laughter.'

Sadness flowed over Bias as he watched the Ugly King wander away.

I still dream of him, you know. I still hear his laughter.

Fourteen summers had drifted by since those dreadful days of death and despair, but for Bias the memory remained, harsh and bright and painful.

During a slave raid on a foreign village Bias had been struck on the left forearm by a club. The bone had snapped, and was long in the healing. Still, they had captured eighteen women, and set sail for the slave markets of Kypros. The slaves had remained silent during the voyage, sitting huddled in the centre of the deck. But when they arrived at the island one of them, a tall woman with fierce dark eyes, had stared malevolently at Odysseus.

'Bask in your triumph, Sacker of Cities,' she said. 'Yet know this: before this season ends you will know the same anguish we suffer. Your heart will be sundered, your soul bathed in fire.'

Odysseus had shaken his head. 'You ungrateful bitch,' he said. 'Were you raped? Were you beaten? Have I not seen you all fed and looked after? You will all be as well off on Kypros as you were in that lice-infested village.'

'And who will give us back the husbands you slew, the children you left behind? The curse of Set sits upon your shoulders, Odysseus. Remember my words when the days shorten.'

Two more succesful raids were made before the *Penelope* and the three other ships returned to Ithaka. Bias had been left there, while his broken arm mended. Odysseus had spent three days with Penelope and his son, the six-year-old Laertes, and had then sailed on one more plunder raid.

Towards season's end Penelope told Bias she was going to Pylos, with Laertes. Nestor had invited them to one of his sons' marriage celebrations. Bias had travelled with her on the short voyage east.

The first three days had been massively enjoyable. Bias had been popular with the female slaves at Nestor's palace. One night two of them had shared his bed, one blonde and big-breasted, the other dark, with huge eyes. It was a fine night. Towards dawn they heard wailing coming from the palace.

Bias did not know it then, nor even sensed it through his joy, but the wailing heralded the days of death.

Plague had broken out ten days earlier in a village close by. King Nestor had ordered soldiers to quarantine the place, allowing no-one out. Later it transpired that a soldier had smuggled his sister from the village, and she had come to the palace. By the fourth day of her visit several slaves had shown the first symptoms: fever, and swellings in the armpits and groin. Within days the plague was rife.

The sick were taken to the stricken village, and placed in a large house owned by the merchant who supervised the flax gathering in the area. He had been the first to die. The villa became known then as the Plague House. Bias had been terrified. Apart from the broken arm he had never been sick in his life, and he dreaded the thought of incapacity almost more than death itself.

Then the child Laertes fell ill. Penelope had insisted on travelling with him to the Plague House. Bias felt like a coward, for he did not offer to go with her. He might just as well have. Two more nights went by, and he woke with a dry throat, sweat streaming from his body.

At first he had tried to hide the symptoms, but the slave girl sharing his bed told her mistress, and soldiers came to escort Bias from the palace, with several others who had fallen sick.

By the time the wagon reached the Plague House Bias was delirious, and he remembered little of the next few days, save that his body was racked by terrible pain, and his dreams were of fire-breathing monsters, whose burning breath blistered his flesh. But he was strong, and he survived the fever and the pus-filled cysts that burst the skin of his armpits and groin. Penelope came to his bedside often during the following days, bringing him broths, and clear, cool water to drink. She looked weary, for she was working tirelessly with three priests of Asklepios. More people were being brought in every day, and now many of the houses in the village were filled with fresh victims of the plague. Death was everywhere, and the screams of the dying echoed throughout the settlement. The sickness killed four in every five of those who contracted it.

Then Penelope had fallen ill. Bias carried her to the wide bed in which her little boy lay, and placed her beside him. Laertes had slept for the previous two days, unable to be roused even to drink cool water.

By the tenth day two of the three priests had also fallen ill. Now only the few survivors tended the victims. Bias had left the house one morning and called out to the soldiers who were guarding the fence that had been erected round the settlement, telling them that more help was needed inside. That afternoon four elderly priestesses of Artemis had arrived with the food wagon. They were stern-eyed, unfriendly women, who took charge with brisk efficiency. They directed Bias and three other male survivors to gather all the bodies and move them to open ground, where a pit was dug and filled with oil and brushwood. Here the corpses were burned.

Bias recalled the bright morning when Odysseus had appeared at the fence, shouting out for Penelope.

Bias had left the house, and saw his king standing at the perimeter, a cape of green upon his broad shoulders, the sunlight glinting on his red beard.

'Where are they, Bias?' he called out. 'Where is my wife, my son?'

'They are sick, my lord. You must stay clear of this place.'

Bias already knew that Odysseus, fearless in battle or storm, was terrified of sickness. His own father had died of the plague. So he was surprised on that day when Odysseus walked to the makeshift gate and lifted the leather latch. Soldiers had surrounded him, grabbing his arms and hauling him back. Odysseus had lashed out, sending one man spinning from his feet. 'I am Odysseus, king of Ithaka,' he thundered. 'The next man who lays hands on me will have that hand cut off!' They fell back then and Odysseus opened the gate and strode in.

Together they had entered the house. Odysseus had faltered then, as he saw the scores of plague victims laid out in the *megaron*. The air was foul with the stench of vomit, excrement and urine. Bias had led his king to an upper bedroom where Penelope lay, Laertes alongside her. Odysseus had slumped down beside them, taking Penelope's hand and lifting it to his lips. 'I am here, my love,' he said. 'The Ugly One is by your side.' Then he had stroked his son's face. 'Be strong, Laertes. Come back to me.'

But Laertes had died that night. Bias had been there. Odysseus had wept, his body shaking. He had hugged the dead child to his chest, his huge hands cradling the boy's head. Bias had seen Odysseus hug the boy many times. Laertes would laugh happily, and kiss his father's bearded cheek. At other times he would giggle helplessly as Odysseus tickled him. Now the child was utterly still, his face as pale as marble. After a long while Odysseus fell silent. Then he looked up at Bias. 'I brought this doom upon them,' he said.

'No, my king. You did not bring the plague.'

'You heard the slave woman. She cursed me. Said I would know the same anguish she had suffered.'

At that moment Penelope gave a soft groan. Odysseus gently laid his son back on the bed and moved to Penelope's side. He leaned over her, brushing the sweat-drenched hair from her glistening brow. 'Don't leave me, girl. Hear my voice. Stay with me.'

And there he had remained for three days, bathing her fevered body with warmed water, changing the soiled bedlinen, holding her to him, talking to her constantly, though she could not hear him. On the morning of the fourth day her cysts burst, her body expelling the poisons. One of the priestesses of Artemis came to see her.

'She will live,' she announced, then left the room.

Fewer and fewer people were brought to the settlement over the next weeks. The survival rate began to rise.

Autumn rains had begun the day Odysseus, Penelope and Bias left the settlement. As they walked along a cliff path towards Nestor's palace sunshine had briefly speared through the thick grey clouds. Bias had looked at his king. In the sunlight he saw the touches of grey at his temples, the weariness in his eyes.

Odysseus never spoke of the curse again. But that was the last summer the ships of Ithaka embarked on slave raids. Odysseus, the Sacker of Cities, the Reaver, the Pirate, became Odysseus the Trader, the Storyteller.

Bias lay back on the sand and stared up at the stars. In that moment he too remembered the laughter of Laertes. The boy would have been twenty now, and a man, handsome and strong.

Yet his death had brought fourteen years of peaceful trading from Odysseus. How many villages would have been raided in that time? How many wives torn from their homes to be sold into slavery? How many fathers cut down in front of their families? The thought surprised him, and he cursed softly. Glancing across the campsite he could see Odysseus sleeping soundly.

Why did you have to talk about threads and tapestries? Now *I* can't sleep!

VI

The three kings

KALLIADES WAS SITTING STARING OUT OVER THE MIST-shrouded sea. There was something sinister about the shimmering white wall, and the smokelike tendrils drifting over the dark, half-submerged rocks. He shivered, drawing his cloak more tightly about him. Easy to believe legends about sea monsters and demons of the deep when you gazed upon such a mist. Anything could be hidden there, watching the sleeping men on the beach. Thinking such thoughts made him remember his childhood, when he had sat at the Gathering Fire listening to the bard tell terrifying stories of night creatures who crept into houses and ate the hearts of the young. He had both loved and hated those stories – loved them while he sat with the other children, and hated them when he was later alone, listening for the soft footfalls of the night beasts. Many of the tales had involved magical mists which covered the movements of demons.

Kalliades suddenly smiled. 'You are not a frightened

child any longer,' he told himself. Then the smile faded.

He had been six years old when the reavers attacked the village, setting houses aflame, killing the men and dragging out the younger women. His fourteen-year-old sister, Agasta, had grabbed him and they had tried to flee. She had hidden him in a flax field. Then strong men had caught her. He remembered the look on Agasta's face: desperation, fear and anguish. She had fought them, scratching and biting as they raped her. In their fury at her resistance they had cut her throat. Kalliades had lain there watching the blood gush out.

Seeking to shut out the memory, Kalliades glanced up to where Piria was sitting beside her small fire. As a child he had been powerless to save his sister. As a man he had, at least, prevented a similar tragedy. Was there some small comfort in that?

A sound cut through his thoughts. Swinging back towards the mist he heard it again, a strange creaking groan. Then he heard muted shouts. The mist parted briefly and for a moment he saw a mast, canted at an odd angle, and the briefest vision of a hull. No sailors chose to spend the night at sea. Journeys upon the Great Green were dangerous enough without the added risk of blindly rowing in the dark, unable to see the reefs or sunken rocks.

Kalliades called out to the men round the campfire, and Odysseus, Bias and the rest of the crew moved out to the sea line. The wallowing ship was swallowed by the mist once more.

'Many of her oars have gone,' said Bias. 'Looks like she's sinking.'

No-one moved. They stood in a ragged line staring out at the wall of mist. Then the stricken vessel appeared again, this time broadside on. In the moonlight they could all see the painted bull's head on the prow.

Odysseus swore colourfully. 'That's Meriones' ship,' he said. 'By the gods, don't just stand there, you cowsons. I have a friend in trouble.'

Instantly the crew ran to the beached *Penelope*, pushing her out, then swarming aboard. Kalliades and Banokles would have gone with them, but Odysseus, the last man to scramble onto the deck, called back to them to stay on the beach. 'Set some signal fires,' he said. 'Likely we'll need some light to guide us back in.'

Odysseus ran to the foredeck and climbed to stand on the prow. The mist was so thick that he could not see the rear deck, or the figure of Bias at the steering oar. Even the sound of the oars dipping into the water was muffled and distant. He heard Bias calling out a slow beat, his voice muted and distorted by the fog.

Glancing to his left, Odysseus stared hard at the shimmering mist. Somewhere close, though invisible now, was a sheer wall of rock, rising from the sea. The blond giant, Leukon, was the lead rower on the port side. Odysseus called out to him. 'Stay watchful. Remember the cliff.' They were not moving fast enough for a collision to damage the *Penelope*. The danger was to the oars.

The *Penelope*'s hull creaked and groaned as the ship scraped slowly against a line of submerged rocks. 'Steady, lads!' shouted Odysseus. 'Lightly now!'

He was tired, his eyes gritty, his muscles aching and bruised from the rescue of Ganny. Sucking in a deep breath he squinted into the mist. 'Can you hear me, Meriones!' he bellowed.

There was no reply, and he called out several times more. A sailor appeared alongside him, a heavy rope looped over his shoulder. Then the *Penelope* began to vibrate. Odysseus swore loudly as another earthquake shivered the sea. The water began to roil. The *Penelope* swung sharply as the undertow took her, then suddenly pitched to port. Odysseus lost his hold on the high prow and started to fall. The crewman with the rope grabbed him, hauling him back to the deck. A large wave lifted the ship and the *Penelope* tilted sharply to starboard. Two of the rowers were thrown from their benches.

Odysseus scrambled back onto the prow. Bias was calling out urgent orders to the men, and the ship steadied. But they had been pushed back towards the cliff. It loomed out of the mist, huge and dark. Rocks began to fall into the sea, sending up great splashes all around them. Odysseus looked up. High above the *Penelope* was a massive overhang, almost as long as the *Penelope*'s keel. A large crack had appeared in it. The wind picked up, lashing the sea against the ship, driving it back towards the black wall.

'Row hard, you cowsons!' shouted Odysseus. The oars bit deep into the heaving water, but against the power of the incoming waves the rowers were struggling just to prevent the *Penelope* from being dashed against the cliff.

A sickening groan sounded from the rock face above. Dust and rock shards tumbled down from the widening crack in the overhang, striking the deck of the *Penelope* like hailstones.

'Ramming speed!' bellowed Odysseus. There was no ram on the *Penelope*, but all the sailors knew what he meant. With all their strength they hauled on the oars. Bias took up the fast beat.

'Pull! Pull! Pull!'

The *Penelope* began to inch forward. Odysseus licked dry lips with a dry tongue, his heart hammering.

'Come on, my girl!' he said softly, patting the prow. 'Bring us clear.'

Then came a thunderous crack from above – and the overhang sheared away. The passage of time ceased for Odysseus. He watched as the colossal rock broke clear, and knew that the ship was doomed. Surprisingly he felt no despair. The face of his wife appeared in his mind, and in her arms she held the infant Laertes. Odysseus heard the child laugh, and it filled his heart with joy.

In that moment a second undertow caught the *Penelope*, dragging her away from the cliff face just as the overhang crashed into the sea no more than a spear's length behind them. The shock wave lifted the small ship, spinning her. Then she straightened. Odysseus' laughter rang out, all weariness vanishing from him. 'The gods love us, lads,' he called out. 'We'll make a story out of this yet!'

'A pox on your stories!' came a voice. 'How about a little help?'

Odysseus glanced to starboard. The listing war galley was close now, the mist swirling round it. On its prow stood a heavily bearded figure, all garbed in black.

'I might have known it was you, Meriones,' called Odysseus cheerfully. 'You couldn't sail a twig across a puddle without it sinking.'

'Good to see you, too, you fat braggart!'

The sailor beside Odysseus looped the rope round the prow, then threw the coil across to Meriones. The war galley had been holed on the port side. Most of the crew had gathered to starboard, their combined weight helping to keep the hole above the water line.

With the rope fastened Odysseus ordered the crew to reverse oars, and slowly they hauled the crippled vessel towards the shore.

The mist was thicker now, and Odysseus made his way along the central deck to the rear. He could see no signal fires, but he could hear the faint sounds of shouting from the distant beach. They were using sound to guide him in, chanting 'Penelope' over and over again. Following the sound of her name the *Penelope* slowly backed water, until the first glimmerings of the fires could be seen. The Mykene warrior, Kalliades, had set a line of small blazes on the hillside in the shape of an arrowhead. Bias grinned. 'That was good thinking,' he said. Odysseus nodded.

'Once we've beached get everyone forward to haul on the rope. We'll bring her in alongside us.'

'Looks like there's been quite a battle,' said Bias.

Odysseus remained silent. The battle would have been with a pirate fleet. No single vessel would have dared attack Meriones. His reputation as a sea fighter was second to none, save perhaps for Helikaon. But why attack a Kretan war galley? It would be carrying no wealth.

The stern of the *Penelope* grounded on the sand. Bias called out for crewmen to take up the rope, and the war galley was pulled alongside. With the two ships safe Odysseus jumped down to the beach. Men clambered down from both ships and waded to the shoreline. A tall man in battle armour and helm strode towards Odysseus and halted before him. 'My thanks to you, Ithaka,' said Idomeneos, the king of Kretos, his voice harsh and grating. Before Odysseus could reply they were joined by the black-bearded Meriones.

Odysseus chuckled. 'So what happened, Meriones? Hit a rock, did you?'

'You know good and well what happened,' answered Meriones. 'We were rammed.'

'Cursed pirates,' said Idomeneos. 'You'd think a king could sail his own seas without such insult. I swear by Poseidon that once I've returned from Troy I'll bring a battle fleet into these waters and butcher all the scum I find.'

'How many were there?' asked Odysseus.

'Six galleys. We sank two, but lost one ourselves,' said Meriones. 'It was a merry time for a while there, flaming arrows, boarding parties, slashing blades. You would have enjoyed it.'

'I'd have enjoyed *watching* it,' said Odysseus. 'The *Penelope* is no warship. There is no ram on her keel. You think they'll still be hunting you tomorrow?'

'No doubt of it,' put in Idomeneos. 'They know who I am. They also know that every king around the Great Green is heading for Troy about now. This was a ransom raid. They thought to capture me and sell me back to my sons.' He glanced across the beach, and saw Nestor walking towards them. 'Ah, this is a fine turn of events. Three kings on a beach and not a warship among them.'

Odysseus directed them to the main fire then waited as injured men were helped from the damaged vessel. It was true: a ransom raid was the most likely explanation for the attack. He chuckled. Not that anyone would pay a copper ring to get Idomeneos back.

Recognizing one of the rescued men, Odysseus walked to where he sat slumped on the sand. 'Thought you'd be dead by now,' he said. The white-haired sailor had a deep gash on his shoulder, and a second puncture wound above the hip. The cut on the shoulder was bleeding badly. Bias came up with a needle and a ball of thin twine.

The wounded man sighed. 'Damn, but I'm sick of stitches, Odysseus. Even my wounds have had wounds.'

'Then what are you doing still at sea, old fool? Last I heard you had a small farm.'

'Still have. I've also got a new young wife, and two young sons.' The sailor shook his head. 'I'm too old to take the noise and the constant demands.'

Odysseus grinned. 'So fighting pirates was preferable?'

'Who would have thought that any pirates would be stupid enough to go against Meriones? Gods, man, we must have killed seventy of them today. Mind you, we lost thirty good men in the doing of it.'

'What happened?' asked Odysseus, as Bias threaded the needle.

'We were sailing for Kios. Pirate fleet came from behind a headland. Six galleys. I thought we were finished for sure.' He glanced across at the kings by the fire. 'We had Meriones, though. Best fighting sailor on the Great Green. Gave us an edge. Not much of one, mind. We were boarded. Hand to hand then.' The man gave a wry chuckle. 'That's when old Sharptooth laid into them. Man, you should have seen the shock on their faces.'

'Sharptooth?' queried Odysseus, pinching two flaps of skin together so that Bias could pierce them with the needle. The old sailor winced.

'King Idomeneos. We call him Sharptooth. He doesn't mind. Truth to tell I think he likes it. He's a fighter, that one. Mean-spirited as a skinny whore, and cold-blooded as a snake, but when it comes to fighting . . . Man, he was in among them so fast, shouting war cries and insults. It was a sight to see. Gladdens the heart to have a brave king.'

'The gods always bless a man with courage.'

'I hope you are right, Ugly One. But we were saved by the stamping feet of the gods. When the sea started to tremble the pirates called off the attack. They will still be there tomorrow, though.'

VII

Circle of the assassin

ODYSSEUS MOVED TO THE FIRE AND SAT DOWN ALONGSIDE the sleeping Ganny. The dark-garbed Meriones was slumped down on the sand, rubbing at his eyes. The man looked exhausted, Odysseus thought. Meriones was strong, but no longer young. The battle with the pirates, and then the long struggle to bring the ship to safety, had drained him. Nestor came and threw brushwood on the fire, then eased himself down, favouring his left knee. The old king's joints were stiffening, Odysseus knew, and pained him greatly. Nearby, King Idomeneos removed his sword belt and laid it on the sand. Odysseus glanced at him. He too was past forty. The whole world is getting old, thought Odysseus glumly. Idly he patted the pig, then lifted the borrowed cloak over its flanks. Ganny gave a little grunt and his eyes opened. His head lifted and he nuzzled Odysseus' hand.

'There just has to be a story there,' said Meriones, with a chuckle.

'I am in no mood for stories,' grunted Odysseus.

'Oh, then I'll tell it for you,' persisted Meriones. 'Odysseus obviously sailed back to the Witch Queen's island. You'll recall it was there some years ago that all his crew were turned into pigs – or so he tells it.'

Odysseus smiled then. 'Ah, but that was a good yarn. And you are right, Meriones. You remember my crewman, Portheos?' He patted the pig again. 'He just couldn't resist the Witch Queen's beauty. Everything was going well until she caught him gazing at her tits. I tell you, my friends, it is not a wise move to gaze at a witch's tits. And this is the result. We kept him on the crew out of loyalty, though he's as much use as a fart at a feast.'

'What was her name again, that Witch Queen?' asked Meriones.

'Circe. The most beautiful woman you ever saw.'

Meriones laughed aloud, then pointed at the brush enclosure where the other pigs were sleeping. 'And who are those unlucky fellows? Did they all stare at the queen's tits?'

'I fear they did,' Odysseus told him. 'Apparently they are all kings from distant isles, beyond Scylla and Charybdis. Each one of them came to the queen's island to woo her. Their missions were doomed from the start, for the queen had already lost her heart to a handsome sailor, a man of great wit and charm and sublime intelligence.'

'And . . . that would be you, of course?'

Odysseus chuckled. 'Did the description confuse you? Of course it is me.'

Nestor laughed. 'You know why she didn't turn you into a pig, Odysseus? It would have been an improvement.'

'Enough of lies about pigs,' snapped Idomeneos. 'What shall we do about the pirates tomorrow? I have less than a dozen men able to fight, and you have a crew of thirty. One small galley against four rammers.'

Odysseus sighed, and swung towards the king of Kretos. 'Why do your men call you Sharptooth?' he asked. 'I see no jutting fang.'

'I'd like to hear the answer to that,' put in Nestor.

'Are you both moon-touched?' grumbled Idomeneos. 'There are more than two hundred fighting men waiting to come against us and all you can think about are pigs and nicknames.'

'No-one is coming against us *tonight*,' Odysseus told him. 'We are three kings, sitting by a warm fire. When golden Apollo rises in the sky tomorrow, that will be the time to concern ourselves with pirates.' He called out to one of his crewmen to bring food for his guests, then lounged back, his arm over the drowsy black pig. 'So, Idomeneos, favour us with the tale.'

Idomeneos rubbed at his face, then removed his helm and laid it on the sand. 'They call me Sharptooth,' he said wearily, 'because I once bit off a man's finger during a battle.'

'His finger?' exclaimed Nestor. 'By the gods, man, that makes you a cannibal.'

'One finger does not make me a cannibal,' Idomeneos objected.

'Interesting point,' Odysseus mused. 'I wonder how

many fingers a man has to eat before he can correctly be called a cannibal.'

'I didn't *eat* the finger! I was struggling with the man, and my sword broke. He had a knife, and I bit him on the hand as we grappled.'

'Sounds like cannibal behaviour to me,' said Nestor, straight-faced. Idomeneos stared malevolently at the old king, and Odysseus, unable to hold it any longer, let out a shout of laughter.

King Idomeneos looked from one to the other. 'A pox on you both,' he said, which brought more guffaws, until crewmen brought them food and they settled down to eat.

'I wonder what has made the pirates so bold this season,' said Nestor, as they laid their empty platters to the sand.

'The death of Helikaon, I shouldn't wonder,' Idomeneos told him.

'What's that?' said Odysseus, his belly tightening.

'Did the news not reach Ithaka? He was stabbed at his own wedding feast,' said Idomeneos. 'By one of his crewmen – a man he trusted. Which is a damn fine reason to trust no-one, I say. Anyway, news of his death has spread around the Great Green these past weeks. Helikaon's fleets are not sailing. So no-one is hunting the pirates. And you know how they feared Helikaon's ship.'

'And rightly so,' put in Meriones. 'The *Xanthos* terrified them, with its Fire Hurlers. You still hear men talking about the day he roasted the pirate crew alive.'

Odysseus pushed himself to his feet and walked away

from the fire. Random images flashed across his mind: the youth Helikaon diving from a cliff top in Dardanos, the child Laertes dying in the Plague House, the older Helikaon on Blue Owl Bay, smitten with love after seeing Andromache. More and more memories flooded him.

Finding a spot away from the crew he sat down, staring out into the mist, thinking back to the death of his son, and how it had clawed his heart – how it still did. He had not realized until this moment that his feelings for Helikaon were so entwined with that loss. The youngster he had taken aboard the *Penelope* had been all a man could wish for in a son, and his pride in the boy had been colossal.

Helikaon's father, King Anchises, had believed his son to be weak and cowardly, but he was wrong. Helikaon had proved himself true. He had fought pirates and sailed through storms without complaint. All he had needed was a mentor who believed in him, rather than a merciless father with a desire to destroy him. Odysseus had been that mentor, and he had grown to love the lad.

Indeed, that love had led him to take a great risk, one which, if discovered, would have left Odysseus a marked man with powerful enemies.

How could it be that a valiant young man like Helikaon should be dead, while old men like himself, Nestor and Idomeneos still joked round campfires?

With a heavy sigh he rose and walked further up the cliff. Reaching the top he saw more campfires on a beach to the north, where four pirate vessels had been drawn up. He stood watching them for a while, his thoughts dark.

He heard a noise and turned. The black pig, trailing its yellow cloak, had walked up the cliff path to stand alongside him.

'I lost my boy today, Ganny,' he said, kneeling down and patting the beast's flanks. His voice broke, and he fought back tears. Ganny nuzzled him. Odysseus drew in a deep breath. 'Ah, but the gods hate a weeper,' he said, a touch of anger in his voice. Rising, he stared balefully down at the pirate camp. 'You know who I am, Ganny? I am Odysseus, the Prince of Lies, the Lord of Storytellers. I will not weep for the dead. I will hold them in my heart, and I will live my life to the full in honour of them. Now down there are some evil cowsons, who tomorrow will seek to cause us harm. We don't have the swords or the bows to outman them, but by Hades we have the guile to outwit them. Ganny, my boy, tomorrow you will be taken away by Oristhenes to a life of idle shagging. Tonight you can come with me, if you have a mind to, and we'll have an adventure. What say you?' The pig cocked its head and stared at the man.

Odysseus smiled. 'You are wondering about the danger, I see. Yes, it is true they may kill us. But, Ganny, no-one lives for ever.'

With that he began to stroll down the long hill towards the pirate camp. For just a moment the pig stood still, then he trotted after the man, the yellow cloak dragging in the dirt behind him.

* * *

Kalliades finished helping with the wounded, then sought out Banokles, who was sitting a little way from the main campfire, watching the three kings talking together. The big man looked dejected.

'I think we angered one of the gods,' he said sourly. 'We haven't had any luck since we sailed back from Troy.'

Kalliades sat down beside him. 'We are alive, my friend. That is luck enough for me.'

'I've been trying to think which one,' persisted Banokles, scratching at his thick blond beard. 'I've always sacrificed to Ares before a battle, and occasionally to Zeus, the All Father. I once took two pigeons to a temple of Poseidon, but I was hungry and traded them for a pie. Maybe it's Poseidon.'

'You imagine the god of the deep has been nursing a grudge because of two pigeons?'

'I don't know *what* causes gods to have grudges,' said Banokles. 'What I do know is we have no luck. So someone must be in a shitty mood.'

Kalliades laughed. 'Let us talk of luck, my friend. When you surged up the stairs to face Argurios and Helikaon you should have died. By all the gods, they are the two most ferocious warriors I have ever seen. Instead you stumbled, took a blade through the arm and survived. Me? I am skilled with a sword . . .'

'You are the best,' interrupted Banokles.

'No – but that is not the point. I too ventured my blade against Argurios, and took a cut to the face. So, we both lived. Even then we should have been doomed.

When we were surrounded by those Trojan soldiers there was no way out for us. King Priam let us go. What is that, if not luck?'

Banokles thought about it. 'I'll grant our luck has not been *all* bad. But fashion something good *now*. A single ship – and not a warship – facing four pirate vessels tomorrow. What chance do we have?'

'We could stay on this island and let the *Penelope* sail without us.'

'Wouldn't that be cowardly?' asked Banokles, suddenly hopeful.

'Yes.'

'What do you mean yes? You're a clever man. Couldn't you find a reason to stay behind that *wasn't* cowardly?'

'I suppose I could, if I could be bothered to try,' Kalliades told him. He glanced across to where Piria was sitting, her cloak tight round her shoulders.

'I think you like her,' said Banokles. 'At least, I hope so, after all the trouble she's caused us.'

'She has no love of men in her,' replied Kalliades. 'But you are right. I like her.'

'I liked a woman once,' said Banokles. 'Or at least I think I did.'

'You have rutted the length of the western mainland. What do you mean *you liked a woman once*?'

'You know! Liked. Even after shagging.'

'You enjoyed her company?'

'Yes. She had green eyes. I used to like to look into them. And she could sing too.'

Kalliades sighed. 'Somehow I can tell that this story

131

is not going to have a happy ending. What did you do? Rut with her sister? Eat her dog?'

'Slavers took her from our village. Most of the men were up in the hills, felling timber, gathering dead wood for winter fires. They took twenty women. I met an old friend from our village a couple of seasons back. He was a crewman on a trade ship. He came across her in Rhodos, wed to a merchant. Four children. He said she seemed happy enough. That's good, eh?'

Kalliades fell silent for a moment, then he clapped Banokles on the shoulder. 'We could stay behind because we are passengers, and we did not name a destination. Therefore we could make *this* our destination, which means we do not have to fight pirates alongside Odysseus. How does that sound?'

Banokles looked glum. 'Still sounds cowardly.' He glanced up. 'Where is that pig going?'

Kalliades swung round to see the pig in the yellow cloak wandering away from the fire and starting up the cliff path. Odysseus was nowhere in sight, and the other kings were settling down beside the fire.

'Never thought to see a king risk his life for a pig,' said Banokles. 'Makes no sense.'

'Nor to me. I will say, however, that I was glad to see the pig make it to shore.'

'Why?' asked Banokles, surprised.

Kalliades shrugged. 'I don't know. It shouldn't have been able to swim so far. Only courage – and a troubled sea – carried it into the bay.'

'A courageous pig?' Banokles snorted. 'You think the meat will taste any different?'

'I doubt we'll find out. Odysseus would likely kill anyone who harmed that beast.' Ganny was almost at the cliff top. 'Come on, let's shepherd it back to camp.'

'You go. I'm tired and I'm comfortable here.'

'You are the man who knows about pigs – or so you claimed. And I doubt I could encourage it back alone.'

Banokles heaved himself to his feet. 'I could have chosen Eruthros for a sword brother,' he said.

'So you keep telling me.'

'He wouldn't bother to chase a wandering pig.'

'Eruthros is dead. If he had the choice I'll wager he'd sooner be chasing a pig than walking through Hades.'

'Truth in that,' agreed Banokles.

VIII

Lord of the Golden Lie

BANOKLES WAS STILL GRUMBLING AS THEY CLIMBED THE
cliff path, but Kalliades closed his mind to it. Thoughts
of Piria were troubling him. Banokles was right. He did
like her. There was something about the tall, slender
woman that touched him deeply. She was proud, strong
and defiant, though it was her loneliness that affected
him most, and he sensed in her a kindred spirit.

Yet why was there such a price on her head? He
already knew she was not a slave, but she was a runaway. Odysseus had said that the bounty on her was
many times greater than that on Banokles and himself.
If that was true then it must have been set by a rich
king. And she could not have come far in that small
sailboat. He thought of the lands and major islands
round about. Odysseus was king of Ithaka and the
islands around it, and Nestor was lord of Pylos. On the
mainland far to the west there was Sparta, but that was
now ruled by Menelaus, brother of Agamemnon, and

he was, as yet, unmarried. And she could not have come that far, surely. Idomeneos, the king of Kretos, was here, and he obviously knew nothing of the runaway woman. If he had then he would have recognized Piria as he walked past her to the campfire.

Then he remembered the great temple. They had sailed past a large island, and on the cliff top he had seen an astonishing sight: what appeared to be a colossal horse, staring out to sea. He had learned from the pirates it was the Temple of the Horse, built with King Priam's gold. 'An island of women,' one of the crew had told him, 'all princesses, or girls of noble birth. I wouldn't mind a few days there, I can tell you.'

'No men at all – not even soldiers?' Banokles had asked.

'Not a one.'

'Then why isn't it raided?'

The man had looked at Banokles scornfully. 'The High Priestess is Mykene, and the women are all daughters of kings. An attack on Thera would bring galleys from every city state and every kingdom in pursuit of vengeance. They'd scour the seas until the last pirate vessel was burned. No-one goes near Thera.'

Kalliades paused in his walk up the hill. Banokles looked at him. 'What is wrong?'

'Nothing. I was just thinking.'

Piria had to have come from Thera. Kalliades knew little about the temple there, but Banokles had been interested and had questioned the pirates about it. As they walked he said, 'You recall that island we passed, with the horse temple?'

'Of course. An island of women.' Banokles grinned. 'Be good to be shipwrecked there, I think. Gods, you'd never want to be rescued, would you?'

'Probably not. Do the women ever leave the place? To get married, or go home?'

'I don't know. No, wait! There was a girl last season, someone said. Sent off to Troy. That's it! Sent to marry Hektor. Don't recall her name. So, yes, they must be allowed to leave.' Banokles walked on, then stopped. 'Although somebody else said that a girl some years back was killed for leaving without permission. Why are you interested?'

'Just curious.'

They crested the cliff and saw Odysseus walking down the path on the other side, the pig ambling beside him. He was heading towards a beach, where four ships had been drawn up.

Kalliades scanned the area. There were close to two hundred men on the beach. In the bright light of their campfires he could see some of them bore wounds. Others were eating and drinking. 'I think they are the pirates who attacked King Idomeneos,' he said.

'Then why is he going down to them?' asked Banokles. 'You think he knows them?'

'Could you recognize a man at this distance?'

'No.'

'And the ships bear no markings. I do not think he knows them.'

'Then it is madness,' said Banokles. 'They'll kill him – and take that golden belt. And they'll eat the pig,' he added.

'I agree – and Odysseus must know that too. He is a clever man, and he has a plan,' said Kalliades. 'And by all the gods he has nerve!'

Banokles muttered a foul oath. 'You are thinking of following him down there, aren't you? What little luck we have left is in a pot, and you are about to piss in it.'

Kalliades laughed. 'You go back, my friend. I have to see how this plays out.' He moved on. After a few moments Banokles caught up to him, as he had known he would. The big man walked alongside him, saying nothing, his expression set and angry.

Kalliades saw Odysseus glance back, but he did not wait for them. He and Ganny went on, then strolled along the beach. Several pirates looked up, then nudged their comrades. A crowd gathered, staring at the odd sight of an ugly man in a gold belt, and a pig in a yellow cloak. Odysseus walked on, apparently unconcerned by the interest.

Kalliades and Banokles were some twenty paces behind him when a lean figure stepped away from a fire and stood in Odysseus' path.

'Whoever you are you are not welcome here,' said the man.

'I am welcome anywhere, donkey face,' responded the Ugly King. 'I am Odysseus, king of Ithaka and lord of the Great Green.' He looked past the insulted man and called out, 'Is that you, Issopon, skulking by the fire? By the gods, why has no-one killed you yet?'

'Because they can't catch me,' replied a burly warrior with a black and silver beard. Heaving himself to his feet, he walked out to face Odysseus. He did not offer his hand, but stood alongside the lean pirate who had first spoken. 'I did not know you were in these waters.'

'The *Penelope* is on the next beach,' Odysseus told him. 'As you would have known, had you the wit to put out scouts. You boys look as if you've been in a fight, but since I hear no singing or bragging I guess you lost it.'

'We did not lose,' snapped the first man. 'It is not over yet.'

Odysseus turned and stared at the four galleys on the beach. 'Well, you didn't fight the *Xanthos*,' he said, 'for I see no fire damage on your vessels.'

'The *Xanthos* is not sailing this season,' Issopon told him.

'You are wrong, my friend. I saw its black horse sail only yesterday. But no matter.' Walking to a nearby sailor, Odysseus leaned down and lifted the man's jug of wine from the sand. Raising it to his lips, he drank deeply.

The silence grew, and Kalliades felt the tension within it. No-one seemed to have noticed his arrival with Banokles. All eyes were on the Ugly King. For his part Odysseus seemed utterly relaxed. He drank a little more, then patted Ganny, who slumped down beside him.

'Why is the pig in a cloak?' asked Issopon.

'I'd like to tell you,' answered Odysseus, 'but poor Ganny here is embarrassed by it.'

'It was the Witch Queen, wasn't it?' someone called out.

'Should never stare at a witch's tits,' agreed

Odysseus. 'No matter how beautiful they are. No matter how plump and inviting. Ganny knew this. We all knew it. But when that cold wind blew, and her nipples pushed out against the gold of her dress ... well, it was just too much for the boy.'

'Tell us!' called out another man. This was followed by a chorus of entreaties. The noise startled Ganny, who lurched to his feet.

'Can't do that, lads. Ganny here would die of shame. But I can tell you a tale of piracy and a fleece that rained gold, and a man with no heart, and a woman of such purity and beauty that wherever she trod flowers sprang up about her feet. You want to hear it?'

A great roar went up, and the pirates settled down on the sand in a great circle round him. Kalliades and Banokles sat down among them, and Odysseus began his tale.

For Kalliades the time spent on that beach was a revelation. It was an evening he would never forget. Odysseus' voice deepened, the sound almost hypnotic, as he told the story of a voyage many years before. He spoke of storms and omens, and a magical mist that shrouded the ship as they sailed close to the coast of Lykia. 'I was younger then, almost a boy,' Odysseus told them. 'The ship was the *Bloodhawk*, captained by Praxinos. You might remember the name.'

Kalliades saw some of the older men nod. 'Aye,' continued Odysseus, 'the name lives on, usually in whispers on cold winter nights. He was a man possessed, for he had heard of the Golden Fleece, and it haunted his dreams and his waking.'

No-one spoke as Odysseus told his tale. Not a man moved, not even to add fuel to the fires. Kalliades closed his eyes, for the words of the storyteller were forming pictures in his mind. He could see the sleek black ship and its blood-red sail, and almost feel the coldness of the mist settling around it as the wind died.

'Now the Fleece had a strange history,' said Odysseus. 'As many of you will know, there are men who use fleeces to collect gold in the high mountains of the east. They lay them down under gushing streams and the gold dust and fragments cling to the wool. But this fleece was different. A wise old woman once told me that it came from a changeling, half man half god. One day, as he was being hunted by angry men, he changed himself into a ram and sought to blend himself into a flock of sheep. However, the shepherd boy saw him, and alerted the pursuers. Before he could change back they fell upon him with swords and knives. Not a man among them wanted to eat the cursed meat, but the shepherd boy skinned the carcass and sold the fleece to a man hunting gold. And that, lads, was where the legend began. He journeyed into the mountains, found a likely stream, and laid the fleece below the water. Soon it began to shimmer and glisten and by dusk it was so laden with gold that it took all the man's strength to draw it clear. And that was only the beginning. He hung the fleece to dry, and then began to brush the gold from it. He brushed and he brushed. Four small sacks he filled, yet still the fleece glimmered like stolen sunshine. All the next day he brushed and he brushed. Eight more sacks were filled. And yet the fleece was still full. Having no more sacks he carefully rolled the fleece and sat back, wondering what to do. Other men began to come down from the mountain, complaining that all the gold was gone. Not a speck of dust remained. The man was no youngster, and he was not consumed by greed. He took his sacks down into the valley, and used his gold to have a house built, and to acquire horses and cattle. He bought a wife and settled down to a life of quiet plenty. He had a son, a beloved son, a child whose laughter echoed in the valleys like springtime. One day, the son was struck down with the plague. The man was in despair, for the boy, who was sun and moon to him, was dying. A workman on his farm told him of a healer who lived in a mountain cave and he journeyed there, bearing his son upon his back.'

Odysseus paused and lifted the jug of wine to his lips, drinking deeply. Even in the silence the spell of his story continued. No-one moved. Wiping his mouth with the back of his hand he told them of the woman in the cave. 'Young she seemed, and beautiful, serene as the sunset. She gazed on the dying boy with eyes of love, and laid a slender hand upon his brow. Then, with a low sigh, she closed her eyes and drew in a long, deep breath. All fever left the child, and his eyes opened. He smiled at his father. So great was the father's relief that he returned to the woman later, and gave her the magical fleece.

'Now Praxinos had heard this story, and he was determined to find the cave, the woman, and the fleece of everlasting gold. Others had tried, it was said, but none had succeeded. For the woman was so pure that no man with even a speck of goodness within him could bring himself to cause her harm. This did not concern Praxinos, for there was nothing inside him but bitterness and bile. He would have the fleece, and kill the woman. This he vowed. One of the crewmen told me he even made a blood pledge to the darkest of the old gods, Kephelos the Devourer, the black-fanged Lord of Shadows.' Odysseus shook his head. 'Perhaps it was he who sent the mist that wrapped itself round the *Bloodhawk* like a shroud. We rowed on, slowly and carefully, expecting at any moment to see land, or to feel the sea floor scrape beneath our keel. But we did not. Around us we could hear ghostly singing and whispering, our names being called by spirits of the night. Ah, lads, it was a frightening time, and I do not know on what sea we sailed that night. Come the dawn the mist disappeared, and we found ourselves upon a wide river, flowing through a mountain range.

' "The Fleece is close by," shouted Praxinos. "I can feel it calling to me."

'We found a landing place and moved ashore. Praxinos split us into hunting parties and we set off in search of the healer's cave. There was me, and old Abydos, plus a youngster named Meleagros and a Hittite called Artashes. Abydos was a foul-mouthed sheepshagger and one of the ugliest men you've ever seen, while the rest of us were little better. Not a handsome one in the group. We walked up through woods of scented pine, and across a pretty meadow, full of yellow flowers. That's when we saw it. There was a cave, and a large crowd of people sitting on the grass outside it. They were villagers, and they'd brought gifts of food for the healer. Must have been fifty people there, old and young, men and women.

'Well, there were only the four of us, so we wandered up to the cave and made no threatening moves. I looked inside. And there she was, sitting on a rug and talking to an old man and his wife. Beyond her, on the wall of the cave, shining like golden fire, was the Fleece. We all saw it, and fell under its spell. Before I knew what I was doing I walked into that cave, jaw hanging, and stood there, gawping. Abydos was beside me, slack-mouthed. The young Hittite whispered something that sounded like a prayer, and Meleagros reached out and touched the Fleece, and his finger came away coated in gold.'

Odysseus fell silent once more. He seemed to shiver at old memories, then shook himself. 'Then the woman rose from her rug. She was no longer young, but a finer looking woman you never saw. She walked over to old Abydos and laid her hand on his shoulder. He smiled at her. Now, I've told you he was an ugly man. But from that day on he was no longer ugly. Strangest thing, for his features did not change. He looked exactly the same, only there was no ugliness in him. "I welcome you," she said, and her voice was like honey, smooth and sweet, a sound you could feast on. Now Meleagros had a boil on his neck, a great angry thing, leaking pus. She touched it, and the redness faded away, leaving only clean, sun-browned skin. Well, not one of us even thought of going to find Praxinos. But then we didn't have to. Just before dusk he stormed into the cave, sword drawn. We had no time to think, and certainly no time to stop him. He rushed across the cave floor, and plunged his blade into the woman. She fell back with a cry. Then he wrenched the Fleece from the wall, and fled with it back to the ship.

'We didn't go with him. We were reeling from what we'd seen. Then old Abydos knelt beside the dying healer. There were tears in his eyes. Meleagros dropped down beside him. "I wish I had magic for you," he said. "Magic like yours." And he laid his hand on her brow. And you know what? That damned boil suddenly flared up again on his neck, and the wound in her chest seemed to close a little. There were some people close by. I swung to them. "Did she heal you?" I asked them. They nodded. "Then have the courage to give back the gift," I urged them. One by one they came forward. It wrenched the heart to see it. One old woman touched her, and the crone's hands began to twist grotesquely, her arms shrivelling and withering. Another man leaned over her, and a huge growth appeared on his throat. And all the while the healer's wound was closing further, shrinking. At the last she sighed and opened her eyes. We helped her up and she gazed round at the cripples and dying all about her. Then she spread her arms and a golden light blazed throughout the cave. I was blinded for a moment, but when my sight came back all the sickness and suffering in the place had passed. Everyone was well again.'

His voice faded away.

'What about the Fleece?' cried a pirate.

144

'Ah, yes, the Fleece. I was angry as I headed back to the ship. I had decided then to gut Praxinos like a fish, throat to groin, and throw his body into the river. A lot of us felt the same way. When we reached the *Bloodhawk* we saw him sitting in the captain's chair, the Fleece on his lap. We scrambled over the side and advanced on him. The light was fading now and we heard him cry out: "Help me! For pity's sake!"

'That was when I saw his hands. They had turned to gold – not covered in dust, but solid metal. And as we watched we could see the gold flowing slowly up his arms. Old Abydos moved alongside him and rapped his knuckles against Praxinos' right leg. It clanged. I looked into the captain's eyes then. By all the gods I never saw such terror. We just stood there. He was dead before the gold reached his face, yet still it spread, until even his hair was gold thread. Once it was over we eased the Fleece from his knees. Not a speck of gold remained. It was just a fleece.'

'What did you do?' asked another man.

'Nothing we could do. Abydos took the Fleece back to the healer, and we broke up Praxinos and shared him among us. I used most of my share to have my first ship built. I did keep one small piece to remind me of the perils of being too greedy.'

Odysseus dipped his hand into the pouch at his side and pulled out a finger of solid gold, which he tossed to the nearest man. 'Pass it around, lad. But don't hold it too long. It is cursed.' The seaman looked at it in the firelight, then handed it swiftly to the man beside him. The finger of gold passed from hand to hand, coming at last to Kalliades. He held it up. It was perfect in every way, from the broken nail down to the creases at the knuckle joint. He offered it to Banokles. 'I don't want it,' muttered the big man, leaning back. Finally it was returned to Odysseus, who dropped it back into the pouch.

'Another tale!' shouted a young pirate.

'No, lad, too tired tonight. But if you are heading northeast you can beach with us tomorrow. I'll likely be in the mood for a tale then. I'll be travelling with King Idomeneos. He's also a fine storyteller.'

'He's the man we are hunting,' said the first man who had spoken to Odysseus upon his arrival.

'I know that, donkey face. It is a foolish mission. You think to take him for ransom. And who would pay? Idomeneos has two sons, and both would like to be king in his place. They wouldn't give you a copper ring. They'd let you kill him. Of course, honour would then insist they brought the entire Kretan fleet in seach of you. Memory tells me it is more than two hundred galleys. They'd scour the seas.' Then Odysseus chuckled. 'But I read men well, and I see you already know this. Therefore your quest is more about blood vengeance than ransom. What did Idomeneos do to you?'

'I don't answer to you, Odysseus.'

'True. You'll answer to them, though,' he said harshly, gesturing towards the waiting pirates. 'They sail for plunder, not revenge. No profit in blood.'

'He stole my wife and killed my sons,' said the pirate, his voice shaking. 'And when he'd finished with her he sold her to the Gypptos. I never found her.'

Odysseus was silent for a moment, and when he finally spoke his voice had lost its harshness. 'Then you have reason to hate. No man would deny that. If anyone took my Penelope I would hunt them down and see them suffer. A man can do no less. But it is a personal matter, and the men with you will risk death for no reward. Idomeneos did not take their wives, nor slay their sons.'

With that the Ugly King prodded Ganny with his toe, then set off back towards the cliff path. The pig stood for a moment, then ran after him. Kalliades and Banokles followed.

'That was a fine story,' said Kalliades. 'Where did you really get that golden finger?'

Odysseus looked tired, and his reply was toneless. 'It is mine,' he said, waggling his index finger. 'I had a goldsmith make a cast for me last summer, and then fill the cast with gold.'

'How many pirate ships will come against us now?' asked Kalliades.

'Probably two, three at worst,' said Odysseus. 'Issopon is a wise old fighter. He heard my words and will draw his galley from the action, I think. Donkey face is another matter entirely. He has a need for blood. And I cannot blame him. Idomeneos always was a cruel and selfish man.'

Piria slept a little, but her dreams were troubled. She saw again the day she and her brother went swimming for the last time in the rock pool beneath the marble boulders. Three years older than she, at fifteen Achilles was already a handsome young man, strong and athletic, delighting in his prowess with javelin and sword. He was also a fine rider and wrestler. Father adored him, pouring compliments upon him, and showering him with gifts. Piria was never jealous. She adored Achilles, and delighted in his successes.

On the day of the last swim the shaded rock pool echoed with their laughter. Such sounds were rarely heard within the palace, high upon the rocky hillside above them. Father was a hard man, and quick to anger. Servants and slaves trod warily, and even retainers spoke in low whispers.

Awake now, in the light of a golden dawn, the dream still clung to her like sea mist upon rock. Piria shivered. He had not been cruel when she was young. Often he would sit her on his knee, twisting his fingers through her long fair hair. Sometimes he would tell stories. Always they were harsh tales, of sword and blood, of gods donning human form to bring chaos and destruction to the world of men. Then a change had come over him. Looking back, she understood now that it mirrored the pubescent change in her. His eyes were on her often, his manner becoming more surly and cold. Piria had been perplexed at the time.

On that terrible day understanding had arrived like a lance. She had been sitting naked with her brother when their father had stormed down the rock path, shouting abuse at her, calling her a whore. 'How dare you cavort naked before the eyes of a man?' he screamed.

It was mystifying, for she and her brother had swum naked together throughout childhood. Father's rage was towering. He ordered her brother to dress himself and return to the palace. When Achilles had gone he grabbed Piria by the hair.

'You want to cavort with men, slut? Then I shall teach you what that means.'

Even now she could not suffer the memory of the rape that followed, and closed her mind to it, her eyes scanning the beach seeking something to divert her.

Odysseus was talking to a stout merchant, who was walking round the pig enclosure, examining the beasts. Kalliades and Banokles were standing apart from the crew, talking quietly. She saw the black man, Bias, approaching her. He was carrying a breastplate of leather, and a round leather helm.

'Odysseus told me to bring you these,' he said. 'There is likely to be a fight, and that will be preceded by a rain of arrows.'

'Who are you fighting?'

'Pirates.'

Fear welled up in her, but she did not show it. Instead, she thanked him, removed the cloak of Banokles, and slipped on the breastplate. It was crudely fashioned, but it fitted her well. The helm was too large, so she put it aside. Moments later she saw Bias take another breastplate to Kalliades. As he donned it he saw her looking at him and smiled. She looked away.

Odysseus approached her. 'Best you get aboard,' he said.

'Did you get a fine price for your pigs?'

'No. Had to pay Oristhenes to look after the wounded we have to leave behind. Idomeneos assures me he will repay me, but the man is a miser with a poor memory when it comes to settling debts. I am still waiting for a wager he lost twelve seasons back.' He smiled and shook his head. 'Kings! Not one you can trust further than you can toss an ox.' He fell silent then, and stood staring back at the pigs.

'I think Ganny will miss you,' she said.

Odysseus laughed. 'He squealed when I took that yellow cloak from him. I think he had grown to like it. I may visit him next time I'm sailing these seas.'

'He will be smoked meat by then,' she said.

'No, not Ganny! Oristhenes assures me he will be treated like a king among pigs. He will be happy here.'

'And you trust Oristhenes to keep his word?'

Odysseus sighed. 'I trust in his sense of self-preservation. I did not sell Ganny to him. Ganny is my pig. Oristhenes can use him for breeding, and for that he will ensure he is well fed. Oristhenes knows me. He will do as he promises.'

'Or you will kill him, Odysseus?'

'I would not kill a man over a pig. I might just burn his house and sell him into slavery. But I'd not kill him. But let us talk about you, Kalliope. Why did you run from Thera? It was foolish, and beyond dangerous.'

'You think me some witless girl?' she snapped. 'My time on Thera was the happiest of my life. No vile and devious men, no betrayers, no rapists. I am seeking a friend, for a seeress told me she would need me before the end.'

'The end of what?'

'I do not know. The seeress saw flames and burning, and my friend fleeing savage killers.'

'And you will save her?' The question was asked gently, with not a trace of contempt.

'If I can I will.'

Odysseus nodded. 'I fear the vision may be true. A war is coming that cannot be long avoided. Your friend is Andromache. I met her on her way to Troy. Fine woman. I liked her. We made a pact, she and I, that I would always tell her the truth.' He chuckled. 'Not a promise I made lightly. Storytellers fashion lies from truth and truth from lies. We have to. Truth is all too often dull.'

'Did she speak of me?' asked Piria, before she could stop herself.

'She spoke of her love for Thera, and how unhappy she was to be leaving. You love her greatly, don't you?'

'She is my life!' said Piria defiantly, looking into his eyes for signs of contempt or disgust.

'Beware who you share that with,' he said softly.

'Are you not going to tell me that my feelings will change when the right man comes into my life?'

'Why so angry?' he countered. 'You think I will condemn you? Love is a mystery. We embrace it where we can. Mostly we do not choose whom we love. It just happens. A voice speaks to us, in ways the ear cannot hear. We recognize a beauty that the eye does not see.

We experience a change in our hearts that no voice can describe. There is no evil in love, Kalliope.'

'Tell that to my father. Tell it to the priests, the kings and the warriors of this cursed world.'

He smiled. 'Ganny is a brave pig, and I like him. I would waste no time, though, trying to teach him the skills of sailing.'

Piria found her anger fading, and she smiled at the Ugly King. 'Now that is a good thing to see,' he said. They stood together for a little while, and Piria felt the warmth of the sun on her face, and the freshness of the sea breeze in her cropped hair. She turned towards Odysseus.

'You said storytellers fashion truth from lies? How can that be?' she asked him.

'A question I have long pondered.' He pointed at Bias. 'I once told a tale about a winged demon who attacked the *Penelope*. I said that Bias, the greatest spear thrower in the world, hurled a javelin so powerfully that it tore through the demon's wings and saved the ship from destruction. Bias was so taken with the story that he practised and practised with the javelin, and finally won a great prize at a King's Games. You see? He had become the greatest, because I lied about it. And therefore it was no longer a lie.'

'I understand,' said Piria. 'And how can the truth be made into a lie?'

'Ah, lass, that is something none of us can avoid.' Bending down, he scooped up the small clay plate upon which Bias had brought her food the night before. 'And what is this?' he asked her.

'A plate of clay.'

'Yes, clay. And it was fashioned by the hands of a man, using water and thick earth and then fire. Without the fire it would not have become pottery, and without the water it could not have been shaped. So it is earth, it is water, it is fire. All these facts are true. So, is this a true plate?'

'Yes, it is a true plate,' she said.

Suddenly Odysseus struck the plate with his fist, shattering it. 'And is it still a plate?' he asked.

'No.'

'And yet it is still pottery, still clay and water and fire. Do you think I changed a truth with my fist? Did I make it a lie?'

'No, it *was* a plate. You destroyed it, but you could not change the truth of its existence.'

'Good,' he said admiringly. 'I like to see a mind work. My point is that truth is a mass of complexities, made up of many parts. What is the truth of you? The High Priestess on Thera would say that you are a traitor to the Order, and that your selfish actions could bring disaster upon the world should the Minotaur awake and plunge us all into darkness. Is that the truth? You would say that you are driven by love to protect a friend, and you are willing to risk your life for her. Would the High Priestess accept that truth? If I hand you over to the Order the same High Priestess will call me a good man, and reward me. Will that be the truth? If I bring you safe to Troy – and it is discovered – I will be declared godless and cursed. I will be named as an evil man. Truth or lies? Both? It depends upon perception, understanding, belief. So, to return to your original question, it is not hard to make the truth a lie. We do it all the time, and mostly we don't even know it.' He glanced at the eastern sky. 'The sun is up. Time to leave.'

IX

Black horse on the water

THE SEA WAS CALM, THE BREEZE A LIGHT NORTHERLY AS the *Penelope* was floated clear of the beach. The last crewman scrambled aboard, and the oars were slid out into the bright blue water. Odysseus stood on the rear deck, watching the rowers. All the crew now wore leather breastplates and helms, and beside them as they rowed lay strung bows and quivers of arrows. Odysseus himself had also donned a breastplate. It was of no better quality than those worn by his men. Beside him stood the brilliantly armoured, high-helmed Idomeneos. Nestor wore no armour at all, just a green knee-length tunic and a long cloak of startling white, but both his sons wore breastplates and carried round shields. They stood close, ready to protect him.

The breeze was fresh with the promise of rain as the *Penelope* eased away from the shore. Once on open sea Bias called out a quicker beat, and the rowers leaned more heavily into their oars.

'You say he had a face like a donkey?' Idomeneos asked Odysseus. 'I recall no such man.'

'He recalled you,' Odysseus told him.

'You might have asked his name.'

'If you cannot recall a man whose sons you slew and whose wife you stole I doubt the name would have helped.'

Idomeneos laughed. 'I've stolen a lot of wives. Believe me, Odysseus, most of them were happy to be stolen.'

Odysseus shrugged. 'I expect you'll be meeting him soon. His face may be the last thing you ever see.'

Idomeneos shook his head. 'I'll not die here. A seer once told me I would die on the day the noon sky turned to midnight. Hasn't happened yet.'

Odysseus moved away from the Kretan king, scanning the sea and the headlands. As he did so he heard the big man, Banokles, complaining to Kalliades. 'Not much fighting room if anyone boards. And if those pirates are also wearing leather breastplates I won't know who I'm killing.'

'Best only to kill those trying to slay you.'

'That is a good plan. Fight defensive. I'm better attacking, though. I'll wager you wish you hadn't left your armour on that pirate ship. I did tell you. That leather breastplate wouldn't turn aside a hurled pebble.'

'I should have listened to your pessimism,' agreed Kalliades. 'But then you are the man who wears armour to a brothel.'

'A man never knows when danger will strike,'

Banokles pointed out. 'And I was once stabbed by a whore's husband.'

Kalliades laughed. 'In the arse. You were running away, as I recall.'

'I liked the man. Didn't want to kill him. Anyway, it was just a nick. Needed no stitches.'

Odysseus smiled. His liking for these two was growing daily.

Piria was standing at the stern, gazing back at the land. Her shoulders were stiff, her features set. Odysseus saw Kalliades move alongside her. 'She is a fine ship,' he said.

Piria's reply was cool. 'I used to wonder why men say *she* when talking about their boats. When I was young I thought it respectful. Now I know differently. The boats go where men tell them. They are merely things for men to ride upon.'

Odysseus stepped in then. 'Love plays a part, Piria. Listen to the crew when they speak of the *Penelope*. You will hear nothing but affection and admiration.'

'Different truths,' she said, which made him smile. Kalliades looked mystified.

Odysseus caught sight of a ship appearing from behind a headland to the north, about a half-mile ahead. It was a big galley, twenty oars on each side, and there were fighting men massed on the central deck. Bias had also seen the ship, and leaned in to the steering oar, angling the *Penelope* away from them. Odysseus moved past Kalliades, dropped to one knee and lifted a hatch before lowering himself down below deck. When he emerged he was carrying a huge bow, crafted from wood, leather and horn. A quiver of very long arrows was hanging from his shoulder.

'You are privileged today,' he told Piria. 'This is Akilina, the greatest bow in all the world. I once shot an arrow into the moon with it.' She did not smile, and Odysseus felt the tension and fear emanating from her. Pride alone was holding her together.

'I have heard of the bow,' said Kalliades.

'Everyone has heard of *that* bow,' put in Banokles. The comments delighted Odysseus, but his attention remained on Piria.

'Andromache talked of her skills with a bow,' he said.

At the sound of her lover's name Piria brightened. 'Sometimes she could best me,' she said, 'though not often.'

'Could you use a bow like this? Are your arms strong enough to draw the string?' he asked, handing her the weapon.

Piria took Akilina from him, stretched out her arm, curled three fingers round the string, then drew back. She managed a three-quarter pull before her arm started to tremble. 'That is good,' said Odysseus, 'believe me.' Retrieving the bow, he leaned towards her. 'If they get close enough to board I will leave Akilina with you. At that range even a three-quarter pull will punch a shaft through a skull.' He swung to the two Mykene. 'You lads will stay close to me, and follow where I go.'

The *Penelope* surged on, her prow cutting the water. The pirate vessel, with its greater oar power, was closing slowly.

'Another one!' yelled a seaman.

A second pirate vessel was coming from the south, some way back. 'If the wind wasn't against us,' said Odysseus, 'the *Penelope* would outsail them easily. As it is, with more oarsmen, they'll come on swiftly. Best you keep your heads down. It will be raining arrows before long.'

Kalliades glanced at the oarsmen on the *Penelope*. They were rowing steadily, but with no real urgency. Their movements were smooth and rhythmic, and they did not even bother to stare at the two enemy ships. Bias called out an order. The right bank of oars lifted from the water, remaining motionless. The left powered on. The *Penelope* swung sharply towards the first galley. Odysseus ran down the central aisle and clambered up onto the curved rail of the prow. Straddling the rail and bracing himself with his legs he notched an arrow to his massive bow. As the two ships closed, enemy archers crowded along the deck of the pirate vessel. Odysseus drew back on Akilina and let fly. The shaft soared through the air, punching into the back of a rower, who cried out and slumped forward. Pirate bowmen let loose a volley of shafts, but they all fell short, splashing into the water off the port bow. Odysseus sent two more arrows into the pirates. One struck a man on the helm, bouncing clear. The other plunged through the shoulder of a bowman. Odysseus threw up his arm, signalling Bias, who yelled out an order, then thrust his weight against the steering oar. The *Penelope* changed course instantly, almost dancing away from the attacking galley. The manoeuvre was accomplished with great skill and timing, but even so, for a few heartbeats, they were in range of the pirate archers. Banokles, Kalliades and Piria dropped to crouch behind the stern rail. A ragged volley of arrows slashed across the rear deck, hitting no-one, but coming close to Bias, who was standing tall at the steering oar. One shaft thudded into the deck rail beside him. Another hit the steering oar and ricocheted up past the black man's face.

Odysseus ran back along the deck, and shot three more arrows from the stern. Only one scored a hit, slicing through the forearm of an archer. Odysseus took a deep breath, then loosed a fourth shaft.

'Ha!' he cried triumphantly, as the arrow took a man through the throat. 'Come at the *Penelope*, will you?' he bellowed. 'By Ares, you'll regret it, you cowsons!' Several arrows flashed by him, but he stood statue still, shooting back into the massed pirates. 'A little more distance would be pleasant,' he yelled at Bias, as another enemy arrow flew past his head.

Now the men of the *Penelope* fully leaned on their oars, sweat streaming from them as they heaved and pulled. The ship picked up speed. Kalliades lifted his head above the stern rail and watched as the distance between the ships began to increase. He saw Odysseus shoot another pirate, the arrow lancing into the man's face. Then the king changed the direction of his shafts, sending them over the heads of the bowmen and into the rowers. Two oars on the port side of the enemy vessel crashed together, and the pirate galley veered. The *Penelope* sped on.

'Hey, donkey face!' shouted Odysseus. 'Don't give up now. Nothing worth having ever comes easy!'

The second galley was closing fast. Bias altered course to keep the distance between them, but that only allowed the first pirate vessel to move back into range.

Odysseus swore softly. If they continued in this way the men of the *Penelope* would exhaust themselves, and the pirates would still catch them. He glanced at Bias. The black man understood this also. 'Which one, my king?' he asked.

'I think we need to kill donkey face,' Odysseus replied.

Bias yelled out orders. The left bank of oars lifted from the water, the men on the right powering their oars at speed. The *Penelope* swung sharply. Meriones, carrying a powerful black bow, ran to join Odysseus.

'Thought you might be bored,' said the Ugly King, 'so I have decided to attack.'

The black-garbed bowman chuckled. 'Let us have a wager first.' He pointed to the first pirate ship. An archer had climbed to the prow rail and was waiting, arrow notched, ready to shoot as soon as they came into range. 'A gold ring says I can knock him from his perch before you do.'

'Agreed!' said Odysseus.

Both men moved along the central deck to the prow, then drew back on their bows, letting fly together. Two shafts slammed into the chest of the enemy archer. His body crumpled, then tipped forward to plunge into the sea, and vanish beneath the keel of pirate vessel.

Meriones continued to shoot as the distance closed

between the ships. Odysseus left him there, running swiftly back to the rear deck. Handing his quiver and bow to Piria, he summoned Kalliades and Banokles to him.

'Bias will swing the *Penelope* at the last moment, and we'll try to shear away their starboard oars. Likely though that they'll haul us to them with grappling hooks. When that happens they'll expect to board us. What they won't expect, because of their greater numbers, is that we'll board them.'

Banokles glanced at the oncoming pirate galley. 'Must be around sixty men on that ship.'

'At least.'

'And another sixty on the second ship.'

'You have a point to make, or are you merely bragging about your ability to count?' Banokles fell silent. 'Stay close to me,' said Odysseus. 'I'm not as nimble as I used to be – and I wasn't the greatest sword fighter then.'

The *Penelope* swung hard to port, as if she was seeking to avoid a collision, then, just as swiftly, moved back to starboard. The two vessels crashed together, but the angle of impact meant the ram on the pirate galley merely slid along the starboard side. The *Penelope*'s rowers tried to drag their oars back across the deck, to prevent them from being splintered, but the collision had come so swiftly that only six of the fifteen oars were saved. Even greater damage was done to the pirate oars as the *Penelope* slid along the galley's hull. Grappling hooks were hurled from the pirate vessel, biting into the *Penelope*'s rail.

This close Odysseus could see the faces of the pirates. Many of them were men who had cheered him yesterday, begging him for more tales. They were garbed now for war, some in leather breastplates, others in makeshift shirts of thick, knotted rope. There were helms of all kinds, some in the high, curved Phrygian style, some of wood, some of leather. Several of the men wore headgear crafted from copper. Most of them were carrying daggers, though many held clubs of wood.

'Follow me,' said Odysseus. He glanced at Banokles and grinned. 'If you have the balls for it.' Drawing his sword, he ran down to the central deck, and hurled himself across the narrow gap and into the mass of fighting men on the pirate ship.

He slammed into the first rank shoulder first, his weight scattering them. Several men fell heavily; others tried to make room to stab at him. Odysseus grabbed a man by his rope shirt, hauling him in to a savage head butt. Blood exploded from the man's ruined nose. Odysseus hurled him aside then slashed his sword in a wide arc. It struck a pirate in the forearm, slicing through flesh and spraying blood through the air.

'Come at Odysseus, would you?' he raged, his sword hacking and slashing, left and right. For a moment the pirates fell back from the fury of his assault. Then they surged at him. The huge form of Banokles clattered into them, spilling men to the deck. Then came Kalliades, his sword stabbing out like a serpent's tongue, lancing into throats, chests and bellies. 'You are all dead men now!' bellowed Odysseus. A pirate darted at him, stabbing for the throat. Odysseus threw up his left arm, blocking the blow, cleaving his sword against the pirate's skull and shearing away his ear. The man screamed and fell back.

Other warriors from the *Penelope* joined in the attack. Banokles shoulder-charged a man, sending him flying. Odysseus continued to rage at the pirates, shouting battle cries and insults as he powered forward. Kalliades had forced his way to the right of Odysseus, and was fighting defensively now, protecting the Ugly King. Banokles was on the left. Even in the midst of the action Odysseus noted the skill they showed. The three had now formed a wedge, with Odysseus as the point. At first they forced the pirates back, but then the weight of numbers began to tell, and the advance slowed.

Odysseus was tiring, for he had fought with no economy of effort, slashing his sword about him with all his might. A pirate hurled himself at him, his club thudding against Odysseus' leather breastplate. The king stumbled, and fell back, hitting the deck hard. Kalliades turned swiftly, plunging his sword through the back of the pirate's neck. The dead man fell across Odysseus. Kalliades took up a defensive position in front of Odysseus to block any further attacks. Odysseus pushed the dead man away from him, and slowly climbed to his feet, sucking in great breaths. The noise of battle was all around him now, the deck slick with blood. His sword arm felt as if it was weighed down with rocks, but his strength was returning.

'Make way, Kalliades!' he thundered. 'Odysseus has more enemies to kill.'

Then he hurled himself once more into the fray.

* * *

Piria stood on the rear deck, the great bow forgotten in her hand. She saw Odysseus jump onto the pirate ship, followed by Banokles and Kalliades, and a dozen men from the *Penelope*'s crew. Then Bias drew two fighting knives and climbed to the rail, leaping down to join the fight. The air was filled with battle cries and screams, and the sound of swords clashing. The Kretan, Idomeneos, rushed to join them, as did the two sons of King Nestor. The fighting was fierce, and she saw Odysseus hacking and slashing his way towards the stern of the vessel, Kalliades and Banokles beside him.

A hand touched her arm. Meriones pointed to port, where the second pirate vessel was closing. Notching an arrow to his bow he sent the shaft winging across the narrowing gap. It struck the high prow. Meriones swore. 'Don't you be telling Odysseus about *that* shot,' he said.

The remaining sailors on the *Penelope* were all armed with bows now, and sent a ragged volley towards the oncoming vessel. Several arrows found their targets. Then came a fierce response. Some forty shafts slashed through the air. Many punched into the deck rail, others skidding across the deck itself. Five crewmen were hit. Piria notched a shaft to the great bow and let fly. The arrow slammed into the chest of an archer. He fell back.

'Good shot,' cried Meriones, loosing a shaft himself. Piria did not see it strike home, for she was already drawing another arrow from the quiver and notching it to Akilina. All fear had gone now, and she continued to shoot, ignoring the shafts that hissed by her.

Suddenly the pirate vessel veered sharply away. Enemy bowmen continued to shoot, but swiftly the ship moved out of range, heading south.

'They are going to turn and ram us,' said Meriones grimly.

But the galley did not turn. Its rowers were labouring hard to put distance between the two ships.

The men on the *Penelope* dropped their bows, drew swords and knives, and ran to join their comrades fighting on the first pirate vessel. Piria turned to watch them – and saw a massive ship coming from the north. It was bigger than any vessel she had ever seen. Forty oars on either side, in two banks, and a mast as tall as a tree. From the mast a huge sail billowed, and upon it was painted a rearing black horse.

'Ah, we are blessed today by all the gods,' said Meriones. 'That is the *Xanthos*.'

'It is . . . colossal,' said Piria.

'Indeed it is – and the bane of all pirates. There are Fire Hurlers on the decks, and a crew of more than a hundred fighting men. And for honest folk like us there is no better sight than that monster.'

Moving to the starboard rail Piria saw that the battle had turned. There were far fewer pirates now, but the fighting was still fierce. She looked for Kalliades, but could not see him. Fear gripped her then, for she saw Banokles still battling alongside Odysseus. Then she caught sight of Kalliades, and relief flowed through her. He had been hidden by the mast. She watched him cut down an enemy, then force his way to stand beside Odysseus.

Some of the pirates threw down their weapons, but there was no quarter, and they were hacked to death. Others threw themselves over the side and into the sea. An ugly man with an unnaturally long face screamed at Idomeneos and threw himself at the Kretan king. Before he could come close he was knocked from his feet by Banokles. Swords plunged down into the man. Piria heard his gurgling death cries.

And the battle was over.

Odysseus sat slumped by the mast, exhausted, watching as the mighty *Xanthos* glided close by. A familiar voice called out, 'Ho, Odysseus! Where are you, sea uncle?'

Wearily he pushed himself to his feet and walked to the starboard rail and leaned upon it. Looking up he saw a tall, wide-shouldered man with golden hair standing at the prow of the giant ship.

'By the tits of Thetis,' he cried, 'what fool put you in charge of a ship?'

Hektor, prince of Troy, laughed. 'Ah, that would be a mighty fool indeed. No, my friend, I am merely a passenger – albeit a passenger with a sword. Are you not a little old to be fighting pirates?'

'Old? I am in my prime, you impudent wretch!'

'I believe you, sea uncle. Looks like you'll need a little help with that galley. I can loan you twenty men.'

'They would be welcome, Hektor, my friend.'

'We'll manoeuvre alongside and send them down to you.'

Odysseus called out his thanks and wandered back to the mast. His hands were trembling now, and he felt nauseous. Bias joined him, kneeling alongside.

'How many did we lose?' Odysseus asked him.

'Eight dead, eleven more with deep wounds, and almost everyone else has been cut or pierced save for me and Leukon. Even then we got off lightly, Odysseus. What of you? You are covered in blood. Any of it your own?'

Odysseus shook his head. 'Who are the dead?'

Bias named them, and a deep sorrow was added to the burden of weariness. Odysseus leaned his head back against the mast. All around him men were stripping the dead pirates and throwing their bodies over the side. The *Xanthos* eased alongside, throwing a deep shadow over the deck. Ropes were lowered, and twenty men shinned down them.

'Damn, but I never used to feel this tired after a battle,' said Odysseus. 'Especially not after winning one.'

'I know,' said Bias. 'I feel it too.'

'You will not tell me we are getting older,' Odysseus warned him.

Bias smiled. 'No, Odysseus. Perhaps we are just getting wiser. The thought of all the men who were alive this morning, and walking the Dark Road now, is dispiriting. And what was achieved? We gained an old galley, a few weapons for trade, and maybe some plunder. None of it was worth the loss of those eight men. Especially young Demetrios.'

Odysseus closed his eyes. 'Go and give the new men

tasks,' he told Bias. 'Transfer any plunder to the *Penelope*.'

'Yes, my king,' said Bias. 'How do you want to proceed?'

'Hektor's men can manoeuvre the galley back to Titan's Rock,' said Odysseus. 'They can pick up the wounded we left behind. We will push on. With a favourable wind we can reach Apollo's Bow by dusk, and if not we'll beach at Humpback Bay.'

Bright sunshine shone across the deck as the shadow of the *Xanthos* moved away. Odysseus heard Hektor call out to him.

'We're going after those pirates, Odysseus. Where are you bound?'

'Apollo's Bow,' shouted Odysseus, as the huge ship glided on towards the south.

Bias moved off to where the twenty new crew members were standing, and the Ugly King sat quietly, gazing down at his blood-covered arms and hands. The fingers had stopped trembling now, but he still felt sick. Young Demetrios had been a good lad, quiet, hard-working, and so proud to have been chosen to replace Portheos. The faces of the other dead men floated across his mind. He had sailed for close to twenty seasons with Abderos, the only man on the crew never to have taken a wife. During winter he lived alone, carving wood and making rope, rarely speaking to anyone. Once back aboard in the spring he would grin widely and embrace his comrades. All he had was the *Penelope*. And now he had died to protect her.

Wearily Odysseus climbed back to his ship.

Banokles strolled over to him and squatted down. He too was blood-spattered, his face and beard bright with red spots and streaks.

'I was wondering,' he said cheerfully, 'if Kalliades and I could become Ithakans. For the Games at Troy, I mean. After all, we can't take part as Mykene.'

Odysseus had no wish for conversation. His mind was still reeling with the loss of his comrades. But this man had saved his life several times today, so he drew in a deep breath and considered the question. 'What is your skill?' he asked at last.

'I'm a fistfighter.'

'And Kalliades?'

'Swordsman.'

'There are no sword events in the Wedding Games. Only the Mykene have death bouts.'

'Ah. He's also a fine runner.'

'Leukon is our fistfighter, Banokles. And you may recall that the last time I saw you in a fist fight you were lying on your back with your arms over your head.'

'True,' said Banokles. 'But there were five of your lads, and I told you I was only catching my breath.'

Odysseus smiled. 'There will be some great fighters in Troy. Truly great. I couldn't enter a man who might shame Ithaka.'

'I wouldn't do that! I'm a terrific fighter.'

'You are a great *warrior*, Banokles. I've seen that today. But fistfighting is different.'

'I could beat Leukon,' said Banokles confidently. Odysseus looked into his eyes.

'I'll tell you what I'll do,' he said. 'Tonight we will be

having a funeral feast for our friends who died today. We will speak their praises, and offer libations for their safe journey to the Elysian Fields. There are not enough men without wounds to stage any Funeral Games. But, if Leukon agrees, you and he can fight in honour of the departed.'

'Wonderful,' said Banokles happily. 'And if I win we can be Ithakans in Troy?'

'You can,' said Odysseus.

He watched the big man amble away. More heart than sense, he thought. Glancing round the deck he caught sight of Leukon, and called him over. Swiftly he told the giant of Banokles' request. Leukon shrugged. 'You want me to fight him?'

'Yes.'

'Then I will.'

'He says he can beat you.'

Leukon stared across at Banokles. 'His reach is shorter than mine, which means he'll take more blows. He's got a good neck, strong arms. Chin looks solid. He has the makings of a fighter. Yes, it will be good practice.'

After Leukon had gone Odysseus felt a fresh wave of weariness. He wanted to lie down on the deck and sleep, but his conscience pricked him. What kind of example will it set if you are seen sleeping as others labour?

A pox on examples, he told himself. I am the king. I do as I please. With that he stretched himself out, laid his head on his arm, and slept.

* * *

Towards mid-afternoon the last of the clouds disappeared and the sky blazed with a brilliant blue. There was no breeze and the heat increased. A section of old sail was raised to create a canopy over the port side of the *Penelope*'s stern deck. Nestor, his sons and Idomeneos rested there.

Piria wandered to the prow and gazed out over the blue water. Sharp pain spasmed through her lower body, the agony so great she almost cried out. Instead she closed her eyes, seeking to steady her breathing and ride the pain, blend with it, absorb it. It did not pass completely – it never had since the savagery of the attack upon her. It merely ebbed and flowed, sapping her strength.

It has only been a few days, she told herself. I will heal. They will not break me. I am Kalliope, and I am stronger than any man's hate. Yet the pain today was worse than before, and it frightened her.

Opening her eyes she tried to concentrate on the brilliance of the blue sea, sparkling with sunlight. It was so peaceful now that the events of the morning seemed almost a dream. She had killed men today, sending sharp arrows to pierce their flesh, just as they had pierced hers. She would have thought that the slaying of pirates by her own hand would have been somehow fulfilling – like a just punishment. Yet where was the satisfaction? Where was the joy in revenge? Piria even felt a little sadness for the death of the young man, Demetrios. He had not spoken to her, but she had observed him with his fellows, seeing his shyness, and sensing that he felt inadequate in the company of such veterans. She had not seen him die, but had watched as they laid his body alongside his seven dead comrades. In death he seemed little more than a child, and the expression on his face was one of utter shock.

Do not pity him, cried the dark voice of her fears. He was a man, and the evil of his gender would have shown itself as he grew older. Do not feel sympathy for any of them! They are all vile.

Not all of them, she thought. There is Kalliades.

He is no different! You will see! His kind words mask the same savage soul, the same need to dominate and possess. Do not trust him, stupid girl.

She saw him walking towards her, and the twin curses of her need and her fear clashed inside her. He is my friend.

He will betray you.

Kalliades smiled a greeting, then looked out over the water, as if seeking for something. She turned to lean on the rail and the pain subsided a little. The relief almost brought tears to her eyes. Kalliades continued to scan the water. His expression was serious, and yet again she thought that he did not give the impression of a man of violence. There was no suggestion of cruelty in him.

'You do not look like a warrior,' she said, the words slipping out before she could stop them.

'Is that a compliment or an insult?'

'Merely an observation.'

'Meriones was impressed with your bow skills. I would guess he didn't expect you to be a warrior either. Though obviously Odysseus did.'

'An astute man,' she said.

Kalliades laughed. 'Astute he may be, but he's terrifying to fight alongside. Twice he nearly took my ear off. I think I spent more time avoiding his wild slashes than I did fighting the pirates.' He fell silent for a moment, and she glanced at him. 'It made me proud when Meriones praised you,' he said.

The dark voice in her head cried out triumphantly, You see! *His* pride. Already he seeks to own you. Anger flared. 'What right do you have to be proud of me?' she stormed. 'I am not like a horse of yours that has won a race.'

'That is not how I meant it. I was just . . .' He glanced down, and his face changed. 'You are bleeding,' he said. 'Are you wounded?'

Piria felt the trickle of blood running down the inside of her thigh. The sea breeze had flicked open her torn gown, exposing the scarlet stain. Pain tore through her, almost beyond bearing. Am I wounded? Stupid, stupid man! My body has been ripped and torn, my flesh pounded and bruised. My heart and soul have been assaulted and defiled.

Are you wounded?

Outrage spilled from her like floodwater bursting through a river bank. Her eyes filled with tears and her vision misted. The figure before her was no longer Kalliades. In that moment he became the father she had loved, who had betrayed her, the brother she had adored, who had spurned her. Hatred and despair vied for control.

Angry words poured from her in a torrent. 'You think I don't know what you really are?' she cried.

'Your soft words are *lies*! Your friendship is a *lie*. You want what all men want. I see it in your eyes. Come on then. Beat upon me with your fists, bite my flesh, curl your fingers round my throat and choke off my breath. Then you can step away from me and say: "Look what *you* made me do, *slut*!"' Her breathing ragged, she backed away from him. In the silence that followed she became aware that her outburst had been shrill, and that crewmen were staring at her. Kalliades remained where he was, and when he spoke his voice was soft, his tone conciliatory.

'I am sorry, Piria. I – I will . . . leave you for a while. We can . . . talk later, if you like. Or not.'

Once more the pain subsided. She saw him turn away. Suddenly terrified to be left alone at the prow, with all men's eyes on her, she called out to him. 'There is no need to go,' she said, her voice breaking. 'I . . . am sorry.'

He hesitated, and she saw him glance towards the crew, noting their interest. Then he walked back to stand between her and their curious gaze. 'It is I who am sorry – sorry for all that you have suffered,' he said gently. 'I will never harm you, Piria. Never cause you pain. Try to hold to that thought.'

She looked up at him. 'Are you in love with me, Kalliades?' The question was out before she could stop it, and she silently cursed herself for her stupidity. Either way she did not want to hear the answer.

He looked into her eyes, and she felt the power of his grey gaze. 'My feelings are my own,' he said at last. 'All I know is that you are sailing for Troy to be with someone *you* love. If you will allow me I will see you safely there.'

'I could never love a man in the way that he would desire. You understand that?'

'Have I asked you to love me?' he countered.

'No.'

'Then the problem does not arise.' Movement out on the waves caught his eye and he turned. 'Look there!' he said, pointing to starboard. Three dolphins, sleek and grey-blue, were leaping and diving through the waves. 'I have always loved watching them,' he said. It was a clumsy change of subject, but she was grateful for it.

'They are very beautiful,' she told him, then glanced up at him, wanting to offer him some indication of her trust. 'My true name is Kalliope,' she said at last.

He smiled. 'We are well named,' he said. 'Beautiful Voice and Beauty Hidden. Your voice is good on the ear. And my name becomes increasingly true with every new scar.' He paused then. 'I take it that this name should remain secret?'

'Yes.'

'I thank you for trusting me. I will not betray you.'

'I know that, Kalliades. You are the first man I ever met I could say that about.' They stood in easy silence now, watching the dolphins, listening to the oars striking the water, and the slow, lazy creaking of the timbers. Banokles joined them. He was still wearing his heavy breastplate and his face was smeared with blood.

'Are we all friends again?' he asked.

'We are friends,' said Piria.

'Good – for I have news!' Banokles grinned at Kalliades. 'We can enter the Games to be held in Troy for Hektor's wedding. There will be wrestling, fistfighting, races – foot, horse and chariot. There will be an archery tourney and a javelin competition. I'm going to enter the fistfighting, and with the gold made on wagers we can live well for a good while. Maybe even buy some . . . some . . .' he glanced at Piria and cleared his throat, 'some horses. Anyway, what do you think?'

'A good plan.' Kalliades nodded. 'With a few flaws. First, we represent no nation or city. Second, we were last in Troy as invaders and might just be considered unwelcome if we make ourselves known. Third – and this, I think, is the most important – you are a brawler who did not reach the final of the contest to find the best boxer in our company of fifty. As I recall Eruthros defeated you.'

'All right,' said Banokles grudgingly, 'I might not become champion, but I'll win a few bouts. So we could still earn gold. And what about the foot races? Was there anyone faster than you in our company?'

'No, but again there were only fifty men in it.' Kalliades sighed. 'Let us say I agreed that we could take part. Whom would we represent?'

'Aha! I have dealt with that,' said Banokles triumphantly. 'I asked Odysseus if we could be Ithakans.'

'And he agreed?' asked Kalliades, surprised.

'Not entirely. He pointed out that Leukon was representing Ithaka in the boxing, and that he was the best fistfighter on the crew. He said I could be an Ithakan if I beat Leukon tonight at the funeral feast.'

'And how does Leukon feel about that?'

Banokles grinned broadly. 'Happy as a pig in shit. He says it will be good to have a practice bout. Apparently no-one else on the crew will practise with him.'

'Have you considered why that might be?'

'Of course. I imagine it's because he hits like a kicking horse.'

'And that doesn't worry you?' put in Piria.

'I've been kicked by a horse before. I got up. I always get up. When I win will you agree to join me for the Games?'

Kalliades glanced at Piria, who was smiling. 'What do you think?' he asked her.

Piria looked towards where Leukon was rowing, then back at Banokles. 'I think that horse you spoke of must have kicked you in the head,' she said.

Odysseus watched his three passengers talking together at the prow. The woman, Piria, was calmer and smiling now. A rare sight. He recalled his visits to her father's palace. She had been younger then, and withdrawn, her face always serious, her blue eyes full of suspicion and mistrust.

'Who is she?' asked Idomeneos.

Odysseus shrugged. 'Just a girl taken by pirates. They raped her. Kalliades and his friend stole her from them.'

'They'll not get much of a price for her. Too loud. Any slave spoke like that to me and I'd have her thrashed.'

'They are not intending to sell her, or keep her.'

'Then why steal her?'

'Why indeed?' said Odysseus.

Moving to the starboard rail, he leaned out and gauged their progress. The wind had picked up, and Humpback Bay was close by off the port bow. The long crescent beach of Apollo's Bow could be seen in the distance. Several ships had already beached there.

Kalliades left the prow and made his way along the central deck to join him. 'May we speak, Odysseus King?' he asked.

'Words cost nothing,' Odysseus replied.

'Your man Leukon is a skilled fistfighter?'

'That he is.'

'Banokles is not,' said Kalliades. 'He has a great heart and courage like a mountain.'

'Then Leukon will fell him like a tree.'

'No, Odysseus King. Leukon will drop him, and Banokles will rise to be struck again. He will continue to rise as long as his heart is beating. He will fight on until he is crippled or dead. That is the nature of the man.'

'I take it you are telling me this for a reason.'

'I tell you because it may have seemed an amusement to allow Banokles to believe he could become an Ithakan. This fight will *not* be an amusement, unless your joy is derived from blood and suffering.'

'Your man requested this,' said Odysseus. 'His fate is in his own hands. Should he wish to withdraw I will think no worse of him.'

Idomeneos, who had been listening, stepped from beneath the tent canopy and joined them. 'That is a fine sword you are wearing,' he said to Kalliades. 'Might I see it?'

Kalliades drew the weapon, reversed it and handed to to the Kretan king. The pommel was a lion head of bronze, the hilt leather-bound, the blade sharp and true. 'Good balance,' said Idomeneos. 'Made by a master smith. Not a blade to let a man down in battle.'

'It was the Sword of Argurios,' Kalliades told him. 'A weapon to cherish.'

'Would you consider trading it?'

'No.'

'For the sword of a hero I would pay well in gold.'

'I will never trade it,' said Kalliades.

'A pity,' said Idomeneos, returning the weapon. The offer made Odysseus uneasy, for he saw the hungry look in Idomeneos' eyes.

'The fight,' he said, 'will be conducted under Olympian rules. Once a fighter has been knocked from his feet five times I will declare his opponent the victor.'

'I thank you, Odysseus King,' said Kalliades.

X

The Hammer of Hephaistos

THE SUN WAS SETTING AS THE *PENELOPE* WAS BEACHED.
Several cookfires were lit. Then the crew moved off to
gather wood for a large funeral pyre upon which they
laid the eight bodies of their dead comrades.

Three other trading ships were also beached on
Apollo's Bow, and their crews watched as the men of
the *Penelope* gathered round the pyre. Odysseus spoke
of the dead, of their loyalty and their courage, and he
called upon the great god Zeus to guide their spirits
along the Dark Road. A large amphora of oil was
poured over the pyre. Four men approached Odysseus
from a nearby campfire. Travelling bards, on route to
Troy, they offered to perform the Song of the Departed.
Odysseus thanked them, and stepped back to sit with
the crew. Two of the bards carried lyres; a third held a
rhythm globe of dark wood, decorated with strips of
bronze. The fourth man had no instrument. He was
older, his neatly trimmed beard shining silver.

Silence fell over the crew as the bards began. Music from the lyres rippled out, the notes sweet and pure. The slim, red-headed man with the rhythm globe pressed thimbles to the fingers of his right hand, and began to drum out a slow, insistent beat. The voice of the silver-haired bard rose above the sound of the lyres, rich and powerful.

The crew sat listening to the familiar lyrics of the Song of the Departed, and such was the skill of the bards that the lament seemed fresh, created solely for this one night. Some among the men shed tears, and all were moved by the performance. When the song was over Odysseus approached the men to thank them, and gave each a silver ring. Then he lit the funeral pyre. The oil-soaked, seasoned wood flared instantly, the blaze so fierce that the crew had to move back from it. Most stood in silence as the fire lit up the beach, each lost in memories. Others, their wounds bandaged, sat upon the sand.

Odysseus strolled over to where Kalliades, Banokles and Piria were standing by the water's edge.

'Are you sure you want to do this?' he asked Banokles. 'I once saw Leukon punch a bronze-reinforced shield and split it down the centre.'

'Was the shield punching back?' asked Banokles.

Odysseus chuckled. 'No,' he said, 'it wasn't.' He looked long and hard at Banokles. 'You've the size for a fistfighter, and your friend tells me you have the heart. I've watched you move, and all your strength is in the upper body. A good fistfighter punches from the shoulder. A great one punches from the heel.'

Banokles laughed. 'This is another tall story. Fists in the feet.'

'No, lad. It's the plain truth. The great fighters twist their whole bodies, bringing all their weight into a blow. Leukon is a great fighter. I expect him to reach the final in Troy and bring yet more glory to the *Penelope* and to Ithaka. So there'll be no shame if you decide not to fight him.'

'Why would I do that?' asked Banokles, scratching at his thick blond beard. He made a fist. 'I call this the Hammer of Hephaistos,' he said proudly. 'Bring me a shield and I'll crack it in half.'

Odysseus transferred his gaze to Kalliades, then shook his head and wandered away. 'He was trying to shake my confidence,' said Banokles. 'Confidence is everything in a fighter, you know.'

'Well, you are not short of that.'

'That's true. But you believe in me?'

Kalliades laid his hand on Banokles' broad shoulder. 'I have always believed in you, my friend. I know that if even the gods lined up against me, you would be there at my side. So, when is this bout to take place?'

'Odysseus said it would be after the *Xanthos* gets here. He says Hektor never likes to miss a fine fight.' He lowered his voice, even though no-one but Piria was close. 'You think he'll remember us from Troy? I'll never forget that big bastard tearing into our boys as if they were children. The only time in my life I've ever been frightened was when I saw Hektor attack. And I don't mind you knowing it – though if you ever mention it to anyone else I'll call you a liar.'

'I won't mention it. I felt the same. For a time there I almost believed he was the god of war himself.'

The evening breeze was cool and the trio wandered up from the beach into a stand of trees where they gathered dry wood. Returning to the rocks, Kalliades lit a small fire. Piria sat quietly with her back to a boulder. Somewhere close by the bards began to sing at a different fire. It was an old song about love and loss. Kalliades shivered, and drew his cloak about him.

As the last light of day faded from the sky he saw the *Xanthos* appear, its great black horse sail furled, its two banks of oars beating slowly as it edged towards the beach. Banokles had stretched himself out on the sand and was asleep by the fire. Piria also watched the great ship. As it came closer to the shore the crewmen surged into their oars, the prow grinding up onto the sand. Weighted rocks, attached to thick ropes, were hurled from the stern to splash into the water below, holding the rear of the vessel steady. Then the crew began to disembark. Kalliades saw Hektor clamber over the prow and leap down to the beach. Odysseus walked over to him, and the two men embraced. Hektor also greeted King Nestor and his sons warmly. Then he clasped hands swiftly with Idomeneos. Although they were some distance away from where he sat, Kalliades could tell there was no love lost between Hektor and the Kretan king. It was not surprising. Even Kalliades, who had not been privy to the councils of generals and kings, knew a war was coming between Troy and the armies of Mykene and its allies. Idomeneos was a kinsman of Agamemnon's and had allowed two

Mykene garrisons on the island of Kretos. Little wonder that Hektor greeted him coolly.

Kalliades thought back to the attack on Troy last autumn. The great gate had been opened to them by traitors, but Kalliades recalled the high walls, and the streets beyond. If an army had to take those walls the losses would be high. Once inside the city the streets could be defended, and every step forward would be paid for in blood. And even then there was Priam's fortress palace, walled and gated. The attackers had been led to believe the Trojans were poor fighting men. This had been a lie. King Priam's personal bodyguard – 200 men known as the King's Eagles – had proved ferocious and defiant, men of courage, skill and stamina. And when other Trojan warriors had arrived they had fought with as much tenacity as any Mykene warrior.

Agamemnon was determined to sack Troy and loot its legendary wealth. To do so would take an army of immense size. Kalliades knew that all the kings of the mainland, and others, would need to be drawn in.

'What are you thinking?' asked Piria softly.

'Nothing of import,' he lied.

She seemed to accept the answer and gazed at the sleeping Banokles. 'He doesn't seem worried by the coming fight.'

'He is not a man given to worry,' he answered, with a smile. 'He does not dwell on the past, nor fear the future. For Banokles the *now* is all there is.'

'I wish I could be like that. The past clings to me, the future threatens me. For a little while I knew where

I was, and was content with my life. It did not last.'

'Then tonight we shall be like Banokles,' he said. 'We sit safe by a fire, food in our bellies. The stars are shining and there is no danger. Let us enjoy it while it lasts.'

Banokles awoke with a start, as Kalliades' sandalled foot nudged him, none too gently, in the ribs. 'What is it?' he asked sleepily.

'In case you'd forgotten, you are due to be fighting Leukon,' said the tall young warrior.

Banokles grinned and sat up. 'I wish I had something to wager,' he said. 'Doesn't seem right to have a fight without a wager.' Pushing himself to his feet he noticed Piria sitting in the shadows of the rocks. She wasn't his type, but it seemed an age since he'd last enjoyed a woman. He grinned at her, and she scowled back. Perhaps she's a witch, he thought, and she knows what I'm thinking. Guiltily he looked away. Over by the *Penelope* campfire he saw Leukon, swinging his arms over his head, then twisting his body from side to side. 'He looks like a fighter, at least,' said Banokles.

'I think we should assume that he is one,' said Kalliades. 'His reach is longer than yours. Best to get under those long arms and go for the body. Fight in close.'

'Good plan,' said Banokles. 'There should be a wager, though.'

'We don't have anything to wager. Everything I took from Arelos I gave to Odysseus for the journey.'

'I could bet my breastplate.'

'Just concentrate on the fight.'

'Then let's get started,' said Banokles. 'I could kill for a jug of wine.'

Together the two men walked across to where the crew of the *Penelope* sat round a large campfire. Banokles saw the Trojan, Hektor, sitting with Odysseus. He didn't seem so daunting on this peaceful spring night, but Banokles' stomach tightened at the memory of his arrival at the battle in Troy. He had looked invincible then.

Odysseus rose to his feet and approached them, summoning Leukon to stand alongside him. Idomeneos joined them. He was wearing his glittering breastplate, inlaid with gold and silver. It gleamed in the firelight.

'Shall we have a friendly wager?' asked Idomeneos.

'I suggested that earlier,' said Banokles. 'But we don't have anything. Except my breastplate.'

'There is your friend's sword,' said Idomeneos. 'I will wager my own breastplate against it.'

'That's right!' exclaimed Banokles. 'The sword, Kalliades. We forgot about that.'

'Yes, we forgot,' said Kalliades, looking coldly at the Kretan king. Banokles saw that Odysseus also looked annoyed. It was mystifying. Here was a chance for Kalliades to win a fabulous breastplate, and he seemed reluctant. A dark thought occurred to him.

'You do have faith in me?' he asked.

'Always,' answered Kalliades. 'The sword it is,' he told Idomeneos.

Odysseus stepped forward. 'We are following Olympian rules for this fight,' he said. 'Are you aware of them?'

'Yes,' said Banokles, who didn't know what he was talking about.

'Perhaps you should explain them,' put in Kalliades swiftly.

'The bout will be closed hand only. No grabbing, pulling, head butting, kicking, or biting. Merely fists.'

'Pah!' Banokles grimaced. 'Where's the skill in that? Head butting is part of the craft of boxing.'

'Oh, I am obviously not making myself clear to you,' said Odysseus affably. 'Let me put it another way. If you break these rules I will smash your hands and feet with a club, and leave you on this beach to rot.' He leaned in close. 'Do not grin at me, you halfwit. It is no jest. Look into my eyes and tell me if you see any humour there.'

Banokles looked into Odysseus' baleful gaze. The man wasn't joking.

'All right,' he said. 'No head butting.'

'And no biting, pulling, kicking or gouging.'

'You didn't mention gouging before,' observed Banokles mischievously.

'I'm mentioning it now. When a man is knocked down his opponent will move away. The fallen man must rise and touch the spear which will be sticking in the sand. If he does not wish to continue he pulls the spear and drops it to the ground.'

'What if he's unconscious?' asked Banokles, his expression innocent.

'By the gods, did a bull stamp on your head when you were a babe?'

'It is a reasonable question,' argued Banokles. 'If

he's unconscious he can't touch the spear, can he?'

'If he's unconscious then he's lost, you moron!'

'You only had to say that,' observed Banokles amiably.

'The first man to be knocked down five times will be judged the loser,' continued Odysseus. 'Is this all understood?'

'Yes,' said Banokles. 'When do we start?'

'Whenever you're ready,' Odysseus told him. Banokles nodded, then slammed a ferocious right into Leukon's mouth, dumping the big crewman to the sand.

'I'm ready,' said Banokles.

Leukon surged to his feet with a roar of anger, and ran at him. 'Got to touch the spear,' yelled Banokles, dancing away.

Odysseus grabbed Kalliades by the arm, drawing him away. Leukon stalked to the spear and slapped his hand against it. Then he turned and advanced. Banokles charged at him – and ran into a straight left that jarred every bone in his body. Only instinct caused him to duck, just as an overhand right slashed through the air above him. Coming up fast he thundered two blows into Leukon's midriff. It was like hitting timber.

This is going to take longer than I thought, he realized – just as a left hook connected with his temple, lifting him from his feet and catapulting him to the sand. He rose groggily, shook his head, then spat blood from his mouth. 'You can hit. I'll give you that,' he told Leukon.

Now the whole crew were gathered round, and other

sailors from camps close by had gathered to watch the bout.

Banokles moved in more warily. It didn't help. Leukon's left hand kept flashing out, through his defences, and slamming against his skull. Twice more he was dumped to the sand, and twice more rose to slap the spear. Leukon grew more cocky, stepping in with combination blows, lefts and rights, coming in a blur. Banokles took them all, seeking an opening. Leukon missed with a straight left. Banokles darted in, sending a wicked uppercut into Leukon's exposed jaw. It hit with all the weight Banokles could muster, and it shook the big man, who staggered back. Banokles rushed in, clubbing two more rights, then a roundhouse left that sent Leukon tumbling to the sand.

He was up swiftly.

Banokles fought on gamely, but he was beginning to realize now that he was outclassed. He caught Leukon with several good blows, but the big crewman merely shrugged and came on, his fists hammering at Banokles' face and body. Banokles was fighting now through a sea of pain, unremitting and unending, but he struggled on, ever hopeful for the one blow that might make the difference.

When it came it was a total surprise. Leukon seemed to slip. His jaw jutted out. Banokles put everything he had into the punch and the big man tottered and fell heavily to the sand. Amazingly he did not rise. The roars of the crowd faded away. Banokles stood blinking in the firelight. He leaned forward to peer more closely at the fallen man, then toppled to his knees. Odysseus moved alongside Leukon, then signalled the fight was over. Kalliades ran to Banokles' side and hauled him to his feet.

'You did it, my friend,' he said. 'Well fought.'

Banokles said nothing for a moment. One eye was swollen shut and his face hurt from the hairline to the jaw. 'A little wine would be good,' he mumbled.

Kalliades helped him back to their small campsite in the boulders. With a groan Banokles lay down by the fading fire. Piria arrived, bearing a bucket of sea water and a cloth. Gently she cleaned the blood from his face. Finally she took a flat stone from the bucket, and pressed it gently against the swollen eye. It was wonderfully cool and Banokles sighed.

Her fingers lightly brushed the blond hair back from his brow. 'You should rest,' she said to him. 'You took a fearful beating.'

'I won, though.'

'You are a brave fighter, Banokles.'

'I think . . . I'll sleep now,' he told her.

And darkness swallowed him.

XI

Back from the dead

KALLIADES GAZED DOWN AT HIS BRUISED AND BATTERED friend, then glanced across to where Leukon was now conscious and talking to Odysseus. Around the *Penelope* campfire a number of local whores had gathered, and were sitting with the men. The sound of laughter drifted across the beach. He sat down, and Piria left Banokles and came to sit beside him.

'I have seen many fist fights,' she said softly. 'Never have I seen anyone take such a beating and stay on his feet.'

Kalliades nodded. 'He doesn't have the sense to know when he's beaten. It was kind of you to bathe his wounds. I thought you didn't like him.'

'He is a hard man not to like,' she admitted grudgingly. He looked at her and smiled.

'This is not the Piria I have come to know.'

'And who is this Piria?' she said, her tone sharp.

'Someone fine and brave,' he told her. 'Truth to tell,

you are like Banokles in some ways. You both have great courage. You too are rash and reckless – though for different reasons. Banokles thinks no further than his next meal, his next battle, or his next woman. You are driven by something else.'

'You see a great deal, Kalliades. Are you as accurate when you glimpse your own reflection?'

'I doubt it,' he admitted. 'Most men rationalize their weaknesses, and exaggerate their strengths. I am no different.'

'Perhaps you are. You wagered a sword you cherished when you believed Banokles could not win. You did that to support him, for you knew if you did not it would sap his confidence.'

'Yes, I treasure the Sword of Argurios, but it is still just a sword. Banokles is a friend. There is not enough gold in all the world to buy such a friendship.'

'And what else cannot be bought?' she asked him.

He thought about the question, as he stared out over the wine-dark sea. 'Nothing of real worth can ever be bought,' he said at last. 'Love, friendship, honour, valour, respect. All these things have to be earned.'

'Speaking of honour, I see that Idomeneos has not yet given you the breastplate.'

'No, he has not,' said Kalliades, anger rising. Why would a man with the wealth of Idomeneos seek to cheat a simple warrior of a sword?

They sat in silence for a while, then she took her cloak and moved to the fire, adding the last of the fuel. Kalliades watched her stretch herself out, pillowing her head on her arm.

Time drifted by, but he was not tired. The fighter Leukon was sitting alone, away from the crew. Kalliades rose and walked across to him.

'What do you want?' asked Leukon, as Kalliades sat down beside him on a flat rock. 'Come to gloat?'

'Why would I gloat?' asked Kalliades. 'You were winning easily and then you decided to lie down.'

'What?'

'You were not unconscious. Banokles was exhausted at the end. He had little strength left – and certainly not enough to punch *you* from your feet.'

'Keep your voice down! Otherwise you will lose that shining breastplate.'

'So why?' whispered Kalliades.

'Odysseus told me to.'

'That does not answer my question.'

Leukon sighed, then pointed across to another campfire further along the beach. 'Did you see the big man with the forked red beard who came and watched the fight?'

Kalliades recalled the man. He was huge and had stood watching the bout, his massive arms folded across his chest. 'What of him?'

'That was Hakros. He is the champion of Rhodos, and a ferocious fighter. Last summer in Argos he killed a man in a bout. Smashed his skull.'

'What of it?'

'He and I will probably fight each other in Troy. There will be big wagers made. All the bigger now that Hakros has seen me beaten already. Losing to Banokles means gold to Odysseus – and to me.'

Kalliades swore softly. 'That was not a good deed,' he said.

Leukon shrugged. 'No harm done. Banokles gained a few bruises, and I feel as if several boulders have been bounced from me. You got a breastplate, and he thinks he's a champion.'

'Yes, he does,' said Kalliades coldly. 'And now he will go to Troy, where some other fine fighter, like Hakros, will break his bones, or perhaps kill him.'

Leukon shook his head. 'There won't be more than four – maybe five – men who could take him. He's strong, and he's tougher than he has any right to be. If he could learn a few good moves he'd do all right. He'll win several of the preliminary bouts, and, with a few wagers, make himself some gold.'

'It will be many days to Troy,' said Kalliades, 'and many nights on beaches such as this. I want you to train him, to show him some of those moves.'

Leukon laughed. 'And why would I do that?'

'There could be two reasons,' said Kalliades. 'One, it would be an act of good fellowship. Two, I could tell Banokles you threw the fight and shamed him. He would then be obliged to challenge you again, this time with swords, and to the death. I don't know what kind of swordsman you are, Leukon, but I'd wager Banokles would kill you in a heartbeat. However, I am a fine judge of men, and I know you will do what I ask because you have a good heart.'

Leukon chuckled. 'I'll train him. But not for fear, and not for good-heartedness. I need the practice. He will do everything I tell him?'

'Yes.'

'And is he a fast learner?'

Now it was Kalliades who laughed. 'It would be easier to teach a pig to dance, or a dog to shoot a bow.'

Men from various crews approached Odysseus, requesting a tale, but he turned them away. He felt a heaviness of heart and had no wish to entertain crowds. So he left the campfire and wandered away down the beach, pausing before the *Xanthos*, the huge warship of Helikaon. He saw Hektor walking towards him. The Trojan was unaware of the admiring, envious glances from the sailors who sat close by. It was one of the traits Odysseus liked about him. There was in Hektor an innocence and a gentleness of spirit, surprising in any warrior, but astonishing in the son of a king like Priam.

Odysseus waited until the Trojan reached him, then led him along the sea shore, away from the crowds.

'There are a great many disappointed men here tonight,' said Hektor. Odysseus glanced up at the taller man.

'I am in no mood for storytelling. So, why are you sailing the Great Green so close to your wedding feast?'

'Father sent me. He was concerned about pirates attacking the wedding guests. With Helikaon . . .' he hesitated, 'with Helikaon injured he thought that word of my involvement would inspire a little fear in them.'

'Injured?' put in Odysseus, his heart leaping. 'I was told he was dead.'

'Do not let your hopes soar, Odysseus. He was

stabbed twice. One wound has healed, but the second blow pierced his armpit and a lung. It is this wound that will not heal. There is corruption there.'

'Who is attending him?'

'The priest Machaon. He is good with wounds. He tended me two years ago, when I almost died. And Andromache will not leave his side.' Odysseus looked up sharply. 'She is a fine woman,' continued Hektor. 'I like her.'

'So I should hope – since you will be spending the rest of your life with her.'

Hektor fell silent, and stood staring out to sea. Odysseus glanced at the young man. There was something wrong here. Hektor seemed distant, and Odysseus sensed a great sorrow in him. Was it fear for Helikaon? The two were great friends.

Hektor glanced back at the campfire. 'I do not like Idomeneos,' he said. 'The man is a lizard. I doubt he will surrender his breastplate to the young Mykene.'

'No, he won't,' said Odysseus. 'But I will make good on his promise.'

'You are a strange man, sea uncle.'

Odysseus chuckled. 'You first called me that fifteen summers back. That was a good voyage.'

'I have fond memories of it. Helikaon and I used to swap stories about you. He told me how you tricked him into diving from that cliff, by pretending you couldn't swim. He will always be grateful for that. He said you made him a man.'

'Pish! He would have found his way without me. Might have taken a little longer, is all.'

Hektor sighed and the smile left his face. 'He is dying, Odysseus. I hear myself say the words and I still can't believe them.'

'He may surprise you yet. Men like Helikaon do not die easily.'

'You have not seen him, Odysseus. He fades in and out, sometimes knowing where he is, but mostly floating in delirium. He is stick-thin and fever-ridden.'

'And is this why you are suffering?'

'In part.' Hektor picked up a stone from the beach and sent it skimming over the water. 'War is coming. That's what Father says. I think he is right. He usually is.'

Odysseus looked at the young man, knowing instantly that his question had been deflected. Hektor never could lie. Whatever it was that had brought him low, the young prince had no wish to speak of it.

'There is always talk of war,' said Odysseus. 'Perhaps wisdom will prevail.'

Hektor shook his head. 'Not wisdom, but gold. Many of the allies Agamemnon needs are fed wealth by my father. That is why the Gathering at Sparta came to nothing. It will not last. Agamemnon will find a way to unite the kings, or he will kill those who oppose him. Either way he will bring his armies to our gates.' He skimmed another stone, then dropped to his knees to hunt for more. 'Do you still carve Penelope's face in the sand?' he asked.

'Yes. Most nights.'

Hektor sat down on the sand, and looked out over the starlit water. 'Those were good days, Odysseus. I had killed no-one then, led no charges, stormed no walls. All that mattered was shipping the olive oil to Kypros and the copper ore to Lykia. I do not see the world as I did then. I look out over a valley and see battlegrounds where once I saw fields and hills, bright with flowers. You know there were six thousand dead at Kadesh? Six thousand!'

'Men will tire of women and song before they tire of war,' said Odysseus, crouching down beside him.

'I am tired of it. So tired. When I was young Father told me I would come to revel in combat and victory. It was never true. I have even come to loathe the fist-fighting, Odysseus. All I want is to live on my farm and raise horses. Yet there is always a battle somewhere. The Egypteians raiding Hittite towns, allies begging for help with insurrections or invasions. Now it is the Mykene, seeking to bring war to Troy.'

'Perhaps . . . but not this spring. This spring you are to be wed. Can you not put off such gloomy thoughts for a while, and enjoy your bride?'

For a heartbeat only Hektor's expression changed, his shoulders sagging. He turned his face away, staring once more out to sea. 'Andromache is wonderful . . . breathtaking and enchanting. She travelled with you, I am told.'

'For a short time. I liked her enormously.'

'And she met Helikaon then.'

'Yes, I believe she did.'

'Did they . . . become friends?'

'Oh, I don't think they got to know each other well enough,' lied Odysseus. 'Why do you ask?'

'She nurses him now, exhausting herself.'

'She did that for Argurios, I am told, after assassins brought him low. It is the nature of the woman, Hektor. Perhaps the nature of *all* women, to nurture and to heal.'

'Yes. I expect you are right.' He smiled. 'Even my father speaks highly of her – and that is rare. He uses women freely, but has no respect for them.'

'She will make a fine wife, Hektor, loyal and true. Of that I have no doubt. She is like my Penelope and will bring you great happiness.'

'We should be getting back to the others,' said Hektor, pushing himself to his feet.

Odysseus spoke quietly. 'You know, lad, sometimes a problem shared grows in weight. Most times, though, it lessens when spoken of. You know that you can talk to me, and that I will not repeat what you say. I tell you this because it seems to me you are carrying a great burden. It should not be so. You are Hektor, prince of Troy. Your fame is known around the Great Green. There is not a man on this beach who would not give ten years of his life to be you.'

Hektor looked into Odysseus' eyes, and when he spoke his voice was full of sorrow. 'I cannot share my burden, sea uncle – even with you. Believe me, though, when I say that if the truth was known not one of those men would wish to be me.'

With that, he strode back to the campfire.

Dawn was breaking, and there were rain clouds to the south when Piria woke. A little way from her Banokles was snoring. Kalliades was stretched out alongside him. He opened his eyes as Piria stirred, and smiled before falling asleep again.

She lay quietly for a while on the soft sand. For the first time in months her dreams had not been troubled, nor had she been woken by the hurt of her injuries. Carefully she sat up. The pain was less now, and she sensed that her body had begun to heal. The rising sun shone down on Apollo's Bow, bathing the cliffs in soft gold, and Piria felt a lightness of spirit that had long been absent. The outburst at Kalliades yesterday had been remarkable in its effect. It was as if she had been holding poison inside her, and it had flowed out with the angry words. Everything was different today, the sky more beautiful, the scent of the sea more uplifting. Even the air felt clean as it filled her lungs. She had not felt this happy since she and Andromache had been together on Thera, with no thought of ever leaving.

Breakfast fires had been lit and Piria wandered across to a stall, where she was given a wooden bowl filled with a nameless stew and a hunk of dry bread. The stew was greasy, brimming with lumps of stringy meat. Yet the taste was divine. She wondered idly whether this same stew would have seemed inedible back on Thera, and decided it probably would. Yet here on this chill morning it was delicious.

The meal finished, she stood and returned to the stall, collecting two more bowls to bring to Banokles and Kalliades. The idea of doing it made her smile. How amazing it was, she thought, to be growing fond of two men.

Kalliades was sitting up when she returned, and he thanked her for the stew. Banokles groaned as he awoke, and took the stew without a word. He ate noisily, complaining of a loose tooth.

Men were stirring now around the *Penelope* campfire, and, further on, the crew of the *Xanthos* were preparing to depart. She saw Hektor sitting alone, and her thoughts darkened as she gazed upon him. This was the man who would chain Andromache's spirit, who would plant his seed in her, who would pin her down and invade her body. In that moment all the old hatreds sought to rise. They had no power over her now, and she pushed them back. Even so she felt uneasy watching Hektor.

Rising to his feet he stripped off his tunic, waded out into the sea and dived forward into the blue waters. He swam with long, easy strokes almost to the edge of the bay, then turned and headed back towards the shore.

'Tell me,' she heard Banokles say behind her, 'did a herd of cattle stampede over me last night?'

'Not that I noticed,' Kalliades told him.

'I am trying to find some part of my body that doesn't hurt,' grumbled Banokles. His right eye was swollen badly, and there were dark bruises on both cheeks.

Piria glanced at him. 'Perhaps your feet,' she said. 'He didn't hit you in the feet.'

Banokles grinned, then winced. 'You are right. My feet are fine.' He looked over at Kalliades. 'I woke last night and saw you talking to Leukon. Does he hurt as much as me?'

'No.'

'I thought not. Bastard! So what *were* you talking about?'

'He has agreed to train you for the Games.'

'Ha!' snorted Banokles. 'Like I need to be trained by a man I beat?'

'Yes, you do, idiot. He is a skilled fighter, and you know it. You beat him with a lucky punch. You know that too. If you are going to win wealth in Troy his training could prove vital. So I have promised him that every night, when we beach, you will do exactly as he tells you.'

'Won't hurt to practise, I suppose,' agreed Banokles. Then he glanced across to where Hektor was emerging from the water. 'I remember him as far more frightening,' he said. 'Very strange. Here he just looks like a big, friendly sailor. Even Leukon is more chilling. And bigger. Back in Troy Hektor looked like a giant – a war god.'

Banokles suddenly leaned forward, shielding his eyes with his hand. 'Trouble looming,' he said. Piria glanced across the beach. Hektor had pulled on a linen kilt and was standing bare-chested, towelling himself dry. Some twenty sailors were walking towards him, led by a massive man with a red forked beard. Piria knew what Banokles meant by trouble looming. The expressions on the men's faces were set and hard, and they were grouped together as if on a hunt, rather than strolling upon a beach.

'That is Hakros, the Rhodian champion,' said Kalliades. 'Leukon told me of him last night.'

'By the balls of Ares he's a monster right enough,' said Banokles. 'Come on, I don't want to miss this.'

The three companions made their way across the sand. Others had spotted the group, and men began to gather, watching intently.

The huge man with the red beard halted before Hektor and stood there, hands on hips, staring at the Trojan prince. Hektor towelled his golden hair, ignoring him. Piria saw the newcomer redden. Then he spoke, his voice harsh.

'So, you are the mighty Hektor. Will you be taking part in your Wedding Games?'

'No,' said Hektor, draping the towel across his shoulder.

'Just as well. Now that I've seen you I know I could break your skull.'

'Lucky for me then,' said Hektor, softly.

Piria saw the Rhodian's eyes narrow. 'I am Hakros.'

'Of course you are,' said Hektor wearily. 'Now be a good fellow, Hakros, and walk away. You have impressed your friends and you have told me your name.'

'I walk when I choose. I am minded to test your legend, Trojan.'

'That would be unwise,' Hektor told him. 'Here on this beach there is no gold to be won, no acclaim.'

Hakros swung to his comrades. 'You see? He is frightened to face me.'

When Hektor spoke there was no anger in his voice, and his words carried to all the watching men. 'You are a stupid man, Hakros, a dullard and a windbag. Now you have two choices. Walk away, or be carried away.'

For a moment there was stillness, then the Rhodian hurled himself at Hektor. The Trojan stepped in to meet him, dropped his shoulder, and sent a thundering right cross into Hakros' jaw. There was a sickening crack and Hakros cried out as he fell. Gamely he surged to his feet – to be met by a straight left that shredded his lips against his teeth and an uppercut that smashed his nose and sent him hurtling unconscious to the sand.

'Oh yes,' said Banokles. 'Now *that* is the man I remember.'

Men gathered around the fallen champion, but Hektor was already walking away.

'His jaw is broken,' Piria heard someone say.

Leukon walked over to stand alongside Banokles and Kalliades. 'Now that man is a fighter,' he said. 'The speed of those punches was inhuman.'

'Could you beat him?' asked Kalliades.

Leukon shook his head. 'I doubt there's a man alive who could.'

'There is one,' said Piria, before she could stop herself.

'And who might that be?' asked Leukon.

'The champion of Thessaly. Achilles.'

'Ah, I have heard of him, but never seen him fight. What is he like?'

'He is bigger than Hektor, but just as fast. But he wouldn't have tried to talk the man out of a fight. The moment the fool stood before him Achilles would have destroyed him. He would have been left dead on the sand.'

'And he *will* be taking part,' said Leukon. 'Not a comforting thought.' Swinging round to Banokles, he clapped him on the shoulder. 'Just as well we'll be practising together,' he said.

'Don't you worry, Leukon,' Banokles told him. 'I'll teach you everything I know.'

Piria walked away from the men and stared out to sea. Somewhere in the far distance was the Golden City, and Andromache. Closing her eyes she pictured her lover's face, the red gold of her hair, the glorious green of her eyes.

'I will be with you soon, my love,' she whispered.

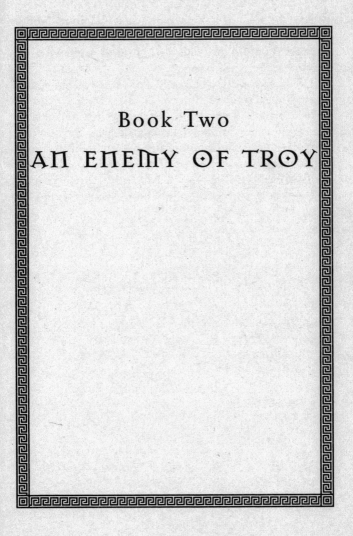

Book Two

AN ENEMY OF TROY

XII

Ghosts of the past

THE SKY ABOVE TROY WAS HEAVY WITH RAIN CLOUDS, AND
to the west Andromache could see the distant lightning
of a summer storm. Thunder rumbled in the cool afternoon, and she pulled her green woollen shawl closely
round her against the cutting wind the Trojans called
the Scythe. Her toes were cold in close-fitting leather
and wool sandals, and she stamped her feet to keep
them warm.

In the Bay of Troy far below she could see a ship
closing fast on the city from the north. It was racing to
beat the coming storm, oars beating rhythmically, sail
stretched taut by the wind.

Andromache's thoughts flew back to her own
journey on the *Penelope* last autumn. Her heart had
been heavy then, the future dark with foreboding. It
seemed impossible that only a single winter had passed
since she had last seen Kalliope, since together they had
performed the calming rites for the soul of the

Minotaur. The island of Thera now belonged to a different age, passing somehow into dream. So much had happened since. In that moment she wished that Kalliope could be with her on this bleak hillside. A selfish thought, she realized, for Kalliope was unsuited to the world of men. Thera was where she belonged, where she was happy and free. Thoughts of Kalliope caused confusion in her now. Unlike her lover, Andromache had never hated men, nor had she ever yearned to be free of them. Her time with Kalliope, especially the nights, tasting the wine on the other's lips, stroking her soft skin, had been wondrous and fulfilling. Yet equally wondrous were the feelings Helikaon had inspired in her.

Her emotions torn, Andromache sighed and turned towards the newly built tomb. It was elaborately carved with bright warriors and fair maidens, and stood facing west towards the lands of the Mykene. No grass yet grew round it, and the marble was white as swan's down. Within it lay the bones of Argurios and Laodike, for ever at rest together.

Andromache felt the familiar ache in her heart, the dead weight of guilt on her soul. If only she had realized the gravity of Laodike's wound, could she have saved her friend? She had asked herself a thousand times. She was sick and tired of the thought; it was an evil demon lying at wait in the corner of her mind, ever eager to leap out and torment her. Yet every day she made her pilgrimage to this tomb and fed the demon anew.

Laodike had been stabbed when the renegade

Thrakians attacked the palace. Andromache had half carried her to the deceptive safety of the queen's apartments, while Helikaon and a company of Royal Eagles had fought a rearguard action against the traitors. The wound had seemed slight. Not a great deal of blood flowed from it, and Laodike had appeared strong. Later, as the dreadful siege wore on, she had become listless and sleepy. Only then did Andromache summon the surgeon to her. The spear had gone deep, and the wound was mortal.

Gentle Laodike, plain and plump, had discovered love in the days before the siege. On that one ghastly night her dreams and her hopes bled from her. Andromache would never forget the moment Laodike's lover came to her. The mighty Argurios, who had held the stairs like a titan, was also dying, an arrow buried deep in his side, the point cutting up close to his heart. Helikaon and Andromache had helped him to his feet and he had made his way to Laodike's side.

Andromache had not heard the words that passed between them, but she saw Argurios draw a small, white feather from the blood-smeared pouch at his side, and place it in Laodike's hand. Then he had covered her hand with his own. Laodike had smiled then, a smile of such joy that it broke Andromache's heart.

So much glory and so much sorrow on that one night.

King Priam had built the white tomb as a tribute to Argurios. Andromache wondered again at the contradiction that was Priam. A lascivious man, sometimes cruel, selfish and greedy, he had nevertheless built a marble tribute to a warrior who had come to the city as his enemy and to the daughter he had had little time for when she lived. They were together now in death, as they would never have been allowed to be in life.

'May your souls be together always,' whispered Andromache, then turned and walked away.

Swiftly she crossed the fortification ditch which surrounded the lower town and started to climb the hill towards the city walls. After the palace siege Priam had speeded work on the ditches. Although hardly more than waist-deep they were wider than a horse could jump and would effectively halt any cavalry charge on the lower town. They were crossed only by three wide wooden bridges which could be set ablaze if necessary.

But the real defence of Troy were the Great Walls. Towering above her, they were grey on this cloudy day and seemed impregnable as the sheerest cliff face. There were four Great Gates piercing the walls – the Scaean Gate to the south, the Dardanian Gate to the north-east, the East Gate, and the western gate called the Gate of Sorrows, as the city's main burial ground lay in its shadow.

Andromache strode up through the Scaean Gate, guarded by the Great Tower of Ilion, and into the city itself. Her gloomy mood lifted a little, despite the weather, at the sight of the golden city, its carved and decorated buildings and green courtyards. It had been her home for half a year and she loved it and hated it in equal measure.

In this cool afternoon the stone streets were teeming with people. Andromache turned to her right, then climbed the wooden steps to the south battlements. Here she paused, feeling the wind more keenly on this high place as it buffeted her and plucked at her long red hair.

She looked to the south, to the verdant slopes of Mount Ida, the sacred mountain where Zeus had his watchtower. Beyond the Ida mountains, unseen, lay Thebe Under Plakos, where her father was king.

Andromache reached the end of the walls at the great northeast bastion. The tower, wider and more massive than the others, faced the northern plains and the lands of the Hittites. Beyond it were horse pastures and the fields of grain which fed the growing population of Troy.

At the moment, in the meadows close beneath the city, rows of sturdy benches were being built and areas of ground paced, measured and roped off to form running tracks and horse racing circuits for the imminent Wedding Games. Andromache watched the preparations thoughtfully, then turned and looked to the south of the bastion where other teams of men were still working on the fortification ditch round the lower town. Not for the first time she thought how odd it was that the western kings who were invited to the Games were the same warriors the ditches were designed to keep out.

The light was beginning to fade, and Andromache headed for Hektor's palace.

As she walked past the House of Serpents, the temple to Asklepios, the god of healing, a young man ran out. Andromache smiled as he approached her. 'Xander, I scarcely recognized you. You're so much taller. I thought you would have returned to Kypros by now.'

The youngster seemed to have grown a hand's-breadth since she saw him last. His chest and shoulders were starting to fill out and she could see the man he would become. But when he grinned his freckled face still showed the near child he had been on the voyage to the city.

'Machaon is teaching me the craft of healing. It is very difficult,' he confessed. 'He told me the lord Helikaon was wounded and that you are nursing him?'

Andromache's smile faded. 'The wound does not heal, and the fever will not subside.'

The youngster was undismayed by the news. 'He is strong, Andromache. A great warrior. He will recover. They say he stood with Argurios and killed a hundred Mykene. Such a man will not let a small wound slay him.'

'It is not a small wound, Xander,' she said, holding back her anger. The boy worshipped Helikaon, but had not seen him since the attack, the flesh melted away, bones jutting from fever-hot skin. Death was close, and, when it came, something in Andromache would die with him.

'What happened?' asked Xander. 'Machaon said he was stabbed by a crewman from the *Xanthos*. That seems impossible.'

'It is true. A crewman named Attalus. Helikaon took a liking to him. He was standing close by when Helikaon walked out to announce his marriage to Queen Halysia. Suddenly he darted forward and plunged a knife into him.'

'Attalus stabbed him!' Xander's face was aghast. 'Attalus helped rescue me from the sea. And he saved Helikaon's life in battle.'

'Does the world of men ever make sense?' snapped Andromache. The sharpness of her words surprised the youngster. Andromache reached out and drew the boy to her in a warm embrace. 'It is good to see you, Xander. It gladdens my heart.'

They stood together for a moment in silence. Then she stepped back. 'Helikaon was stabbed twice,' she said. 'First in the chest, although the blow was turned by the reinforced shirt he wore. That wound has closed well. Then Attalus stabbed him in the armpit. The blade bit deep.'

'Was the dagger poisoned?' asked Xander.

'Machaon says not. But the bleeding inside will not stop. Queen Halysia sent him here to Troy in the hope of a cure.'

'Can I see him?'

'You will need to prepare yourself, Xander. He is not the young god you remember.'

They walked together to Hektor's palace and climbed to a high chamber on the east of the building. It was light and airy, and overlooked the Street of Bright Dancers and the barracks and stables of the Heraklion regiment. Machaon had told her it was good for recovery to face the rising sun, and he believed the sounds and smells of the horses and the daily commotion of soldiers arriving and leaving would be stimulating to the stricken man.

They were met at the doorway by a powerful

black-bearded man, who grinned widely when he saw the boy. 'Xander!' He reached out and grabbed Xander in a crushing embrace. Xander, red-faced and pleased, said, 'Gershom! I thought you would be on the *Xanthos*.'

Gershom shook his head. 'No, boy. Helikaon needs a guard, and I never liked rowing anyway. Have you come to visit him? He will be glad to see you.'

The bed was wide and draped with white linen. Beside it sat a pregnant young woman working on a piece of crumpled embroidery.

Helikaon was deathly pale and asleep. Andromache glanced at Xander. His face too had gone pale, as he saw the true condition of his hero. Sweat glistened on Helikaon's thin face, and the closed eyes were sunken, the skin around them dark. There was a smell in the room, of putrefaction and decay.

Xander stood silently, and Andromache saw there were tears in his eyes. The young pregnant woman was staring up at the youngster.

Andromache said, 'Xander, this is Helen, a princess of Sparta who is now the wife of Prince Paris.' For a moment he seemed not to have heard her, then he took a deep breath, and tore his gaze from the stricken man.

Helen smiled shyly. She was a plain girl, with fair hair and warm brown eyes, and her smile lit up the sickroom.

Just then the sick man cried out. 'Argurios, to your right! Good man! Dios, another sword!' He sat up in bed, his stick-thin arm waving at unseen enemies. Gershom and Andromache pushed him gently back and he was instantly asleep, the shadows under his eyes dark against the white sheets.

As they walked out of the chamber, Andromache said, 'The nights are bad, when the dead parade before his bed. Zidantas, and Argurios, and his brother Diomedes. And others whose names I do not know.'

She saw Xander staring at her, and regretted speaking so openly. 'You look tired, lady,' he said gently, and the kindness in his tone almost made her weep.

When he had gone, escorted from the palace by Gershom, Andromache returned to her own chamber and threw herself on her bed, her body gripped with dread, eyes dry and staring at the ceiling.

She thought back to the day on the beach after the siege. It had been the last time she had seen Helikaon well and whole. They had agreed they must part; that Andromache must stay and marry Hektor, that Helikaon must return to Dardanos and take up the burden of kingship.

He had said to her, *There is nothing on earth I want more than to sail away with you, to live together, to be together.* They both knew it was impossible then. Now she wished they had left together at that moment, throwing the call of duty to the four winds, and sailing far from the woes of the world.

She rested there for a while, then rose from the bed and returned to the sickroom. Helen stood as she entered, and hugged her briefly. Helikaon was asleep, his breathing ragged.

'I must go,' said Helen. 'I will return tomorrow.'

Alone now with Helikaon Andromache sat by the

bed and took his hand. The skin was hot and dry. 'I am here, Helikaon,' she said. 'Andromache is here.'

Gershom bid a cheerful farewell to Xander, and watched as the youngster ran off, back towards the House of Serpents. Only then did the appearance of good humour leave Gershom's face.

Helikaon was dying.

There was no doubt now in Gershom's mind. The wound would not heal and only the last vestiges of the man's enormous stamina were holding him to life.

So, it had to be tonight. Gershom stood for a while in the moonshadows of the palace gateway. Cthosis the Eunuch had given him directions to find the Prophet, but these would take him through the Egypteian quarter of the city.

'If you are recognized, my prince,' Cthosis had warned him, back in Dardania, 'then nowhere will be safe for you. And there are many there who will have seen you in your grandfather's palace.'

'It may not be necessary,' Gershom had replied. 'They have great healers in Troy.'

'If that is so,' said the slender merchant, 'then you should remain in Dardania, where there are few Egypteians.'

'Helikaon is my friend. I will travel with him. This prophet is a desert dweller?'

'A prophet of the One. He is a harsh man. And, as with you, the pharaoh has spoken the words of his death.'

'You have met this man?'

'No,' replied Cthosis. 'Nor do I wish to.' He lowered his voice. 'He had a servant once who displeased him, and with one gesture he turned him into a leper. You must understand, my prince, that he hates all Egypteian nobles. If he guesses who you are – and he may well, for his powers are great – he will curse you, and you will die.'

'It will take more than a curse to kill me,' Gershom had told him.

Now, standing in the shadows, Gershom was not so sure. He had no doubt that many of the stories Cthosis had told him of the Prophet had been exaggerated, but even so the man must have some magiks. And to reach him Gershom would need to walk through the eastern quarter, an area teeming with Egypteian merchants and envoys. Any who recognized him could claim their weight in gold as a reward.

A foolish risk to take for a dying man, whispered the voice of reason.

'Not if his death can be prevented,' he said aloud.

Lifting the hood of his dark cloak over his head he set off through the moonlight, skirting the Street of Bright Dancers, and heading down the long hill towards the eastern quarter. In the distance he could hear the sounds of hammers, as workers continued under torchlight to complete the buildings for the Games. Not for the first time Gershom considered the bizarre nature of these peoples of the sea.

All the enemies of Troy invited to attend a wedding. And while they were here they would be protected by Trojan soldiers, as if they were friends. Where is the sense in this, he wondered? Enemies should be cut down, their bones left to rot. Instead they would bring their retainers and play games, running and throwing, wrestling and racing. And the prizes these men cherished above all others? Not the riches of victory, the gold rings, or silver adornments. Not the ornate helms, the cunningly crafted swords, or the glittering shields.

No, the warriors longed for the small circlets of laurel leaves brought from the trees beneath Mount Olympos, and placed on the heads of the champions.

They struggled and fought, and sometimes died, for a few fading leaves.

Pushing thoughts of such idiocy from his mind Gershom strode on.

Unlike the upper city, with its fine palaces, court-yards and gardens, the lower town was cramped and crowded, the stench of urine and excrement hanging in the air. The streets were narrow, many of the buildings squalid and poorly built. Gershom moved on. Several women accosted him, offering him 'favours', and several young men, their faces painted, called out to him. Gershom ignored them all.

Coming at last to the Street of Bronze he cut right and began searching for the alleyway Cthosis had described. As he scanned the buildings a heavily built man approached him. 'Are you lost, stranger?' he asked.

'No, I am not lost,' Gershom told him. He saw the man's eyes flicker to the right and heard sounds of stealthy movement from behind.

Gershom suddenly smiled, feeling all tension leave him. Stepping in swiftly he grabbed the man before him and spun him into the path of the man behind. The two would-be robbers collided and fell heavily, before scrambling to their feet. Gershom stood, hands on hips, and observed them. The second man had a dagger in his hand. Gershom did not draw his own. 'You are not very skilful thieves,' he said.

The man with the dagger swore at him, and charged. Gershom swatted the knife-thrust aside and hammered a thunderous left into the attacker's jaw. The man hit a nearby wall head first and sank to the stone unmoving.

The first man stood blinking in the moonlight. 'You do not seem to be armed,' said Gershom. 'Do you wish to retrieve your friend's dagger?'

The robber licked his lips. 'Is he dead?' he asked.

'I do not know, nor do I care. You know this area?'

'What? Yes, I know it.'

'I am told there is an alley near here, where they have a small temple to the God of Deserts?'

'Yes. Not the next turning, but the one after, on the right.'

The man on the ground groaned, and tried to rise. Then he slumped back.

Gershom walked on. He felt better than he had in days.

The alley was dark, but further down he could see lamplight shining from a low window. Picking his way carefully along the narrow way he came to a gateway and a small courtyard. Five men were sitting there, on low stone benches. They looked up as he entered. They were wearing the pale, flowing robes of the desert people, garments Gershom had not seen since leaving Egypte.

'I am seeking the Prophet,' he said. No-one spoke. He repeated the statement in the language of the desert.

Now they stared at him, but still no-one spoke.

'I have a friend who is dying,' he continued. 'I am told the Prophet is a man with great healing power.'

'He is not here,' said a young man, hawk-faced and stern. His dark gaze was cold, almost malevolent. 'And if he was, why would he see you, Prince Ahmose?'

The other men rose smoothly, and spread out to form a half-circle round him.

'Perhaps out of curiosity,' replied Gershom. 'When will he be back?'

'I had a brother,' said the first man, his voice trembling. 'He was flayed alive. And a sister whose throat was cut because she looked up into the face of an Egypteian prince. My father had his hands cut off for complaining that there was not enough straw to make bricks.'

'And I had a dog that fell down a hole once,' said Gershom. 'Such a shame. I loved that dog. But I didn't come here to listen to your miserable life story, or mourn with you the ill luck of your family.' The young man tensed, his hand moving towards the hilt of a curved dagger at his belt. 'And if you draw that weapon,' said Gershom, 'some other member of your blighted family will be telling the terrible tale of how you ended up wearing your balls as a necklace.'

The dagger flashed into the young man's hand. His

comrades also drew weapons. Gershom stepped back, his own knife now in his hand. His mind was cool. When they attacked he would kill the youngster first, then hurl himself into the group, slashing left and right. With luck he would down three of them swiftly, and then make a break for the alley.

Just as the young man tensed for the attack a commanding voice rang out. 'Yeshua! Sheathe your blade! All of you, stand back.'

Gershom saw a tall man standing in the doorway of the small temple, lamplight shining on a beard that was thick and white.

'This man is the enemy, holy one,' Yeshua called out. 'It is Ahmose!'

'I know who it is, boy. I have been expecting him. Come through, Ahmose. Yeshua, bring food for our guest.'

Gershom sheathed his knife, though he noted the others still held their weapons in their hands.

'Do some of you yearn to be lepers?' asked the old man, his voice cold. Instantly the blades vanished, the men returning to the stone benches. Gershom walked past them. As he approached the Prophet he saw that, despite the white beard, the man was not so very old, probably in his mid to late forties. He too was wearing the long robes of the desert dweller. The width of his shoulders showed him to be a man of great strength. He was as tall as Gershom, his eyes dark beneath jutting grey brows. There was a glint in those eyes that was not welcoming. In the moment their gaze met Gershom knew he was not safe from danger, for there was a burning hatred in the man's dark eyes. The Prophet gestured for Gershom to precede him. Gershom smiled.

'After you, holy one,' he said.

'Wise to be wary,' answered the man, turning on his heel and marching into the building. The room inside was circular, and devoid of decoration. There were no statues, no mosaics, merely a few chairs, and a small, plain rectangular altar of stone with blood channels at the corners. Several lamps were burning, but the light was not strong.

The Prophet moved to a simple rug before the altar and sat down cross-legged upon it. Gershom sat opposite him. Neither man spoke. Yeshua entered, and laid a bowl of dried figs and nuts, baked with honey, in the space between them. The Prophet took a handful and began to eat. Gershom also dipped his hand into the bowl, taking only a single nut, which he ate swiftly.

'So,' said the older man. 'You have a dying friend. Why do you think I can help him?'

'A follower of yours told me you were a great healer.'

'You speak of Cthosis. He spent too long in the halls of your grandfather. His mind is full of superstitions.' He shrugged. 'Yet he is a good man in his own way. You saved him from Rameses, I recall. Why did you do that?'

'Must there always be reasons for our actions?' countered Gershom. 'Perhaps I just didn't want to see a slave killed for so small a slight. Perhaps I simply disliked Rameses. In truth I do not know. I have always been subject to whims.'

'And the royal guardsmen who attacked one of our women? You slew them. Also on a whim?'

'I was drunk. And I didn't know she was a slave.'

'You would have acted differently?'

'Perhaps.'

The Prophet shook his head. 'I think not, Ahmose.'

'I am called Gershom now.'

The older man laughed. 'How apt that is. You chose a word known among the desert folk, a word for stranger. A man with no home, no place in the world. No tribe, no nation. Why did you do that?'

'I did not come here to answer your questions. I came to ask for your help.'

'To save Helikaon.'

'Yes. I owe him my life. He plucked me from the sea, where I would have died. He gave me a place among his followers.'

'Do you not find it strange, Gershom, that the only two good deeds of your life should have been on behalf of my people, and that the name you chose also comes from us?'

'More questions? Is this the price I must pay for your help?'

'No. The price I demand will be high.'

'I have little wealth.'

'I do not seek gold or trinkets.'

'What, then?'

'I will one day call for you, and you will come to me, wherever I am. You will then do as I bid for one year.'

'I will become your slave?'

The Prophet's answer was softly spoken, and

Gershom heard a subtle note of contempt in it. 'Is the price too high, Prince Ahmose?'

Gershom swallowed hard. His pride swelled, urging him to shout out that, yes, this price was too high. He was a prince of Egypt and no man's slave. Yet he did not speak. He sat very quietly, scarcely able to breathe through his tension.

'I agree,' he said, at last.

'Good. And fear not. You will not be any man's slave. And the time is not yet, when I shall call upon you.'

The Prophet ate some more dates. Gershom breathed more easily. Not a slave, at least.

'Could you truly have made your men lepers?' he asked.

'They believe that I can. Perhaps they are right.'

'Cthosis told me you once cured a Hittite prince of leprosy.'

'There are those who say that I did,' said the Prophet. 'The Hittite prince would be among them. He came to me with his skin white and scaly, pus-filled sores on his body. When he left his skin was pink and unmarked.'

'Then you *did* heal him?'

'No. I ordered him to bathe for seven days in the River Jordan.'

'So, you are saying your god healed him after seven days.'

'My god created the river, so I expect you could say that.' The Prophet leaned forward. 'There are many skin diseases, Gershom, and many treatments for them. In summer the Jordan can stink. The water and the mud are noxious. But there is goodness there, within the stench. My family have long known that many skin ailments are healed by scrubbing the body with mud from the Jordan. The Hittite prince did not have leprosy. Merely a skin ailment that the mud and the water washed from him.'

'No miracle then,' said Gershom, unable to keep the disappointment from his voice.

The Prophet gave a cold smile. 'I have discovered that miracles are merely events that happen just when they are needed. A man dying of thirst in the desert sees a bee flying through the air. He decides that Jehovah has sent him the bee and follows it – to a glistening pool of cold, clear water. Is it a miracle?'

'It sounds like one,' said Gershom.

'A desert dweller will tell you that bees are never far from water. Of course this begets the question: "Who sent the bee?" However, your friend is not dying of thirst. He was stabbed.'

'Yes, twice. The second wound has rotted, deep within his body.'

'I can take away the putrefaction, but you will need to have great trust in me. For what I do will seem madness. Do you trust me?'

Gershom looked into the Prophet's dark eyes. 'I am a good judge of men,' he said. 'I trust you.'

'Then I will come with you tonight, and we will begin the cure.'

'You will bring medicines and potions?'

'No, Gershom. I will bring that which feeds upon putrefaction and disease. I will bring maggots.'

XIII

The worms of healing

THE SMALL LAMP GUTTERED AND DIED, BUT ANDROMACHE scarcely noticed it. Sitting by the bedside, holding Helikaon's hand, she gazed at his face, ghost-pale in the soft moonlight shining through the open window.

Tonight there had been no fever dreams, no calling out to lost loved ones.

Andromache sensed the end was near. Anger, unfocused and raw, surged in her. She loathed this feeling of abject helplessness. All her life she had believed in the power of action, that she alone would determine her fate, and the fate of those she loved. When Argurios had been attacked by assassins, and could not regain his strength, she had coerced him into swimming in the sea, believing it would restore him. And it had. Back in Thebe, when little Salos had been stricken, and had lain unconscious for many days, she had sat by his bedside, talking to him, calling gently to him. He had awoken and smiled at her. Always, in the past, she had found a way to bend events to her will.

But then had come the death of Laodike. That had caused a crack in the fortress of her confidence. Now the walls were breached, and she saw that what lay beyond was not confidence, but vanity.

The night was cool, yet still there was a sheen of bright sweat upon Helikaon's handsome face. Such a face, she thought, reaching up to stroke the fevered cheek.

One kiss was all they had exchanged, on that night when the world was bathed in blood, and the enemy was close. One kiss. One declaration of love. One hope, that if they survived they would be together. A night of ultimate victory, and terrible desolation.

Hektor, believed to be dead, had returned in glory. Hektor! How she wished she could hate him for the grief she had known. Yet she could not. For it was not Hektor who had ordered her to leave the island of Thera, nor Hektor who had haggled over the bridal price. It was not even Hektor who had chosen her.

Her father had bargained with King Priam, gaining treaties and gold, selling Andromache like a market cow into the Trojan royal family.

A cool breeze whispered through the window, and a soft groan came from Helikaon. His eyes opened, the brilliant blue of them seeming silver grey in the moonlight.

'Andromache,' he whispered. She squeezed his hand.

'I am here.'

'Not . . . a dream . . . then.'

'Not a dream.' Filling a cup with water she held it to

his lips and he drank a little. Then his eyes closed once more.

'Helikaon,' she whispered. 'Can you hear me?' There was no response. He was sleeping again, drifting away from her towards the Dark Road. She felt the muscles of her stomach tighten painfully. 'You remember the beach at Blue Owl Bay,' she said, 'where first we met? I saw you then in the moonlight, and something inside me knew you would be part of my life. Odysseus took me to a seer. His name was Aklides. He told me . . . he told me,' tears began to fall, and her voice shook, 'that I would know a love as powerful and as tempestous as the Great Green. I mocked him, and asked him whom I should watch for. He said the man with one sandal. When Odysseus and I left his tent I saw a common soldier some distance away. His sandal strap broke, and he kicked it clear. I laughed then, and asked Odysseus if I should call out to this soldier, this love of my life. I wish I had, Helikaon, for it was you, disguised to trick the killers. If I had called out then . . . if you had turned towards me . . .' She hung her head and fell silent.

Hearing sounds in the corridor beyond she swiftly wiped her eyes with the sleeve of her green dress.

The door opened, and Gershom stepped inside, holding the door to usher in a stranger, a tall, powerfully built man in long flowing robes. Andromache rose from the bedside and faced the newcomer. He had fierce eyes under thick, bristling brows.

'This is a healer,' said Gershom. 'I asked him to come.'

'You look more like a warrior,' said Andromache.

'And I am,' the man told her, his voice deep. Moving past her to the bedside he leaned over Helikaon, drawing back the bedlinen to gaze down on the open wound. 'Bring light,' he ordered.

Gershom left the room and returned with two lamps, which he placed by the bedside. The bearded healer knelt down and lifted Helikaon's arm, exposing the wound further. Then he sniffed at it. 'Very bad,' he said, reaching up and resting his hand on Helikaon's brow. 'Worse than I feared.'

From his shoulder bag he removed a small pottery jar, covered with gauze, then a thin wooden spoon. In the flickering light Andromache saw him carefully smear the wound with what appeared to be a white paste. She blinked and looked more closely. The paste was writhing!

'What are you doing?' she screamed, launching herself at the man. Gershom grabbed her, hauling her back.

'You must trust him!' he said.

'They are maggots!'

'Yes, they are maggots,' said the man at the bedside. 'And they are his only chance of life. Though it may be too late.'

'Are you both insane?' shouted Andromache, struggling in Gershom's grip. 'They are creatures of filth.'

'You are Andromache,' said the healer, his voice displaying no emotion. 'Daughter of Ektion, king of Thebe Under Plakos. I know of you, girl. A priestess of the Minotaur. Betrothed to Hektor. Stories of your courage abound in Troy. You saved the king from an assassin. You took up a bow and fought against the Mykene when they attacked Priam's palace. You helped to heal the warrior Argurios.' All the while he spoke he continued to apply the tiny white worms to the wound. Then he laid a section of gauze across it. 'You are fierce and you are proud. But you are also young, and you do not know all there is to know.'

'And you do?' cried Andromache.

'Listen to me!' snapped the healer. 'The maggots will eat away the decaying flesh, and devour the sickness within it. You are correct, they are creatures of filth. They feast on filth – on the filth that is killing him. Release her, Gershom.'

Andromache sensed the reluctance in the big man, but his hold loosened, and she pulled free of him. 'Why should I trust you?' she asked the healer.

'I don't care if you do or you don't,' he responded. 'I have lived long in this world, and I have seen glory and I have seen horror. I have witnessed the compassion of evil men, and the darkness in the hearts of the good. I am not here to convince you, woman. All that matters is that you should know I have no interest in Helikaon's survival. His world and mine do not inter-act. Equally, I have no interest in his death. I am here because Gershom came to me. When I leave you can either trust in my wisdom, or clean the maggots from the wound. I care not.'

In the silence that followed she looked into the healer's broad, fierce face, then swung towards the dying man in the bed. 'And he will recover if I leave the worms?'

'I cannot say that. He is very weak. The maggots should have been applied as soon as the flesh began to putrefy. However, Gershom tells me he is a brave man, determined and decisive. Such a man will not die easily.'

'How long . . . must they feed on him?'

'Three days. The maggots will then be fat, ten times their present size. I will remove them, and perhaps add more. In the meantime someone must be with him at all times. Whenever he wakes he must drink. Water mixed with honey. As much as he will take.' Swinging his bag to his shoulder, he rose, and looked at Gershom. 'I will return.'

Without another word he left the room, and Andromache stood silently as his footsteps faded away. Gershom moved to the bedside, laying his hand gently on Helikaon's shoulder. 'Fight on, my friend,' he said softly.

Helikaon gave a shuddering breath, and his eyes opened. Andromache was instantly beside him. 'Was . . . someone here?'

'Yes, a healer,' answered Gershom. 'Rest now. Build your strength.'

'So . . . many dreams.'

Andromache filled a silver cup with water. Gershom lifted Helikaon's head and he drank a little. Then he slept again. For the rest of the night Andromache remained by the bedside. Gershom left with the dawn, and Andromache dozed for a while. She awoke when Helen arrived, carrying a jug.

'Gershom said to mix honey with the water,' she said, placing the jug by the bedside.

Andromache rose and stretched, then walked out onto the wide balcony above the Street of Bright Dancers. Helen joined her there.

'They say that more visitors are arriving every day,' said Helen. 'Kings and princes to celebrate your wedding. The bay is full of ships. Paris says many of the nobles are unhappy at being asked to remove themselves from their palaces to make way for all the foreigners.'

'They are not here to celebrate anything,' said Andromache. 'They come for Priam's golden gifts, or to win riches in the Games. They care nothing for any wedding. Many of them are little more than bandits who have seized lands and named themselves kings.'

'Like Agamemnon,' said Helen sadly. 'He seized Sparta and named his brother king.'

Andromache put her arm round the young woman's shoulder. 'I am sorry, Helen, that was thoughtless of me.'

'Oh, don't apologize, Andromache. My grandfather took Sparta by storm, enslaving the people of the land. My father merely fought and died to hold on to what his own father had stolen. It was foolish. He thought he could reason with Agamemnon and the Mykene. But the lamb does not reason with the lion. Father gave my sister to Agamemnon, and declared him his son. Then he offered me to Agamemnon's brother, Menelaus. All for nothing. What Agamemnon wants he gets. And he wanted Sparta.' Helen shrugged, then gave a wan smile. 'So now Menelaus sits on the throne, and my father's bones moulder in some field.'

'Perhaps Menelaus too will be overthrown,' observed Andromache.

'I think not. Father had no sons, no heirs. There will be a few revolts, but though the Spartans are a proud people there are not enough of them to defeat the Mykene.'

Andromache lifted her head to the sky, enjoying the warmth of the new sun on her face. 'At least your father was wise enough to send you to Troy,' she said. 'Here you are safe.'

'That's what Paris says, and Antiphones, and Hektor. Oh, Andromache, I have seen the army of Mykene on the march. Nowhere is safe from Agamemnon's ambition. Paris says Agamemnon tried to form a coalition among the kings of the west to lead an attack on Troy.'

'And he failed. The kings know such an expedition would be disastrous.'

Helen looked doubtful. 'My father said the same. The Mykene would not march on Sparta.'

'Troy is not Sparta,' Andromache pointed out. 'We are far across the sea, with mighty towers and walls. We have Hektor and the Trojan Horse. All around us are allies, and beyond them is the Hittite empire. They would not allow Troy to fall.'

'You have never seen Agamemnon,' said Helen. 'I went to the Lion's Hall when he wed my sister Klytemnestra. I stood close to him. I heard him speak. And, once, he turned towards me, and looked into my eyes. He said nothing to me, but those eyes terrified me. There was nothing in them, Andromache. Not joy, not hate. Nothing. All the treasure in the world could not fill the emptiness I saw there.'

On the third day the healer came again. Andromache and Gershom took him to the sickroom. Helikaon's colour had improved, though he was still feverish. Andromache watched as the healer removed the gauze. Bile rose in her when she saw him pinching out the fat, writhing maggots and dropping them into an empty jar. They were bloated and swollen. However, the wound, though open and raw, looked cleaner, less inflamed.

'You need to add more?' she asked.

Leaning forward, the Prophet sniffed the wound. 'There is still corruption here,' he said. 'Three more days.' With that he took a second jar, and once more placed tiny maggots within the wound, covering them with gauze.

The days passed slowly. Helikaon had more moments of clarity, and once even managed a bowl of meat broth and a little bread. The nights remained fraught. He would cry out in fever dreams, calling for his friend, Ox, or his murdered brother Diomedes.

Andromache was exhausted by the time the healer returned the second time. The wound was almost closed and the healer, having cleaned it, declared it was ready to be stitched.

'Are all the worms free of it?' she asked him. 'What if there are some inside still?'

'They will die.'

'They will not become flies and eat away at him?'

'No. Flies are living creatures and need to breathe.

Once the wound is closed any maggots left inside will suffocate.' Taking a curved needle and some dark thread, he began to close the wound. As he worked he asked her about Helikaon's moments of lucidity, and what he spoke of during those moments. He listened intently, and did not seem happy with her responses.

'What is it you fear?' she asked him.

He looked down at the sleeping man. 'He is a little stronger, and his body is fighting hard. It is his mind that concerns me. *That* is not fighting. It is as if his spirit does not want to live. It has given up. Tell me of the attack on him.'

'I know little of it,' said Andromache, turning towards Gershom. 'Were you there?'

'Yes, I was. He was coming from the cliff path with Queen Halysia. She was radiant and happy, and holding to his hand. As they approached the crowd Attalus stepped out to meet them. Helikaon greeted him with a smile, and then – so swiftly there was no chance to react – Attalus drew his dagger and plunged it into Helikaon. As he fell back I ran forward with several others and we bore Attalus to the ground. Someone stabbed the villain in the chest. He died soon after. That is all.'

'No,' said the Prophet. 'That is not all.'

'It is all that I know,' said Gershom.

'Did Attalus die swiftly, or did anyone discover why he had stabbed his friend?'

'Helikaon came to him. He knelt by Attalus. By then the assassin was almost dead. Helikaon asked him something, then leaned in. Attalus replied, but I did not hear it.'

'How did Helikaon take what he heard?'

'That is hard to say, Prophet. He was wounded – though we did not think it so serious. His face went white, and he recoiled from the dying man. Then he stood, shaking his head as if in disbelief. He staggered then, and we all saw the amount of blood he was losing. That was when we fetched the surgeon.'

'And he has not spoken of what he learned?'

'Not to me. Is it important, then?'

'I would say so,' answered the Prophet.

'What can we do for him?' asked Andromache.

'Watch him carefully, as before. Let him hear laughter, song, music. When he is stronger perhaps bring a woman to his bed, or a young man if that is his preference. Have someone lie naked alongside him. Have them stroke his skin. Anything to remind him of the joys of life.'

He finished stitching the wound, then stood. 'I am leaving tomorrow for the south. There is little more I can do for him.' He turned towards Gershom. 'Remember your promise. For I shall.'

'I will come when you call, Prophet. I am a man of my word.' Andromache stared at the two men, sensing that this moment had importance, and not knowing why. It struck her then that they were very similar in look, both powerfully built, deep-eyed and stern. They could have been father and son.

The Prophet glanced at Andromache. 'In the desert life is harsh and dangerous. Men yearn for women of strength to walk beside them, fearless and proud. You would do well in the desert, I think.'

With that he strode from the room. 'I think he liked you,' observed Gershom.

'What did he mean about your promise?'

'It is nothing,' he told her.

Later that day the physician Machaon came to the palace. He was a round-shouldered young man, with receding dark hair, and a permanent air of weariness. Andromache greeted him warmly, then led him to the bedside.

'He still clings to life?' he asked.

'Better than that,' Andromache told him. 'The wound is clean and sealed.'

Machaon looked doubtful, but followed Andromache to the sickroom, and examined Helikaon himself. Andromache saw his amazement. 'This is not possible,' he said. 'The wound was rancid, and beyond healing.'

She told him about the Prophet and the maggots. He sat unbelieving as she described the process.

'He is lucky that such a ghastly nonsense did not kill him,' he said. 'There must be another reason. Has he eaten anything, or been given potions I have not been made aware of?'

Andromache stared at him. 'Nothing he has not had before. I do not understand you, Machaon. Your own eyes have seen the efficacy of the treatment. Why then do you doubt it?'

Machaon looked at her pityingly. 'Maggots are creatures of foulness. I can understand how some barbaric desert dweller might believe in them, but you are an intelligent woman. I can only assume that exhaustion has dulled your senses.'

Andromache felt a cold anger rise in her. 'Oh, Machaon, I did not expect *you* to reinforce my belief in the stupidity of men. I thought you different . . . wiser. Now I have a question for you. There are many treatments for illness and disease. How many of them were created by you? What cure have you discovered in your time as a healer?'

'I have studied all the great works—' he began. She interrupted him.

'Not the works of others, Machaon. Tell me the cures *you* have devised.' The young physician remained silent, his expression tense. 'And *that* is something to consider,' she said, witheringly. 'There have been no potions, Machaon, no secret elixirs. A man came and explained that maggots ate rancid flesh. I did not believe it, but I have seen it to be true. He had a cure not written down in your ancient scrolls.'

His face darkened, and he rose to his feet. 'Helikaon is beloved of the gods,' he said. 'What we have here is a miracle. I will give thanks to Asklepios and to the goddess Athene. I have brought healing potions which I will leave with you.'

Gershom stood aside in the doorway, allowing the physician to depart. Then he looked at Andromache and smiled. 'You were hard on him. He is a good man, and he works tirelessly for the sick.'

'I know. But he is arrogant. How many wounded men will die under his care because of it?'

'You should get some rest,' he said. 'I'll sit with him. Go and sleep. You will feel better for it.'

Andromache knew he was right. She was almost

reeling from exhaustion. When she reached her rooms a young servant girl asked her if she wanted hot water brought for a bath. Andromache shook her head. 'I need to sleep,' she said. Dismissing the girl, she walked into the bedroom, threw off her clothes, and stretched out on the broad bed. A cool wind blew through the open window and she drew the covers across her body.

Yet sleep would not come. Images swirled in her mind: Helikaon upon the beach at Blue Owl Bay, young and handsome; Kalliope laughing and dancing in the moonlight. All her life people had talked of the wonders of love, the joy of it, the strength of it, the music and the passion of it. She had perceived love then to be an absolute: unchanging and solid as a marble statue. Yet it wasn't. She had loved Kalliope, luxuriating in her company, in the warmth of her skin, the softness of her kisses. And she loved Helikaon, yearning to be with him, her heart beating faster even as she sat by his sickbed, holding his hand. It was very confusing.

Bards talked and sang of the one great love, the meeting of souls, exquisite and unique. The seer on the beach at Blue Owl Bay had talked of *three* loves, one as tempestuous as the Great Green, one like the oak, solid and true, and one like the bright moon. Helikaon was the first, for he had been the man with one sandal. When she had asked about the others the seer had told her that the oak would rise to her from the filth of pigs, and the moon arrive in blood and pain.

None of them was Kalliope.

Yet I do love her, she thought. I know that to be true.

Her thoughts drifted, and she saw the isle of Thera, and the great Temple of the Horse. It was almost mid-day now, and the priestesses would be preparing the wine to offer the Minotaur. Twelve women would walk to the trembling rock. They would chant and sing, then pour the wine into the hissing crack, trying not to breathe the noxious fumes that rose from below the ground.

The hot breath of the Minotaur.

Kalliope might be with them. The last time Andromache had taken part in the ritual Kalliope had winked at her, and been rebuked by the High Priestess.

Alone now in her bed Andromache closed her eyes. 'I wish you were here,' she whispered, thinking of Kalliope. Then Kalliope's image blurred, and once again she found herself picturing the brilliant blue eyes of Helikaon.

For Helikaon the world he had known no longer existed. He floated wraithlike through a chaotic jumble of dreams. Sometimes he was lying in a broad bed, by a magical window that flickered in a heartbeat between sunlight and moonlight; at others he was standing on the deck of the *Xanthos* as it sailed the Great Green, or on the cliffs of Dardanos, watching a fleet of ships, all burning, the screams of the sailors sounding like the cries of demonic gulls. Images shifted and shivered. Only the pain was constant, though this was as nothing to the agonies he suffered when the visions came.

His little brother Diomedes, playing happily in the sunshine. Helikaon looked on, hearing the boy's merry laughter – then noticing that an edge of the child's tunic had begun to burn. He cried out to warn him, but the boy went on playing as the flames roared about him. Helikaon tried to reach him, but his limbs were leaden and every step forward only served to increase the distance between them. Diomedes' skin blackened, and only then did he turn towards his brother. 'Help me!' cried the boy. But Helikaon could do nothing but watch him burn.

Then he was on the *Xanthos* again, standing alongside his old friend Ox. Sunlight was bright, the breeze fresh. Ox turned towards him, and Helikaon saw a trickle of blood, like a thin red necklace round Ox's throat. Helikaon reached up to touch the wound – and the head came away in his hands.

His eyes opened, and once more he was in the broad bed, moonlight shining through the window. He heard movement, and saw Andromache's face above him. Her hand was cool upon his face. 'Come back to us, Helikaon,' she whispered.

The plea confused him. From where should he come, and to where? He was already everywhere, sailing the Great Green, walking the Seven Hills with Odysseus and Bias, the black man complaining about the midges coming off the marshes; standing on the battlements of Troy, looking out over the sunset sea, riding with Hektor against the Amorites. All the events of his life playing again and again, from childhood fears and the suicide of his mother to adult tragedies and the deaths of those he loved.

Now the sun was shining, and he was walking with

golden-haired Halysia towards the palace. She was to be his wife, and he knew she was happy now. The previous year the Mykene had killed her child, and raped her, leaving her for dead. Her life since had been one of sorrow and fear. Now he would protect her – even if he could not love her. He felt the warmth of her hand in his, her grip tight, as if afraid he might pull away from her. As they approached the crowds he saw Attalus step out. The man darted forward, a knife in his hand. Instinctively Helikaon tried to block the blow, but Halysia, in her surprise at this sudden movement, held to him even more tightly. The knife plunged into his chest. Tearing himself loose from Halysia's grip he threw up his arm. The blade tore into his armpit. Then men surged around him, bearing Attalus to the ground. Helikaon saw one of his bodyguards thrust a dagger into Attalus' belly, ripping it up through the lungs. Helikaon pushed himself through the mass of men, and dropped to his knees beside the assassin.

'Why?' he asked the dying man.

'I . . . am . . . Karpophorus,' Attalus told him. 'It is . . . my holy duty.'

'You killed my father!'

'Yes.'

'Who hired you for that?'

As the killer whispered the name Helikaon cried out and the scene darkened. A hand was stroking his face, and his eyes opened once more. Moonlight was shining against the dark frame of the window, and he could see patches of clouds in the night sky. 'You must live, Helikaon,' said a vision that looked like Andromache.

'Why?' he answered wearily.

And now he was fighting on the stairs once more, Argurios beside him. He was so tired, and the Mykene kept coming, surging up at them. A hand touched his arm, and a voice said: 'Walk with me, Golden One.'

'I have to fight,' he shouted, plunging his blade into the neck of an advancing soldier.

'The fight is already won,' said the voice of Argurios. 'Come with me.' The world spun and Helikaon was standing alongside the great warrior, looking down at the fighting, seeing himself, blood-spattered, struggling on. Then he saw the vile Kolanos draw back on his bow. And he knew the arrow was aimed at Argurios, knew that it would punch through his broken cuirass.

'No!' he shouted. 'Argurios, beware!'

'I am here,' said the Argurios standing beside him. 'The arrow has already flown. You see?' Helikaon looked at him, and saw the shaft, buried deep in his side. 'You cannot stop what is to be, Helikaon. This was my time. Walk with me.'

And then there was sunshine, the glory of an autumn sunset. They were in a garden, watching the last light of the dying sun fade in the west. Argurios was dressed now in a simple tunic of white, his face bronzed by the sun. Gone were the signs of struggle, the deep-etched lines, the dark circles beneath his eyes. 'Go back to the world, Helikaon. Live,' he said.

'I don't know how,' Helikaon replied.

'Neither did I – for all but the last few days of my life.

We are tiny flames, Helikaon, and we flicker alone in the great dark for no more than a heartbeat. When we strive for wealth, glory and fame, it is meaningless. The nations we fight for will one day cease to be. Even the mountains we gaze upon will crumble to dust. To truly live we must yearn for that which does not die.'

'Everything dies,' said Helikaon sadly.

'Not everything,' said Argurios. A shaft of sunlight illuminated a white stone bench at the end of the garden. Helikaon saw a woman sitting upon it, watching the sunset. She turned to him and smiled. It was Laodike. Argurios walked away from him to where Laodike sat, and kissed her. Then the two of them sat together on the bench, arm in arm as the light faded. Helikaon felt lost and alone. Argurios turned towards him. 'Go back,' he said. 'She is waiting!'

His mind flickered, and his eyes opened. He was lying down now, and could see the enchanted window to his right, bright stars shining in the sky.

'Come back to us, my love,' whispered a vision of Andromache.

Helikaon felt the warmth of a naked body slide alongside his, her arm over his chest, her leg touching his thigh.

'Andromache?' he whispered. It did not matter that she was a phantom. The moon shone bright and he saw her face, her beautiful green eyes looking down into his.

'Yes, it is Andromache,' she said. Her lips touched his and he felt his heart quicken. Her hand moved down over his belly and he groaned as arousal stiffened his loins. Her lips parted and the kiss became more

passionate. The pain from his wound faded. This was a
new dream! A part of his mind expected her to burst
into flame, or the scene to shift to one of horror. But it
did not. The warmth in him grew, his heart pounding.
His good arm circled her back, drawing her down and
across him. Her thigh slid over his hip, and now she
was above him, straddling him.

The nightmare visions had no claim on him now. He
felt the soft, wet warmth of her and surged up to meet
it. She cried out as he entered her, then pressed down
upon him, her hands cradling his face, her lips pressed
to his own.

Deep within him something awoke, and he felt it
grow. It was a yearning for life, for joy. The phantom
above him began to shudder and moan, and cry out.
The sound filled him. Then white light exploded behind
his eyes, and he passed out.

He awoke to bird song and the bright light of day.

Helikaon took a deep breath, and could taste the salt
upon the air. A plain-faced woman was leaning over
him. He struggled to remember her name. Then it came
to him. She was the Spartan princess, Helen, and he
had seen her with Paris at the palace of Hekabe.

'How are you feeling?' she asked him.

'Hungry,' he told her. He struggled to sit, and she
helped him, lifting the pillows behind him.

'I have some honey water,' she said, 'but I will fetch
you some food.'

'Thank you, Helen.'

She smiled shyly. 'It is good to see you recovered. We
were all very worried.'

He drank some honeyed water and Helen left the room to fetch him breakfast. Leaning to place the empty cup on the table beside the bed he winced. The wound under his armpit was still painful. He glanced down at his chest and arms. So thin, he thought, touching the jutting collar bones and tracing the lines of his ribs.

The door opened and Andromache came in, carrying a bowl of fruit. She was wearing a long dress of shimmering scarlet, her red hair held back from her face by a head band of ornate silver, set with emeralds. She looked thoughtful and concerned as she laid the fruit bowl beside the bed. She did not sit beside him, but stood watching him.

'It is good to see you,' he said. 'By the gods, I feel I have been torn back from the grave.'

'You were very sick,' she said softly, her eyes on his.

'You need have no more fear for me,' he told her. 'My strength is returning. I slept last night with no dreams. Well, save one of you.'

'You dreamed of me?'

'I did, and it was a fine dream – a dream of life. I think it was that dream which cured me.'

She seemed to relax then, and sat down by the bed-side. When she spoke her voice was cool, her tone distant. 'Everyone thought you were dying, but Gershom found a healer. He cleansed your wound. Once it is fully sealed you will need to swim, and to take walks to build your strength.'

'What is wrong, Andromache?' he asked.

'Nothing is wrong,' she replied. 'I am . . . pleased you are recovered.'

'You talk like a stranger. We are friends, you and I.'

'We are not friends,' she snapped. 'We . . . I . . . I am to be wed to Hektor, and you to Halysia.'

'And that means we cannot be friends?'

'I do not see you as a friend, Helikaon. I cannot.' She looked away, staring out of the window.

'You know that I love you,' he said, softly. 'As I have never loved another woman. That will always be true.'

'I know,' she said, her voice bitter. She swung back towards him. 'I feel the same. And that is why we cannot be friends. I cannot sit with you and make idle chatter, and laugh at silly jests. You fill my mind, Helikaon. All the time. Even in my dreams.'

'I told you I dreamed of you last night,' he said.

'I do not want to hear it,' she told him, rising. 'Gershom is waiting to see you. And Antiphones. Xander came yesterday too. He said he would return.'

'Where is Hektor?'

'He sailed with the *Xanthos*, in search of pirates. He is expected soon.'

Helikaon looked into her face. 'I thank you for saving me, Andromache,' he told her.

'It was not me. I told you. Gershom found a healer.'

'No,' he said sadly. 'It was you.'

XIV

Black galleys in the bay

ANDROMACHE STRODE OUT INTO THE LONG GARDEN behind the palace, her bow in her hand, a quiver of arrows slung across her shoulder. Targets of bound straw had been set by the far wall, cunningly crafted in the shapes of deer, boar, and men. Andromache notched a black-feathered shaft to the string, drew back, and loosed.

At a distance of thirty paces the arrow tore into the straw deer at the belly. It was a poor shot. Had it been a real animal the arrow would have ripped through its guts, causing an agonized death, and ruining the meat. With a deer, she knew, the arrow needed to pierce both lungs. Death would then be swift, the meat tender. Calming herself she sent four more shafts into the target. These were better aimed.

'You are a fine shot,' came the voice of Antiphones. Andromache swung towards him, masking her irritation at having been interrupted.

'You are looking well, Antiphones,' she said. He was still colossally large, but he had shed a great deal of weight since the autumn. His face now looked healthy, and he no longer wheezed as he moved.

'Still fatter than five pigs, but I am working on it,' he replied. 'As you know, Father has given me command of the Ilos regiment. By next spring I'm hoping to be able to mount a horse and ride out with the cavalry.'

She smiled. 'I am glad he rewarded you, Antiphones. Had you not discovered the plot we might all be dead now.'

His face stiffened, but then the smile returned, though a little forced, she thought. 'Yes, Father was grateful. I have discovered, though, that his benevolence is always short-lived.'

'My own father is the same,' she said. 'Perhaps all kings are. They feel they have nothing to be grateful for. People are born only to serve them, therefore those who do so faithfully are only behaving as expected.'

'Well, at least he has taken a liking to you,' said Antiphones, easing himself down on a stone bench in the shade of a flowering tree.

'It is not affection,' she told him. 'It is merely lust – and a desire to have that which has been refused him.'

Antiphones shrugged. 'You can continue to say no, Andromache. He may be many things, but he would not force a woman against her will.'

Andromache shook her head and laughed. 'How naïve that sounds, Antiphones. What you mean is he would not force her down with the strength of his arms. You think the palace girls he beds, or the daughters of the nobles, spread their legs for him because of his charm? His golden hair is streaked with grey. He is old, Antiphones. Young girls do not clamour for the old. They share his bed because they must. Because he is the king and they are afraid of his wrath.'

'But you are not afraid of his wrath?'

'I fear no man.'

'Then you are safe from his advances.'

'Yes, but I still feel his eyes on me. I can almost hear his heartbeat quicken when I am close. I imagine it will stop when I am Hektor's wife.'

'It hasn't stopped him with other men's wives,' said Antiphones, softly, looking round in case any servants were close by.

'There are no whisperers here, Antiphones,' she said. 'Surely he will stop. Is not Hektor his favourite son? Even Priam would not risk angering him.'

'Yes, he is the favourite,' replied Antiphones, without bitterness. 'For years that was hard for me to swallow. Harder for Agathon, for Polites. Hard for all the sons. How could any compete with the *mighty* Hektor?'

'Do you hate him?'

'Father?'

'No. Hektor.'

Antiphones shook his head. 'No-one ever hates Hektor. Even Agathon, who I discovered hated just about everyone in Troy. Including me – and I was his brother as well as his friend. Why do you ask? Do you dislike Hektor?'

'How can I dislike someone I have never really met?'

Antiphones looked confused. 'But Hektor has been in Troy throughout the winter.'

'Yes, and somehow rarely where I am. Strange behaviour for a man soon to be my husband.' She felt anger rise, and tried to quell it. 'But then the daughters of kings are merely breeding cows sold to the highest bidder. Why should a man wish to speak to a breeding cow?'

Antiphones chuckled. 'I have never known a woman like you, Andromache.'

'A compliment, I trust?'

'You know, I am not sure. I was raised to believe women yearned to be subservient, and longed to be dominated.'

'Had you been raised by Priam alone that would be no surprise, but Hekabe is not a subservient queen, and I would imagine no man ever dominated her.'

'That is true,' said Antiphones. 'Priam and Hekabe, passion and poison, strength and cruelty. She would eat her young for the sake of power.' Antiphones sighed. 'What a loving family we are.'

Stepping away from him, she sent an arrow flashing down the garden and into the straw boar. Two more shafts sliced into the target.

'I notice you don't shoot at the man,' said Antiphones, pointing towards the tallest of the straw targets.

'I don't hunt men,' she said.

'Yet you killed the man trying to stab Father.'

She swung towards him. 'I can hit a target eighty paces distant one hundred times in a hundred. Do men

253

say, what a fine archer? No. Kill one assassin a mere thirty paces away and they are so impressed. What is this link between men and death, Antiphones? Why did I have to kill to become respected?'

'You do yourself an injustice, Andromache. It is not about killing. The man was running at Father, a spear in his hand. You had a heartbeat to react. You did not recoil. Fear and shock did not stiffen your limbs. You acted swiftly and surely, while others froze. And your arrow was true.'

'As I said, a simple shot. Did you see Helikaon?'

'For a while. Then he fell asleep. He looks better today. There is colour in his cheeks, and the fever has broken. He will recover. And he will need to . . . rather swiftly.'

'Why?'

'The city will soon be filled by warriors from the west, come to take part in the Games. Helikaon is hated by them. Agamemnon has ordered his death. It is almost certain there will be more attempts on his life.' He drew in a deep breath. 'And not just Helikaon. Many of the kings loathe one another. Before long the streets will be crawling with assassins.'

'But the Games . . .' said Andromache, 'by the laws of Olympos any city that stages Games in honour of the gods is neutral. All enmities are put aside. There will be a truce.' Antiphones was looking at her quizzically. 'What is it? Am I suddenly speaking in a foreign language?'

'Almost. You are a curious mixture, Andromache. One moment you are speaking with authority about the nature of kings, and the next . . .' He hesitated, then shook his head. 'You accused me of being naïve. Surely you must understand that the truce is illusory. Everyone knows it. Priam will have soldiers everywhere. All the family will walk surrounded by bodyguards. Agamemnon will have his Followers with him at all times, hands on daggers, ready to strike down anyone who gets too close to their king. It will be a time of tension and menace. Helikaon will be a prime target. Of that you can have no doubt. Once he is stronger have him taken to his own palace.' He pushed himself ponderously to his feet.

'Perhaps he should go back to Dardania,' she said.

'He won't do that. That would signify weakness to his enemies.'

'And seeing a stick-thin man tottering around in the sunlight will make them gasp at his strength?'

Antiphones laughed, with genuine good humour. 'You have a tongue on you like a whip. I am chastened, and I flee from your company.'

Andromache smiled. 'It was good to talk with you, Antiphones. I hope you will visit me again. As long, of course, as it is considered seemly for a future brother to attend me in the absence of my betrothed.'

'Oh, no-one will worry about me,' he said brightly. 'It is well known that my tastes have never been for women. Pies, pastries, and handsome young men. No, Andromache, we do not have to concern ourselves with seemly behaviour.' Stepping forward he kissed her lightly on both cheeks. 'And remember what I said. Speak to Gershom. He is a fighting man and will know how to protect Helikaon.'

* * *

The whore known as Big Red watched the rising pandemonium on the beach and laughed. A fistfight would break out soon, maybe several, she thought as the beachmasters fought a losing battle to organize the incoming galleys. The other whores who had gathered were not amused. Bad tempers meant poor business, and the women had believed there would be gold and silver rings to be earned with so many ships arriving together. In fact, as Big Red had surmised almost as soon as she reached the beach, there were just too many ships. Few of the sailors, and even fewer of the passengers, were in any mood to let loose the one-eyed snake.

Red moved away from the line of whores, looking for a spot in the shade. Later tonight there would be gold aplenty to be made in the streets of Troy. For now she might as well rest and enjoy the entertainment. Reaching a low stone bench she brushed her hand across its surface, scanning it for bird shit. Her red gown was new and she had no wish to see it stained. Satisfied the bench was cleaned, she eased her considerable weight down upon it. The relief was instant. Her left knee had been paining her recently, and long periods of standing caused the joint to stiffen and swell. Comfortable now, she watched the chaos upon the long beach.

As far as the eye could see in both directions the Bay of Troy was packed with vessels large and small, and scores more were gliding in quietly through the afternoon mist. There was no room for them all, and the beachmasters, backed up by soldiers, were forcing some boats off the sand to make way for incomers. Those leaving were impeding those rowing in and the clash of oars and cursing of sailors echoed round the waters.

She heard the angry complaints of fishermen, furious at losing berths their families had used for generations, being forced to travel far up the Scamander to beach. Foreign captains shouted scorn at the beachmasters when told to disembark their important passengers then return the way they had come to beach in the Bay of Herakles, far from the city. Merchants and pedlars who had just arrived were milling about, uncertain where to go, anxious for their cargoes in the heaving throng.

Red found it all highly amusing. Clouds of flying insects from the low marshes about the bay were buzzing round the sweating, red-faced beachmasters, who were trying to maintain order and placate tempers while rapidly losing their own. Red was never troubled by insects. They did not like the heavy perfume with which she doused her henna-dyed hair.

'You poxy son of a river-rat!'

Red watched with delight as a Gyppto mechant took a swing at the beachmaster Dresos. Fat Dresos tried to dodge but lost his footing and sprawled in the sand. Soldiers stepped forward and prodded the furious Gyppto back to his ship at spearpoint.

Others joined in the laughter as Dresos got to his feet, but he swung angrily on the red-headed whore.

'Shut your mouth, you filthy bitch!'

This just made her laugh harder, but one of the young soldiers stepped over to her.

'Better get back beyond the wall, Red. Likely to be trouble before long. Wouldn't want to see you get hurt.'

'Sweet of you, Ipheus,' she said, and felt a sinking of the spirits. The young man had treated her with polite concern, but there had been no hint of desire as he spoke to her. He had not looked into her violet eyes and blushed. He had not licked his lips, or shifted from foot to foot, awed by her sensuality. Red glanced down at the flowing crimson gown she wore to disguise her growing weight. Once – and not so long ago – she *had* been desirable. But those were the days before she became known as *Big* Red. She sighed.

'Are you all right, Red?' asked Ipheus.

'Come ride me and find out,' she replied, with a practised wink.

The soldier laughed. 'Couldn't afford you, Red,' he said, then moved off towards another group of angry men.

The young man's compliment did not lift her mood, and Red decided to go home, and drown her sorrows in wine. She never had been beautiful. Her large and powerful frame precluded that. But there had once been power in her violet eyes, in the days when the gods blessed her with radiant youth. Now that youth was passing. Many of the older whores sought out husbands in the autumn of their careers – old soldiers or lonely merchants. Red wanted no husband, as she had never wanted children.

She began the long walk up towards the city, and

paused. The noise on the beach had faded away. All argument and cursing had ceased. It seemed even the seabirds had stopped their screeching. The crowds on the beach were all looking towards the bay. In the ominous silence Red realized she could hear her heart beating.

Three black galleys were moving slowly through the mass of ships. Oarsmen on other vessels hurriedly backed up, making room for them. No-one complained or shouted insults as the galleys headed for shore, ahead of those who had been waiting impatiently since midday.

As the first galley closed on the beach black oars were raised. The ship glided on for a few heartbeats, then the keel bumped quietly on the sand.

Red walked back down to where Ipheus was standing silently, his expression tense.

'You'd think the god of the dead was arriving,' she said.

'And you wouldn't be far wrong. Those are Mykene vessels. Agamemnon is here.'

Agamemnon, a long black cloak over his thin shoulders, his black chin beard jutting like a sword blade, stood on the prow and gazed up at the golden city of Troy. His dark, brooding eyes scanned the high walls, his expression unreadable. Beside him stood the fleshy, dissolute Peleus, king of Thessaly, and his son Achilles, a huge, black-haired young warrior dressed in a white knee-length tunic edged with gold thread.

'See how they fear you,' said Peleus enviously. For a

moment only Agamemnon had no idea what he meant, then he realized that the crews of the waiting ships had fallen silent, and no-one complained as the galleys of Mykene eased through to the beach. He was not uplifted by the knowledge. It was no more than he expected.

On the beach Agamemnon saw courtiers waiting to greet him, but he did not move, or acknowledge them.

'Strong walls,' said Peleus. 'Impressive. You'd lose men on a ratio of ten, maybe fifteen to one, trying to scale them. Better to breach the gates, I think. You have been here before?'

'My father brought me, when I was a child. We walked the walls. They are weakest in the west of the city. That is where Herakles breached them.'

'He had the war god Ares in his ranks, they say,' remarked Peleus.

Agamemnon glanced at him, but said nothing. Always men spoke of gods walking among men, but Agamemnon had never seen such a miracle. He believed in the gods, of course, but he felt them distant from the affairs of men, or at least indifferent to them. His own armies had conquered cities said to be protected by the gods, and none of his men had been struck down by the lightning of Ares, or the hammer of Hephaistos. His own priests were, in the main, dissemblers. If the army suffered a reverse, then it was the will of the gods. If a victory, then the will of the gods. It seemed to Agamemnon that the gods favoured the men with the sharpest swords and the greatest numbers. Even so, he sacrificed to the gods before every battle. He had even taken to following the old Hittite practice of human sacrifice before particularly important conflicts. Whether this aided him super-naturally he neither knew nor cared. What was more important was that such disregard for human life caused fear and panic among his enemies – as indeed did the practice of slaughtering the inhabitants of towns and cities that resisted his ambition. Other cities then surrendered without the need for lengthy sieges, their lords pledging undying allegiance to Mykene rule.

On the beach the courtiers were still waiting, their long white cloaks fluttering in the faint breeze.

'Are you feeling strong, Achilles?' Agamemnon asked the young warrior beside Peleus.

'Always,' answered Achilles. 'You think Hektor will take part in the Games?' His dark eyes gleamed as he asked it, and Agamemnon saw the longing in him for combat and glory.

Agamemnon thought about the question. It was an interesting one. King Priam would be seeking to impress the kings of the west with the power of Troy. How better to show that power than having the mighty Hektor humble the champions of those kings? And yet . . . what if Hektor did not prevail? What if the ultimate champion of the Games was from the west? He looked at Achilles. The man's strength was obvious, his shoulders broad, his muscles finely honed. He had proved himself in battle, and in bouts, where his massive fists had pounded valiant opponents to the dust. Could Hektor defeat Achilles? Would Priam risk such a bout?

Would I, he wondered?

But then I am not Priam, he reasoned. The king of Troy was addicted to risk, and he wondered if Priam's vanity would dictate that Hektor would stand with the athletes. He saw that Achilles was still waiting patiently for his answer.

'No,' he said, 'I do not think Hektor will take part. But it could be we might engineer it. We will see.'

'I pray that he does,' said Achilles. 'I tire of the stories of Hektor the Man Killer, Hektor the Hero. Whom has he fought? What men of worth? A few skinny Gypptos, a handful of Hittite rebels. Thrakian renegades, ill armed and poorly led. His legend is built on straw. I will tear it down for him.'

'Ha!' said Peleus, with a broad smile. 'There speaks a prince of Thessaly! By the gods, Agamemnon, my son will humble that proud Trojan.' As he spoke he clapped Agamemnon on the shoulder.

'I have no doubt of it,' replied the Mykene king, masking his irritation at the touch. One day, he thought, I will take great pleasure in having hot irons thrust through your eyes. His loathing of Peleus was absolute, though he never allowed it to show. Peleus was important to his ambition, and that was all that mattered at this time. The attack on Troy, when it came, would need huge numbers of warriors, and Peleus had 8,000 fighting men under his command, and a son worth 100 more. For those men Agamemnon could bury his hatred beneath smiles of comradeship and promises of alliance. He could ignore the gross excesses of the man, the rape of children, and the casual murders of female slaves, tortured and throttled. Peleus was a brute, who killed for pleasure. Agamemnon would wait. When Troy was his then Peleus would be the first to die. The first of many. For a moment only the festering hatred he felt for his brother kings surged to the surface; the spindly Nestor, the braggart Idomeneos, and the ugly storyteller Odysseus. And more. He swallowed hard, licking dry lips with a dry tongue. All enemies will be despatched, he told himself, but each in their day. Today was not the day to think of the vile Peleus, or any of the other kings of the west. Today was about Priam.

Once more he glanced up at the golden city. A chariot decorated with gold, and drawn by two pure white horses, emerged. It was being driven by a broad-shouldered man in a tunic of pale blue, and a white cloak embroidered with silver thread. His long golden hair and close-cropped beard were streaked now with white. Priam was growing old, but still he radiated authority. Crowds drew back, and many cheered as the king rode his chariot down to the beach. Agamemnon felt his emotions surge – a heady mixture of hatred and admiration. Even strangers to this city would be in no doubt they were in the presence of a king as Priam steered his chariot through the throng.

Agamemnon was well aware that he himself did not look mighty, with his rounded shoulders, slim frame and ungainly gait. Nevertheless, despite this drawback he had made himself the most famous warrior king in the western world. He knew exactly why. What he lacked in physical majesty was more than compensated for by his utter ruthlessness. Enemies died. Their families died. Their mothers, their fathers, their uncles and their friends died. Agamemnon engendered fear. It enveloped his opponents like a sea mist. And he could plot a campaign, or a battle, and wage it mercilessly and brilliantly until it was won.

He gazed up again at the mighty walls of Troy. This was a prize worth taking, he thought.

Cold dread struck him, causing an involuntary shiver. Troy was no longer merely a prize, a city to be plundered. The conqueror of Troy would have immortal fame and the opportunity of empire. To fail here would be to lie in a forgotten grave in the midst of a ruined nation. Pushing such dark thoughts from his mind, he turned to his companions.

'Now we go ashore,' he said, as the Trojan king's chariot drew up on the beach below the ship. 'The fox has come to greet us. We will stroke his ego, and smile at his jests. And as we smile we will picture the day he is on his knees before us, his city in flames, his sons dead, his life a few heartbeats from its end.'

XV

The Eagle Child

ANTIPHONES STOOD ON THE BEACH, HIS BROTHER POLITES beside him, with several courtiers in attendance. He was there to greet the Mykene king, but soon realized Agamemnon would not leave his ship until Priam deigned to make an entrance.

The heat was strong, and Antiphones began to sweat. His vast bulk was bearing down on his knee joints, which were beginning to ache. Beside him the skinny Polites was dabbing at the bald spot on his crown with a piece of embroidered linen. Neither man spoke and Antiphones wished he could be anywhere but here.

He looked up at the prow of the black galley, where he could see a round-shouldered man with a black chin beard. Was this the dreaded Agamemnon, butcher of cities? Antiphones sighed. Though he was losing weight fast he was still grotesque in his own eyes; a soft, plump creature other men looked upon with either scorn or pity.

That he had become a hero during the attack on the city the previous autumn meant little to him, for when men referred to his slaying of the assassins and his warning of the raid on Priam's palace they spoke of the *fat hero*.

Even in that they were wrong, he thought darkly.

He remembered the day Father had come to his sickbed, where he was recovering from the stab wounds he had suffered – wounds that would have killed a thinner man. The blades had been defeated by the wealth of flesh guarding his body.

Priam had walked into the room and stood by the bed, regarding his son with eyes that shone with both contempt and concern.

'Well, boy, I am told you acted with courage. I must say I am surprised.'

'Why would that be, Father? Am I not the son of Priam and the brother of Hektor?'

Priam had shrugged. 'Let us not argue, Antiphones. Let us merely say I misjudged you. Helikaon tells me that without your warning we would not have been able to shut the gates in time. Then the Thrakians would have been upon us before we had a chance to muster a defence.'

'That was all he told you?'

'Is there more?'

'There is always more, Father.' Anger had ripped through him then, making his wounds burn. 'Would you like to hear it?'

'Well, I am here, so I might as well,' answered the king, sitting down upon the bed. 'Will there be more surprises?'

'I plotted with Agathon to kill you. I only turned away at the last because he planned to murder all my brothers and their families.' Antiphones had expected rage, and then that soldiers would be summoned to drag him from the bed and murder him. Instead Priam had merely shrugged.

'I knew that,' said the king. 'No other way you could have learned of his plans. I take it you were foolish enough to confront him – hence the assassins?'

'Yes. Foolish Antiphones. I thought I could reason with him. Just kill the old man, Agathon. No need for innocent people to die. Just one ghastly old man.'

Priam had laughed then, his manner changing. 'Agathon would have made a terrible king, Antiphones. You would have been better. You have a sound mind, and a fine grasp of the intricacies of trade and the acquisition of profits.'

'Really? And that is why you made Polites your chancellor? A man who needs to kick off his sandals to count to twenty? That is why you chose me to be your Master of Horse, a fat man who could not ride? You are a monster, and I hate you.'

'Nothing wrong with hate, boy,' said Priam indifferently.

'So what now, Father? Banishment? Death?'

'I considered death – had you not admitted to me your part in the plot. As it is I am rather proud of you. Which, as you can imagine, is a rare thing where you are concerned. I am giving you command of the Ilos regiment.'

'Why?'

Priam had stood and stared down at him. 'I am a king, boy. Kings never have to explain. You want the command?'

'Yes.'

'Good. Well, you rest and recover. We'll talk more when you leave the houses of healing.' He walked to the door, then swung back. 'I take it there will be no more plots from you?'

Without waiting for an answer he was gone.

Back at his own house, some weeks later, Antiphones found that his servants had prepared a feast for him, loading the tables with his favourite sweetmeats and pies. He had stared at them, with no longing, which surprised him. Little Kassandra had been there. The twelve-year-old had looked at him with serious eyes. 'I did tell them, Antiphones, but they didn't believe me.'

'What did you tell them, sweet girl?'

'That you would have no taste for such food again.'

'And how did you know that?'

'Xidoros told me. He said you had spent years eating your pain, and you could never be filled. Now the pain is gone, and you are no longer hungry.'

Antiphones had kissed her on the brow, and questioned her no further. Xidoros was her first teacher, and he had died four years before.

The imaginary spirit had been correct, though. His taste for sweetmeats had vanished. However, years of excess would take more than a few months to overcome. He stood now on the beach, his joints aching, sweat coursing down his face, wishing that he could sit down.

Then – thank the gods – his father's chariot came into sight.

Now there was movement on the ship and several men lowered themselves to the beach. The first was the man with the black chin beard, the second a florid-faced, middle-aged man, clean-shaven. The third was a god!

Antiphones stared at the young warrior in the white, gold-edged tunic. His body was lightly tanned, his muscles sleek and well defined. His face was the most beautiful that Antiphones had ever seen, deep dark eyes over high cheekbones, full lips above a strong chin. Antiphones could not stop staring at him. His mouth was dry, and all thoughts of pain in his joints disappeared in an instant. Other men, officers of Agamemnon, climbed down to join their lord. Antiphones tore his gaze from the beautiful young man and tried to concentrate on the meeting of kings.

'At last you return to Troy,' said Priam, stepping in and throwing a powerful arm round Agamemnon's shoulder. 'When last I saw you here you were no taller than a jackrabbit, and clinging to your father's cloak. Welcome back, Agamemnon. May your visit be a happy one, and rich with the company of friends.'

'It is always good to be among friends,' said Agamemnon. 'It is good to be here, and to be able to tell you in person of my sorrow that Mykene renegades should have joined your son in his revolt. You should know that I had them put to death upon their return. I take it that is why you freed them, so that justice could be served by my own hand?'

'I freed them because they weren't worth killing,' said Priam, with a wide smile. 'They fought like children. Quite the worst fighters I've ever seen. By Athene, I'd be ashamed if they were part of my army. No wonder they were renegades. No king worth the name would have such men under his command. But enough of chatter in the sunshine.'

Antiphones listened to the exchange, and suppressed a smile. The Mykene invaders had been the elite of Agamemnon's forces, and had fought like lions.

'Let me introduce my sons, Antiphones and Polites,' said Priam. The introductions went on until Antiphones stood before the godlike Achilles.

'I have heard wonderful tales of your bravery,' said Antiphones. 'It is a great honour to have you in our city.'

Achilles smiled at him, seeming to appreciate the warmth of the greeting. 'I too have heard of the wonders of Troy,' he said. 'Where is your great hero, Hektor?'

'At sea, hunting pirates. He should be here within the next few days. At least I hope so, or he will miss his own wedding celebrations.'

'Will he participate in the Games?'

'I do not believe that he will.'

'Ah, that is a shame,' said Achilles. 'Now my victory will not be as sweet.'

'But it will be wondrous to see,' said Antiphones. 'I shall look forward to it.'

Achilles seemed puzzled, and leaned close. 'You are so sure of my winning?'

'I cannot believe any man could ever defeat you,' answered Antiphones.

'Not even Hektor?'

'That I could not say,' answered Antiphones honestly. 'Hektor is not a man. He is like you – a young god. Mere mortals cannot make judgements on such matters.'

Achilles laughed. 'I like you, Antiphones. Come dine with us one evening.' Then he moved away.

Priam took Agamemnon in his chariot, while the other officers and dignitaries walked up the slope towards the great gate.

Antiphones remained where he was, lost in the wonder of the moment.

'They hate each other,' cried Kassandra, pointing from the high wall down towards the chariot carrying her father Priam and the Mykene king. 'Look at all that red mist flowing around them and behind them, like a great cloak.'

Andromache smiled down at the fey child, and stroked her dark hair. Kassandra looked up at her and grinned. In that moment Andromache saw that Kassandra's childhood was passing. She was in her thirteenth year, and already there were tiny breasts showing under her thin tunic, and her hips were no longer quite as thin. 'I don't see any mist,' said Andromache.

'Of course you don't. Silly of me.' She leaned far out over the wall, trying to see as the golden chariot passed through the gates beneath.

'Be careful,' said Andromache, reaching out and taking her arm.

'I shall not fall,' Kassandra told her, then ran back across the battlements to watch the chariot moving on towards the upper city. 'Helikaon is unhappy,' she said suddenly.

'He has been ill. He is recovering now.'

'Helen says he asked for you, but you would not go to him.'

'Then Helen says too much,' snapped Andromache. The sunshine was bright, and Andromache felt a sudden nausea. It was the third time that day.

'Oh look, there is fighting on the beach again,' said Kassandra. 'Lots of men whacking each other with fists and sticks.' She laughed. 'And there go the soldiers, dragging them apart. What fun!'

Andromache moved into the shade of the high gate tower, and sat down, breathing deeply and slowly.

Kassandra came and sat beside her. 'You are looking very pale,' she said.

'I ate smoked fish yesterday. It must have been bad.'

Kassandra moved closer, laying her head on Andromache's shoulder. 'Your bodyguards are very handsome,' she whispered. 'I like Cheon.'

The nausea passed away. Andromache sighed, and looked up at the tall young soldier standing some ten paces distant, with his comrade Teachos. As Antiphones had foreseen, Priam had ordered all the royal family to be accompanied by guards during the Games and the wedding celebrations. Cheon and Teachos were pleasant enough company, though

Andromache would have preferred the more gregarious Polydorus. His conversation was always bright and engaging. However, he had been assigned to Helen.

'You like Cheon because he winks at you,' said Andromache. Kassandra giggled.

'He has beautiful forearms,' she said. 'I love the way the muscles ripple on them.'

'You sound like a girl in love,' said Andromache.

'Oh no, I don't love him,' Kassandra replied, with great seriousness. 'Anyway, there wouldn't be any point. Cheon will be dead long before me, and I won't live very long.'

'You shouldn't say such things,' Andromache admonished her.

'Why does everyone become so agitated about death?' asked Kassandra, sitting up and looking into Andromache's eyes. 'Everyone dies.'

'Not everyone dies *young*, Kassandra.'

'Laodike did.'

'Laodike was killed by evil men. I don't want to talk of it.'

'It wasn't your fault, you know. She was dying from the moment the spear struck her.'

Andromache pushed herself to her feet. 'It is too hot out here. Let's go back to the palace. We can sit in the garden.'

'Will you show me how to use your bow?'

'Yes.'

The child smiled happily, but then her expression changed. She cocked her head, as if listening to someone. Then she nodded and sighed. 'You won't be able to,' she said. 'When we get to the palace a messenger will tell you father wants to see you.'

'Whom are you listening to?'

'Xidoros.'

'Has Xidoros nothing better to do than haunt small girls?'

'I suppose it would be very tedious for him,' said Kassandra, 'if it was just me. But he has lots of other spirits to talk to.'

Andromache asked no more questions. Conversations with Kassandra were always difficult. The child had been struck down by a brain fever when very young, and since then had heard voices. Sometimes she seemed almost normal, as when speaking about Cheon. Mostly, though, her thought processes were unfathomable.

Together they walked down the gatehouse steps, emerging into the shadows of the Scaean Gate. Crowds were moving through and Andromache waited for Cheon and Teachos to move ahead, clearing a way. Then they slowly strolled back through the upper city and on to the palace of Hektor.

Andromache left the guards in the main entrance and took Kassandra through to the garden. Fetching her bow and her quiver, she called the girl to her. 'You see, there is no messenger from Priam, and I am going to teach you the bow.' She notched an arrow to the string, then handed the weapon to the child. 'Draw back upon the string as far as you can, and then sight it towards the straw deer.'

Kassandra tugged back on the string – which broke,

spilling the arrow to the ground. In that moment a servant came into sight. 'Lady Andromache, there is a messenger from the king to see you.'

Andromache thanked the man, then took the broken weapon from Kassandra's hand. 'Very well, you were right, little seeress. Perhaps you would like to tell me why the king wishes to see me.'

'He wants you in his bed,' said Kassandra. 'He is going to seduce you.'

'That is not prophecy,' replied Andromache. 'I would think everyone in the palace has guessed his intention. He is not discreet with his compliments. Tell me something no-one could possibly know.'

'That's a silly game,' said Kassandra. 'If nobody knows then you would not know it either. Then when I told you there would be no way to prove it. Like if I told you that a sparrow had died on the roof of the palace and had been eaten by a crow. Anyway, why do you want to test me?'

Andromache sat down on a stone bench. 'I suppose I would like to know if the voices are real or imaginary.'

Kassandra shook her head. 'No, you *want* them to be made up. Everybody wants them to be made up. I told Father that Hektor wasn't dead. He was angry and shouted at me. But Hektor wasn't dead. He came home, just like I said. Father thinks it was a coincidence. I told you that you would need your bow and put it in your hand on the night the Thrakians later attacked. No-one ever believes in my gift, Andromache. No matter what I tell them.'

Andromache drew the girl to her, and kissed her

cheek. 'Sadly, I think you are right, Kassandra. We all get frightened by prophecy. So, from now on, I will not question your powers, nor seek to test you. And I will teach you to use the bow. I will, won't I?'

'Yes, you will,' answered Kassandra, with a shy smile.

'And now I must go and resist your father's charms. You stay here and flirt with Teachos. I shall be back before sunset.'

'Take some water with you,' said Kassandra. 'The sickness will come again as you walk.'

'I shall avoid the salt fish in future,' Andromache told her.

'It isn't the fish,' the child replied.

Andromache crossed the square in front of the great temple to Athene, with its copper and amber doors, and paused for a moment at the base of the huge statue to the goddess. Elaborately carved, it showed Athene in her war helm, holding a spear in one hand, the shield of thunder at her feet. Andromache gazed at the stone shield. It was perfectly round, and a lightning bolt had been carved upon its centre.

'You always pause here,' said the soldier, Cheon. 'Then you reach up and touch the shield. Why do you do that?'

'Why do you always tug on your ear before asking a question?' she countered.

He gave a boyish grin. 'I was not aware of it. Is Athene the patron goddess of your home city?'

'No, Hermes has pride of place there. My father

loves wealth and Hermes is the god of travellers and merchants. But my mother was a follower of the goddess. She learned the mysteries. On the night of my birth she almost died, but a priestess of Athene saved her – and me.'

Andromache walked on, thinking of the long-ago day when she had sat on her mother's knee and heard of that terrible night. 'You were blessed by the goddess, dearheart. She flew over the palace, disguised as an eagle,' Olektra had told her.

'How do we know that?'

'Many people saw her.'

'They saw an eagle. How did they know it was the goddess, Mother?'

Olektra had looked momentarily uncertain. Then she had smiled. 'You'll understand when you are older and wiser.'

'But do *you* understand, Mother?'

Olektra had hugged her close and whispered in her ear, 'Perhaps I will when *I* am older and wiser.'

Andromache smiled at the memory.

From here in the upper city she could see all Troy laid out before her, the shining roofs of its carved and decorated palaces, its wide streets, its high golden walls and towers, the Great Tower of Ilion dwarfing them all. Beyond there was the lower town, and beyond that the Bay of Troy crowded with ships. To the southwest she could see Hekabe's summer palace, King's Joy, shining whitely in the sunlight. In the distance she could just make out the black dots that were galleys on the Great Green.

She glanced at Cheon. Although the square around them was not busy, one hand lay on his sword hilt and his eyes constantly watched for peril.

Her stomach moved with nausea again and she stood quietly for a moment until the feeling ebbed. Then she set off, striding quickly towards Priam's palace.

The place was in turmoil, the red-pillared portico seething with people. Royal guards – the King's Eagles in armour of bronze and silver – were questioning them, then letting them in one at a time. Andromache slipped through the line of warriors, smiling her thanks at the armoured Eagle who recognized her and stepped aside, ushering her in. The *megaron* beyond was more crowded than she had ever seen it. Merchants and petitioners waited in huddles, watched by soldiers; slaves ran around on errands, and scribes moved back and forth, their wicker baskets filled with soft clay tablets. There were royal courtiers, counsellors to the king, foreign visitors in outlandish costumes, and soldiers everwhere.

'Shall I stay with you, lady?' Cheon asked, frowning at the throng.

'No, I'll be all right. Go and get something to eat. I'll be here a while.'

He dipped his head and moved back towards the *megaron* entrance. She knew he would be there waiting for her when she came out, whenever that was.

Andromache looked round for someone she knew. She saw the king's chancellor, Polites, coming down the stone steps from the queen's apartments, and tried to move through the crowd towards him, but a portly merchant stepped on her foot and she nearly lost her balance. She scowled at the clumsy fat man, but he, not knowing her, merely glanced past her.

Then came a welcome voice. 'Sister, let me get you out of here.'

'Dios! What a bearpit this is!'

Hektor's half-brother smiled at her with genuine affection. She was reminded of their first meeting, when he had confronted her on the royal beach, accusing her of immodesty. 'Prince Deiphobos' he had insisted she call him, standing on his dignity in front of his courtiers. Then came the day of the siege. Dios had changed that day, as had so many others. Guarding the stairs, placing his body and his life in front of his king, he had grown in everyone's eyes. Now he was less arrogant, and his ever-present mob of lickspittle flunkeys and courtiers had melted away. He had become a good friend to Andromache during the long winter.

'Come out into the gardens,' he said, taking her arm. 'It's not so bad out there. Where's your bodyguard?'

'I sent him away. I thought he would not be needed in here, with all these soldiers.'

He shook his head and laughed. 'Andromache, why do you always seek trouble? You are surrounded by a press of people, so you send your guard away. It is true that if you were attacked, about a hundred Eagles would fall on the attacker and kill him, but that might be too late for you. It was almost too late for Helikaon, remember?' His face sobered. 'How is he now?'

'Better, much better. He has returned to the House

of Stone Horses, and will go back to Dardanos soon.'

'I am glad to hear it. Now, why are you here?'

'Priam wishes to see me.'

'Does he?' A cloud passed over Dios's face and she felt his concern. Does everyone know of Priam's intentions for me, she wondered? Dios said, 'He has been closeted with Agamemnon for most of the day. You might have a long wait.'

'It is the king's privilege to keep his subjects waiting,' she said, but in her heart she was angry at Priam's games. Bile rose again in her throat, and she swallowed it down.

Protected by high walls from Troy's ever-present wind, the royal gardens smelled of fragrant flowers and salt sea air. On the far side of the gardens Andromache spotted Kreusa, Priam's favourite daughter. The dark-haired beauty saw Dios and, smiling, started to walk towards him, then she noticed Andromache and scowled, turning abruptly back the way she had come. Not for the first time Andromache wondered about Kreusa. Where was she on the night of the siege? It was said she was at a friend's house, that she was late leaving and was warned of the attack before she reached the palace. Priam called it the mercy of the gods. Andromache called it highly suspicious.

'I hate to leave you here, Andromache,' said Dios, 'but Polites and I must attend the king. Can I have some food or drink sent out?'

She declined, then watched him walk back into the *megaron*.

The afternoon passed slowly into evening, and

torches were lit in the gardens. The crowds finally drifted away. The air cooled and Andromache wrapped her green shawl around her. The moon rose above the palace roof, and still she sat, her anger simmering. She thought of returning to Hektor's palace, but knew Priam would only call her out in the depths of the night instead. So she waited, quelling the rage in her heart and the nausea in her belly.

At last she saw a tall Eagle walking towards her through the torchlight.

'The king will see you now, lady,' he said. 'He is in the queen's apartments.' His eyes shied away from her. It was common palace knowledge that Priam used the apartments for assignations with women, be they palace slaves or noblewomen.

She followed the soldier back into the *megaron*, and up the great stone staircase. She had not been to the queen's apartments since the night of the siege. The remembered sounds of battle echoed in her mind: the clash of metal, the grunting of the warriors, and the cries of the wounded. She passed through the room where Laodike died. It was empty now, cold and silent. A single faded rug lay on the stone floor and dust motes swam in the air, swirling in the light from the torches.

The Eagle led her to a large room draped with heavy tapestries. There was a wide bed, several cushioned couches, and a table heaped with sweetmeats. It was warm and stuffy. Servants were clearing away food and bringing fresh flagons of wine. Priam sat on one of the couches. He looked tired, and much older than when they had first met, she thought.

'Andromache. I am sorry to keep you waiting.' He gestured to a couch and she sat down, looking around her.

'You entertained Agamemnon here?'

'Man to man,' he said, shrugging. 'We quaffed wine together and laughed. If I greet visiting dignitaries in the *megaron* they feel immediately subordinate.'

'What is wrong with making Agamemnon feel subordinate? I hear he is a snake.'

'Oh yes, he is a snake. But a dangerous snake.' He smiled wearily. 'So I charm him and play him sweet music. Until I am ready to cut his head off. Will you take some wine?'

'Water would be good.'

He stood and served her himself with a goblet of water. She noticed the servants had all left the chamber and they were alone.

'You visited Hekabe yesterday,' said the king. 'How is she?'

Andromache thought of the ruin that was the dying queen: yellow skin stretched like thin papyrus on brittle bones, a voice like the rustle of dead leaves on an icy pond, feverish black eyes which pierced you like a spear.

'She is determined on seeing her favourite son wed,' she answered. 'I have no reason to think she will not do that.'

'Is she in pain?'

Andromache raised questioning eyes to the king. 'Have you never asked that of anyone before?'

'I cannot chat about the queen's condition with

anyone passing through the palace. That is why I ask you.' Priam's face showed sadness. 'You must understand, Andromache, she was a woman I honoured above all others.'

Then, thought Andromache, you should show that honour by visiting her in her dying days. She bit her lip and remained silent.

Priam took a swig of wine and leaned towards her, looking into her eyes. 'Why do you think I summoned you here tonight?' he said, changing the subject.

'To ask after your dying wife?'

Priam flushed. 'Your thoughts are like ice and your words a spear. That is the reason I value you. One of the reasons,' he added, smiling a little. His eyes strayed to her long strong legs and slender hips. 'You are a beautiful woman, Andromache. Most men value golden-haired milkmaids with simpering smiles and buxom hips. You have the stern beauty of Athene. It fires my blood. You know this.'

Andromache was too tired to play his games. 'I will not be your mistress, Priam,' she said, standing, hoping he'd let her leave.

'I think you will.'

'Never. I am to wed your son Hektor. I *do* understand the nature of duty. I will be a dutiful wife.'

He sat back, smiling and relaxed again. 'Sit down, girl. I will not touch you until you invite me to.'

'And that will be never!'

'Then I shall amuse myself by telling you a story. You might enjoy it – for it is about you. Many years ago – long before you were born – I visited Thera with my young and lovely queen. We were travelling to Kretos to see the king of the day, Deukalion, father of this braggart Idomeneos. There was a terrible storm at sea. It was feared the ship would founder. Hekabe was pregnant and sick. I don't remember which child it was. We survived the storm, but we had to put in to Thera for a night. We offered pleasantries to the chief priestess, a hachet-faced woman I recall. After the dreary duties were done, the queen wished to be closeted with a young seeress she knew from her days there as a priestess. The two spoke for hours, well into the night. Then the seeress – her name was Melite – walked with Hekabe to the prophecy flame. When the fumes overcame her Melite fell to the floor and began to shout. Much of what she said was lost on Hekabe, for Melite shrieked out words in tongues that were unfamiliar to her. But, just before Melite lost consciousness, her voice changed, becoming that of a young child. She then spoke a pretty verse. You want to hear it?'

Andromache was silent for a moment. Her interest was piqued. She too had known Melite, and recalled only too well that the old woman had prophesied her departure from Thera, weeks before the ship arrived with the message from Hekabe. 'Yes, I will hear it,' she told him.

'I think you will find it interesting,' said the king. '*Beneath the Shield of Thunder waits the Eagle Child, on shadow wings, to soar above all city gates, till end of days, and fall of kings*. Hekabe was very taken with the verse, but the meaning was hidden from her. For years she consulted mystics and seers. Then, in late winter two years back, she encountered a Hittite sooth-sayer. He finally interpreted the verse to Hekabe's liking. The Shield of Thunder, he said, was not an object, but a person. A woman. The Eagle Child would be born to her. As you know, the eagle is the symbol of kingship. So, this woman would bear the son of a king. *To soar above all city gates* means he will never be defeated in battle, and *till end of days* means his city will be eternal.'

'Even if the prophecy is a true one,' said Andromache, 'there are hundreds of kings, and thousands of young women who serve Athene. All of them would at some time have stood before her statue and effectively have been beneath the Shield of Thunder.'

'Indeed so.' Priam leaned forward. 'But how many of them were born with the image of the shield upon their heads?'

Andromache sighed. 'I was told of my birthmark – but that is all it is, lord; a patch of red skin with a slash of white upon it.'

Priam shook his head. 'My ambassador, Heraklitos, was there that night. He saw the shield, and heard the words of the priestess. But there is more. When Melite was babbling on Thera she spoke of a woman with the strength of a man. Hekabe remembered that – albeit not swiftly enough. Your father's people came from across the sea, and with them they brought many words of the western tongue. *Andros* for man, and *machos* for strength. Your name is derived from these two words.

You are the Shield of Thunder, Andromache, and your child will be the son of a king. He will make my city greater, eternal and undying.'

'Suppose it is true,' said Andromache, rising, 'and I do not believe it is, what makes you believe that you will be the father? You could die, Priam, and then Hektor will be king, and his son will be the Eagle Child. Had you not thought of that?'

'Oh, there is little in all of this that I haven't thought of, Andromache. But you can go now. We will talk again once Hektor returns.' Turning away from her, he filled a goblet full of wine and drained it.

'Might I ask one question, sire?'

'Make it brief, for I am tired.'

'If I am the Shield of Thunder, why then did you send for my sister Paleste to be wed to Hektor?'

Priam sighed. 'A stupid error of Heraklitos. He told us that Paleste was the child who bore the shield. He was very sick then, and his mind was not what it was.'

'He was not wrong, lord. At my birth my mother named me Paleste, but my father changed it when he returned from his campaign.'

But Priam was not listening. Taking the jug of wine and the goblet he walked back through the apartments to the bedroom, pushing shut the door behind him.

Andromache felt the nausea strike once more, but swallowed it down. Sweat was on her brow as she left the apartments and made her way down to the *megaron*. A servant brought her some water, and she sat quietly, waiting for her stomach to settle.

She thought then of shy and gentle Paleste. How

awful the workings of this city would have been to her. Did Priam seek to seduce her? Was she awed and frightened by the dying Hekabe? She suddenly shivered, as the full import of Priam's careless words struck home. Paleste had been 'a stupid error'.

How convenient then that innocent Paleste, trusting and sweet, should have sickened and died.

Andromache rose from her seat and walked out into the cool night air. Cheon was waiting for her. As he approached her, Andromache fell to her knees and vomited on the path. The soldier was instantly beside her, supporting her. Twice more Andromache retched, then her head cleared and her stomach ceased to cramp.

'Do you need a physician?' Cheon asked, concern in his voice. Andromache shook her head.

They walked slowly through the empty streets, and Andromache felt stronger by the time they reached the gates of the palace. Once inside she ordered a servant to bring her some bread and cheese, then went to her rooms.

Kassandra was sleeping on a couch, but she awoke when Andromache entered. 'I was dreaming of dolphins,' said the girl, yawning.

Andromache sat beside her. 'You spoke earlier of my sickness. You said it was not the fish.'

Kassandra leaned in and smiled. 'It is the Eagle Child,' she whispered. 'The son of Helikaon.'

XVI

The death of a king

THE PALACE AGAMEMNON HAD BEEN ASSIGNED OVER-
looked the temple of Hermes and the bay beyond. The
location was excellent, but the standard of work-
manship, Agamemnon saw, was not of the highest
quality. The finish on the dressed stone was clumsy, and
many of the carvings seemed to have been completed in
haste. Also the architect must have been a man of little
imagination, for huge windows had been set in the
main apartments upstairs, facing west into the setting
sun. In the height of summer the rooms would be like
ovens.

Agamemnon sat now in the spacious walled garden,
three guards close by, as his men searched through the
fifteen rooms. The Mykene king did not expect them to
find assassins hidden anywhere, but the search alone
would keep his men focused on the dangers he faced.
All the food in the kitchens had been removed and
dumped, the wine poured away. Fresh food was being

purchased in the market. Agamemnon gazed balefully over the garden. Garishly coloured flowers had been planted, and their scent would draw insects.

'Whose palace is this?' he asked his aide.

'The king's son, Polites'.' Kleitos winced as he spoke, lifting his hand to massage his jaw. Three teeth had been broken when the renegade Banokles attacked him. Two had been successfully pulled, but the third had snapped off at the gum line. The angry stump ached constantly.

A soldier, wearing the long black cloak of a Follower, entered the garden. 'The rooms are clear, Agamemnon King.'

'Check the roof,' Agamemnon told him.

'Yes, lord.'

Kleitos waited until the man had left and then asked, 'You think Priam would hide an assassin on the roof?'

Agamemnon ignored the question. 'What did you find out about Helikaon?'

'He is recovering, my lord. He is at his palace in the lower town.'

'And well guarded?'

'First reports are that he has nine servants, all men. But no Trojans guard him, and he brought no Dardanian soldiers with him to Troy. He has one companion, a big man, named Gershom. It is said he's a Gyppto.'

Agamemnon leaned back in his chair. How many assassination attempts could one man survive? Kolanos had had him trapped on Blue Owl Bay, but Helikaon had slipped by the killers dressed as a simple soldier.

Then, last autumn, a group of warriors had confronted him in the grounds of the temple of Hermes. Helikaon had survived that too. Now even the dagger of the legendary Karpophorus had failed to kill him. 'He is blessed by luck,' he said.

'It is said that he is the son of Aphrodite herself,' said Kleitos, in a low voice. 'Perhaps he is protected by the goddess.'

Agamemnon controlled his rising anger, and waited for several moments, so that his voice would appear calm and controlled. 'His mother was a madwoman, Kleitos, who chewed too much *meas* root. She threw herself from a cliff top and was killed upon the rocks below. And do not tell me the story of how she was seen flying from the cliff to distant Olympos. I have spoken to a man who gathered up her remains for burial. One eye was hanging from her shattered skull and her jaw had been torn off.'

'Yes, my king. I was only repeating what I had heard.'

'Is the Thrakian here yet?'

'Yes, my lord. King Eioneus arrived yesterday. He is lodged in a palace on the outskirts of the city. He brought two war horses with him and desired to be close to the open hills so that he could ride them.'

'How many retainers?'

'Thirty soldiers, and his son, Rhesos. There is also the Thrakian contingent for the Games – some twenty men.'

Agamemnon considered the information. 'Eioneus is a man of routine. Have him watched, then ride out over

the route he chooses. There will be a perfect spot somewhere for a man to lie in wait.'

'We have some fine archers with us, my lord. Okotos
can hit a bird on the wing.'

'No, not a bowman. Use a slinger. Eioneus is an old
man. A fall from a running horse could kill him. Even
better if the stone strikes unseen by those with him. His
death would then seem ill fortune.'

As the light began to fade Agamemnon rose and
entered the palace. Lamps had been lit, and he could
smell roasting meat from the kitchen. A soldier brought
him a goblet of watered wine and Agamemnon drank
sparingly. Some time after dusk King Peleus arrived.
The man was angry, his face flushed.

'By the gods, they have given me a hovel,' he complained. 'Close to the dyemakers. The stink is
stomach-churning.'

'Where is Achilles?'

'He and two of his companions are out running in
the hills.'

'Do they have guards riding with them?'

Peleus laughed. 'You think anyone would be foolish
enough to attack Achilles? He would tear out their
lungs.'

'Or an arrow could pierce his,' Agamemnon pointed
out.

'You think Priam would break the truce?'

'Not all men are as honourable as you and I,' said
Agamemnon.

Day by day Helikaon's strength grew. On his return to

his own palace in the lower town he had barely been able to climb the stairs, and only then after stopping several times to catch his breath. His once lean and powerful frame was now skeletally thin, his muscles wasted. However, the absence of infection allowed his appetite to return, and Gershom supervised the preparation of his meals. There were no sweetmeats, no wines, but an abundance of fruits and fresh meats. 'My grandfather was a great warrior in his day,' he told Helikaon, 'and he was wounded more than twenty times. He maintained that an injured body needed simple fare: water to flush through the system, fruits and meats for strength. And like a fine horse the body needed to work in order to grow stronger.'

Soon, Helikaon's skin began to lose its ghostly sheen, the dark rings under his eyes disappearing. Gershom borrowed two horses from Priam's stables, and the two men rode bareback out over the hills. The ride tired Helikaon, and Gershom led them down through several fields to a farmhouse, where a well had been sunk. Tethering their mounts, the companions sat in the shade of the house. Helikaon was holding his hand over his wound. There were no bandages now, and when he raised his arm the deep scar was red and vivid.

'How is the pain?' asked Gershom.

'Almost gone. But the wound itches.' He glanced at Gershom. 'How could you allow a stranger to cover me in maggots?' he asked, with a weary smile.

'I was bored,' Gershom told him. 'I thought it would be entertaining.'

Helikaon leaned back against the wall and closed his

eyes. 'I have had no dreams since that last night,' he said. 'In a way I miss them. It was as if I could float across the world in an instant. I thought the room was enchanted. Day would pass into night and back to day in a heartbeat.'

'From what I heard when you were delirious your dreams were all of blood and death and pain.'

'Mostly they were. But I also dreamed I saw Argurios and Laodike. That was like balm upon the spirit. And I . . .' He fell silent.

'What?' asked Gershom.

Helikaon sighed. 'I had a healing dream. Andromache was in it. It felt as if I was being lifted from a dark pit into bright sunshine.'

Gershom glanced at his friend. Helikaon was staring away into the distance and Gershom could feel a sense of sadness emanating from him. Why this should be was mystifying. Helikaon had returned from the shores of Hades. He was a young king, with everything to live for. He had a beautiful wife waiting for him in Dardania, and a fleet of ships to sail the Great Green, bringing him wealth. Yet not once since he had begun his recovery had he laughed, or made a jest.

A growl sounded from close by, and a large black hound came padding around the wall, lips drawn back, teeth bared. The horses shifted nervously. Gershom's hand moved to his dagger.

'No, my friend,' said Helikaon, 'do not harm it. The hound is doing what it should, protecting its master's home. Ignore it. Turn your head away and do not stare into its eyes.'

'So that it can take a bite out of my rump?'

Helikaon slowly reached out his hand, softly clicking his fingers. The hound stood still, but the snarl remained, and the hackles on its neck were raised. Suddenly Helikaon snapped his fingers and called out, 'Here! Come!' Instantly the hound padded over to him. 'You are a fine, brave fellow,' Helikaon told it, slowly raising his hand so that the hound could sniff at it.

'And you, I fear, are an idiot,' grumbled Gershom. 'With jaws like that he could have taken off your fingers.'

'You know the problem with a royal upbringing in Egypt, Gershom? You can look but you do not have to see. Slaves everywhere to do your bidding, bring you food, lay out your clothing.' The hound wandered away, padding back past the well, where it slumped down in an area of shade. 'The hound is an old one. Grey round the jaws. It is not young and reckless. People will visit this farmhouse all the time. No farmer would keep an ill-trained guard dog unleashed. Daylight visitors will generally be welcome. Had we come at night the story would have been different. And then there are the horses. If that dog was in a killing mood they would have sensed it and panicked. Instead they merely shifted a little and grew wary. Therefore we were in no danger. All we had to do was show the dog we had no evil intent.'

Gershom shook his head. 'You do not convince me, Helikaon. You rationalize your actions and, because the end result is favourable, you become right. However, the dog *could* have been suffering with toothache, or been rabid, and therefore would not have acted according to its training. The horses might *not* have scented its purpose. Horses are not generally considered to be great thinkers. Your method of dealing with the situation involved danger. Mine, to stab the beast, would have achieved the same end result, with no risk.'

'Except you would have killed a fine dog,' Helikaon pointed out.

'It is not my dog.'

As they were speaking two men came walking in from the fields. Both were broad-shouldered and red-headed, though the first man was older, and there was grey in his hair.

'You seeking me?' he asked.

Helikaon eased himself to his feet. 'No. We were merely riding and sought to rest here a while.'

'Ah, well, you are welcome,' said the farmer. 'Lucky, though. Cerberos there took a lump out of the last traveller who arrived unannounced.' Gershom's laughter boomed out. 'It wasn't amusing,' grumbled the farmer. 'Cost me two sheep in compensation. He's getting old and forgetting his training. Are you heading up to the city?'

'Yes.'

'Best avoid the low woods. Been an accident there, and there are soldiers swarming everywhere, stopping travellers and asking questions.'

'What happened?' asked Helikaon.

'Some foreigner fell from his horse and died. Important man. Come for the wedding feast, I expect.

Anyways, I am losing daylight standing here, so you'll need to excuse me. Here, Cerberos,' he called, and the black hound padded after him as he walked off.

'Do not say a word,' Helikaon warned Gershom.

'What could I say? I who was born in a royal palace and look but do not see?'

Helikaon sighed. 'How long are you going to hold this over my head?'

'Difficult to say. Most of the summer, for sure.'

Helikaon laughed then, and swung his horse. 'For that you can eat my dust all the way to the palace,' he said, heeling his mount into a run.

Gershom set off after him. Both horses were powerful and fast, but Gershom was considerably heavier than the Dardanian king, and could not close the gap. Only as they came closer to the city did Helikaon slow his horse and allow Gershom's mount to canter alongside. There was good colour in Helikaon's cheeks, and his mood seemed to have lifted. As they crested a hill the bay beyond came into sight, brilliantly blue in the sunshine. A light breeze was blowing over the hills. Helikaon reined in his mount and sat staring out over the sea. Gershom saw his mood change once more, his expression hardening.

'What is it?' he asked.

'There is a man coming to Troy whom I have sworn to kill.'

'Well, your strength is returning fast. A few more weeks and you will be able to challenge him.'

Helikaon said nothing more, and heeled his horse. By the time they reached the palace his strength was done, and he took to his bed. Gershom returned the mounts, and while at the stables heard that the king of Thraki, Eioneus, had been the man killed in the fall from the horse. He had been riding ahead of his companions, and when they rounded a bend in the path they had found him sprawled on the ground, his horse standing close by.

The death was considered an ill omen for the coming wedding, and an evening of tribute was being arranged by King Priam, to be held in the temple of Poseidon in five days, when all the kings of west and east were hoped to be present. The Mykene king, Agamemnon, had volunteered to speak the words of praise for the departed.

The awful knowledge that she was pregnant filled Andromache's days and sleepless nights with anger and self-loathing. How could she have done something so stupid? How could the gods have punished her so harshly?

She tried to convince herself she had only slid into Helikaon's bed to follow the advice of the Prophet, putting a warm body next to the dying man to draw him back to life. But Andromache had never been swayed by self-deceit. Almost from the moment she had seen Helikaon on the beach at Blue Owl Bay she had yearned to be close to him, naked, skin on skin. Even now, with the dreadful consequences of her action hanging over her like a stormbird, she felt the thrill of that moment.

Her maid, Axa, was moving through the apartments,

chattering as she gathered up discarded clothing. She was in a happy mood, as she had been throughout the winter. Her husband, feared dead with Hektor, was home again, and Axa's joy was complete. Her babe was healthy, her man alive, and the world shone with delight.

'Perhaps the saffron gown today,' she said. 'The sun is shining and I could braid your hair with golden wire. That would catch the light.'

'I want no braid today,' said Andromache. 'And the yellow is too bright. Bring me the pale green.'

'You always wear green,' complained Axa. 'Did you see the *Xanthos* on the bay yesterday? Perhaps the Lord Hektor will come to visit now. The yellow gown will dazzle him.'

'I do not want him dazzled. And he will not come.'

Axa looked puzzled. 'You think not?'

Andromache turned towards her. 'How many times has he visited his own palace since I have been here?'

'Several times. I saw him once.'

'He came to see Helikaon, and always when I was absent.'

'Oh, I am sure he—'

'Please, Axa, make no excuses. This is an arranged marriage which Hektor obviously does not want. My guess is he will go to his farm and I will not see him until the wedding feast.'

Axa's face fell. 'Oh, you mustn't think that, my lady. Hektor is a wonderful man. Mestares worships him. He told me Hektor thinks you the most beautiful woman.'

'So beautiful that he cannot bear to spend time with

me. Enough of this. You are right – let it be the saffron gown.' Andromache had no wish to wear such a bright colour, but knew acquiescence would deflect Axa. The plump maid beamed happily and rushed off to fetch the robe.

Andromache walked out onto the balcony. It was still in shadow, but she could see sunlight dappling the city, and hear the sounds of workmen preparing the Games area. Farther off she saw men building an embankment along the length of the hippodrome, where the chariot and horse races would be held. The city was becoming filled now with travellers and contestants, eager to win gold in the Games. The plain to the north had become a city of tents and hastily built huts.

A feeling of nausea swept over her and she took a deep breath.

Back on Thera she had walked with the other priestesses on the slopes of the angry mountain, chanting hymns to placate the Minotaur rumbling beneath the ground. She felt now a similar danger. On the surface she was Andromache, virgin princess of Thebe, about to wed the heir to the throne of Troy. But growing within her was her own minotaur, whose presence, when known, would bring about her destruction.

When Priam discovered her infidelity he would have her killed. The king, despite his desire for her, could be ruthless. He had, in recent years, ordered the deaths of several wayward sons. And with her his rage would be towering, for she had spurned his advances on what he would see now as merely the pretext of honour. She would, in his eyes, have sought to fool him. Priam's ego would not tolerate that.

So what can I do, she wondered? Go to Helikaon? Tell him his dream was no dream at all? Her heart sank. He would seek to protect her, and earn the enmity of Priam. Could Dardania's small army stand against the might of Troy? She knew the answer.

Andromache thought then of Hektor. She could try to seduce him. If successful he would believe the child was his. Even as the thought came to her she dismissed it. All her life she had believed in honesty – especially between lovers. Andromache had never lied to Kalliope. How then could a marriage begin with such a lie? It would sit like poison in the heart. No, there was only one honourable course – go to Hektor, admit everything, and accept what followed as the will of the gods.

Axa returned and helped her into the saffron gown. It was a beautiful dress, threaded with delicate golden wire and silver embroidery.

'I am going to take a walk,' she said, as Axa knelt down to tie the thongs of her sandals.

'Shall I come with you?'

'No, Axa. I will not need you any more today. Go home and see your babe.'

'He is growing well,' said Axa, 'and he is going to be handsome, like my Mestares, not dull and plain like me.'

Andromache stared down into Axa's moon face, and felt a lump in her throat. 'Axa, you are not plain. Everything you are shines from your face: your strength, loyalty, love and courage.'

Axa blushed. 'You say the strangest things some-times, my lady,' she said. 'Now what about gold thread in your hair?'

'No, I shall let it fall free.'

Axa rose and stared at Andromache's flame-red hair. 'The sun has caught it,' she noted critically. 'There are golden streaks in it. You should wear a veil more often.'

Andromache laughed, her mood lightening momentarily. 'You are never satisfied, Axa. One moment you want to put gold in my hair, and then you complain because it is already there.'

'You know what I mean,' argued Axa. 'Only peasant women have such streaks in their hair, because they are out in the sun all day.'

'Then I must be a peasant,' said Andromache. 'Now be off with you.'

At the palace gates she saw Cheon sitting quietly on a bench, his glittering bronze helm beside him, his breastplate gleaming in the sunshine. He rose as she approached.

'Are we going to the tomb?'

'No. We are walking to Hektor's farm.'

'It is a fair distance in this heat, lady. Shall I call for a chariot?'

'I like to walk.'

He said no more and together they strolled out into the city. Cheon donned his helmet. It was a full-faced helm which, happily for Andromache, made conver-sation near impossible. Cheon led the way through the crowds in the city centre, and then through the Dardanian Gate and onto the stone road beyond.

301

Cheon was right. The walk was long in such heat and by midday they were still far from their destination. Andromache's pride would not let her admit her error, and she strode on, sweat staining the saffron robe, her sandals chafing her ankles. Cheon glanced at her.

'If you do not object, lady,' he said, removing his helm, 'I would appreciate a halt in the shade.'

She looked at him and smiled. 'You are a gracious man, Cheon, and there is not a bead of sweat upon you. And, yes, thank you, I would really like to rest awhile.'

He grinned at her, then pointed to a small stand of trees. A white shrine had been set there. Within an alcove there was a statue of a woman, holding a bow. Dried flowers bedecked it. Reaching out, Andromache stroked the statue and smiled. It reminded her of Kalliope. Just behind the shrine she heard the sounds of running water. She moved through a screen of bushes and found a stream, bubbling over white stones. Kneeling down, she cupped her hands and drank. The water had an indefinable aftertaste that was not entirely pleasant. Cheon stood by, his hand on his sword hilt.

'You are not drinking?' she asked him.

'I am not thirsty.'

She dipped the sleeve of her gown into the stream and dabbed some water to her face, then rose to stand beside him in the shade. 'Whose shrine is this?'

'The mother of the wrestler Archeos built it to honour the goddess Artemis. It is said Archeos won more Games than any man living.'

'He was a Trojan?'

'No, lady. He was from Samothraki.' He tugged at his ear, and seemed about to speak. Then he drew in a breath and stepped away from her.

'What is it you wish to ask?' she said.

'I was wondering why you were going to Lord Hektor unannounced.'

'How do you know I am unannounced?'

'He would have sent a carriage for you, and a company of horse.'

'You know him?'

He shook his head. 'He has spoken to me, but I do not know him. Great man, though.'

'So everyone keeps telling me.'

He glanced at her, then grinned. It made him seem suddenly boyish. 'My brother serves with Hektor. Was with him at Kadesh.'

'Yes, yes, a great warrior. I have heard it all before, Cheon.'

'I wasn't going to speak of war, lady. All men know Hektor is a fighter. His greatness, though, lies in the small things. He knows the names of his men, the names of their wives. My brother is not an officer. He spoke to Hektor once, as they sat by a stream. He told him of his pregnant wife. When the child was born Hektor sent a gold cup as a birth gift.' He turned away. 'I suppose that it doesn't sound much.'

'Yes, it does,' said Andromache. 'It would surprise me to learn that my father knew any soldier's name. He would never consider sending a gift to one.' She stepped out into the sunlight and walked on. Cheon fell into step beside her. A breeze began to blow and a few puffballs of cloud blocked the sun. As they made their way downhill it was cooler, the breeze whispering over puddles from yesterday's rain.

At last they saw the farm and the horse pastures beyond. The main building was old, stone built, single-storeyed and flat-roofed. The three structures round it were timber built and tall, with wide doors. One was obviously a stable; the other two, Andromache guessed, were either storehouses or barns.

In front of the main house men were trying to catch a pig that had broken through a fence. The beast turned and charged at the men, scattering them. Then it slipped in the mud, rolled over and collided with the broken fence. In that instant a huge man, bare-chested and mud-covered, hurled himself at the animal. It darted away, and the giant slithered face first into the fence, to loud laughter from his fellows.

Andromache heard their laughter carried on the wind and her heart lifted. As she and Cheon made their way down the hill the men formed a semicircle round the pig, trying to herd it back behind the fence. But it ran at them again. This time the mud-covered giant timed his leap better, massive arms circling the pig's shoulders. It grunted and struggled, but the man pinned it down. Amazingly he then surged to his feet, the enormous pig in his arms. Slithering in the mud, he staggered into the enclosure.

The others grabbed a fence rail and slid it into position. The man dropped the startled pig, then turned and ran back for the fence. Instantly the pig gave chase. The man reached the fence just ahead of the angry beast and vaulted it. He landed on a slick patch of mud and skidded from his feet. Once more laughter burst out. The man sat up, trying to brush the mud from his face and hair. Then he saw Andromache.

Slowly Hektor climbed to his feet. 'This is an unexpected pleasure,' he said.

Andromache did not reply. Her mind fled back to the tent of the seer, Aklides, who had predicted the three great loves of her life. The first was Helikaon. The second was the Oak.

'And how will I know him?' she had asked.

'He will rise from the mud, his body caked with the filth of pigs.'

Andromache's mouth was dry, her head spinning. The now familiar feeling of nausea swept through her. 'We need to speak, you and I,' she managed to say.

XVII

Andromache's choice

ANDROMACHE WAITED IN THE COOL OF THE MAIN ROOM, its windows shuttered against the bright sunlight. A young servant brought her a bowl of fruit and a jug of water. Sliced yellow fruit floated on the surface. The girl filled a cup and passed it to her. Andromache thanked her. She was slim and fair, with large blue eyes. For a moment Andromache was reminded of Kalliope. 'You are very lovely,' she told the girl, reaching out and stroking her face.

'Thank you, Princess,' replied the girl, and Andromache saw her pupils widen.

How strange are the emotions, thought Andromache. Here I am, about to face my doom, and yet I can feel my blood stirring, and the need in me to draw a servant into an embrace. With a soft sigh she turned away from the girl and looked round the room. The furnishings were functional, with not a sign of gilding or engraving. There were three long couches, and five deep chairs.

Upon the stone floor was a huge rug, decorated with autumnal colours. Despite the lack of adornment the room had a welcoming feel. Without the burden she now carried it would be a place Andromache could enjoy.

She sipped her water, trying to think of what to say when the Trojan prince returned from his bath. But her thoughts were clouded, random images intruding. Helikaon crying out in the ecstasy of delirium, Kalliope dancing on the Night of Artemis, herself standing on the upper gallery of the king's *megaron*, shooting arrows down into the Mykene. So much had happened in these last few months.

And now this. The seer's vision must have been mis-interpreted, she thought. Yes, he had seen this moment – no doubt of it – and had somehow, perhaps, sensed the power of Andromache's emotions. Yet Hektor could not be a great love of her life. She felt no rush of blood when she gazed upon him, no yearning to touch him, to be close, to feel his lips upon hers.

Moving to the far wall she gazed up at the shield hanging there. It was an old piece, black oxhide stretched over a wooden frame. There was a white decoration at the centre, of a leaping stag.

'It was carried by a Thrakian rebel,' said Hektor, entering the room behind her. 'He gave it to me. I rather like it. Simple, well made.'

She swung towards him. His golden hair was wet from the bath, and he was dressed now in a tunic of pale gold. For a moment it seemed the large room had shrunk, and, as he approached her, the size of him was daunting.

'You move very quietly for a big man.'

'I have learned to walk softly around women,' he said, with a shy smile.

'Or indeed not to walk around them at all.'

His gaze shifted from hers. 'I apologize, Andromache. I have neglected you.'

'It is of no matter. I am here to ask you to release me from this duty of marriage.'

He said nothing, but filled a cup with water and drank. The silence lengthened. Andromache had not known what to expect, but she had thought there would be some angry response. Instead he gave a rueful smile and moved to a couch. 'Come, sit,' he said, gently. 'Let us talk awhile.'

'What is there to say?'

Hektor regarded her gravely, and when he spoke his tone was regretful. 'If only it were that simple I would grant your request in an instant. You are a fine, brave woman, and you deserve far more than I can offer. However, this match was not made by me, but by Hekabe and Priam. I am as much bonded to their will as you are. In this we cannot escape our fate, Andromache.'

'It is not a question of escape,' she told him. 'I cannot wed you.'

He gazed at her and she felt the power of his blue eyes. 'You love another. I can understand that. Not many of royal birth get to marry those they love.'

'Yes, I love another,' she said, drawing in a deep breath, 'but that is not the problem.' The moment was here, and she could avoid it no longer. 'I am with child.'

Her green eyes looked defiantly at him, awaiting the eruption of his righteous fury. But there was no angry outburst.

'Father never did waste time,' he said. 'And now you know Hektor's shame.' He did not look at her, but took a deep breath and leaned forward. 'I have faced many dangers in my life, and many fears, but this moment is the worst. Of course I can understand why you would not wish to wed me. Who would?'

Andromache sat quietly for a moment. That he thought the father was Priam was obvious, but the rest left her nonplussed. Rising to her feet, she crossed the room to sit beside him.

'I have not been bedded by Priam,' she told him. 'I refused his advances.'

He turned towards her then, blue eyes locking to her green gaze. 'Then who is the father?' The question was softly asked. In that moment several thoughts struck her. She was sitting close now to a man of enormous physical strength, and yet she felt no threat. Instead there was a curious comfort in his nearness, and she was surprised by it. In all her thoughts of this meeting she had never expected to feel so . . . so safe. All tension faded from her, and, sitting quietly in the shaded room, she told him of Helikaon's sickness, and the words of the Prophet, and of her foolishness in sharing his bed. He listened quietly. 'So, it is Helikaon you love?'

'Yes.'

'And he loves you?'

'He said that he did, when we both thought you were dead.'

'And he has married Halysia. What foolish people we nobles are. Does he know of the child?'

'No. Nor will he. He was delirious, and believes it was a dream he had. He has no memory of our lying together.' And then the walls of her resistance crumbled to dust, and despair overwhelmed her. Tears began to flow, and she was sobbing. Hektor leaned towards her, drawing her close. Not since a child in her father's arms had she felt so protected. Hektor said nothing, merely holding her quietly, his hand gently patting her back, as if she was a babe.

After a while she managed to halt the sobs, and to draw in deep, shuddering breaths.

Only then did Hektor speak. 'Priam must not find out, Andromache. I love him, but he would have you walled alive, or strapped into a box and hurled into the sea. His rages are towering, his punishments barbaric. But I do not know how we can fool him.'

'Are you still willing to marry me?'

Hektor smiled at her. 'I can think of no greater honour for me.'

Relief swept through her. 'Then the problem is solved. The wedding is soon now. My pregnancy is new, and no-one will question it if I give birth a few days early.'

'The problem is not solved,' he said, sadly. 'Father will know the child is not mine.'

'How?'

Hektor leaned back from her. 'You do not know then?' He closed his eyes and turned away. 'I have dreaded this moment,' he said. 'It has hung over me, haunting even my dreams.'

She reached out and took his hand. 'If I am to be your wife I will stand by you loyally. Nothing you tell me will be breathed to another.'

For a while he remained silent. Then he walked to the table and poured himself a goblet of water. 'I would sooner face armed men than have this conversation,' he said.

'Then don't have it,' said Andromache. 'I do not want to cause you pain.'

'No, it needs to be said. I may not be a man, but I am not a coward.' Returning to the couch, he sat alongside her. 'Two years ago I was wounded, and like to die. Spear thrust into the groin. I regained my strength, but something vital was lost to me.' He took a deep breath. 'I cannot father children, Andromache, nor enter a woman. Only Priam and the surgeon knew this, and Priam had the surgeon strangled. He could not bear any to know his son's shame.'

Andromache stared at him, her own fears and concerns diminished by the weight of his grief. 'A man is not defined by his prick,' she said. His head jerked round, and she saw his surprise. 'Yes,' she said, with a smile, 'even a priestess knows the vulgar words. The one-eyed snake, the red spear, the spitting serpent. Listen to me, Hektor. If I didn't know before today, then I know now that you are a fine man. And I grieve for your loss, for I understand how men prize their parts, bragging about the size of them, the thickness of them. And I will not lie to you. Your loss will be my loss also. Understand this, though: I would sooner have a man with heart, who cares for others, and will love my child, than an uncaring idiot with a stiff prick. Not a man? That is nonsense.'

He turned to her and took her hand, lifting it to his lips. 'I thank you for that,' he said. 'It was gracious of you.'

'No,' she said. 'Do not allow yourself to believe I am some sycophant trying to please you. I am Andromache and I speak the truth. Look into my eyes, Hektor, and tell me if you see a lie there.'

She gazed at him frankly, and watched him relax. 'No,' he said, at last. 'I see no lie.'

'Will you trust me to deal with this problem, and not question my decision?' she asked him.

'I will trust you,' he told her.

'Good. Then have a carriage brought round, to take me back to the city. And tomorrow I will move here. So that we can sit and talk and learn of one another.'

A little while later, as they stood beside the wagon, Hektor took her hand. 'I will be a good husband to you, Andromache of Thebe,' he said.

'I know that, Hektor of Troy,' she replied. Emotion surged in her again, and tears formed. 'You will be my Oak,' she told him, her voice breaking.

Ordering the driver to take her and Cheon to the gates of Priam's palace, she sat back in her seat. Cheon, apparently sensitive to her need for reflection, said nothing during the journey. Once at the palace she instructed Cheon to wait for her, then strode through the *megaron*, telling a servant that she wished to see the king on a matter of urgency.

This time she was not made to wait.

Priam was in the queen's apartments. He rose as she was ushered in, then waited until the servant had departed. 'What is so urgent?' he asked.

'I have been to see Hektor,' she said, and was struck by the physical similarity between the two men. Priam was not as hugely built, but the shape of his face and the power of his eyes were almost identical to his son's.

'And?'

'I now understand why you pursue me.'

'He told you? That must have been hard for him. So, why are you here?'

'You know why,' she said, anger in her voice.

'You seek to dissolve this marriage?'

'No. If I did I would not survive. I would die like the surgeon who treated him.'

He nodded. 'You are an intelligent woman.'

'I will grant your desire, but I have conditions.'

'Name them. I will grant them all.' She could see the eagerness in his eyes now, his face flushing.

'I will come to your bed only once in every full phase of the moon. I will do this until a doctor confirms I am with child. After that you will never attempt to bed me again. You agree?'

'I agree.' He laughed then, opening his arms. 'So come to me, Shield of Thunder.'

And she stepped into his embrace.

XVIII

The fear of Kalliades

WORKMEN HAD LABOURED ALL NIGHT UNDER TORCHLIGHT to complete the Games areas. A large section of flat ground had been levelled and stamped to create a stadium for the runners and javelin throwers, the jumpers, the boxers and the wrestlers. A long hippodrome had been created some 400 paces west of the stadium, with a high embankment that was now set with benches and seats for the privileged. Here the chariot and horse races would be held. The main judges' dais had been erected at the hippodrome, with intricately fashioned seats of ivory and wood, inlaid with gold. A second, smaller dais had been constructed at the stadium. The organization of the Games, under the direction of the king's son, Polites, had been fraught with difficulties. No-one had known how many competitors would seek to participate, or, indeed, the size of the crowds. Initially Polites had thought a few hundred athletes would travel to Troy. Already there were more than a thousand. As to those wishing to enjoy the spectacle, the estimates had risen from six to around sixteen thousand. Even this figure was beginning to look conservative.

Polites paced back and forth before the smaller judges' dais in the stadium. The dawn sun had not long cleared the horizon, and the last of the work was being completed, carpenters putting in place lines of benches, labourers dragging trestle tables from the backs of carts, or hoisting linen canopies to shade the seating areas of the nobles.

Sixteen thousand! Polites rubbed at his temples. The headache had been with him now for the last five days. Sixteen thousand people needing to eat, to urinate, to defecate; needing to be kept cool in the midday with supplies of water. For the common people there were latrine pits dug, but special buildings had been constructed where nobles could piss into pots like civilized folk.

Polites strode across the stadium, passing under the columned roof of the new *palaistra*, where athletes would prepare. Closed off from public scrutiny, the competitors could discuss tactics with their trainers, or hire masseurs, or take cold baths. Here too were the rooms of Asklepios, where physicians and surgeons would tend those wounded in the more dangerous events. Cuts to the faces of boxers would be stitched here, and the broken limbs of charioteers would be set. The greatest number of injuries would result from the chariot races – especially the four-horse contests. Not so much, Polites knew, from collisions, but from the sharp turns at either end of the long, narrow track. The course was set between two strong posts. In order to minimize the distance travelled a skilful charioteer would rein in the inner horses, while allowing the outer beasts their heads. This would swing the chariot round the posts at speed. However, timing was crucial. Two years ago, in Thraki, Polites had witnessed one ghastly accident. The charioteer Kreunos, famous for his skill, had been in the lead when he had mistimed his turn. The hub of his wheel struck the post, splintering the axle, and catapulting the chariot into the air. Entangled in the reins, Kreunos was helpless. The horses ran wild, and Kreunos had been smashed into the rails separating the crowd from the racers. His right leg was almost torn from his body and he had died a few days later.

Inside the *palaistra* Polites saw workmen filling the newly built baths under the guidance of the foreman, Choros, a slender Thrakian. Polites had come to trust the man implicitly. Beneath a gentle demeanour Choros was ferociously efficient, and only the very foolish gave less than their best when working for him.

'Greetings, my lord,' said Choros. 'Fear not – we will be ready.'

'The regiments will be here soon,' said Polites. It was a redundant comment. Choros was well aware that this was the Day of the Judges. Polites' mouth was dry, his heart hammering. Priam would be arriving soon after the regiments, and with him would be many of the guests. It would be appalling should anything go wrong on this first day. Priam would shame him before the kings.

He will shame me anyway, he thought. If a seabird

shits on the running track it will somehow be my fault. Though maybe not today. Polites had seen Priam earlier that morning, and the king had seemed in a joyous mood. May the gods cause that to last for the five days of the Games, he prayed.

Leaving Choros with the workmen he moved through the building, emerging at the rear onto a narrow walkway leading to the stables. They were empty at present, but later today the first of the horses would be brought in to be examined by the judges, and marked for competition. Polites went on, down past the stands where the crowds would gather, then through the gate and onto the race track. Here he kicked off his sandals. Slaves had been working for days to remove all the loose stones from the surface, before tamping it flat. Even so the chariot wheels would bite deep on the turns, and it was almost certain that some jagged piece of rock would be dug up and flung into the crowds. Polites slowly walked the length of the course between the turning posts, scanning the ground. The new judges would be performing the same task a little later, and their eyes would be keener than his, he knew.

At the last Games, five years before, Polites had been merely a spectator. He had not appreciated the intensity of the work involved in preparation. Had it not been for the involvement of his half-brother Antiphones he knew he would have made a mess of it. It was a depressing thought. Polites left the track and climbed up onto the embankments, seating himself on a new bench, and running his hand lightly along the polished wood. No sign of splinters.

'The first thing to do,' Antiphones had told him, when Father first gave Polites his role, 'is to find good foremen, men you can trust to see the work through. Assign each man a specific task, then appoint an overseer to co-ordinate the work.' Antiphones had been recovering from his wounds then, but he had kept a brotherly eye on the organization. Polites was grateful, and yet curiously resentful. Antiphones was clever and quick-witted, his mind able to grasp complexities with ease. Polites always needed time to think problems through and would invariably become lost in alternatives, unable to make a decision.

As he sat on the bench his heart sank. In what do you excel, Polites, he asked himself? You cannot run, and you cannot ride well. You are no fighter, nor are you a thinker. He thought of his garden then, and the joy it gave him. Even this did not lift his spirits, for many of the new seedlings would die now that he had been forced to turn his palace over to Agamemnon. Uncared for, they would wither in the fierce sunlight.

In the distance Polites could hear the sound of marching feet. The regiments were moving, gathering here to select the hundred judges, the *Incorruptibles*. Now *there* was something to be grateful for, he thought. You could have been a soldier, and then chosen for such a thankless role. He wondered why any common soldier would agree to become a judge. For five days, under the baleful gaze of kings and nobles, the judges would make decisions on races and events upon which fortunes had been wagered. They would endure the wrath of monarchs, and sometimes the fury of the crowds. For this they would receive no reward, save a small silver token shaped like a discus and bearing the embossed image of Father Zeus. For five days these former peasants would have powers beyond those of kings, and be expected to use them wisely and without favour.

Well, that was the theory. Would any judge go against Priam, knowing that within five days he would once again be no more than a soldier, and subject to the whims of the king? Hardly.

Polites rose from his bench and made his way back along the race track, put on his sandals, and returned through the stables and the *palaistra* to watch the selection of the judges. Soon Father would be here. Polites' stomach turned. What have I missed, he wondered? What hideous error will he discover?

In the midst of a large crowd Kalliades and Banokles made their way up the long slope to the Scaean Gate. Banokles was happy to be free of the ship, but Kalliades had felt a sinking of the heart as they sighted the city. The voyage had been dreamlike, with no sense of the passing of time. Kalliades had stood with Piria on the deck of the *Penelope*, walked with her on moonlit beaches, laughed with her and joked with her. Now here they were, at the end of their journey. Soon he would be saying farewell to her, and the thought frightened him. She can never love you, he told himself. Better to say farewell than to watch her run into the arms of her lover, with never a backward glance towards you. No, it was not better. To wake to a day when he could not gaze at her face was unthinkable.

'You ever seen Odysseus that angry?' asked Banokles. 'I thought he was in a rage when we fought the pirates, but today his face was so red I thought he'd bleed from the ears.'

'He was furious,' agreed Kalliades, recalling the moment when Odysseus had tried to steer the *Penelope* towards Priam's private beach. A small boat manned by a beachmaster and several sailors had cut across them.

'You cannot beach here,' the master yelled.

Odysseus had rushed to the prow and stared angrily down at the man. 'You moron,' he shouted. 'I am Odysseus, king of Ithaka. With me are Nestor of Pylos, and Idomeneos of Kretos. This is where all the vessels of kings beach. Now move away, or I'll sink you.'

The beachmaster called out to some soldiers on the beach. Some twenty of them came running forward, hands on their sword hilts. 'My orders are explicit, King Odysseus,' replied the beachmaster. 'No more ships are to beach here. You may sink this craft if you will, but those soldiers will still prevent your landing. There will be blood shed. I promise you that.'

Kalliades had moved away from Odysseus. The man had been shamed before his crew, and before his fellow kings. The Ugly King stood there, blinking in the sunlight, almost unable to speak. It was Bias who called out for the men to reverse oars and draw back, and the *Penelope* had sailed further along the bay. They beached some way from the city, and the men clambered down to the sand. Odysseus remained at the stern, arms folded across his chest. The other kings,

Nestor and Idomeneos, did not speak to him as they too departed the ship. Even Bias walked away without a word.

Piria approached Kalliades. 'The slight has pierced him like a dagger,' she said.

'I fear so. Banokles and I are going into the city to enter for the Games,' he said. 'Would you like to accompany us?'

'I cannot. I could be recognized by . . . by those who would cause me harm. Odysseus says I should remain here.'

And so Kalliades and Banokles had left her.

Kalliades stopped to ask directions from some soldiers at the Scaean Gate. Then the two comrades moved on, angling away from the crowd. Banokles spotted two whores, standing in the shade of a building, and waved at them.

'We need to find the gathering field,' said Kalliades.

Banokles sighed. 'And we've no wealth. Should have known that bastard would not surrender his breastplate. A curse on all kings!' Kalliades had paused. Streets branched off in all directions and he was gazing at the columned buildings. 'Are we lost?'

'Not yet,' Kalliades replied, heading on.

'Do we have a plan yet?'

'For what?'

'For life in Troy. Like . . . where are we going to stay?'

Kalliades laughed. 'You were there when Odysseus told us we would be lodged at Hektor's palace. You were standing right beside me.'

'I wasn't listening. I leave that sort of thing to you. Did you notice the size of the walls as we walked up to the city? They looked large the last time we were here, but in daylight they are massive. I wouldn't want to be on a ladder trying to scale them.'

'You won't have to. We are Mykene no longer. Which reminds me . . . should we see anyone we know, do not shout a greeting, or walk up to them.'

'Why would I do anything that stupid?'

'I am sorry, my friend. I was merely thinking aloud. The city is under truce for the Games, but there is still a bounty on our heads. And there will be many Mykene here.'

Finally they found their way to the gathering field, northeast of the city. Scores of tents had been erected here, and scribes were taking down the names of contestants at dozens of bench tables.

Eventually both Banokles and Kalliades registered to take part, and were given thin copper tokens embossed with numbers and an image of the entered event. They were told to return tomorrow at dawn for the preliminaries.

At the edge of the field a cooking area had been set up, two charcoal pits in which bulls were being roasted on spits. The two men sat in the shade of a large canvas canopy and ate. 'I think this bull died of old age,' grumbled Banokles. 'I haven't eaten meat this stringy since we invaded Sparta. You remember? That old goat Eruthros killed? I swear it was all hoof, bone and sinew. Not a piece of meat on it.'

'Rations were short,' recalled Kalliades. 'I remember

digging up roots and ripping bark off trees to add to the stew.'

'Good fighters those Spartans. If there'd been more of them we'd have been in real trouble.' Banokles laughed. 'They must really have angered the gods, eh? First they get beaten in a battle and then they end up with Menelaus as king.'

'I always liked him,' said Kalliades.

'Nothing to dislike,' agreed Banokles, 'but the man's as soft as puppy shit. He's got a belly on him like a pregnant sow.'

'I talked to him once,' said Kalliades. 'The night before we took Sparta. He was terrified, and couldn't stop throwing up. He said all he wanted was to be back at his farm. He'd been cross-breeding his herds with bulls from Thessaly. He claimed the milk yield from his cows had almost doubled.'

'Milk yield?' snorted Banokles. 'By the gods, anyone can get to be a king these days.'

'They can if they are brothers to Agamemnon. But be fair to Menelaus. Though he was frightened he still donned his armour and joined us in the attack. He didn't have to. He could have waited with the rear guard.'

Banokles did not look convinced. Then he brightened. 'You think there will be slave girls at Hektor's palace?' he asked.

'I don't know.' Kalliades chuckled. 'If there are I doubt they'll be ordered to rut with sailors.'

'They might, though.'

'Better, I think, to find a whore. That way you won't risk offending Hektor.'

'Oh, good plan,' mocked Banokles. 'Whores have to be paid for.'

Kalliades reached into the pouch at his side, and drew out five silver rings. Banokles was astonished. 'How did you come by them?'

'Odysseus gave them to me. And he says there will be fifty more. I sold him the breastplate of Idomeneos.'

'It is worth more than fifty-five silver rings.'

Kalliades shook his head. 'Not to me. Idomeneos is a king. I cannot demand he honour his debt. Odysseus can. It is that simple. Now, do you want the rings?'

Banokles grinned. 'I want what they'll buy,' he said.

'Well, first let us locate Hektor's palace.'

The two friends left the gathering field and wandered back through the city.

'How many women will five silver rings buy me?' Banokles asked.

'I neglected to ask Odysseus about the price of whores.'

'Not like you to forget the important things,' observed Banokles. 'Will you be coming whore hunting with me?'

'No. I'll return to the beach. Odysseus has told Piria to sleep on the *Penelope*. She'll be coming to the palace later.'

'Why?'

'Odysseus wants to find out if any of the other kings are staying close to Hektor's palace. It could be dangerous for her, if she is recognized.'

'So you will spend the night guarding her?' Banokles shook his head. Ahead, the road widened, and they saw a marketplace packed with stalls. There were shops there, and several eating places, with tables set out beneath brightly coloured canopies. Banokles grabbed Kalliades by the arm. 'Come on,' he said. 'We need to talk.'

'We were talking.'

'I need a drink for this kind of conversation,' Banokles said. Kalliades followed him to a small table placed against a cool stone wall. Banokles ordered wine, filled a goblet and drained it. 'Are you moonstruck, Kalliades?' he asked.

'I don't know what you're talking about.'

'I think you do. You've fallen in love with her.'

'I am merely concerned for her safety.'

'And pig shit smells like jasmine! I like the girl, Kalliades, so don't misunderstand me. She has courage and she has heart, and, if it was in her nature, she'd make a fine wife. But it *isn't* in her nature. You know as well as I do that the lover she is searching for is a woman.'

Kalliades sighed. 'I didn't *choose* to love her,' he said. 'But I did choose to protect her, and I did promise to see her safely to her lover. I will do that, and then we will part.'

'Is that a promise?'

Kalliades poured himself a cup of wine, and sipped it. The silence grew.

'I thought not,' said Banokles. 'So what are you really hoping for? That her lover will turn her away? That she will fall into your arms? That you will take all her sorrow from her? It cannot happen. Brothers cannot do that for sisters. And that is how she sees you. How she will always see you.'

'I know that,' replied Kalliades. 'I know that everything you say is true, and yet . . . I also know there is a reason why she came into my life. I cannot explain it, Banokles. I was *meant* to meet her. That is a truth that my soul understands.'

Looking into his friend's pale eyes he saw no similar understanding there. Then Banokles shrugged and smiled. 'You do what you must, my friend. You go and walk in the moonlight with the woman you love. I'll find someone who doesn't love me, and shag her until my eyes bulge.'

The tension between them evaporated and Kalliades laughed. 'That is a good plan,' he said. 'Simple and direct, with clear objectives. I hope you can stick to it.'

'Why would I not?'

'Because when full of wine you tend to look for brawls to take part in.'

'Not tonight,' said Banokles. 'Tonight is for wine and women. I give you my oath on that.'

XIX

A bow for Odysseus

MANY PEOPLE SPOKE OF THEIR LOVE FOR TROY, GROWING misty-eyed about its beauty. To Big Red it was just a city of stone, a place to earn silver rings and gold trinkets. The truth, she believed, was that this emotion men spoke of was merely love of wealth. Troy was rich, and those who prospered within it became wealthy. Even the old baker, whose house she was now walking wearily towards, wore rings of gold and had a carriage to ferry him about the city. His breads and his cakes were purchased by the nobles and served at feasts and gatherings. The baker owned six slaves and a farm close to the city, which supplied his grain. He was a fine client. His erections were semi-soft and easily dealt with, his gratitude rich and rewarding. At the end of a long day Red had no wish to spend time with a younger client.

She plodded on through the back streets, the silver rings she had earned that day neatly threaded on a thong and hidden within the folds of her long red robe. Between each silver ring was a thin piece of wood, to stop the metal clinking as she moved. These streets in the lower town were seething now with cut-purses and thieves, most of them working for Silfanos, and although she paid – as did all the lower town whores – a monthly tribute to Silfanos it was still sensible to hide her wealth. In a pouch at her side she carried a handful of copper rings, in case some enterprising robber should accost her.

The day had been profitable, and were it not for the fact that the baker paid her in kind she would have returned home and sat in her small garden with a jug of wine. There was, however, no food in her larder, and she had a taste for the honey cakes he made.

Her lower back ached as she walked and she was hungry. The thought of the honey cakes drove her on.

Passing through a low alleyway she emerged onto a small square. The sound of laughter carried to her and she glanced across to where a group of men were sitting. One of them was Silfanos. He and three of his men were drinking with a young, powerfully built warrior in an old breastplate. It was obvious the blond man was drunk and happy. A man should always die happy, she thought. Once night had fully fallen and the streets were empty Silfanos and his men would fall upon the drunk and rob him. The breastplate was probably worth a score of rings.

Red moved on, but the drunk saw her and heaved himself to his feet. He staggered towards her. 'Hold!' he called out. 'Please!'

She stared at him malevolently, ready to brush aside any clumsy advance. He did not seek to touch her, but stood open-mouthed before her. 'By the gods,' he said, 'I think you are the most beautiful woman I ever saw.'

'All women look beautiful to a man soused with wine,' she snapped.

'I've had wine before,' he said. 'But I've never seen anyone like you. Here.' He pulled a silver ring from his pouch and thrust it into her hand.

'Take it back,' she said. 'I have nothing for you.'

'No. That is for your beauty alone. Merely seeing you gladdens my heart. By the gods, it was worth travelling across the Great Green just to stand here and gaze upon you.' Glancing beyond him she saw thin-faced Silfanos gesturing for her to depart. She nodded at him and moved away.

'What is your name?' the big man called out.

'I am called Red.'

'I am Banokles. We must meet again, Red.'

Ignoring him, she walked on. Silfanos was a wretch and a killer. If she and the drunk were to meet again, it would not be on this side of the Dark Road.

By the time she reached the house of the baker the streets were dark. Red found she was still holding the silver ring the man had given her. She paused before the baker's door and slipped the ring into her pouch. The fool had paid just to look at her. Despite herself she was touched. Then anger swept over her. He was an idiot, she told herself.

The baker had prepared a tray of sweet cakes, but despite her hunger she ignored them, telling him how much she had looked forward to seeing him, and stroking his face, and kissing his cheek. Putting his arm round her he led her into his bedroom, then lay back as she cooed and stroked him.

'Why won't you wed me, Red?' he asked her, as he had asked her many times before.

'Be content with what you have,' she told him.

'I want more, Red.'

'All men want more.'

'I cannot imagine a life without you.'

'Nor do you need to. I am here now.' With that she began to apply the skills of her twenty years as a whore. His happiness was complete within a few heartbeats. She lay beside him for politeness's sake until he dozed, then walked out into his kitchen and ate several of the cakes. If he had been as good a lover as he was a baker she would have wed him in an instant.

He had also prepared a basket of bread for her. Gathering it up, she left the house. She had intended to return home by a different route, having no wish to pass the body of the blond man, or worse to be there when Silfanos and his men were still in the act of murder. But she was tired, and in no mood for a detour. She decided to creep to the edge of the square, peep round the corner, and then if necessary keep to the shadows, moving silently.

When she reached the corner she could hear no sounds of laughter or song, and guessed that the crime had already been committed. Peeping into the square, she was amazed to see the blond man still sitting there, nursing a cup of wine. Sprawled out on the ground around him were the bodies of four men. Involuntarily, she gasped. The warrior heard her and looked up.

'Red!' he shouted happily. 'You came back!'

He stood up, then slumped back. 'Oh,' she heard him say, 'I think a little too much wine has flowed.'

Red moved across the square, scanning the bodies. Silfanos was not among them. 'Are they dead?' she asked.

He considered the question solemnly. 'Could be, I suppose.' He kicked out at the nearest man, who groaned. 'Probably not, though.'

'Where is the other one?'

'Ran off. By the gods, I've seen hounds who couldn't run that fast.' He chuckled, then burped. 'It's been a good day, Red. I've eaten my fill, shagged . . .' lifting his hand, he counted his fingers, 'four times, and had a fine fight. Best of all, though, I've seen you.'

'You need to leave here,' she said. 'The other man will come back, and he'll bring more robbers with him.'

'I'll swat them like flies,' he shouted, swinging his arm, and falling off his seat. He grunted, then pushed himself to his feet. 'Need a piss,' he said, lifting his tunic and urinating on the unconscious man lying closest to him. 'Stupid thieves,' he muttered, as he finished. 'All the time I had rings they sat and drank with me. Then when all the rings were gone they sought to rob me.'

'They wanted your breastplate,' she said. 'Now come along. It is time to go.'

'I haven't got any rings, Red. Nothing to give you.'

'Just walk with me, idiot!' she stormed. 'Otherwise

you'll be lying here dead!' Stepping in, she took his arm and dragged him across the square. He grinned at her, then glanced down at the basket she was carrying.

'Oh, bread!' he said. 'Can we stop and eat? I'm a little peckish.'

'In a while,' she assured him, pulling him on. 'Where are you staying?'

'Palace,' he said. 'Somewhere. With Kalliades. My friend.'

'I don't know any Kalliades.'

They walked on, through narrow alleys and side streets, emerging at last onto a broad avenue. 'Need a little sleep now,' Banokles told her, slumping against the wall of a building.

Red heard the distant sound of angry shouts. 'You can't sleep here,' she said. 'My house is close by. Can you walk that far?'

'With you? To your house?' Grinning at her again, he sucked in a huge breath and pushed himself away from the wall. 'Lead on, beauty!'

They made it to another side street. Banokles halted there, fell to his knees and vomited. 'That's better,' he said.

Two men ran round the corner. Red stepped swiftly back into the shadows. The men rushed at Banokles. One of them had a club. Banokles saw them, gave a great shout and charged. Red saw him strike the first man, who was catapulted from his feet. The second attacker leapt upon Banokles. The warrior grabbed the man, hoisted him high, then hurled him into his unconscious comrade. Banokles staggered back a step, then rushed in as the man struggled to rise. A huge fist cracked into the attacker's chin and he slumped senseless to the ground.

Sweeping up the club, Banokles staggered back towards the avenue. Red ran after him. 'Not that way, you fool!' she hissed.

'Oh, hello, Red. Thought you'd left me.'

'Follow me,' she ordered him. Obediently he swung behind her, the club on his shoulder. She led him through the gate at the rear of her house, then dropped the locking bar in place behind them.

Once inside the building she lit a lantern. Banokles slumped into a chair. His head fell back, and his breathing deepened. Red stood there, looking at the man in the lanternlight.

'Built like an ox, brain like a sparrow,' she said.

Leaving him in the chair, she walked through to her bedroom at the rear of the house. Stripping off her gown, she laid it over a chair, then hid the thong of silver rings behind a recess in the wall before climbing into bed. She was just falling sleep when she heard the big man moving about. He called her name.

'I am in here,' she replied, irritated.

A naked figure loomed in the doorway. He stepped inside, stumbled over a chair, then bumped into the bed. Pulling back the covers, he slid in alongside her.

'I take no clients in my own bed,' she told him.

'Oh, don't worry, Red,' he replied sleepily. 'I couldn't possibly shag just now.'

Within moments, his warm body nestled alongside her, he was asleep.

* * *

Odysseus strolled across the gathering field, his bow Akilina in his hand, a quiver of long arrows hanging from his shoulder. He stared straight ahead, walking as if without a care in the world, but his heart was hammering, and he felt as nervous as a colt. Of all the pleasures in the wide world there were only two to compare with the joy of competing in a Games: holding his wife close on a cold winter's night, and watching the first of the spring breezes billow the sail of the *Penelope*.

Even the huge satisfaction of storytelling paled against the exquisite moment of true competition, when he would notch an arrow to beautiful Akilina and send a shaft hurtling into the target. Odysseus cared not if they were moving targets hauled on carts, or straw models of beasts and men. If there was one talent Odysseus believed he possessed it was to shoot a bow better than any man alive.

A huge crowd had gathered at the far end of the field, and many of the contestants were already standing by. Odysseus could see Meriones – who had beaten him once in five contests – and the callow sons of Nestor, who would be lucky to progress to the later rounds.

It was a fine day, the sun high and bright, a subtle breeze whispering across the field. Licking his finger Odysseus tested the breeze. It was not strong enough to divert an arrow shot from Akilina.

Despite his excitement the tensions of yesterday remained. The beaching of the *Penelope* a long ride from the city gates had both enraged and shamed him.

To suffer such an indignity was bad enough, but to endure it in the company of Nestor and Idomeneos was unbearable. Neither of his fellow kings had commented on the slight, which made it worse. A little joshing would have given Odysseus the opportunity to make a jest of it.

Today, however, the world was beginning to look brighter. As soon as he had reached the city Odysseus had enquired after Helikaon, and had discovered that he was recovering from the assassin's wounds. This joyous news lifted his spirits, but even so, in the back of his mind the insult of yesterday slowly simmered. The beachmaster would not have dared make such a decision had someone in higher authority not ordered it. That someone could only be Priam. This was baffling to Odysseus, for though not a friend to the Trojan king, he was a neutral. In these troublesome times, with the world on the brink of war, it would be an act of madness to make an enemy of him. Perhaps, he decided, it was not about him at all. Perhaps it was intended as a slight to Idomeneos and Nestor. Even so, it would be foolish, for Priam would need both those kings in his camp if he were to thwart Agamemnon.

Pushing such thoughts aside, Odysseus strolled onto the archery field. He could feel all eyes on him as he approached the men waiting to participate in the tourney. He glanced down the shooting line, and saw that the targets were dummies of straw, set no more than fifty paces distant.

'By Hermes, Meriones, a man could throw an arrow over such a paltry distance,' he complained.

'Indeed he could, my friend,' responded black-bearded Meriones. 'At this range almost no-one will be eliminated.'

To entertain the crowd both he and Meriones stepped forward, sending shaft after shaft into the furthest targets. Men began to cheer and stamp their feet. Eventually, their quivers empty, the two old friends wandered out onto the field to gather their arrows.

'A strange event yesterday,' said Meriones.

'It was a slight, right enough,' Odysseus told him. 'Perhaps it was not intended for me. Priam has little love for Idomeneos.'

Meriones nodded. 'True enough, but would he risk alienating him with so much at stake? Have *you* done anything to incur Priam's wrath?'

'Not that I'm aware.'

As they made their way back to the other bowmen a Trojan soldier, wearing the yellow sash of a judge, came walking along the line, calling out for those with tokens marked from one to twenty to step forward.

Odysseus, whose token was embossed with number eleven, strode forward with Meriones.

The judge was a handsome young man, with fiery red hair and keen blue eyes. He glanced at the bows the men carried. 'Be so good as to leave your weapons with friends,' he said. 'All archers are to be issued with standard bows from the city armoury.'

'What?' roared Odysseus, his anger erupting. Similar cries of outrage came from some of the other bowmen.

The judge raised his arms for silence. 'By order of the king this contest is to be fairly judged on the merits of each archer. Many of you carry beautifully made bows, some of horn, some of wood and leather. You, King Odysseus, have the legendary Akilina. It is well known that it can shoot an arrow further than any bow in the world. Would any contest therefore be fair? We have men here who have no wealth, and who have cut their own bows from shrivelled trees. Should they be at a disadvantage because you have Akilina?'

Odysseus said nothing, but then Meriones spoke. 'It is a fair point,' he agreed. 'Bring on your bows. Let us at least practise with them.'

Several soldiers then marched out, carrying slender weapons of the Egypteian style, each carved from a single length of wood, with no composite to give extra strength and elasticity. A young soldier approached Meriones. He was carrying two bows, and as he offered the first to the black-bearded archer he seemed to hesitate. Then he drew it back and turned towards the judge. 'Go ahead,' he was ordered. The youngster then reached out with his right hand, offering a bow to Meriones, who took it and drew back several times on the string. The second bow he offered to Odysseus.

'By the gods,' said Odysseus, loudly, as he hefted it. 'I could shape better weapons than this from dried cow dung. Strike a rabbit with a shaft from this and it would scratch its arse and wonder which flea had nipped it.' Laughter broke out among the crowd.

Other soldiers brought buckets of arrows, which they placed before the men. Then the judge spoke again. 'Each archer will have five shots. The leading ten archers will progress to the second round.'

'These are flimsy weapons,' complained Meriones. 'Not enough pull to offset the breeze.' He turned to the judge. 'Are we at least allowed to practise with these bows?'

The judge shook his head, and called the archers forward.

Upon the order to shoot each man drew back on his bowstring. There was a sudden crack. The bow of Odysseus split, his arrow dropping to the ground. 'Fetch another bow!' he called.

A soldier brought him a second weapon. Odysseus calmed himself, sighted carefully, then let fly. The arrow, caught by the breeze, drifted a hair's-breadth wide of the dummy. Now with a feel for the bow he sent his next three shafts hammering into the straw chest. Then he called out for his fifth arrow.

'You have had five, Odysseus,' the judge told him.

'Are you an imbecile? The bow broke on the first.'

'Such was the will of the gods. You have scored three in five. I am sorry, King Odysseus, you are eliminated.'

The crowd was utterly silent. Odysseus, greatest of archers, famed around the Great Green, had not made it through the opening round. Hurling the bow to the ground, he snatched up Akilina and sent a long arrow ripping through the furthest target. It struck the pole holding the dummy in place with such force that the target was ripped from its ties and fell to the grass.

Odysseus swung on the judge. 'You ignorant cowson! You think this crowd came to see grown men playing with sticks and string? They came to see the finest archers and the greatest bows. They came to see

Akilina and the black bow of Meriones. They came for an exhibition of greatness, not an embarrassing display of mediocrity.' With that he stalked away, burning with shame.

Meriones ran to catch him. 'My friend, wait!' he called. 'Come, let us find something cool to drink.'

'I am in no mood for company, Meriones.'

'I know. In your place neither would I be. But hear me, Odysseus. The judge was over-zealous. You should have been allowed another shaft.'

Odysseus paused. 'I don't like losing, Meriones. All men know that. But there is something in the air here, and I do not like the smell. Did you notice the young soldier when he went to give you the bow? He offered it from the left hand, then drew back, and gave you the right-hand weapon.'

'Aye, I saw that. What of it? You think you were cheated?'

'I do not know, Meriones. What I do know is that I have now been shamed twice in a single day.'

The judges called out for the archers to resume their positions. Meriones leaned in to Odysseus. 'I am sorry, my friend. But whatever happens here all men know you are still the greatest archer in the world.'

'Go! Go and win the damned tourney.'

Meriones ran back across the field. Odysseus wandered round the gathering field, watching other contests. Bias progressed through both early rounds of the javelin, and Leukon despatched two opponents in the boxing tourney. Even the big lout Banokles battered his way into the later rounds. Bored and hot, and with the opening ceremony not until late afternoon, Odysseus returned to the *Penelope*.

Piria was sitting quietly beneath the canopy on the rear deck as he climbed aboard. 'I had not expected to see you so soon,' she said. The comment did not help his mood. Piria handed him a cup of water. 'Have you seen Andromache?'

Draining the cup, he shook his head. 'She has left the palace and moved to Hektor's farm.'

'I shall go there, then.'

'Yes, you must. But not yet. The city is teeming with foreigners. Your father is here, and your brother, and quite an entourage, I'm told. The risk of your being recognized is too great. In five days all the kings will be leaving.'

'I am willing to risk the journey now,' she said.

The anger that had been simmering below the surface all day erupted. 'You stupid girl!' he roared. 'Of course *you* are willing to risk it. And if you are captured while scampering witlessly off to your lost love, then every man on this crew might face death. The last man who helped a Thera runaway was burned alive, along with his family. You think I would allow my men's lives to be put further at risk for the sake of five days? By the gods, girl, you seek to disobey me on this and I'll hand you over myself.' She sat very still, her eyes wide and fearful. Odysseus felt his anger drift away. What are you doing, he asked himself? This girl has suffered great abuse – and not just during these last few days. And now you terrorize her? 'Forgive that outburst,' he said at last. 'This has been an ugly day and I am not, by nature, a calm man. You are safe with me, Piria. But give me the five days and I will have you at Andromache's side.'

'I am sorry too, Odysseus,' she said. 'I spoke without thinking. I would not want any one of your crew to suffer because of me. I will, of course, wait. Who am I to be when we reach Hektor's palace?'

He reddened then. 'I have given that much thought. I cannot call you a slave or a servant, for then you would be left among those in Hektor's employ. You would be given tasks for which you are not trained. I cannot say you are family, for it is known that I have no family, save Penelope. Therefore – and do not bridle before I have finished – I shall say you are my concubine. You will then be given your own rooms, and I shall send out for clothing for you to replace that tattered gown. You need have no fear. I shall not be requiring you to play the role.'

Surprisingly, she smiled. 'I thank you, Odysseus.'

'Yes, well. That is settled then. And now I shall cool myself with a swim and then don my kingly robes for the opening ceremony.'

Walking to the prow he lowered himself to the sand. Then, doffing tunic and sandals, he waded out and dived forward. The cold of the sea refreshed him, but niggling doubts continued to gnaw at him.

It was just a broken bow, he told himself. No more, no less.

XX

The enemy of Troy

DRESSED IN A LONG ROBE OF WHITE, AND WEARING A wide-brimmed straw hat, Odysseus travelled to the stadium in one of Priam's chariots. He was greeted there by Priam's son, Polites, a shy and dull young man of limited conversation. The prince led him to an enclosure, where he found himself in the company of Agamemnon, Peleus, Idomeneos and Nestor. The Mykene king nodded in greeting. 'I hear fortune did not favour you at the archery tourney,' he said.

'Bow snapped,' answered Odysseus, trying for a lightness of tone, as if he cared nothing for the result. It did not fool Agamemnon, he knew. The man had a mind as sharp as a viper's fang.

Out in the stadium a dark-haired young soldier, wearing a cloak of gold, was pacing out the running track. Three hundred long paces, imitating the stride of Herakles, who had established the first known sprint race generations back. 'The Lord of the Games should be of noble birth,' muttered Idomeneos, 'and not some peasant in armour.'

Odysseus let the comment pass. The grandfather of Idomeneos had been a peasant warrior, who had seized a section of Kretos and declared himself king. Nestor looked at him, raising an eyebrow. He too knew of Idomeneos' ancestry.

Once the track was established the turning posts were carried out, then hammered into the ground. Across the field the first of the athletes were leaving the *palaistra* and moving into position. Odysseus saw Kalliades swinging his arms and loosening his muscles.

'I know that man,' said Agamemnon. His expression darkened. 'He is a Mykene renegade.'

'Which one?' asked Odysseus innocently.

'There! The tall one,' said Agamemnon, pointing at Kalliades again.

'Member of my crew,' said Odysseus. 'He runs for Ithaka.'

'The man with the Sword of Argurios,' added Idomeneos.

'Another traitor,' snapped Agamemnon.

'The world is full of traitors,' agreed Odysseus. 'So how is it you know this man?'

'He killed Kolanos, a loyal Follower, and was sentenced to death for it. However, he escaped justice and fled . . . to you, apparently.'

'Had I but known,' said Odysseus. 'Naturally I shall dismiss him from my crew when the Games are over.'

'He should be dragged out now,' Agamemnon maintained. 'I shall send word to Priam.'

'That might cause a problem or two,' said Odysseus. 'I seem to recall that following the attack on Troy last autumn King Priam released all prisoners. It is said he requested they kill the general of that raid, a man who had offered to betray his king.'

'A foul Trojan lie!' snapped Agamemnon. 'Kolanos would never have betrayed me.'

'Even so, the killing of Kolanos was ordered by Priam. You can hardly ask him to punish a man who carried out his order. And, on the surface at least, Kolanos had already betrayed you by attacking Priam, who was – and remains – your ally.'

Agamemnon hesitated. 'Your words are wise, Odysseus,' he said at last. 'It saddens me that we are not allies. Surely you can see the threat Troy poses? You think Priam, with all his wealth, and his growing armies, has no designs on the lands of the west?'

'I do not know the mind of Priam. I think, however, that wealth is all he desires. And he has no need to invade others to see it grow. Troy sucks in gold by the day, in every ship, in every caravan.'

'I have agents here in Troy,' said Agamemnon, keeping his voice low. 'Priam recently purchased a thousand Phrygian bows, and he is shipping copper and tin to his armouries. Breastplates, helms, shields, swords. If we do not deal with this man now he will descend on us all.'

Odysseus smiled. 'I am the man with no enemies, Agamemnon. Not Troy, not the Mykene, not the Hittites or the Gypptos. My ships are welcome in all bays, and all ports.'

Agamemnon appeared to relax. 'I appreciate your

frankness, Odysseus. I shall be equally forthright. When the war comes – as it must – then those who continue to trade with Troy will be considered enemies. There will be no neutrals.'

'It is getting dangerous to be neutral these days. Old Eioneus was neutral. I hear he fell from his horse and died.'

'A tragic loss for his people,' said Agamemnon. 'And I fear he will not be the last. I am told that another of us is to be declared an enemy of Troy. Whoever it is will be lucky to leave the city alive.'

'You are suggesting Priam killed Eioneus?'

'I had no quarrel with him. Perhaps he was preparing to renounce his alliance with Troy.'

Odysseus did not believe the lie for a moment, but he kept his own counsel. 'And who is this other enemy to be named?' he asked.

'I don't know. I wish I did. It is a most odd story.'

Just at that moment there came a great roar from the crowd, as the runners were called to the starting line at the western end of the track. The Lord of the Games lifted his arm. The vast crowd fell silent. 'Away!' shouted the lord. The twenty runners sped out, sprinting towards the finishing post. Several judges were waiting there to note the first five to cross the line. These would progress to the next round.

Kalliades finished second. Other races followed. Odysseus watched them, sometimes wagering with Idomeneos and Nestor. Then he left the enclosure and walked round the stadium to where the later rounds of the javelin were being contested. Bias was throwing well, but Odysseus saw the black man rubbing at his shoulder. He looks weary now, thought Odysseus. By the later rounds his shoulder will be a sea of pain.

Then, some distance away, standing close to Priam, he saw Helikaon. His heart lifted, and he waved to catch Helikaon's eye. He was convinced he had, for the dark-haired young man glanced in his direction, then turned away. Odysseus watched as he eased his way back through the throng until he was out of sight.

The boy looks thin and weary, he thought. And with so many Mykene in Troy he should not be out in public. But I will lift his spirits when we speak. Helikaon would be glad to know that supplies of tin from the Seven Hills had exceeded expectations, and the profits last season had been enormous.

Hungry now, Odysseus made his way to a food stall, where he stood in the shade munching on a Trojan delicacy, meat and herbs wrapped in a broad leaf that had been marinated in wine. Then he walked back round the stadium, coming at last to the enclosure where Agamemnon was standing with King Peleus and his tall son, Achilles.

Odysseus looked at the fleshy king, and thought of Piria, and of how she had hacked away her blond locks as a child. He knew, as did many of the kings of the west, of the man's abhorrent sexual tastes, but he knew now of one more evil committed by him.

Now look what you made me do, slut.

Appalling enough to have raped the child, but to make her believe it was somehow her fault was vile beyond belief.

'Well met, Odysseus,' said Peleus, thrusting out his hand.

'You must forgive me,' replied Odysseus, avoiding the handshake. 'I have been munching on sweetmeats and my hands are sticky with honey.' He swung to Achilles. 'Good to see you, lad. The word is you will be Champion of the Games.'

'There is no real competition,' said the young man sourly. 'Save perhaps your man, Leukon.'

'He is a canny fighter.'

More races began. Peleus and Achilles wandered away to stand with Idomeneos, and the Athenian king, Menestheos.

Agamemnon leaned towards Odysseus. 'You are not overly fond of Peleus?'

'I hardly know him. So, tell me of this enemy of Troy.'

'I have the story in fragments only. Given time I will learn more. You recall the assassin, Karpophorus?'

'By reputation only.'

'He died stabbing the ghastly Helikaon. He did not die immediately, however. It seems that Karpophorus was also responsible for the murder of Helikaon's father.' Odysseus felt suddenly cold, and his belly tightened. 'What is it?' asked Agamemnon, his dark eyes watching the Ugly King.

'Too many sweetmeats,' answered Odysseus. 'Go on.'

'There is little more that I can tell. Karpophorus told Helikaon the identity of the man who ordered his father's death. Helikaon passed the information to

347

Priam. As you know, Priam was blood kin to the father. Cousin or such like. So honour demands he declare the man who hired the killer an enemy of Troy. Now I doubt the man is a mere merchant, so it is likely he is a king. The question is who? Anchises was not an enemy to the Mykene. There is a dark mystery here, I think.'

Odysseus saw that Agamemnon was staring at him intently. 'I don't doubt light will shine upon it soon,' he said, moving away. Then he caught sight of Kalliades and Banokles strolling close by. Stepping out, he called the two friends to him. Banokles had a swelling under his right eye, and a cut lip, but he was in a fine mood.

'Did you see me, Odysseus?' he asked. 'Downed that Hittite six times.' He lifted his fist. 'Hammer of Hephaistos!'

'You did well,' said the king. 'Are you returning to the palace now?'

'No,' said Banokles. 'I'm off to the lower town to meet a friend.'

'I'm heading for the *Penelope*. I'd be grateful for your company,' said Odysseus, staring at Kalliades. The warrior's eyes narrowed. Then he nodded.

'And we would be privileged to walk with you, Odysseus King.'

'We would?' queried Banokles.

'The Law of the Road,' Kalliades told him.

'Stay close and watchful,' said Odysseus, setting off towards the upper city. The two warriors fell in behind him.

As he walked a cold anger began in Odysseus, far more powerful than the volcanic rages for which he was renowned. It ate into him, burrowing deep, awakening thoughts and feelings he had put behind him almost fifteen years before.

Priam now knew that Odysseus had hired Karpophorus to kill Helikaon's father.

As a result he was to be declared an enemy of Troy. This, in itself, would have been a matter of great regret for the Ithakan king. But understandable.

But Priam had not been satisfied with the honourable course, summoning Odysseus to the palace and banishing him from Troy. Instead he had set out to humiliate and shame him. The icy anger swelled, seeping through his body. What had to follow now was obvious. During the Games Priam would set out to divide the kings of the west, to bribe and coerce the weaker or greedier elements. He could not allow Odysseus to leave Troy alive to ally with Agamemnon. Priam would know that Nestor of Pylos and perhaps even Idomeneos would be swayed if Odysseus joined the ranks of the Mykene plotters.

As Odysseus walked he watched faces in the crowd, seeking any sign of tension, anyone who looked too long, or too hard, at him. Glancing to his left he saw Kalliades doing the same. To his right Banokles was walking warily, also scanning the crowd for signs of trouble.

Pushing thoughts of assassination from his mind, he returned to the larger problem. There has to be some way to resolve this, he thought. You are Odysseus, the thinker, the planner. You are known for your cunning and your stratagems. One by one he considered courses of action. What if he went to Priam and tried to set the matter right? Priam would not listen. Odysseus had caused the death of blood kin. Blood demanded blood.

What else to do? He could gather his men, slip out of Troy at dawn, then make his way back to Ithaka, on the other side of the Great Green. And then what? Live the rest of his life in fear of assassins sent by Priam? Then there was Helikaon. The fact that he had gone to Priam meant that he too would declare Odysseus an enemy. The dread *Xanthos* would sail the Great Green hunting down Ithakan ships, as would the other fifty galleys under Helikaon's control. If they blocked the trade route to the Seven Hills, Ithaka would within a year – two at the most – be poverty-stricken and ruined.

Face the truth, Odysseus, he told himself. Priam's decision to make me an enemy has left only one viable choice. You are like a ship, being driven by storm winds you cannot control, towards a land of hatred and blood you have no wish to visit. The realization of it grieved him. He loved Helikaon, and felt great fondness for Hektor and his new wife, Andromache. In the war to come his every sympathy would lie with Troy. He disliked the megalomaniac Agamemnon and loathed the ghastly Peleus. He had contempt for the mean-spirited Idomeneos, and felt no warmth towards the Athenian, Menestheos. In fact, of all the kings of the west, he felt affection for only Nestor. Anger swelled again, cold and all-consuming.

Odysseus gazed up at the towering walls, and the mighty Scaean Gate. He saw the hilltop palace of

Priam, and the buildings on either side of the narrow, twisting streets. He no longer viewed them as impressive works of architecture. Now he saw them through different eyes. Coldly he estimated the numbers of men needed to scale the walls, and pictured the streets as battlegrounds.

As they eased their way through the crowds Kalliades leaned in to him. 'Four men,' he said. 'Following a little distance behind. They have been with us since the tourney fields.'

Odysseus did not look back. Neither Kalliades nor Banokles was armed, and Odysseus himself carried only a small, curved knife in a jewelled scabbard. The weapon was useful for cutting fruit, but little else.

'Are they soldiers?' he asked.

'Perhaps, but they are not wearing armour. They have knives, not swords.'

Odysseus pictured the route ahead. Soon they would leave the main concourse and move through narrower residential streets. Pausing by a market stall he picked up a small bracelet, of silver inlaid with opal.

'A fine piece, sir,' said the stallholder. 'You won't see better anywhere.'

Odysseus replaced it and walked on. 'Two of them have cut through the alley on the left,' whispered Kalliades.

'They know we are going to the ship,' Odysseus told him. 'There is a small square with a well close by. The road we are taking intersects with the alley there.' He glanced at Banokles. 'You have the Hammer of Hephaistos ready?'

'Always,' answered Banokles.

'Then prepare to use it.'

Odysseus swung on his heel and walked back the way he had come. Two men, both tall and broad-shouldered, and wearing long cloaks, suddenly halted. Odysseus strode up to them. Without a word he clubbed his fist into the first man's face. Banokles leapt at the second, downing him with a ferocious right hook. The first man staggered back. Odysseus followed in, kicking his legs out from under him. As the man fell Odysseus dropped to his knees, wrenching the man's knife from its scabbard. The victim struggled to rise, then subsided as his own dagger blade touched his throat.

'You want to say anything?' Odysseus asked. The man licked his lips.

'I do not know why you are attacking me, stranger.'

'Ah,' said Odysseus with a smile. 'Now I know you are lying, for you were in the crowd at the archery tourney, and you know I am no stranger. I am Odysseus, king of Ithaka. And you are an assassin.'

'That is nonsense! Help!' the man suddenly shouted. 'I am being attacked!' Odysseus struck him. His head bounced down against the stone of the road. He groaned once. Odysseus clubbed him again. Then there was silence.

Odysseus rose and, gesturing to Kalliades and Banokles, approached the road leading to the square. Behind them several people from the crowd had gathered round the fallen men. Tossing the stolen knife to Kalliades, the king set off down the narrow road.

Banokles, armed with the second man's knife, took up a position on his right.

'Keep the weapons in clear view,' said Odysseus. 'I want the other two to know they are in for a fight.'

They walked on, coming at last to the small square and the well. The remaining two assassins were waiting there. They looked across at Odysseus, noting the knives his companions carried. Then they looked past the trio, seeking their comrades. Odysseus glared at them, and continued walking. The assassins glanced at one another, then turned and moved away.

'You want us to follow and kill them?' asked Banokles.

Odysseus shook his head. 'Let us get back to the ship. I need to think. Hekabe the queen has asked to see me later. I'll want you both with me for that.'

Helikaon did not remain for the full afternoon of Games. His strength was all but gone as he and Gershom moved back through the crowd towards the waiting carriages. Helikaon stumbled, and Gershom caught his arm. The heat from the sun was intense, almost as great as a mid-summer day, and Helikaon was sweating freely.

Climbing into the six-seat chariot, Helikaon slumped down gratefully. Gershom sat opposite him, scanning the crowd, his hand on his dagger hilt. Helikaon smiled. 'I doubt even Agamemnon would seek to kill me in front of Priam.'

The charioteer flicked the reins and the two-horse carriage moved out. The ride was bumpy across the newly broken ground outside of the new stadium, but soon they reached the road. Gershom relaxed a little as the chariot picked up speed, but still kept a wary eye open for bowmen or slingers.

'We shouldn't have come,' he grumbled. 'All men can see how weak you are. It will encourage them to try an attack.'

'They will attack anyway,' answered Helikaon, 'when they perceive that the time is right. And it will be while Agamemnon is still in Troy. He will want to rejoice at my death.'

The chariot clattered on through near empty streets. 'Odysseus was there,' said Gershom. 'He waved at you.'

'I saw him,' said Helikaon. 'If word comes to the palace that he wishes to see me, make some excuse.'

'He is your closest friend,' said Gershom.

Helikaon did not reply. Pulling a cloth from his belt, he dabbed at his sweat-streaked face. Gershom looked closely at him. Helikaon's colour was good, his skin having lost the ashen texture it had acquired during his illness. He was close now to recovery, needing only to rebuild his stamina.

The carriage moved down through the lower town until it reached Helikaon's palace. Two armed guards stood there, drawing open the gates to allow entry. Once inside the building Helikaon walked through to a large room and stretched himself out on a couch. A servant brought a pitcher of cool water and filled a cup for the Dardanian king. Helikaon drank deeply, then closed his eyes, resting his head on a cushion. Gershom left him there and strode through to the rear garden, where two more guards were patrolling. He spoke to them for a little while, then returned to the palace. The guards were for little more than show. It was not a building to be easily defended. There were windows on two sides leading to the streets, and the walls of the gardens were low. Assassins could force entry in any one of twenty places without alerting the sentries. And, sometime during the next five days, they would do exactly that. A sensible plan of action would be to leave and return to Dardania, but Helikaon would not hear of it.

Returning to the cool of the main room Gershom saw Helikaon sitting forward, elbows resting on his knees. He looked tired and troubled.

'Why do you not wish to see Odysseus?' asked Gershom, seating himself alongside the Dardanian king.

'I will see him, but I need time to prepare my thoughts.' Idly he rubbed at the healing wound beneath his arm. Then he leaned back. 'When Attalus was dying he spoke to me. It is a strange thing, Gershom, but I think his words were more poisonous than his blade.'

'How could that be?'

'He told me Odysseus paid to have my father murdered.'

The words hung in the air. Gershom knew little of Helikaon's past, save what the sailors had spoken of. A sad and lonely childhood, redeemed by two years with Odysseus on the *Penelope* and in Ithaka. Upon his return to Dardania his father had been murdered, and Helikaon had refused the crown, instead offering his support to his half-brother, the child Diomedes, and the boy's mother, the king's widow, Halysia.

Assassination was common enough, between rivals and enemies, but even Gershom, whose Egypteian heritage had involved little education in the ways of the sea peoples, knew that Ithaka was far distant from Dardania. There was no reason for enmity, and apparently no cause for Odysseus to desire the death of the Dardanian king. Where would be the profit in it?

'Attalus was lying,' he said, at last.

'I do not think so. That is why I need more time to prepare myself for a meeting.'

'What would Odysseus have gained from such an act? Was your father blocking his trade routes? Was there ill feeling from some act in the past?'

'I do not know. Perhaps when they were younger there was a feud.'

'Then you should ask Odysseus.'

Helikaon shook his head. 'Not as simple as that, my friend. I swore an oath on the altar of Ares that I would hunt down and kill the man responsible for my father's murder. If I ask Odysseus outright, and he admits it to be true, then I will have no alternative but to declare him my enemy and seek his death. I do not want that. Odysseus was more than my friend. Without him I would have been nothing.'

'You loved your father?'

'Yes – though he did not return that love. He was a hard, cold man and he saw in me a weakling who would never have the strength to rule.'

'Does anyone else know what Attalus told you?' asked Gershom.

'No.'

'Then let it go. A man who despised you died. A man who loved you lives. Surely even your gods would understand were you to renege on your oath.'

'They are not known for their understanding of mortal dilemmas,' said Helikaon.

'No,' agreed Gershom, 'they are more interested in disguising themselves as swans and bulls and suchlike and rutting with mortal men and women. Or feuding with one another like children. I have never heard of such an unruly bunch of immortals.'

Helikaon laughed. 'You obviously do not fear them.'

Gershom shook his head. 'When you have learned from childhood of the horrors of Set, and what he did to his brother, your gods seem no more worrisome than squabbling puppies.'

Filling a cup with water Helikaon drank. 'You make it sound so easy, Gershom. But it is not. I was raised to believe – as all our noble houses teach – that family and honour is everything. The unity of blood. It is what binds us together. An attack on one member of a family is an attack on all. Enemies, therefore, know that if they seek to harm any one of us the rest will descend on him with swords of fire. Such unity offers security. Honour demands vengeance on any who seek to come against us.'

'It seems to me,' said Gershom, 'that you sea people spend a great deal of time talking about honour, but strip away the high-sounding words and you are no different from any other race. Family? Has Priam not killed wayward sons? When a king dies do his sons not go to war on one another to succeed him? Men speak of how you reacted to your father's death. They say it was amazing, for you did not order your little brother's execution. Your race thrives on blood and death, Helikaon. Your ships raid the coasts of other nations, stealing slaves, burning and plundering. Warriors brag of how many men they have killed, and women they have raped. Almost all of your kings either seized their thrones with swords and murder, or are children of men who seized power with swords and murder. So put all this talk of honour to one side. The only fact I know about your father is that he sought to dispossess you, declaring your brother to be his heir. Odysseus, you tell me, helped make you a man and asked for nothing in return. Do you see any balance, any harmony, in killing your friend to avenge the murder of an enemy? For that is what your father was to you.'

Helikaon sat silently for a while. Then he looked at Gershom. 'What of your family?' he asked. 'You have never spoken of them. Would you forgive the man who killed your father?'

'I never knew my father,' said Gershom. 'He died before I was born. So I cannot answer your question. The fact is that you believed Attalus – Karpophorus, whatever his name was. If he *was* telling the truth then it could only be a part of it. Odysseus has the other part that can make it whole. You have to talk with him.'

Helikaon rubbed at his eyes. 'I need to rest, my friend,' he said, 'but I will think on all you have said.'

After Helikaon had taken to his bed Gershom left the

palace building. Two men were apparently loitering close to a well on the other side of the avenue. Gershom wandered over to them. Both were lean, and cold-eyed.

'Anything?' asked Gershom.

'Three came today,' answered the first man. 'They walked round the palace, staring at the windows. I followed them to the palace of Polites. They were Mykene.'

Gershom returned to the palace, moving through the lower levels and checking the locking bars on the shuttered windows. There was little point in such activity, he knew, for the shutter locks were flimsy, and not intended to prevent a determined intruder. A dagger blade would lift the locking bars with little difficulty.

Back in the main room Gershom lay back on a couch and closed his eyes. He had taken to sleeping in the afternoons, and then remaining awake and watchful through the night. He slept a little, but bad dreams haunted him.

He was awoken by a servant just before dusk, who told him that Prince Deiphobos had arrived to see King Aeneas.

Bleary-eyed, Gershom sent the servant to wake Helikaon and walked out to greet the slim, dark-haired young prince. Dios seemed troubled, but said nothing as they returned to the main room. Another servant brought a tray of food, and a pitcher of watered wine. Dios refused both and sat quietly.

When Helikaon entered Dios rose and embraced him warmly. 'You look better each day, my friend,' he said.

Gershom sat silently as the two men chatted, but

there was a tension in the air. Finally Dios said: 'Odysseus is to be declared an enemy of Troy.'

'What?' exclaimed Helikaon. 'Why would he be an enemy?'

Dios seemed surprised. 'For ordering the murder of your father, of course.'

All colour leeched from Helikaon's face. 'Priam ordered this?'

'Yes.'

'How could he know?'

'He came to see you when you were sick and delirious. You told him about Karpophorus.'

'I have no memory of it,' said Helikaon. 'And this is the worst news I have heard in a long time. Priam is about to make a terrible mistake and one he will come to regret, unless we can get him to change his mind.'

'On that day the sun will turn green,' said Dios. 'But I don't understand you, Helikaon. What mistake? Odysseus had your father killed.'

'Only according to Attalus,' replied Helikaon, desperation in his voice. 'We should at least give Odysseus the opportunity to deny it.'

'Hektor urged exactly that,' said Dios. 'Father would not listen. However, such thoughts are academic now. *You* believed the assassin, and *you* passed on that belief to Father. He will not be swayed, Helikaon. Honour demands vengeance, he said. Blood must avenge blood.'

Gershom needed to hear no more. Rising from his seat he left the two men alone, and wandered out into the fading light.

XXI

A queen of poison

HEKABE THE QUEEN FELT LIKE ONE OF THE GODS ALOFT ON Olympos as she gazed down upon the two bays far below. From her high vantage point at King's Joy she could see, to her right, the shallow Bay of Troy, its water brown and brackish, churned by ships still jostling for beach space. To her left was the deeper Bay of Herakles, the water here sparkling and blue. Even here there were scores of ships, the beaches being swiftly filled. Hekabe seldom smiled now, but the thought of all those angry ships' captains and flustered beachmasters brought a dry chuckle to her throat.

Pain, sharp and hot, began to seep through her belly and into her lower back. These days she thought of herself as a vessel, a vessel filled each day with fresh agony. With trembling fingers she reached for the medicine phial, running a sharp fingernail through the thin wax that sealed it. Once opened she lifted it to her dry lips, then paused. Not yet, she decided. For she could still see the ships in the bays, and the people swarming across the beaches. Once the opiates began their work those ships would become great monsters, the people merely magical insects flying and swooping across the line of her vision. Despite the temporary relief from pain Hekabe loathed these moments, when her mind was dulled and confused. Age and illness wrecking her body she could tolerate, but not this. Her fame had once been based on her beauty, but during these last twenty years she had become known, revered and feared for the power of her mind; her ability to outwit, outplan and outmanoeuvre the enemies of Troy. To see dangers almost before they arose, and nip them out like pricking weeds from a garden.

She sat very still and sought to detach her mind from the agony of the spreading cancer, allowing her thoughts to drift, back to her childhood, to her early glorious years with Priam, to her son's wedding in just a few days' time. Her work was almost complete and the prophecy about to be fulfilled. Once Andromache was pregnant Hekabe could die at last, the future of Troy secure.

The crocus-yellow canopy raised above her head to shade her from the bright morning sun gave everything a garish, violent hue. Hot knives began to pierce her belly, causing her to cry out. Taking a deep breath, she reluctantly lifted the phial to her lips and drank. The medicine was bitter, burning her tongue. Then the pain began to fade a little. When first she had been given these phials they had eliminated the suffering altogether. Now the cancer was stronger, and nothing could entirely mask its effects. She could hardly remember now a day without suffering.

From time to time slow figures crossed her vision. Sometimes they seemed to swim in the air. She had no idea who most of them were. People spoke to her but their voices were hollow and distant. She ignored them.

A figure moved across her, blocking the sun. Irritably she blinked and tried to focus. She started to speak, but her mouth was dry and crusty as an old sandal. The figure came closer, a hand extending a goblet to her. It was filled with cool water. Hekabe drank gratefully, the taste of the medicine washing away. Her vision cleared, and she saw the visitor was her new daughter, the flame-haired Andromache.

So like me, she thought, fierce and proud and full of life and vitality. She gazed fondly at the girl. 'Andromache,' she whispered. 'One of the few visitors I can tolerate.'

'How are you today, Mother?' asked the girl.

'Still dying. But, by Hera's will and my own strength, I am making Hades wait for me.' Hekabe took another sip from the goblet. It writhed in her hand, becoming a sharp-fanged serpent. Hekabe held fast to its throat. 'You will not bite me, viper,' she told it. 'I can still crush you.'

Andromache gently took the serpent from her. 'Be careful, girl,' warned the queen, 'its bite is deadly.' Then she saw it had become a goblet again, and relaxed. Andromache kissed the queen's dry cheek, then sat down beside her. Hekabe reached out and patted the girl's arm. 'So alike, you and I,' she said. 'Even more now.'

'Why now?' asked Andromache.

'My spies tell me Priam has taken you to his bed. I told you he would. Now you have experienced the joy that has been denied me for so long.'

'It was not joyous,' said Andromache. 'Merely necessary.'

Hekabe laughed. 'Not joyous? Priam has many faults but being a bad lover is not among them.'

'I do not wish to talk of it, Mother.'

'Soon you will be pregnant, and the child will ensure the future of Troy. The prophecy will be fulfilled. Another son for Priam,' the queen said with satisfaction. 'The people will love the boy because they will believe he is Hektor's son. They will call him Lord of the City.'

She looked assessingly at Andromache. 'Hmm. You are slender, like me. Childbirth is never easy for us, not like the big-hipped women of the countryside. You will suffer, girl, but you are strong. I bore Priam eight children. Each one of them I wrestled into the world with blood and pain. Each time I was victorious. Now look at me . . .'

Her voice drifted away and she sat in silence for a while. She saw the dark figures of gods stalking across the horizon. There were horses and bears walking with them, and a great horned creature she did not recognize. She could feel the vibrations of their footsteps tremble through her spine.

She leaned towards the girl, her voice low and insistent. 'The house of Priam will go on for a thousand years, and I played my part in that. I played my part well. I did what I had to do.' She nodded to herself, remembering that day nearly a year ago, the slender Paleste writhing in agony on the floor of the queen's apartments, her vomit staining the rugs, her screams muffled by an old shawl.

Her thoughts floated free and she returned to the days when she and her lord had sailed the Great Green. They had lived aboard ship, and her memories were sea-green, the taste of salt upon her lips. Young and in love, they visited verdant isles and cities of stone, meeting kings and pirates, sleeping in beds of ivory and gold, or on cold beaches under the stars. She tried to remember the name of the ship that carried them . . . but it was out of reach.

Unaccustomed sadness touched her.

'*Scamandrios*!' she said suddenly. 'That was it, *Scamandrios*.'

Andromache looked curious. 'Who was that, Mother?'

Hekabe shook her head, confusion fogging her mind again. 'I don't remember now. Perhaps he was a king. We met so many kings. They were like gods in those days. They are small and petty men now . . .

'Tell me of the Games,' she said, rallying, her mind fighting the dulling drugs. 'What is the gossip? Are these small kings killing each other yet? A good Games always ends with some deaths. A few minor thrones change hands. It is the way of the world. I hear the king of Thraki is dead already. Agamemnon's responsible for that, I have no doubt. Have you met Agamemnon? He's not the man his father was, they say.'

'The Games have barely started,' said Andromache. 'I have not heard much gossip. Although,' she said, smiling a little, 'I heard Odysseus lost the archery tourney. He was not allowed to use his own great bow and the one he was given broke. He was said to be very angry.'

Hekabe felt a surge of anger in her frail breast. 'Odysseus,' she said malevolently. 'He will not see Ithaka again. I will see to that.'

'What do you mean?'

'Hah! Odysseus the Tale Spinner. Odysseus the buffoon. That is how people see him these days. But I know him of old. He is a cold killer. He paid an assassin to murder Anchises. Blood kin to Priam.'

'How can you know this?' The girl's face looked sickly under the yellow awning. 'Not Odysseus.'

'The assassin, the same one who wounded Helikaon, told Helikaon so with his dying breath. And Helikaon himself told Priam.'

'It is nonsense,' said Andromache. 'What would Odysseus have gained from such an act?'

Hekabe leaned back in her chair. 'That is what Priam wonders. All his advisers are mystified. They talk of ancient feuds, and trade agreements. Stupid men! The answer is there for any with the wit to see it. Odysseus loves Helikaon. Perhaps the boy was his catamite. Who knows? Anchises loathed the boy and dispossessed him. I knew Anchises. He was a sound ruler and a man with no sentiment. It was probable he would have had Helikaon quietly murdered. Odysseus is wily, and he would have guessed this. So, to save the boy, he had the father slain.'

'He did it to save Helikaon's life?'

'Of course.'

'Why should that make him an enemy of Troy?' asked Andromache. 'Helikaon is our friend, and, if you are right, Odysseus saved him.'

'I care nothing about the murder of Anchises,' answered Hekabe. 'Neither does Priam. But before this war begins we must be sure of our friends, and eliminate all possible outside threats. Odysseus' part in the death of Anchises has given us the opportunity to kill him, without alienating our allies.'

'I do not understand,' whispered Andromache, obviously mystified. 'Odysseus is neutral. Why would he be a threat?'

Hekabe sighed. 'You have much to learn, child, about the nature of politics. It is not about what Odysseus is *now*. It is the danger he represents for the future. If his lands were closer to Troy we could bind him to us with gold and with friendship. But he is a western king, with close links to the Mykene. And, yes, there is a small chance that he would remain neutral. But we cannot risk the future of Troy on a small chance. The truth is that once the war became inevitable Odysseus had to die. Agamemnon is a man of battles, and will be a worthy foe, but we can defeat him. But Odysseus is crafty and a planner. More than this he is a charismatic leader, and where he leads other kings will follow. We cannot risk him joining with Agamemnon.'

'Then you always intended to murder Odysseus?' said Andromache.

'Of course. I have invited him to attend me here this eve. He will suspect nothing of a dying old woman. They say the Ugly King is cunning, but he has never dealt with Hekabe. He will leave King's Joy alive – and then sicken and die back in his bed. Stay with me, Andromache. You can chat and laugh with him, and put him at his ease. He will be here soon.'

She nodded her head again in satisfaction, thinking of the poison phial which had long been her servant and friend. 'Rulers are never short of enemies, Andromache,' she said. 'We must be ruthless in order to survive. Kill them all. Tonight Odysseus will die, and tomorrow I will have fat Antiphones here. Priam is a fool to have forgiven him for his treachery. A man who betrays you once will do so again, when the time suits him.'

Hekabe's mouth was dry once more and her goblet empty. 'Andromache, fill my water goblet. I don't know where the servants are.'

The girl was gone for some time. Hekabe dozed in the sunlight. She awoke suddenly with Andromache beside her again. Her daughter carefully poured a small phial of medicine into the goblet, added water, then handed it to her. The queen drank gratefully. The bitter taste of the medicine was sharp upon the tongue, and there was an unaccustomed aftertaste that Hekabe could not identify. She sat in silence, as the medicine began to dull the agonies. After a while, miraculously, all traces of pain vanished. She felt free for the first time in months.

'This medicine is new,' she said, her mind beginning to clear.

'Machaon gave it to Laodike last autumn,' said Andromache. 'Is your pain gone now?'

'It is. I almost feel I could dance.' Hekabe smiled. 'It is a beautiful day, don't you think?'

'I am with child,' said Andromache calmly. 'And the father is not Priam.'

Hekabe frowned. 'Not Priam?'

'The father of my child is Helikaon. Now tell me about Paleste.'

Hekabe's eyes narrowed. Was the girl insane? When Priam found out about her deceit he would be furious. 'Foolish girl,' she hissed. 'You have doomed Helikaon and the child. Priam will have them killed. If you are lucky he will keep you alive to fulfil the prophecy. I thought you were sharper than your sister. It seems Ektion's daughters are as stupid as each other.'

Andromache knelt by the old woman's side. 'You do not understand, Hekabe. I slept with Priam so he would think this child is his. The king will never know. Now tell me how you killed Paleste.'

Hekabe saw again the image of the agonized child, and her lip curled. 'She was a mistake, a stupid mistake by the fool Heraklitos. She was nothing. The future of Troy's family was all that mattered. It must be protected. Paleste was nothing,' she repeated.

Andromache sat back on her haunches and looked at her for a moment. Hekabe thought there were tears in her eyes, but her own vision had misted. She looked around her feebly.

'Where is Paris?' she asked.

'Gone with Helen to watch the Games.'

'There are no servants. Where are the servants?'

'I told them to leave us alone.'

Andromache stood up and dusted down her gown, as if preparing to leave. The phial she had left on the table she dropped into a pouch at her side.

Then, like sunlight piercing the mists of morning, Hekabe's mind finally cleared. Medicine given to Laodike months ago. Strong medicine. Why had she not been offered it before? Understanding swept through her. It was meant to have been the gift of release, when the pain became unbearable. She knew then what the aftertaste had been. Hemlock! Hekabe rested her hand on her skinny thigh and pressed the flesh. She could feel nothing. Death was creeping along her veins. She sighed.

'Do not think me a fool for being so tricked, Andromache,' she said. 'It was the medicine that made me stupid. Ah well, you have avenged your sister, and that is honourable. I would have done the same in your place. You see, I was right. We are very alike.' She looked into Andromache's green eyes and saw a flash of anger there.

'If I believed that to be true, Hekabe, I would have taken the poison myself. This is not for Paleste, though perhaps it should have been, for she was sweet and kind and loving, and deserved better than to be drawn into your world of deceit, treachery and murder. This is for Odysseus, a fine man, good and proud, and for Antiphones, who is my friend, and for who knows how many other innocents your evil would seek to destroy.'

'Innocents?' replied Hekabe, her voice rich with

contempt. 'On the mountains of ambition there are no innocents. You think Priam would still be king if I had viewed the world through such naïve eyes? You think Troy would have survived against the avarice of powerful kings had I not dealt with them, bribed them, seduced them, befriended them, and killed them? You want to live among the *innocents*, Andromache, among the sheep? Yes, in every peasant village they will live their loving lives, among true friends, and they will sing and dance together on feast days, and weep when their friends and loved ones die. Sweet little sheep. Brings a tear to my eye. We are not sheep, stupid girl! We are lions. We are wolves. We devour the sheep and we rend and tear at each other. Just as you have done – and will do again when needs must.'

'You are wrong, Hekabe,' Andromache told her. 'I may be stupid, as you say, to believe in honour and friendship and loyalty without price. But these are virtues to be cherished, for without them we are no more than beasts roaming the land.'

'Yet you pretended to befriend me,' said Hekabe, her mind beginning to swim. 'You lied and you cheated your way into my favour. Is this honour?'

'I did not pretend, Mother,' she heard Andromache say, her voice breaking. 'I have liked you from the moment we met, and I admire your strength and your courage. May the gods grant you rest and peace.'

'Rest and peace! You foolish, foolish girl. If Odysseus lives then Troy will face ruin.' Hekabe fell back into her chair, her eyes staring up at the blue of the sky. Her thoughts were of plans wrecked on the shores of other people's weakness and error. And then she found herself once more upon the deck of the *Scamandrios*, and up ahead she could see a golden figure, shining with a dazzling light. She thought it must be Priam, and her joy soared. 'Where do we sail today, my lord?' she whispered.

XXII

The Sacker of Cities

A FULL DAY OF MOURNING WAS DECLARED BY PRIAM. ALL
contests ceased, and even the market traders were
refused permission to sell their wares. A hundred bulls,
60 goats and 200 sheep were sacrificed to Hades, Lord
of the Underworld, the meat then hauled off to feed the
thousands thronging the hillsides around the city.
Hekabe's body was carried back into the palace,
wrapped in robes of gold, and there laid in state in the
queen's apartments.

The High Priest of the temple of Zeus maintained
that even the heavens wept, for dark clouds gathered,
rain pouring down for most of the day.

Some priests whispered that the death of the queen
was an ill omen for the wedding of her son, but these
views were not widely spoken.

In the palace of Polites the Mykene king,
Agamemnon, struggled to conceal his delight at the
news. Hekabe was a fearsome opponent, whose agents

had caused the deaths of a number of Mykene spies. In the past her counsel had checked many of Priam's more rash decisions. Without her Priam was weakened and Agamemnon's invasion plans could move ahead more smoothly.

The doors in the main room had been closed and guarded for most of the afternoon, and the words spoken here could not be overheard. The gathered kings had talked of logistics and supply, the movements of armies, and the defences of the city.

Agamemnon listened as they spoke, offering little. He knew how the war should be fought, and most of his plans were already moving forward in secret. There was, however, no harm in letting others put forward ideas, thus allowing them to believe they were more important to the project than was the actuality. Idomeneos had spoken at length, as had Peleus.

Odysseus had said little, nor offered any objections to the wilder ideas of Idomeneos. Still, even if Odysseus was more the storyteller than the strategist, at least he had drawn the others in, and more would follow. There were now 16 rulers pledged to the war, with 470 ships and close to 60,000 fighting men. Agamemnon glanced at Idomeneos. There was still a chance the Kretan king would draw back at the last, bribed by Priam's gold. Idomeneos would always be for sale to the highest bidder. It was the nature of the man, bred as he was from peasants. Agamemnon transferred his gaze to the elderly Nestor. He was not of peasant stock, yet his mind also sang with the music of commerce. The war would cost him in trade goods and gold. But he would join with them – especially now that Odysseus had declared himself.

What a boon that had been. The Ugly King, accompanied by five bodyguards, had arrived at the palace yesterday evening. Agamemnon had invited him in, and the two men had walked through to a small side room.

'I cannot stay this evening,' said Odysseus. 'There are matters I must attend to. I came merely to tell you that Ithaka, with fifty ships and two thousand men, will be available to you, Agamemnon.'

Agamemnon had stood silent a moment, looking into his eyes. Then he said, 'That is good to hear – though, I must say, I am surprised.'

'We will talk more,' said Odysseus grimly. 'Do you have plans for tomorrow eve?'

'None that cannot be changed.'

'Then I shall come here, with Idomeneos and Nestor.'

'They are also with us?'

'They will be.'

Agamemnon had thrust out his hand. 'I bid you welcome, Ithaka,' he said. 'You are a brother now to the Mykene. Your troubles are our troubles, your dreams our dreams.'

Odysseus took his hand. The grip was strong. 'I am grateful, Mykene,' he replied, solemnly. 'With this bonding of hands your enemies become our enemies, your friends our friends.'

Inside the main room now the king of Thessaly was drunk, his head lolling back on his chair. 'Farewell to the old witch,' he said, raising his cup.

'Do not gloat, my friend,' said Agamemnon. 'Even in

the midst of enmity we should feel some sympathy for Priam, for it was said he had great love for her.'

'A pox on sympathy,' muttered Peleus. 'The old hag outlived her time.'

'We all do,' said Odysseus. 'Some sooner than others.'

Peleus sat up in his chair, his bleary eyes on the Ithakan king. 'What does that mean?' he snarled.

'Did it seem I was speaking in some obscure Hittite dialect?' countered Odysseus, his tone bored.

Peleus observed him malevolently. 'I never liked you, Odysseus,' he said.

'Hardly surprising. You've never liked anyone this side of puberty.'

Peleus surged out of his chair, scrabbling for his dagger. Agamemnon moved with speed to stand between the men. 'Now that is enough, my friend,' he said, grasping Peleus by the wrist. 'It is not necessary for us to like one another. There is a common enemy who requires our focus.' He felt Peleus relax, and sensed the man was grateful to have been blocked. The Mykene king turned to Odysseus. 'Your mood has been foul all evening. Walk with me in the garden. The air will clear your mind.'

Pushing open the doors as he spoke, Agamemnon strolled out into the cool of the evening. The Ugly King followed him. The guards moved back out of earshot.

'Are you still torn, Odysseus?' asked Agamemnon softly.

'Emotions are complex beasts. I loathe Peleus. I like Hektor and Helikaon. Now Peleus is my ally and my two friends are my foes. Of course I am torn. But my course is set, my sail rigged. They have declared me an enemy of Troy, and now they will discover what that means.'

Agamemnon nodded. 'You speak of Helikaon. Tonight my men will kill him.' It was a lie, but Agamemnon needed to see his reaction.

Odysseus laughed. 'I think you will try at some time,' he said. 'It is a sensible plan. Helikaon is a fine fighter, a good general and a brilliant sailor. But it will not be tonight.'

'Not tonight? Why?'

'Two reasons. One, you are unsure of me, Agamemnon. I could leave here and warn the boy. That might mean your men taken alive, and implicating you. Or, if they succeeded, I could go to Priam with information about your plot and you would be dragged to justice for breaking the truce. Priam's gratitude might then extend to putting aside his enmity and declaring me a friend once more.'

Agamemnon nodded. 'You have a sharp mind, Odysseus.'

'Yes, I do.' He looked at Agamemnon and sighed. 'I would tell you to put your fears aside concerning me, but it is not in your nature. So I will continue to speak frankly until you realize that my alliance is a true one. I hope Helikaon survives. Yet in order for us to succeed in this venture Dardania must be in turmoil. Only then can your troops cross the Hellespont from Thraki and invade to the north of Troy.'

Agamemnon blinked and felt shock flow through

him with needles of ice. No-one knew of his troops'
moving into Thraki. If it was discovered before the end
of the Games he would never leave Troy alive.

'I don't know of what you speak,' he managed to say.

'Let us play no games, Agamemnon. Troy cannot be
taken by frontal assault. You could camp an army
across the Scamander, as Idomeneos suggests, and the
roads north and east would remain open, supplies and
mercenaries flowing in. To fully surround Troy you
would need a hundred times more soldiers than any of
us possess. The feeding of such a multitude would
require thousands of wagons, and, more important,
farmlands and stock, and slaves to gather crops. An
army of that size would denude the land all the way to
the horizon, and cause consternation in the Hittite
capital. Being huge it would be difficult to manage, and
slow to respond to threat. Troy's allies would attack its
flanks, severing its supply routes. Hektor and the
Trojan Horse would sally out from the city, striking like
lightning, then fleeing back behind the walls. Within a
season our treasuries would be bare, our armies
demoralized. Then what if the Hittites won their own
civil war, freeing their forces to come to the aid of
Troy?

'No, Agamemnon, there is only one way to take this
city. It needs to be slowly squeezed from above and
below, with the sea routes blocked. North is Dardania,
south Thebe Under Plakos. Dardanos guards the
Hellespont, and across the narrow straits there is
Thraki – an ally of Troy. So, first you must take Thraki,
and hold it, preparing it to be a supply base for our

troops. Only then can an invasion force cross the Hellespont into Dardania, and continue to be resupplied. In the south it will be more simple. Troops and supplies can be shipped from Kos, Rhodos and Miletos. Then Thebe Under Plakos can be taken, closing off the routes through the Ida Mountains, and preventing the coming of reinforcements from the Fat King, Kygones, in Lykia, and others friendly to Troy.'

Agamemon looked at Odysseus as if seeing him for the first time. The broad face, which had seemed so jovial, was now hard, the eyes glittering. Power radiated from him. 'Your words are fascinating,' said Agamemnon, playing for time. 'Do go on.'

Odysseus laughed. 'Fascinating they may be, but you already know all that I am about to say. For you understand strategy as well as any man alive. This is not a city to be raided and sacked in the course of a few days, or even a few seasons. But it cannot take too long. We both know that.'

'And why would that be?'

'The gold, Agamemnon. Priam's mighty coffers. He will need gold to hire mercenaries, to buy allies. If we block his trade his income will wither, and slowly his treasury will be sucked dry. I do not want to fight my way into a ruined city in ten years' time to find it barren. Do you?'

Agamemnon said nothing for a while. Then he signalled to a guard to bring them some wine. As they drank he said, 'I have misjudged you, Odysseus. For that I apologize. I saw only the genial storyteller. Now I truly understand why you were once called the Sacker of Cities. All that you say is true.' He paused. 'Tell me, what do you know of the Shield of Thunder?'

Now it was Odysseus' turn to be surprised. 'Athene's shield? What of it?'

Agamemnon watched him closely, but Odysseus obviously knew nothing. 'One of my priests suggested we make sacrifice to Athene, and ask for the Shield of Thunder to protect our efforts. I wondered if you'd heard any tales concerning it.'

Odysseus shrugged. 'Only what every child is taught. The shield was given to Athene by Hephaistos, which angered Ares, for he desired it. Ares was so enraged he smashed Hephaistos' foot with a club. But I have never heard of anyone calling for protection from the Shield before. Still, why not? Sacking this citadel will require all the help we can get. Worth a few bulls at least.'

Later, when his guests had gone, Agamemnon climbed to the roof of the palace, and seated himself in a wide, wicker chair beneath the stars. His thoughts roamed over the events of the past few days, re-examining them. Time and again, though, he returned to the conversation two nights before, when the Trojan prince Antiphones had joined them for supper. The fat man had been dazzled by the splendour of Achilles and sat staring at him as if moonstruck. Much wine had flowed, and Antiphones, eager to entertain Achilles, had told many amusing stories. As Agamemnon had instructed, Achilles flattered the Trojan prince, hanging upon his every word, laughing at his jests. Nevertheless they had learned little, even with Antiphones drunk, until Achilles had talked admiringly about Troy and its wonders.

'It is a great city,' said Antiphones. 'Immortal soon.'

'How will it be immortal, my friend?' Achilles asked him, as Agamemnon sat quietly back in the shadows.

'There is a prophecy. Priam and Hekabe believe it, and many seers have declared it to be true.' And then he had quoted a verse: *'Beneath the Shield of Thunder waits the Eagle Child, on shadow wings, to soar above all city gates, till end of days, and fall of kings.'*

'Interesting,' said Achilles. 'And what does it mean, this doggerel verse?'

'Ah!' said Antiphones, tapping his nose. 'Secret. Hekabe's secret. I shouldn't know it, really. But sweet Andromache told me.' He chuckled, then drained his cup. 'A fine girl. She'll ... be a splendid wife for ... Hektor.'

'I heard she killed an assassin as he was about to murder Priam King?' put in Agamemnon, softly.

'Shot him through the heart,' said Antiphones. 'Stunning girl! Deadly with the bow. She is my friend, you know. Sweet Shield of Thunder.' His face had fallen then, and he had wiped his fat hand across his mouth, as if pushing back the words. Then he had heaved himself to his feet. 'Need to ... go now,' he said. At a signal from Agamemnon Achilles helped Antiphones from the palace, and walked him back to his own apartments.

Agamemnon had sent for his advisers and questioned them about the prophecy. None had heard of it. For most of the following day the words had continued to haunt him. Messages were sent out to Mykene spies and informers to gather all information on Andromache. Finally they located a merchant who had once been based in Thebe Under Plakos, and knew something of the royal family there. He told the story of the child born with a curious birthmark upon her skull, round like a shield, with lightning through the centre.

So, then, Andromache was the Shield of Thunder, and the Eagle Child who would soar above all city gates would be her son, by the Prince Hektor. Priam and Hekabe were setting great store by this prophecy. It was obviously false, for all true followers of the gods knew that the Shield of Thunder sported a snake, and not the lightning bolt these eastern kingdoms believed. Even so, *they* believed in the prophecy.

Whether it was true or merely wishful thinking made little difference. Agamemnon knew that such a belief would stiffen the resolve of Priam when the war came. It followed, therefore, that if the woman of the prophecy were to die, then great would be the grief and despair that followed her death. It would also show to Troy, its citizens, and the world that Priam could not protect his own. The Games and the wedding celebrations would turn to ash and the coming war would fall upon a people cowed by disaster and tragedy. It was perfect.

Sitting on the rooftop he made a decision, and summoned Kleitos to him. The tall warrior came immediately.

'Pull all men back from the Palace of Stone Horses. We will not attack Helikaon.'

'But, lord, we are almost set.'

'No, the time is not right. Instead have the woman

Andromache followed. Find out if she sleeps in the king's palace, or in Hektor's. How many guards attend her? Does she wander in the marketplaces, where a stray dagger can cut her down? I want to know everything, Kleitos. Everything.'

Back in the great courtyard of Hektor's palace, where the crew of the *Penelope* had made their camp, the mood was sombre. Bias, though through to the final of the javelin, could scarcely lift his arm, and there was a tingling in his fingertips that did not bode well. Leukon was nursing a swelling on his cheek and a small cut over his right eye. His left fist was also bruised and swollen, all these wounds coming from a gruelling victory over the Mykene champion, a tough and durable fighter with a head made of rock. Leukon's hopes of becoming champion in the boxing contest were shrinking fast – especially as he had watched Achilles demolish opponents with gruesome ease. Kalliades had lost in the short race, taking an elbow in the face from a canny sprinter from Kretos, who had gone on to win. And even the usually cheerful Banokles was downcast, having lost in a savage bout the previous afternoon.

'Could have sworn I had him with that uppercut,' Banokles told Kalliades, as they sat in the moonlight. 'Big Red said she thought I was unlucky.'

'It was a tight contest,' agreed Kalliades. 'However, look on the cheerful side – had you won we would have been once more bereft of wealth. As it is we have fifteen gold rings, thirty-eight silver, and a handful of copper.'

383

'Not sure about *that* at all,' said Banokles. 'You bet against me.'

'We agreed to follow Leukon's advice,' said Kalliades wearily. 'He would tell me when you were facing an opponent you couldn't beat. And I would wager on him.'

'Doesn't feel right,' grumbled Banokles. 'You might have told me.'

'If I had told you what would you have done?'

'*I'd* have bet on him.'

'And that would certainly not have been right. Anyway, did you really want to come up against Achilles? That's who your opponent faces in tomorrow's semi-final. As it is we have wealth, a roof over our heads, and you have no broken bones.'

Leukon strolled over to them, bearing a jug of wine and filling Banokles' cup. 'A few more weeks of training on your footwork and you would have had him, my friend,' he said, slumping down beside the bruised warrior. 'You kept walking into that looping left.'

'Felt like being struck by an avalanche,' said Banokles. 'Looking forward to seeing Achilles taking a few of those blows. Wipe the smug smile off his face.'

Leukon shook his head. 'Achilles will finish him in a few heartbeats,' he said, gloomily. 'And that looping left won't touch him. Never seen a big man move so fast.'

'You'll beat him in the final,' said Banokles. Leukon did not reply, and the three men sat quietly, drinking their wine.

Odysseus, with his five bodyguards in tow, came

through the gates and crossed the courtyard without speaking to anyone.

'I'm going to visit Red,' said Banokles. 'Hand me a few of those silver rings, Kalliades.'

Kalliades opened the bulging pouch at his side and pulled out several rings, which he dropped into Banokles' outstretched palm. 'Not like you to offer your favours to only one woman,' he observed.

'Never was a woman like Red,' replied Banokles happily, draining the last of his wine and setting off for the gates.

They watched him go, and then Kalliades turned to Leukon. 'Banokles is a man without cares. Unlike you, it seems.'

Leukon said nothing for a while, and the two men sat in silence. Finally the blond sailor spoke, his voice almost a whisper. 'Achilles has no weaknesses. He has speed, strength and enormous stamina. And he can take a punch. I saw him demolish an opponent yesterday. I fought the same man last summer. Took me an afternoon to wear him down. Achilles finished him in less time than it takes to drink a cup of wine. The truth is I do not have the skill to take him, and that is hard for me to admit.' Filling his cup, he drank deeply. Kalliades clapped him on the shoulder.

'Cheer up, my friend. With luck you won't win the semi-final and your opponent will have to face Achilles.'

'Why would I not win the semi-final? I have fought the man three times. I have the measure of him.'

'I was jesting.'

'Leukon is not the man to jest with,' said Odysseus, joining them. 'How is the fist?' he asked the big fighter.

'The extra day's rest will help, as will the strapping for the fight.' Leukon glanced across the courtyard to where Bias was rubbing olive oil into his shoulder. 'The same cannot be said for Bias. His shoulder is aflame, and swollen badly.'

'I will speak to him later,' said Odysseus, 'but now you and I need to talk. Come with me.'

Kalliades watched the Ugly King and the fighter move into the palace, then strolled across to where Bias was kneading his injured muscles. 'Here, let me,' he said, taking the phial of oil and pouring it into his palms.

'Thank you,' said Bias. 'Can't reach the point by the shoulder blade.'

Bias's skin felt hot to the touch, the muscles round the shoulder inflamed and swollen. Gently Kalliades kneaded them, easing out knots and adhesions. 'I saw Banokles heading out,' said Bias. 'Gone whoring again?'

Kalliades chuckled. 'It is what he does best.'

'That's what I miss about youth,' said Bias. 'That and the fact I could throw a damned javelin without ripping every muscle in my back.'

'Even so only three men outthrew you.'

'They'll *all* outthrow me tomorrow.'

'Perhaps not,' said Kalliades. 'We'll soak some cloths in cold water and take some of the heat from those muscles.'

Later, as the two men sat in the cool of the night, Bias

asked: 'Have you thought what you'll do when the Games are over?'

'Head south, probably. Down to Thebe Under Plakos, and then perhaps on to Lykia. Join a mercenary regiment.'

'Will you be taking the girl with you?'

'No. She will be staying in Troy with a friend.'

There was no-one close by, but even so the black man leaned in close, dropping his voice. 'She may not be welcomed by this friend. You know that?'

'They are more than just friends,' answered Kalliades.

'I know that, lad. The crew do not know who Piria is, but Odysseus tells me that you do. The temple on Thera was built with Trojan gold. Priam is its patron. You think he will allow a runaway to live free in Troy? As long as she is here she will be a danger to any who give her shelter.'

'What are you suggesting, Bias?'

'I know you are fond of her. Take her with you. Far from the city, where she will never be recognized.'

Kalliades looked into the black man's broad face. 'And this concern is purely for Piria?'

'No, lad. It is for me, and the other lads on the *Penelope*. If she's captured in Troy and questioned, then we will be implicated. I have no wish to be burned alive.'

Kalliades fell silent. In his recent conversations with Piria she had spoken of Andromache with enthusiasm and love, her face shining with happiness and anticipation. What would be the effect if she was rejected by her? Or worse, if Hektor's guards took her into custody? The thought of such an outcome left him sick with fear. She had great courage, but her personality was fragile. How many more betrayals could she take?

'She will not be captured,' he said at last. 'I will keep her safe.'

XXIII

A gathering of wolves

PRIAM SAT ALONE IN THE QUEEN'S APARTMENTS, THE shrouded body of Hekabe laid out on a bier at the centre of the main room. The scent of heavy perfumes rose from the linen, masking the stench of death. Priam could not approach the body. He sat on the far side of the room, a half-empty wine cup in his hand. As was the funeral custom of the house of Ilos, his white tunic was rent at the shoulder, and grey ash had been rubbed into the right sleeve, and also sprinkled over his hair.

Priam drank the last of the wine. He was aware of the presence of Hekabe in the room, standing there, staring down at him. He could feel her disapproval.

'I should have come to you,' he whispered. 'I know that. But I could not. It was more than I could bear. You understand that, Hekabe. I know you do. You were once the most beautiful of women. I wanted to remember you that way, and not as some cancer-eaten hag, all yellow skin and gleaming bone.'

He gave a furtive glance towards the body, and closed his eyes, seeing again the glorious days of youth, when it seemed they were both immortal. He recalled when these apartments had been finished, and he and Hekabe had stood on the balcony, looking out over the city. She had been pregnant then, with Hektor. 'There is nothing we cannot do, Priam,' she had told him. 'We are the mighty!'

'We *were* the mighty,' he said aloud. 'But now you are gone from me, and the wolves are gathering. They are all in the *megaron* below, waiting for your funeral feast. They will come to me, offering their condolences, their fine wishes. They will stare at me through hooded eyes, and they will sense my weakness. Agamemnon will be jubilant. The ghastly Peleus, the greedy Idomeneos, the wily Nestor, and the cunning Odysseus.' He rose and walked back and forth, not looking at the shrouded body. He gazed into the depths of the empty wine cup, then hurled it against the wall. 'Where are you now that I need you?' he shouted. Then he sagged back to his chair. An image flickered into his mind, of Andromache disrobing before him, turning her back to him as the gown fell to the floor. He saw himself stepping forward, his hands sliding over the soft skin. The same image had been haunting him for days now. He woke to it, walked with it, fell asleep to it.

'My mind is clouded, Hekabe,' he said, trying to push it away. 'I took Andromache to my bed, as you knew I would. I thought that would end the constant need for her. It did not. It fired my blood in a way I

390

have not known since . . . since you and I were young. Is that what you hoped for? Was this your gift to me? She is so like you, my love. I see you in her eyes, hear you in her voice.' He fell silent, then staggered across the room to where the wine jug stood on a small table. Hefting it he drank deeply, red liquid swilling over his cheeks and dripping to his tunic. 'Now she will not come to me. She reminds me of the agreement we made. Once in every rising moon. She reminds *me*! Am I not the king? Is it not for me to make, or break, agreements?' He rubbed at his eyes. 'No, I cannot think of her now. I must consider the wolves. They are becoming a pack, and I must break it, separate them. I can bribe Idomeneos, and some of the smaller petty chieftains. Nestor may still be reasoned with. The rest I must find a way to intimidate. And Odysseus must die.'

He heard the door and swung round to see his son, fat Antiphones, enter quietly. 'What's the matter with you?' he shouted. 'Can't you see I am talking to your mother?'

'I can, Father, as can others, but I fear *she* cannot hear you.'

Priam swung towards the body, lost his balance and began to fall. Antiphones grabbed him, hauling him upright, then half carried him to a couch. 'Get me wine,' ordered the king.

Antiphones shook his head. 'You have enemies coming to your hall. This is not a time for such maudlin behaviour. I will fetch you water, and you will drink it and piss away this weakness. Then you will come down to your guests as the mighty king of Troy, and not as a drunken sot bleating for his poor dead wife.'

The words cut through Priam's grief, and his hand snaked out, grabbing Antiphones by the tunic and dragging him across the couch. 'You dare speak to me in this way? By thunder, I'll have your tongue ripped out!'

'And *that* is the Priam we need to see now,' said Antiphones softly.

Priam blinked, his anger fading. Drawing in a deep breath, he released Antiphones. His son was right. The room began to swim and he leaned back into the couch.

'Fetch water,' he mumbled.

Antiphones took hold of his arm. 'Let us get out to the balcony. The air will help clear your head.'

Priam managed to stand, and, supported by his son, staggered out into the moonlight. Once there he leaned over the balcony rail and vomited. His head began to pound, but he felt the effects of the wine weakening. Antiphones brought him a jug of water, which he forced himself to drink. After a while he took a deep breath and pushed himself upright. 'I am myself again,' he said. 'Now let us walk among the wolves.'

The kings of west and east sat at the great table in Priam's *megaron*, beneath flickering torches, in the shadows of gilded statues of Trojan heroes. Servants bearing golden trays on which stood golden cups brimming with wine moved along the huge, horseshoe-shaped table. Priam had still not appeared, and the kings were growing restive. The Athenian king, Menestheos, was the first to complain. The stocky, red-bearded Athenian had a notoriously quick temper. 'How much longer will he keep us waiting?' he growled. 'This is intolerable!'

'Be calm, my friend,' said Agamemnon, from across the table. 'The man is in despair, and not thinking clearly. He does not intend to insult us, I am sure. In his grief he has merely forgotten his manners.'

Alongside him the golden-haired Hektor reddened. 'I thank you for your courtesy, Agamemnon,' he said coldly, 'but my father needs no-one to apologize for him.'

Odysseus was sitting quietly, close to the great doors. He had no wish to be at this feast, and had felt no affection for the queen. She was, he knew, a poisonous mixture: the smile of a siren, the eyes of a leopard, and the heart of a snake. Odysseus did not mourn her passing, nor had he any desire to offer platitudes to Priam. However, courtesy dictated he be here for the oration. So, he would listen politely as the High Priest of Athene extolled the queen's countless virtues, and watch as they sliced the throats of seven white doves, which would then, so fools believed, fly to distant Olympos and regale the gods with the story of Hekabe's life. What kind of gods would not already know of Hekabe's life, and all the deceits and treacheries that stained it? Such a stupid ritual, thought Odysseus.

A servant placed a golden goblet before Odysseus, but he ignored it. He glanced along the table, to where Helikaon sat, between Agapenor, the young king of Arcadia, and Ektion, the middle-aged king of Thebe Under Plakos, father to Andromache. Helikaon did not once look in Odysseus' direction.

The doors at the far end of the *megaron* opened, and six Royal Eagles entered, clad in armour of bronze and silver, with white cloaks and white-crested helms. Stepping aside, they clashed their spears on their round shields, announcing the arrival of King Priam.

He entered followed by his large son, Antiphones. Odysseus watched the king with a cold gaze. Priam was still tall and broad-shouldered, but age sat upon him like a crow, picking at his strength. His face was flushed, and he had obviously been drinking heavily. Even so, he walked steadily to his place at the head of the horseshoe table and sat without a word to his guests. Then he gestured for the priest to begin the oration.

The man was tall and spindly, and younger than most high priests. Probably another bastard son of Priam's, thought Odysseus. But his voice was rich and deep, and he spoke movingly of the life of Hekabe. He told of her strength and her loyalty, and her love for Troy. He spoke of her sons, and her pride in the achievements of her hero-son, Hektor. The performance was excellent, and when he had concluded, the kings hammered their hands upon the table in appreciation. Then Priam heaved himself to his feet.

'I thank you for coming tonight,' he told his guests. 'Many here have been friends of Troy for longer than my life. Others may become friends. That is my hope. We all of us here have been men of war. Sometimes it has been forced upon us. Sometimes we have sallied out to engage in it, in pursuit of glory or riches. War is a noble pursuit, and oft-times necessary, to right wrongs against our houses, or to deal a death blow to those who would wish the same upon us. Tonight, however, we dine as friends, and mourn the passing of beauty. Eat and drink, my friends, and enjoy the entertainments my sons have organized. We have dancers from Kretos, jugglers from Miletos, singers and musicians. This night should be one of joy, in thanks for a life that meant much to me.' Priam clapped his hands, and music began. Servants rushed forward, placing golden platters brimming with food upon the table.

Odysseus ate sparingly, and once the meal was over, and the entertainments had begun, he stood from the table and made his way towards the door. He was surprised to hear Priam call out, 'Leaving us so soon, king of Ithaka? No words of commiseration?' As the king spoke the music died away. Odysseus turned slowly into the silence.

'What would you have me say, Priam King? That I am sorry for your loss? I am sorry for any man who loses one he loves. But I'll offer no honeyed words to you. Honour and custom dictated I be here tonight. Honour and custom dictate I will attend the Games tomorrow. Then I will sail from here, without a backward glance.'

'You will sail from here as an enemy of Troy!' thundered Priam. 'As a hirer of assassins, and an oath breaker. And when we meet thereafter be sure to have a weapon in your hand.'

'I will indeed,' replied Odysseus angrily. 'And it will be Akilina, and not some ruined twig your lickspittle judges place before me. I had no desire for a war with Troy. You remember that, Priam. You remember that when your sons die and your influence shrivels. You remember that when the flames consume your palace. '

'I feel my bones trembling,' sneered Priam. 'Little Ithaka against the might of Troy. You have a weapon to throw down my walls? You have an army to defeat the Trojan Horse? No, you do not! Not you, nor a hundred like you gathered together, would make more than a fleabite on the body of Troy. A hundred thousand men could not take this city. You have a hundred thousand, little king?'

In that moment Odysseus realized Priam had engineered this clash in order to make exactly this point to the assembled kings. He stood silently for a moment, then laughed. 'I want you to remember that boast too, Priam,' he said. 'I want all the men here to repeat it across the Great Green. Not I, nor a hundred like me gathered together, would make more than a fleabite on the body of Troy. Let the valleys echo to that boast. Let the mountains ring with it. Let the seas whisper it across the beaches of the world.' With that, he swung away and strode through the doors.

Hearing someone follow him he glanced round and saw Helikaon. Odysseus felt a great sinking of the spirit. 'Make your threat swiftly,' he said. 'I am in no mood to tarry.'

'I have no threat, Odysseus,' said Helikaon sadly. 'I did not desire any of this.'

'A consideration best remembered *before* you ran to Priam,' the Ugly King replied. 'Did our friendship mean so little to you that you could not wait to hear what I might have to say before having me declared a rogue and an outcast?' Caught between sorrow and rage, he swung away from the young man, but Helikaon moved swiftly, taking hold of his arm.

'It was not as you believe!' he cried. 'No man has a greater call on my affection than you, Odysseus. I have no recollection of Priam coming to me. I was delirious, poison in my blood. I scarce recall any conversation then. I drifted in and out of dreams; dreams of death and despair.'

Odysseus felt the rage seep out of him. His shoulders sagged and a terrible weariness settled on him. 'Best ask me now what you need to know,' he said.

'Did Karpophorus lie? Tell me that he did and we can put all this right.'

Odysseus saw the need in Helikaon for this lie to be true. It shone in his eyes. 'It cannot be put right now, Golden One. The assassin did not lie. I paid him a sheep's weight in silver to kill Anchises.'

Helikaon stood silently, staring at him, his expression showing his disbelief. 'I don't understand. Why would you do it? You had nothing to gain. My father loathed me, but he had no enmity towards you. Tell me, and put an end to the anguish.'

Odysseus sighed. 'I fear it will only bring a different form of anguish, and I would willingly have surrendered ten years of my life rather than have you discover the truth. Even now I hesitate to tell you.'

'I need to know, Odysseus.' Helikaon looked at him closely. 'Though, even as I say it, I think I can guess the answer.'

Odysseus nodded. 'On that last voyage, when we sailed to Dardania, we had three passengers. Two merchants and a traveller. The traveller was Karpophorus. I recognized him, and I guessed the purpose of his trip. We spoke one night, away from the crew. I made it clear to him that I knew his target, and I made him an offer. He had no choice but to accept, for to refuse would have resulted in his death there and then, by my own hand.'

'And I was his target?'

'Yes. Anchises had already dispossessed you, and declared you illegitimate. He had nominated Diomedes as his heir. But he wanted to be sure you would not cause him problems.' Odysseus sighed. 'He wanted you dead. I knew this already because he had offered me wealth to kill you while you sailed with me. I believed, wrongly, that when he saw the man you had become he would be filled with pride, as I was. When I realized he had hired Karpophorus I knew he would stop at nothing to see you slain. So I paid Karpophorus to kill him. And, even now, I don't regret it.'

Helikaon walked away a few steps, and stood with his back to Odysseus. 'Why did you not tell me before this?' he asked. 'I would have understood.'

'Yes, you would. But despite everything you still admired Anchises. I saw no reason to hack at his memory. Now I wish I had.'

'I need to walk,' said Helikaon, swinging back to face him. 'Let us get away from this place, stroll down to the beach, and feel the sea air on our faces.'

'No, Helikaon. We cannot walk together,' said

Odysseus, sadness in his voice. 'My bodyguards are waiting beyond the gates. It is possible Priam will have more assassins out to waylay me. As for you, you already know that Mykene killers are seeking you. There will be no more carefree walks for either of us.' For a few moments there was silence between them. Then Odysseus spoke again. 'The great war is coming, and we are to be enemies, you and I. That saddens me more than words can convey.'

'And you will side with Agamemnon? He will drench the world in blood.'

Odysseus shrugged. 'This is not of my making, Helikaon. I did not declare myself an enemy of Troy. And even if I wished it there is nowhere to run and hide. Priam has sought now to shame me three times. I am a king, and kings do not reign long if they let other kings piss on their shoes. My ships will not attack Dardanian vessels, and I will have no part in any invasion of your lands. But I will bring war to Troy, and I will see Priam fall.'

'And I will fight alongside Priam and Hektor,' said Helikaon.

'The only honourable course,' agreed Odysseus. 'But get yourself strong again, boy. You are all skin and bone.'

'What of the Seven Hills?' asked Helikaon. 'We built the settlement together, and there are Dardanians and Ithakans working there side by side.'

Odysseus considered the question. 'It is far from this coming war. You can trust me to oversee it, and ensure your profits are held for you. I will do my best to see there is no friction between the peoples there. Let us hope that one day we can walk the Seven Hills together, as friends once more.'

'I will pray for that day, Odysseus, my friend.'

Tears in his eyes, Odysseus drew the younger man into an embrace, and kissed his cheeks. 'May the gods favour you,' he said.

'And may they watch over you, Ugly One. Always.'

The Games resumed the morning after the funeral feast for Hekabe. The sky was clear, a fresh breeze blowing across the hills. Thousands flocked to the hippodrome and the stadium, and fortunes were wagered on this final day. Not one copper ring, however, was placed on Achilles, for none could be found who would bet against him.

Despite the warnings of his friends Helikaon walked among the excited throng, watching the contests. The parting with Odysseus weighed heavily on him, and he had no interest any longer in the Games. He had come only for a glimpse of Andromache. Gershom was with him, his hand constantly on his dagger hilt, his dark eyes scanning the crowd for signs of assassins. 'This is foolish,' said Gershom, not for the first time, as they eased their way through a pack of spectators at the hippodrome.

'I will not live in fear,' Helikaon told him. 'I tried it once. It does not suit me.'

Wooden bench seats had been set into the raised banks round the racing area, but these were already full. Helikaon led Gershom through the crowd to a canopied royal enclosure, where he was recognized by the two Royal Eagles guarding the entrance. 'Good to see you back among the living,' said one, a wide-shouldered veteran with a black and silver beard. The man had been one of the soldiers who had fought alongside Helikaon the previous autumn, during the attack on Priam's palace. Helikaon clapped the man on the shoulder as he walked into the enclosure, Gershom beside him. A servant brought cool drinks of pressed fruits, flavoured with spices.

At the back of the enclosure Helikaon saw the slender, dark-haired Dios, and the huge Antiphones. They were arguing about the merits of the charioteers about to race. Dios saw Helikaon and smiled broadly, stepping forward to embrace him. Then Antiphones shook his hand.

'You are looking more like yourself,' said Dios. 'It is good to see.'

'But still a little thin,' added Antiphones. 'I think I have lost more weight than you carry, Helikaon.'

Out on the hippodrome track they saw Polites and some twenty judges walking in a line, examing the ground, searching for small stones that might be lifted by the spinning wheels of the chariots and hurled into the crowd.

'He has done well,' said Helikaon. 'The Games have been splendidly organized.'

Once the judges had completed their examination of the track the charioteers came out, riding in single file so that the crowd could see the horses, make their judgements and decide upon their wagers. The red-haired Athenian king, Menestheos, led the line, his four black geldings looking sleek and powerful. Behind him was the Lykian charioteer, Supolos, followed by the Mykene champion, Ajax. He was the only man sporting a helm and a breastplate of leather. All the other charioteers wore simple tunics.

Helikaon scanned the line, watching closely the behaviour of the horses. Some were nervous, tossing their heads and stamping their hooves, others seemed serene. The black geldings of Menestheos continued to catch his eye. 'Are you wagering?' asked Dios.

'Perhaps.'

'The Lykian, Supolos, has been magnificent throughout. Never seen a team with such speed.'

Helikaon smiled. 'I'll wager a hundred gold rings that Menestheos and his blacks finish ahead of him.'

'Done!'

Having completed a full slow circuit the twelve chariots were led to their starting positions. The chariots would race towards the first turning pole, spin round it, then thunder back towards the second pole for ten circuits. The starting line was staggered, so that the distance to the first pole was the same for all. Menestheos had drawn the outside position, the Lykian, Supolos, the inside. The charioteers looped the long reins around their wrists and waited for the trumpet blast.

The crowd fell silent.

The trumpet sounded.

Forty-eight horses surged into their traces, and the race began. The four black geldings of Menestheos thundered away, cutting across the next team, causing the following charioteer to swerve and haul back on his reins. On the inside the team of Supolos pulled ahead with blistering speed. Supolos reached the turn first, his chariot lifting on one wheel as he reined in the inner pair, while the outer increased their speed. It was a breathtaking display of skill, his chariot wheel missing the pole by no more than a hand's breadth. Menestheos was just behind him, the Mykene, Ajax, in close pursuit in third place.

The crowd were baying now, the excitement rising. Two chariots in the rear collided on a turn. One lost a wheel, the other spun over, throwing the charioteer to the dust. Soldiers ran onto the course, dragging the damaged chariots clear. Both charioteers rose uninjured.

By the fifth turn it seemed that Supolos would claim the laurel crown, but Menestheos and Ajax were both driving with skill and nerve, awaiting the one mistake that would allow them to surge through.

It came on the ninth turn. A moment of mis-judgement saw Supolos swing too wide. Ajax lashed his team, seeking to drive through the narrow space created. Supolos, recovering swiftly, tried to close him off. Down the straight they thundered, side by side. At the next turn they were too close, and their wheels collided and locked together. The Lykian's wheel was torn clear, and his damaged chariot hammered into the guard rail. The vehicle shattered – but the horses ran on. Supolos, the reins tight round his wrists, was dragged along the ground. The collision had forced

Ajax to slow down, and the Athenian, Menestheos, seeing his chance, lashed his reins and cried out in a loud
voice: 'Go, beauties! Go!'

The blacks came out of the turn and powered into a
gallop. The hapless Supolos was directly in their path.
The outside gelding leapt across his flailing body, but
the chariot wheel struck his neck with awful force, and
all in the crowd knew instantly he had been killed.

Menestheos raced to the final turn, just ahead of
Ajax, and executed a perfect swinging manoeuvre.
Then he lashed the black horses into one last surge for
the finish. Ajax could not close the gap and finished
second, the other seven charioteers trailing in without
mishap. Only then did stretcher bearers run onto the
track to retrieve the body of Supolos.

'My luck is cursed,' said Dios.

'Not as badly as the Lykian's,' Helikaon pointed out.

'Menestheos could have avoided him,' observed
Antiphones. 'He only had to rein back and swerve.'

'Would have cost him the race,' said Dios.

Helikaon waited to applaud as Menestheos received
the laurel crown, then he and Gershom made their way
down the columned walkway to the stadium entrance.
Gershom continued to watch the crowd around them
with suspicion.

The final of the javelin tourney was under way as
they arrived. It was won by a Rhodian, with an
enormous throw, but Helikaon was delighted to see his
old friend, Bias, finish second. The crew of the
Penelope surged around him, lifting him to their
shoulders as if he had won. As Bias was being carried

aloft he spotted Helikaon and waved, grinning broadly. Helikaon lifted his hand and smiled back. Sadness touched him. Will we both be smiling when next we meet, he wondered?

On the far side of the stadium was the second royal enclosure. Helikaon and Gershom eased their way through the crowd until they were close to it. Then Helikaon stopped. Two gilded thrones had been placed at the front, and seated upon them, beneath gold-embroidered canopies, were Hektor and Andromache. Her father Ektion, a slender man with deep-set, wary eyes, was seated at her right, while Priam sat beside his son.

Helikaon stood silently staring at the woman he loved. She was wearing an ankle-length gown of shimmering yellow, and a belt of gold. Her long red hair had been bound with golden wire, and was held back from her face by a golden circlet upon her brow. Her beauty struck his heart like a lance.

'Are you going in?' asked Gershom.

'No, you would not be allowed to enter. We will stay together,' Helikaon replied.

Gershom chuckled. 'Believe me, my friend, I would *prefer* you to go in. Walking around with you, watching for assassins, is shredding my nerves. I will meet you here after Achilles has won his bout.'

Taking a deep, calming breath Helikaon walked past the guards and entered the enclosure. Priam saw him and smiled a greeting. Seeing the king brought back the events of the previous night. Odysseus had responded to the taunts of Priam with words of war. And in that moment, Helikaon knew, the world had changed. He remembered then the vision of his wife, Halysia, of flames and battle, and a fleet of ships upon a sea of blood.

A sense of unreality gripped him now. No more than fifty paces distant the kings of the west were in their own enclosure, watching athletes and joking amongst themselves: Odysseus, Agamemnon, Idomeneos, and the Athenian king Menestheos, still sporting his laurel crown. Close by were Peleus of Thessaly, Nestor of Pylos, Pelemos the Rhodian ruler, and tall Agapenor of Arcadia. These men would leave Troy and sail back to their homelands, there to gather armies and return. There would be no friendly contests then, no competition for laurel wreaths. Armoured in bronze, sharp swords in their hands, they would seek to slaughter or enslave the very people who now watched happily as their future killers raced against one another. As the foot race was won by a slender Mykene the crowd cheered and clapped their hands. They could be cheering the man who would one day slit their throats and rape their wives.

Helikaon eased back to the rear of the enclosure, where servants stood ready to offer cool drinks to the nobles. Taking a cup he sipped the contents. It was the same mixture of fruits and spices being served in the hippodrome. Then he saw Andromache rise from her seat, and walk back towards him. His heart began to race, his breath catching in his throat, his mouth instantly dry. Andromache accepted a cup of water from a servant, then, without acknowledging

Helikaon, started to walk back to her seat.

'You look beyond beautiful,' said Helikaon.

She paused, her green eyes observing him gravely. 'I am happy to see your strength improving, King Aeneas.'

Andromache's tone was cool, and despite her physical closeness he felt as distant from her as the moon from the sun. He wanted to find some words to bring her close, to make her smile at least. But he could think of nothing. Just then Priam moved into his line of sight. He crossed to Andromache and slid his arm round her waist, broad fingers resting on the curve of her hip. Helikaon felt his stomach tighten at the familiarity, and was surprised to see Andromache accept the touch without complaint.

'Are you enjoying your day, my daughter?' asked Priam, leaning over to kiss her hair.

'In truth, I am looking forward to returning to the farm tonight.'

'I thought you might stay at the palace,' he said.

'That is kind of you, but I am weary. The farm is quiet and cool, and I enjoy it there.'

Helikaon saw the disappointment in Priam. The king's gaze swung to him. 'You are looking better, Aeneas. It is good. What did you think of the words of Odysseus last night? You think I should fear his fleabite?'

'Yes, I think you should,' Helikaon told him. 'Of all the enemies to choose you have picked the most dangerous in Odysseus.'

'I did not choose him,' snapped Priam. 'He slew my

blood kin. Your own father. I would have thought that would have earned your hatred.'

'He is my enemy now,' agreed Helikaon. 'That will have to suffice, for I could never hate him.'

'I thought the dagger had entered your chest – not sliced off your balls,' hissed Priam, his pale eyes glinting with anger.

Helikaon's reply was icy. 'I see your desire to make new enemies has not yet been sated. Have you not enough already, Uncle? Or do you seek to drive *me* into the camp of Agamemnon?'

'True! True!' replied Priam, forcing a smile. 'We should not fall out, Aeneas. My words were hasty and ill judged.' With a final lingering caress of Andromache's waist he moved back to his seat to watch the Games.

Andromache lifted her cup of water and sipped it. Then she glanced at Helikaon. 'You are truly an enemy now to Odysseus?' she asked.

'Not from choice,' he said, 'for I love him deeply.'

'And he will be a great enemy,' she said, her voice low.

'Indeed he will. Agamemnon is blood-hungry and greedy. Odysseus is a thinker and a planner. The war he brings will be many times more threatening than anything Agamemnon could initiate.'

'I spoke to Hekabe before she died. She said he was a threat. I did not believe it. When will you be returning to Dardanos?'

'Tomorrow, after the Games are concluded. Unless Agamemnon has other plans. Mykene spies have been circling my palace. Assassins will probably follow.'

She paled then, and fear showed in her eyes. 'Why do you tell me this?'

He leaned towards her. 'To see if there is any trace of concern in your eyes. We declared our love for one another, Andromache. The Fates decreed we could not be together, but that love has not died – at least not in me. Yet you have become cold, and I know no reason why that should be.'

'It is not seemly to talk of love on my wedding day,' she said, and he thought he detected sorrow in her voice. 'I know what is in my heart. I know what my soul cries out for. But I also know I cannot have what I desire, and to think of it, and to talk of it, does not help ease the pain. Go home to your *wife*, Helikaon, and I will return to my *husband*.' She turned away, paused, then swung back to face him. 'I do not worry about these assassins, Helikaon,' she said. 'I know you. You can be kind, and you care for those close to you. But you are also a killer, cold and deadly. When they come you will slay them without mercy.' And then she turned away.

As the day wore on the heat began to mount, the sun blazing down from a clear sky, the breeze fading away. The final of the archery tourney was won by the young Trojan soldier, Cheon, who narrowly beat Meriones into second place.

As the day neared its end the ropes holding back the crowds were released, and thousands of spectators moved across the stadium, eager to see the last event, and watch the mighty Achilles claim the champion's crown.

Helikaon watched the Thessalian prince stride across the open ground. He was wearing a short kilt of fine, pale leather, his upper body bare to the sunlight, his raven hair drawn back from his face. The crowd followed him, but not pressing in too closely. He looked, thought Helikaon, like a lion surrounded by sheep. The Dardanian glanced round, seeking out the challenger, but there was no sign of him. Achilles halted before the two thrones and stood quietly.

The kings of the west, led by Agamemnon, left their enclosure and strode across the open ground, the crowd parting for them. Odysseus walked forward to stand before Priam.

'I have just learned,' he said loudly, 'that my fighter, Leukon, has suffered an injury. He tripped and fell on the way here, breaking two of his fingers. He cannot fight today.' A roar of disappointment went up from the crowd. Helikaon felt his stomach tighten. He did not believe for a moment that the story was true, and he sensed danger looming.

Priam rose from his seat, raising his arms for silence. 'That is, indeed, grim news, Odysseus,' he said. 'It is always regrettable when a man becomes champion by default. However, few can deny that Achilles is worthy of the crown.' So saying, he reached down and lifted the laurel band, preparing to offer it to the Thessalian.

At that moment Achilles spoke. 'By your leave, Priam King,' he said, 'it seems to me that your people gathered here deserve to see a contest. Why not then allow them an exhibition bout? It is said by some that your son, Hektor, is a fine fighter. I would deem it a privilege to spar with him, and I am sure the Trojan people would enjoy viewing it.'

A great cheer went up, and the crowd began to chant: 'Hektor! Hektor!'

Anger swept through Helikaon. Hektor had not trained for these Games, and had been sitting all day, eating and drinking. Achilles spoke of an exhibition bout, of sparring. That was a lie. The moment the two men faced up to one another it would be a fight to the finish. He realized then that this was the plan: for the Games to finish with the Trojan hero sprawled senseless in the dust, and Troy humiliated by the might of the west.

With any other opponent Helikaon would have had no doubts as to the outcome. Hektor was a magnificent fighter. But for the first time he found himself wondering if Hektor might be outclassed. It seemed like a betrayal of friendship even to think it, but Helikaon had now seen both men in action. Hektor was enormously strong and brave and fast. But Achilles was colder, and there was a cruelty in him that made him deadly. Helikaon glanced at Priam, hoping he would see the danger. His heart sank – for there was a gleam in Priam's eyes that spoke of triumph. Here was a man who could not conceive of defeat for his son. As far as Priam was concerned Hektor was the physical personification of Troy itself, and therefore unbeatable. Priam once more lifted his hands for silence, and as the chanting died away he turned towards his son. 'Will you honour your people, and take up this challenge?' he asked.

Hektor rose, his expression grim. 'As always I will obey my father's bidding,' he said. Stepping down from the dais, he pulled off his jewelled belt and removed his tunic. A soldier brought him a leather kilt, which he swung round his waist and tied into place. Helikaon moved down to stand alongside him.

'You know this will be no sparring match?' he whispered.

Hektor nodded. 'Of course I know. This is about blood and humiliation.'

XXIV

The fallen hero

MORE THAN TWENTY THOUSAND PEOPLE WERE PRESENT AT the fight, though less than a tenth could say truthfully that they witnessed it. People further back than the first few rows could occasionally see a glimpse of the two men, while those at the rear could only listen to the roars of the crowd. And yet, decades later, men from all nations would say their fathers or their grandfathers had stood close by on that day. Two hundred years on a king from Macedonia named Antipas would insist that his ancestor had held the cloak of the victor. For seven generations his family claimed the title Cloakbearer. Bards would later sing of the battle, maintaining that Zeus and the gods had descended on Troy that day, disguised as mortals, and that ownership of the stars was wagered by them.

Odysseus saw no gods as he stood on the far side of the circle with the kings of the west. He saw two proud men, in the full glory of youth and strength, circling one another under a blazing sun. Achilles made the first attack, stepping in and feinting with a left, before flashing a right hand that thundered against Hektor's face. The Trojan champion reacted with an uppercut that hammered into his opponent's belly, and a left cross that glanced from Achilles' temple. Then they pulled back and circled again. This time it was Hektor who moved in. Achilles swayed back from a straight left, then stepped inside, throwing a combination of blows that drove Hektor back. The punches were blindingly fast, each one pounding into Hektor's face. The Trojan covered up, blocking further blows with his forearms, then counter-attacked with a left hook that clubbed into Achilles' cheek.

Achilles was bigger and faster than the Trojan and landing more punches. Odysseus watched intently as the fighters circled once more. Each man had now tested the other, and both knew there would be no swift conclusion.

Odysseus stood quietly, the roars of the crowd washing over him. He knew Achilles was the stronger man, but he knew also that skill and speed alone would not dictate the outcome. The plan had been Agamemnon's and Odysseus had offered no argument against it. If Hektor could be defeated it would damage the morale of the Trojans, whereas if Achilles lost it would dent only the confidence of the Thessalians, and have little effect on men from other nations drawn into the battle for Troy.

Even so he was torn as he watched the combat. He liked Hektor, and had no desire to see him humbled.

Equally he longed to see the look on Priam's face when his beloved son was defeated. Odysseus glanced at the Trojan king. Priam was watching the fight, his expression calm and untroubled.

That will change, thought Odysseus.

Both fighters now glistened with sweat, and there was a swelling beneath Hektor's right eye. Achilles was unmarked. He surged forward, ducking under a murderous right, then smashing two blows into Hektor's face, opening a cut under the left eye that sprayed blood over the nearby spectators. A gasp went up from the crowd. Hektor countered with a left hook that slashed above Achilles' ducking head. Achilles hammered a blow into Hektor's belly and a right cross that cracked against his chin. Off balance, Hektor tumbled to the dirt and rolled onto his back.

Odysseus flicked a glance at Priam and smiled. The Trojan king was ashen, his mouth open in shock.

Hektor rose to his knees, shook his head and remained where he was for a moment, dragging in deep breaths. Then he stood, walked to the spear plunged into the ground and patted the haft. Blood was running down his face.

The crowd was silent now.

Achilles launched a swift attack, but he was over-confident, and ran into a straight left that jarred him to his heels and an uppercut to the belly that lifted him from his feet. Hektor followed in, but Achilles spun away, sending a stinging right that further opened the cut on Hektor's face.

The day wore on, the sun sinking slowly over the sea.

Hektor was slowing, fewer of his punches hitting the target, whereas Achilles seemed to be growing in strength. Twice more Hektor was downed, and twice more he rose to touch the spear haft.

At this point, Odysseus thought, the end was inevitable. Hektor's strength was being leached away by every blow. Only pride and courage kept him on his feet.

Achilles, sensing victory was close, stepped in, thundering two right crosses into Hektor's face, hurling him from his feet.

Hektor hit the ground hard and rolled to his knees. He struggled to rise, fell back, then slowly made it to his feet to touch the spear.

Then Achilles made a terrible mistake.

'Come on, you Trojan dog,' he sneered. 'There is more pain here for you.'

Odysseus saw the change come over Hektor. His head came up and his pale eyes narrowed. Then, amazingly, he smiled.

Achilles, oblivious of the change in his opponent, charged in. Hektor stepped in to meet him, blocking a right cross and sending yet another uppercut into Achilles' belly. Breath whooshed from the Thessalian's lungs. A clubbing left hook exploded against his forehead, splitting the skin above his right eye. Achilles tried to back away. Hektor hit him with a ferocious left, then a right that pulped his lips against his teeth, shredding them. Desperately Achilles ducked his head, trying to protect his face with his forearms. An uppercut swept between the raised limbs. Achilles' head snapped back. A straight left shattered his nose. Achilles stumbled back, but there was no escape. Hektor moved in, hammering punch after punch into Achilles' ruined face. Blood was flowing into both eyes now, and Achilles did not see the blow that ended the fight. Hektor stepped back and, with all his strength, hit his opponent with an explosive right that spun the Thessalian through a full circle before his unconscious body hit the dirt.

A huge cheer went up from the crowd. Hektor turned and strode back to the dais, where he lifted clear the laurel wreath of victory. Walking back to where Achilles lay he dropped the wreath onto his chest, then swung to face Odysseus and the kings of the west. As the cheering faded away he pointed down at the fallen hero. When he spoke his voice was cold.

'Hail to mighty Achilles,' he said. 'Hail to the Champion of the Games.'

Banokles was furious to have missed the fight. He'd had no desire to watch Leukon humbled by the awesome Achilles and had walked down to the lower town to enjoy the company of Big Red. Only later, as he walked back to Hektor's palace, did he learn of the contest he had missed. Crowds streaming away from the stadium were talking of nothing else, their mood jubilant.

Back at the palace the crew of the *Penelope* were gathering their belongings for departure. Banokles found Kalliades sitting in the shade of a flowering tree in the rear gardens. Slumping down beside him, he said: 'I would have wagered on Hektor.'

Kalliades laughed. 'You said you thought Achilles was unbeatable. In fact you said even Hektor would have no chance against him. I remember that.'

'You always remember too much,' grumbled Banokles. 'Was it a great bout?'

'The best I have ever seen.'

'And I missed it.'

'Do not be so downcast, my friend. In days to come you will brag about being there, and no-one will be the wiser.'

'That's true,' said Banokles, his mood lifting. Several crew members left the palace building, carrying their bedrolls. 'Where is everyone going? I thought they were going to sail in the morning.'

'Odysseus is leaving the city now,' said Kalliades. 'Says he will find a bay somewhere up the coast.'

'Why?'

'The neutrality of the Games ends tonight. I hear most of the kings of the west are leaving with him.'

'What will we do?' asked Banokles.

'We'll head south, down to Thebe Under Plakos. The king there is troubled by bandits raiding his trade caravans.'

'Is that a long distance from Troy?'

Kalliades glanced at him. 'Are your legs weary?'

'No. Just asking.' Banokles called out to a passing servant for some wine, but the man ingored him. 'Seems like we are not welcome any more,' he said.

Odysseus came strolling from the palace. 'You lads can stay with the *Penelope*, if you will. I have spoken to

Agamemnon, and he has lifted the sentence from you. As far as he is concerned you are Ithakan warriors, and I would be glad to have you.'

'That's good,' said Banokles. He glanced at Kalliades. 'It is good, isn't it?'

Kalliades rose to stand before Odysseus. 'I thank you, Odysseus King, but I promised to take Piria to her friend. To see her safely to the end of her journey.'

'A man should always honour his word,' said Odysseus, 'but I fear nowhere is safe for that girl. You understand?'

'I believe I do.'

'Her actions, though inspired by love and prophecy, have been reckless. I think she is beginning to realize that now.'

'Not so long ago,' said Kalliades, 'you told me she would need friends. Loyal friends. She has those, Odysseus. We will keep her safe. Banokles and I will allow no-one to harm her, or take her. If she is not welcomed by her friend she can accompany us to Thebe Under Plakos. There she will not be known.'

'I do not think her friend will turn her away,' said Odysseus, 'though good sense would dictate otherwise.' Reaching out, he gripped Kalliades' hand. 'You lads take care. If ever you are in need of a friend you can look to Ithaka, or to any Ithakan ship. You tell them you are friends of Odysseus, and they will carry you wherever they are sailing.'

'That is good to know,' Kalliades told him.

'My last words of advice are these. I have given Piria directions to Hektor's farm. Get her to wait until dusk.

There are a number of Thessalians still in the city who might recognize her in daylight.'

'We will see her there safely,' promised Kalliades.

Odysseus turned to Banokles. 'I did not see you at the fight, big man.'

'Oh, I was there,' insisted Banokles. 'Wouldn't have missed it.'

'Aye, it was something to see, and I doubt Achilles will ever forget it. You don't taunt a man like Hektor. Heroes can always delve deeper than ordinary men. They have a well of courage that is bottomless. I think both of you understand that. It has been good to know you.'

As he walked away, Bias, Leukon and others of the crew wandered over to say their goodbyes, and then Kalliades and Banokles were alone in the garden.

A little while later Piria joined them. She was wearing a long, hooded cloak of dark green and carrying a Phrygian bow, and a quiver of arrows was slung across her shoulder.

'Going hunting?' asked Banokles.

'No,' said the blonde girl. 'This is Andromache's bow. A servant told me she had asked for it to be brought to the farm. I said I would carry it. Why are you still here?'

'We thought you might like our company upon the road,' said Kalliades.

Piria gave a shy smile. 'I would like that . . . my friends,' she told them.

Banokles strolled away to the room he shared with Kalliades. There he donned his old cuirass and strapped his sword belt to his side. Tonight they would leave Troy. The thought hung heavily on him. He pictured Big Red as he had last seen her, sitting in an old wicker chair in her small garden. She had been mending a tear at the hem of a gown. She looked up as he prepared to leave. 'You have cake crumbs in your beard,' she said.

Banokles had brushed them away. 'See you tomorrow?' he had asked. Red had shrugged.

'The Games are over today,' she said. 'Everyone will be leaving.'

There had been no hugs, no farewell kiss. He considered going back to the lower town and seeking her out. But what would be the purpose? He didn't want to say goodbye to her. With a sigh he left the room and strode through the palace. There will be plenty of women in the countryside, he told himself. With luck he could buy some slave girls to tend him.

Curiously, the thought saddened him.

Andromache held tightly to the bronze rail of the war chariot as Cheon guided the vehicle along the paved roads of the city and out towards the open land leading to the farm. The chariot, drawn by two bay geldings, was of flimsy construction: a narrow, wickerwork base of heat-moulded wood, strengthened at the upper rim by copper wire. There was a rack, which would normally hold four javelins, and two bronze hooks for stowing a bow and a quiver of arrows. There was scarcely room for two people on board. But then the vehicle was built for speed and manoeuvrability on the battlefield, to bring an archer into range of the enemy and away again before a counter-attack could be mounted. Cheon had commandeered it at the palace, since all the passenger carts were in use, and Andromache had been eager to return to the farm.

Andromache glanced at the handsome, dark-haired soldier. His helm was hanging from the bow hook, for he was still sporting the laurel wreath of victory he had won at the archery tourney. Along the way he was recognized by the crowds on the streets, and they cheered him loudly.

Once they were clear of the city the crowds thinned, and Cheon allowed the geldings to slow to a walk. Andromache was relieved, for the vehicle had juddered alarmingly on the stone streets, and her knees ached from trying to remain upright.

'I am sorry to have missed your victory,' she told the young soldier. He grinned at her.

'I was lucky that Meriones did not have his own bow. I have practised with mine for almost a year. Yet he came close to beating me with a weapon he had never handled before. And as for regret, nothing can match mine, for I was in the *palaistra* being massaged when Hektor defeated Achilles. You must be very proud.'

Andromache did not reply, but the question echoed in her mind. Was she proud? Was that the feeling she had experienced as the two champions had pounded their fists against one another, splitting skin and spraying blood? Was it pride that caused her stomach to turn, so that it required all her will to prevent herself from vomiting? She had turned her eyes away during much of the contest, watching instead the reactions of the men surrounding her. Priam had, at first, seemed unconcerned, merely waiting for the inevitable victory. Slowly she had watched his confidence fade. The man seemed to age ten years in a matter of heartbeats. Only at the end, as Achilles fell for the last time, did he surge from his seat.

Yet despite her revulsion at the brutality of the fight Andromache was elated by the outcome – especially as she gazed upon the stricken face of Peleus, the Thessalian king. This was the man who had raped Kalliope, ripping her childhood from her. This was the wretch who had left his daughter damaged beyond repair. Even in the sanctuary of Thera, where men were forbidden, Kalliope would wake screaming, her body bathed in sweat. Then she would fall into Andromache's arms, weeping at the awful memories.

With the fight over Andromache had returned to the king's palace with Hektor. He had said little during the walk. His breathing was laboured and he held his left arm to his side. Andromache had been with him when the physician came. Three ribs were broken, and several of his teeth had been loosened. She had sat with him for a while, but then he had patted her arm. 'Go back to the farm,' he said, forcing a smile. 'I will rest here awhile.'

'You fought well,' she told him, 'with great courage.'

His reply surprised her. 'I hated it,' he said. 'Every brutal heartbeat of it. It hurts me to think of what Achilles must be feeling at this moment, his pride in the dust.'

She gazed at him, at his bruised face and his bright

blue eyes. Without thinking she lifted her hand and gently stroked the golden hair back from his brow. 'We are what we are, Hektor. You need have no sympathy for Achilles. He is a brute, from a family of brutes. Come to the farm when you can.'

His huge hand reached out and he took her fingers gently and raised them to his lips. 'I am glad you are my wife, Andromache. You are everything I could ever have desired. I am sorry I cannot be—'

'Do not say it again,' she said, interrupting him. 'Rest now, and come to the farm when you can.'

Leaving the room she had walked out onto the gallery beyond, her eyes misting with tears. Sadness clung to her. It struck her then that Hektor and Kalliope were not so unalike. Both had been damaged. Both, in different ways, cursed by the Fates.

Servants moved by silently, and she could hear the sound of raised voices from the *megaron* below. Priam's voice suddenly boomed out.

'Are you insane? She is the wife of my son.'

Andromache moved away from the balcony to the gallery rail, staring down into the columned *megaron*. Priam was seated upon his throne, facing the Mykene king, Agamemnon, and some of the kings of the west. Andromache recognized the vile Peleus, and Nestor, Idomeneos and Menestheos. Helikaon, Antiphones and Dios were standing alongside Priam.

'You must understand, Priam King,' said Agamemnon, 'that there is no intent here to cause undue offence. You sanctioned the marriage of Paris to the woman Helen. This was not your right. Helen is a princess of Sparta, sent here by her father during the recent war. My brother, Menelaus, is now king of Sparta, and Helen is his subject. He has decided, in the interests of his people, to wed her.'

Priam's laughter was harsh. 'Menelaus led a Mykene army into Sparta and killed the king. He seized the throne and now faces insurrections. In order to bolster his fabricated claim to the crown he seeks to wed someone of royal blood. You think I would send Helen home to rut with the man who murdered her father?'

Agamemnon shook his head. 'You have no choice. All of us here are allies, and we are allies because we have agreed to respect each other's rights and borders, and internal laws. Without such respect there can be no alliance. Let us suppose that one of your daughters was to visit a kingdom of the west, and that the ruler there suddenly married her to one of his sons. What would be your reaction? And what would you expect when you demanded her return?'

'Spare me the clever words, Agamemnon. You desire a war with Troy, and you have been seeking allies in that venture for years now. I tire of your duplicity, the fair speeches that cloak foul deeds. Let me make it simple for you. Helen remains in Troy. The alliance is at an end. Now get you gone from my city.'

Agamemnon spread his arms, and his reply was full of regret. 'It saddens me to hear you speak in this way, Priam King. However, as you say, the alliance is at an end. You may come to rue this decision.' With that he turned and strode out, followed by the other kings.

Back in the present the voice of Cheon cut through

her memories. 'Do you wish to stop by the shrine to Artemis?' he asked, as the chariot neared the little stream.

'Not today, Cheon. Take me home.'

The journey seemed interminable, and the afternoon sun blazed brightly in a cloudless sky. By the time they reached the old stone house Andromache felt weary beyond belief. They were greeted by Hektor's housekeeper, the elderly Menesthi, a Hittite woman, whose true age was a mystery. Cheon maintained she was the oldest woman alive – a claim Andromache could well believe, for the old woman's face had the texture of pumice stone.

Inside the main building Menesthi's husband, the equally ancient Vahusima, prepared a bath for her. Shedding her yellow gown she stepped into it, laying her head back on a folded towel. The feeling of the cool water on her overheated skin was exquisite. She called Menesthi to her, to remove the gold wire that bound her hair, then ducked her head below the surface.

Menesthi brought her fresh clothing, a simple loose robe of white linen. Rising from the bath Andromache stood naked, allowing the warm air to dry her body. Then she moved to the rear window and stared out over the fields towards the wooded hillside.

In that moment she saw two men duck into the trees. It seemed to her they were acting furtively. She stared out, seeking another glimpse of them, but there was no further sign of movement. The first of the men appeared familiar to her, but she could not place him. He must be one of Hektor's woodsmen, she thought.

Donning the robe, she walked back through the house. Cheon was sitting on the porch in the shadows, watching two youths leading a powerful grey stallion round the paddock. The beast was high-spirited and nervous, and when one of the boys tried to mount him he reared and threw him to the grass. Cheon laughed. 'He has no wish to be ridden,' he said. 'Those lads will have some deep bruises by this evening.'

Andromache smiled. 'I see you are still wearing your laurel crown. Are you intending to sleep with it on?'

'I think I will,' he said. 'I think I will wear it until it rots and falls off.'

'Does that not seem a little vain, Cheon?'

'Entirely,' he agreed, with a grin.

Andromache seated herself beside him. 'The farm seems deserted.'

'Most of the men went to the city for the last day. They'll be getting drunk about now. I doubt we'll see them until tomorrow, when they will drift in looking sheepish and bleary-eyed.'

As the light began to fade Andromache moved back inside. Menesthi brought her a simple meal of bread and cheese, and a dish of sliced fruit. Andromache finished it and stretched out on a couch, resting her head on a thick cushion.

Her dreams were confused and full of anxiety, and she awoke with a start. Suddenly she remembered where she had seen the man in the woods before. He was not one of Hektor's men. She had noticed him as she stood with Kassandra on the day Agamemnon arrived in Troy.

The man was a Mykene soldier.

Fearful now, she rose and went towards the main rooms. Perhaps they were assassins come to kill Hektor, not realizing he had remained at the palace. She needed to find Cheon and warn him.

As she neared the front of the house she saw a red glow through the window. Pulling open the door, she saw old Vahusima and the two boys running towards a blazing barn. From within the building she heard the sounds of terrified horses, and ran out to help them just as Cheon emerged from behind the house.

One of the boys suddenly stumbled and fell. Vahusima reached the doors of the stable, and struggled to lift clear the locking bar. Then he cried out – and Andromache saw an arrow jutting from his back.

Dark figures came rushing from the shadows, swords in their hands.

XXV

Blood for Artemis

THE MOON WAS PERFECTLY ROUND, ITS EDGE SHARP AS A knife, as the three companions made their way out of the twilight city.

They left by the East Gate and crossed the fortification ditch in the shadow of the great northeast bastion, then headed north. The way was easy, a gentle walk through rolling hills and meadows, and they travelled quickly. They carried with them all they possessed, for they did not expect to return. Kalliades had the Sword of Argurios at his side. Banokles was carrying a small sack of provisions on his shoulder, including a heavy pottery jug which glugged a little as he walked. Piria, in her hooded cloak, carried only Andromache's bow and quiver.

Her thoughts were in chaos and the easy walk did nothing to calm them. Had she been still on Thera she would have run on the black sandy beach, or across the barren hilltops, until her body hurt, exhaustion purging her fears for a little while. Or she would reach for Andromache, who could always calm the turmoil in her heart.

Yet now it was thoughts of Andromache that caused her fear. For the past season her only ambition had been to reach the woman she loved. Her entire will had been engaged in achieving that one goal. But now, at the end of her journey, she was overwhelmed with doubts.

What if Andromache no longer wanted her?

Her treacherous mind played out possible scenes. She saw Andromache standing at a farmhouse door, her face stern, her eyes cold. 'What are you doing here?' she would ask. She would reply: 'I have travelled across the Great Green to be with you.' Andromache would say, 'That life is ended. You are not wanted here,' and the door would close firmly in her face.

She tried to recall the joyous scene she had nursed in her heart for so long – Andromache running into her arms, confessing she hated her husband Hektor, begging Piria to take her away from Troy, to a life of quiet bliss together in a small village overlooking the sea. But black doubts now assailed this pretty picture. How would you live in this village, they demanded? Raising goats, or sewing garments for peasants, or making bread? The pair had no such skills. Two princesses, hunted by their families, and by the great powers of Troy and Thera, living unrecognized in a quiet country retreat? She knew now that it was impossible. So what would they do? The thought brought fresh despair, and she sighed.

'You seem troubled.'

Kalliades had dropped back to speak to her as Banokles strode ahead. She could find nothing to say. He did not press her, and they walked on in silence, following Banokles' long moon-shadow up a gentle hillside.

The two years she had spent on Thera with Andromache had been the only truly happy time she could recall. I should have stayed on the Blessed Isle, she thought, seeing again the farmhouse door closing on her and her dreams.

She realized she had stopped walking, and the two men were looking at her curiously.

Her breathing was shallow, and she felt the beginnings of panic, a trembling in her hands, a tightness in her belly. They had reached the brow of a low hill, and ahead by the roadside she could see a small white shrine, shining in the moonlight. Not wanting her companions to see her distress, she walked over to it. The bones of small creatures lay at its base and the statue of a woman with a bow had been placed in an alcove.

The statue was of the huntress goddess, Artemis, who despised men. On Thera there was a temple to her on the highest point of the island, a spur of limestone rock standing proud of the rest of the isle. She and Andromache had often climbed to that temple, to walk the sun-drenched corridors and hear the wind whistle among the white columns. They both felt safe in the halls of the moon goddess, who welcomed men only as sacrifice.

Piria looked at the bow in her hand, feeling the

leather grip smooth against her hand, just as it had nestled in Andromache's hand perhaps days before.

There were many small offerings laid on the shrine: wooden figures of pregnant women carved without skill but with great care, bronze arrowheads, coloured pebbles painted with images of the goddess, and many clay animals – deer, hounds and quail.

'O Lady of the Wild Creatures,' she whispered, 'I have nothing to give you.' She had only her shabby tunic and her sandals. She held the bow of Andromache and the dagger of Kalliades. She had nothing of her own. Even her blond hair she had hacked away.

She stood before the shrine, with its offerings of wood and clay and bright bronze. 'I have nothing to give. I have nothing to give,' she repeated.

Suddenly she took the knife from her belt and stepped towards the shrine, arm raised. 'Accept my blood, moon goddess,' she whispered. 'Accept this offering.' She felt a hand on her arm and spun round, eyes wide and angry.

Kalliades said gently, 'Artemis does not seek the blood of women.'

'I have nothing else,' said Piria, tears flowing.

He stood for a moment, then slowly lifted his left palm towards her. She looked into his eyes, her brow furrowed.

'The goddess will accept *my* blood,' he said softly. She hesitated for just a moment, then made a small cut in the flesh of his hand. Moving to the shrine, he clenched his fist above the statue. Crimson drops splashed down, dark against the white stone. He moved back and glanced at Banokles.

Mystified, the big man looked from one to the other, then he shrugged and stepped forward. Gently, Piria nicked the side of his left hand and his blood joined that of Kalliades.

Piria spoke. 'Artemis, virgin lady, moon goddess, I give you this offering of the blood of men. Give us your light in the darkness, and bring us to our hearts' desire.'

Suddenly the woods and fields around them were plunged into silence. The small breeze dropped, and all sounds – the rustle of leaves and bushes, the night noises of small creatures – suddenly ceased, as if the world was holding its breath. The moon seemed huge in the still, dark sky.

For the first time in days Piria's heart calmed. She smiled at the two men. 'Thank you,' she said. 'I am ready now.'

Banokles cleared his throat and said gruffly, 'If you find you are not welcome . . . well . . . you could always come with us, you know. With Kalliades and me. We are going south. To the mountains.'

Her vision misted, and she nodded her thanks to him, not trusting herself to speak. Kalliades leaned towards her. 'Let us find your friend, and then you can decide where your road will lead.'

They returned to the road. As they approached the crest of the hill Piria glanced at the two warriors beside her. A sense of peace and security, lost to her since she was twelve years old, flowed over her. She was with men she trusted and in whose company she felt safe.

They stopped at the brow of the hill and looked down into the valley beyond. They could see a fierce red glow, and the acrid smell of smoke assailed their nostrils. As their eyes adjusted they could see flames leaping from a group of buildings. The sounds of animals in distress reached their ears.

'Fire!' shouted Kalliades. 'The farm is on fire!' Dark figures moved across the flames and they could hear the clash of swords and the cries of wounded men.

Piria started to run down the hill. 'Andromache!' she cried.

Unsheathing their swords, her two friends followed.

For a moment only Andromache froze. Then she heard a voice call out: 'There she is! Kill her!' She saw a bearded swordsman pointing at her. Cheon, sword in hand, ran at the first of the killers, swaying aside from a sword thrust and plunging his own blade into the attacker's face. The man fell back. Cheon followed in – but an arrow ripped into his side. Other dark-garbed men rushed in, hacking and slashing at the dying Trojan.

Another arrow flashed past Andromache's face. Leaving Cheon's body, five men ran at her. Spinning round she raced across the open ground towards the hillside. Then she heard a woman's voice cry out.

'Andromache! Come to me!' Even through her fear she recognized the voice, and glanced up.

There was Kalliope on the steep hillside above her, a bow in her hand. There were two warriors with her, one tall and dark, the other powerful and blond, wearing a leather cuirass covered with gleaming bronze discs. 'Look out!' shouted the tall man. Andromache spun away once more. A bearded assassin was closing in on her, a dagger in his hand. 'Got you now, bitch!' he snarled.

Andromache leapt at him, her foot cracking against his chest, knocking him from his feet. More attackers were close behind. An arrow from Kalliope's bow lanced into the throat of the nearest, then the blond bearded warrior ran past Andromache, blocking a sword thrust before sending a backhand cut slashing into the face of an assassin. Blood sprayed out from the wound. He shoulder-charged another man, then rushed in to the following group, his sword hacking and cutting. The tall warrior raced in to fight alongside his comrade. Andromache saw more assassins, some nine in all, converge on the two men, and it seemed they must be overrun. Beyond them one of the youths who had earlier been trying to tame the stallion staggered to the doors of the blazing barn, and managed to raise the locking bar. Terrified horses came thundering out, racing in panic away from the flames.

'Come to me, my love!' shouted Kalliope.

Andromache ran up the hillside towards her. Kalliope was still shooting arrows at the attacking men. As she scrambled up towards her lover Andromache caught sight of a bowman some fifty paces distant. He loosed an arrow. Andromache hurled herself to the ground.

But the shaft had not been aimed at her.

She saw Kalliope stagger back, her bow falling to the

grass, a black-feathered arrow jutting from her chest.

Anger, fierce and cold, swept through Andromache. Surging up, she ran to Kalliope's side, sweeping up the bow and notching an arrow to the string. The bowman loosed another shaft that slashed through her white robe, scoring the skin of her hip. Ignoring the pain, she took aim. The man, suddenly fearful, dashed towards the protection of the trees. Andromache gauged his speed, altered her aim, and let fly. For a heartbeat she thought she had missed, but the arrow clove into the side of his neck. His legs gave way and he fell.

Taking another arrow she swung to see the two warriors standing back to back and fighting furiously. The bodies of four assassins lay close by. Another killer cried out as the sword of the tall man lanced into his chest. Then one of the assassins at the rear darted round the fighting men and sprinted towards Andromache.

She let him come – then sent a shaft ripping through his lungs. He staggered on for several steps, then, in a last desperate attempt to complete his mission, hurled his sword at her. It did not come close, and he pitched forward onto his face.

Below her she saw the blond warrior stumble, but his comrade stepped in to block a sword thrust, and hauled him to his feet. Six bodies now lay around the pair, and the two surviving attackers suddenly turned and fled, heading out past the blazing barn. Andromache shot at one of them, but missed. Then they were gone.

Hurling aside the bow, Andromache dropped to her knees alongside Kalliope, who struggled to rise, but fell back with a cry. The two warriors came then, the tall man casting his sword aside and also dropping to his knees. Andromache saw his anguish.

A sense of unreality flowed through Andromache. This is a dream, she told herself. Kalliope cannot be here, and if she was, it would not be in the company of men. Assassins could not have attacked Hektor's farm, so close to the city. I will wake, she thought, still on the couch. Just a dream!

Then, as she moved, pain lanced through her hip. She glanced down at the blood on the slashed white gown. Kalliope's hand touched her arm. 'I came for you,' she said. 'Don't send me away! Please don't send me away!'

'I never will!' Andromache cried. 'Never!'

Once again Kalliope tried to rise. The tall warrior gently lifted her into a sitting position. 'Rest your head on my shoulder, Piria,' he said, his voice breaking.

'Am I hurt?' she asked him.

'Yes, you are hurt, sweet girl.'

Kalliope's left hand reached up, her fingers finding the arrow shaft. Her eyes flared wide with fear, then she smiled and sighed. 'He killed me, didn't he? Tell me the truth, Kalliades.'

Andromache saw the man's head bow down. 'I promised to see you safe,' he said. 'And I failed you.'

'Don't say that! You did not fail me, Kalliades. Not once. You gave me my life back. You and Banokles. Your friendship restored me.' Her gaze shifted to Andromache, who leaned in close and kissed her. 'It was Melite,' said Kalliope, her voice fading. 'She told me wicked men would come for you. I . . . I had to . . . be there.'

'And you were,' whispered Andromache.

Kalliope fell silent. The huge, blond warrior leaned in close, and Andromache saw there were tears in his eyes.

'You are all so sad,' said Kalliope. 'I am not sad. All the people . . . I love . . . are with me.' Her eyes fastened on the bright moon above. 'And there . . . is . . . Artemis . . .'

Then she was silent.

Andromache stared down at the pale, still face of her lover, and heard again the words of Aklides. His vision had been true, but misinterpreted. He had seen Helikaon with one sandal, and Hektor rising from the ground, covered in the filth of pigs.

But he had also seen a figure coming to her in the moonlight, with blood and pain. And, seeing the short hair, he had mistaken that vision for a young man. Reaching out, Andromache lifted Kalliope's hand, kissing the fingers. 'You are my moon,' she whispered, tears filling her eyes. 'Stay with me, Kalliope. Please!'

Banokles laid his hand on her arm. 'She has gone, lady. The brave girl has gone.'

Book Three

THE BATTLE FOR THRAKI

XXVI

The treacherous hound

THE SANDY SHORELINE BENEATH THE HIGH GREY CLIFFS OF
Ithaka lay silent save for the cry of gulls. The group of
wooden huts which housed fishermen and their families
seemed deserted under the hazy afternoon sun.

The old galley *Penelope*, her exposed hull heavily
barnacled, was pulled up high on the sand. Forgotten
and neglected, her once gleaming timbers were
bleached now by the blistering sun, her planks warped
and twisted.

From the shaded portico of her palace the queen of
Ithaka gazed at her namesake with sadness. For three
long years the ship had been abandoned here, forsaken
by Odysseus in favour of the war galley *Bloodhawk*.
Though ideal for a cargo vessel, the *Penelope* was no
fighting ship. For one season only she had continued
plying her trade for an Ithakan merchant, but the
bloody war on the Great Green had made trading by
sea increasingly dangerous and the galley was discarded

in favour of smaller, faster ships which risked the triangular run between Ithaka, Kephallenia and the mainland, or northwest towards the distant settlement of Seven Hills.

Penelope drew her blue shawl around her and peered out to sea. It seemed so calm today, yet far beyond the line of her sight there would be men dying in despair as their ships foundered, or their villages burned. In lands all round the Great Green wives and mothers would be weeping for the lost, their dreams impaled on the spears of angry men. The seed of new hatreds would be spread with every raid, planted in the hearts of those who survived; children who would grow into men filled with a desire for vengeance.

Yet, even with the knowledge of the evils of war, she had supported Odysseus in his actions. 'You could do no less, my husband,' she had said when he returned to her three years ago cursing and fuming still over his insulting treatment in Troy, 'for such slights cannot be ignored.'

In her heart she wished they could have been. If the kings of the world were reasonable men, clear-thinking and far-sighted, such wars would never occur. Yet reasonable men rarely ascended to thrones, and when they did it was even more rare for them to survive for long. Successful kings were brutal and greedy, men of blood and death, warriors who believed in nothing but the power of sword and spear. Penelope sighed. The husband she loved had tried to be a reasonable man. Yet beneath the affable surface there had always lurked the warrior king.

He had spent that first winter with her, nursing his

anger through the long nights, then in spring had left to go raiding in the lands of his new enemies. The name *Bloodhawk* now inspired fear from the coasts of Thraki down the great isles of the eastern mainland to Lykia in the south. She had last seen her king early in the year. After being forced to winter on Kypros while his damaged ship was repaired, Odysseus had hurried back to Ithaka for a brief visit. Penelope smoothed down the front of her dress, remembering the few precious days and nights they had spent together.

Her sadness grew with each passing season, for each time he returned to her he seemed to be moving backwards in time. At first he had entered the war with some regrets, spurred on by anger and pride. But now she knew he was revelling in re-experiencing his youth. Odysseus the bluff genial trader, sliding slowly into comfortable old age, was gone, to be replaced by Odysseus the reaver, the cool and calculating planner, the *strategos*. Her heart ached for the man he once was.

Shading her eyes with her hand, Penelope saw movement on the horizon, and a line of ships appeared there. They were heading straight for the island. Her heart leapt for a moment. Could it be Odysseus? The hope lasted mere heartbeats. She had heard only days before that the *Bloodhawk* had been seen heading north from the Mykene settlement on Kos.

She could see now it was a large fleet, with one great ship plunging through the waves far ahead of the others.

The *Xanthos*! A warship that size, it could be no other.

She heard running feet behind her and turned to see Bias. The old warrior had a sword in his left hand. A round wooden buckler had been clumsily strapped to the stump of his ruined right arm.

'Lady! It is the *Xanthos*! We must make for the hill fort.'

Behind him fisherfolk were emerging from the huts, and the small garrison of Ithaka, many of them merely boys or ancients, were racing down to the beach, some faces grim, many frightened. Odysseus had left a force of 200 to guard his fortress and his queen. Penelope studied the fleet. Thirty-one ships she counted. Close to 2,000 fighting men.

She said to Bias, raising her voice so the soldiers could hear, 'I am the queen of Ithaka, wife to the great Odysseus. I do not hide like a frightened peasant.'

The *Xanthos* was heading towards the shore at ramming speed, its great prow carving the waves with the speed of a running horse. Penelope could hear the lusty chant of the rowers and clearly see the bearded face of a sailor looking over the prow.

'Hold!' came the bellowed order from the ship, and the chanting ceased suddenly as oars were raised. There was a moment when the *Xanthos* seemed suspended above the beach, then she crashed onto the shore, her keel ripping into the sand and spraying gravel on all sides.

As the huge galley lurched to a halt, sluicing water from her planks, the queen turned to her small force. 'Go to the fort and prepare to defend it. Now!' For a moment they stood unmoving. 'Go!' she repeated.

Reluctantly they retreated, past the palace and up the hillside to the ephemeral safety of the wooden stockade. Bias did not move.

'Does the queen not have your loyalty?' she asked him.

'She has my love, and my life. I'll not hide behind wooden walls while you risk yours.'

Anger touched her, and she was about to order him back, when the round buckler slid from his shrivelled stump, and clattered to the sand. She felt his embarrassment and his shame.

'Walk with me, Bias,' she said. 'It will be comforting to have your strength by me.'

They strode side by side down the beach. Penelope had never seen the *Xanthos* before, and she marvelled at its size and beauty, though her face remained serene.

A rope was thrown over the side, and Helikaon climbed down to the beach. Penelope looked with sadness upon the notorious killer who was once a boy she loved. He was wearing a faded linen kilt and his black hair was pulled back with a leather thong. He was bronzed dark by the sun, and bore a stitched, barely healed scar on one thigh, and a recent, unhealed one on his chest. He glanced at the hulk of Odysseus' old ship as he strode up the beach, but his face betrayed no expression.

'Greetings, lady,' he said, bowing his head slightly. She looked into his violent blue eyes and saw tension and tiredness. Why was he here? To kill her and her people? She realized she knew nothing about him now, save his reputation as a killer without mercy or restraint.

She avoided looking at the other ships as they sailed towards the beach, and forced a welcoming smile.

'Helikaon, greetings! It is too many summers since we last welcomed you here. I will have food and wine brought down. We can talk of happier times.'

He smiled tightly. 'Thank you, lady, but my ships are well provisioned. We enjoyed the hospitality of old Nestor and his people on our way here. We have food and water for many days.'

Penelope was shocked, although she would not show it. She had no idea Pylos had been attacked. How many dead, she wondered? She had many friends there, and kinsmen.

'But you will break bread with me, the way we used to?' she asked, ruthlessly dismissing from her mind thoughts of the dead of Pylos. She could not help them; she could only save her own people.

He nodded, and gazed assessingly at the old fort, and the armed men who now lined the stockade walls. 'Yes, lady, we will break bread.' He turned to Bias. 'I heard you lost that arm at a battle off Kretos. I am glad you survived.'

The black man's eyes narrowed. 'I hope you burn, Helikaon,' he said coldly, 'and your death ship with you.'

Penelope gestured for him to move back, and the old man, staring balefully at Helikaon, retreated several steps. The queen turned to him. 'I am in no danger now, Bias. Return to the fort.' Bias bowed his head, glared once more at Helikaon, then strode away.

Servants brought a blanket to lay on the sand and

Helikaon and the queen sat down. Though the sun blazed in the sky Penelope ordered a welcome fire lit, as was the custom when entertaining friends. Wine and bread were laid before them, but they ate and drank little.

'Tell me news, Helikaon. Little reaches us here in far Ithaka.'

Helikaon looked into her face. 'The only news is of war, lady, and I'm sure you have no genuine wish to hear of it. Many are dying, up and down the Great Green. There are no victors. Your husband lives, I am told. We have not encountered one another. I have no recent news of the *Bloodhawk*. I came here for one reason, to pay my respects to you . . .'

'I know the reason you came here,' Penelope said angrily, leaning forward, her voice low. 'To show Odysseus that you could. You threaten his people . . .'

His face tightened. 'I have not threatened you, and I will not.'

'Your very presence here is a threat. It is a message to Odysseus that he cannot guard those he loves. Your first words to me were to boast of attacking my kinsmen at Pylos. I am not a fool, Helikaon. I was queen here when you were a babe in arms. I *know* why you are here.'

'He left you poorly guarded,' he said, gesturing at the small Ithakan force.

They sat in silence for a while. Penelope was furious with herself. Her first priority was to save her people from attack. Antagonizing Helikaon was more than foolish. She could not believe he would set his killers on

447

her people, yet tension etched into the skin round his eyes told of unresolved conflicts in his mind.

Calming herself, she asked pleasantly, 'How is your little son? He must be three now.'

Helikaon's face lightened. 'He is a joy. I miss him every day I am away. But he is not my son. I wish that he was.'

'Not your son?'

Helikaon explained that the queen had been raped at the time of a Mykene attack and the boy was the result. 'I had hoped it would remain secret – for Halysia's sake. But such things rarely do. There were servants who knew, and the whispers began.'

'How does Halysia feel about him?' she asked.

Helikaon's face darkened again. 'She cannot look upon him without pain. To see him merely reminds her of the horror of the attack, her own child set ablaze and hurled from the cliffs, her body brutalized, raped and stabbed. Such are the men your husband is now allied to.' She saw him struggling to contain his anger.

'But you love the boy,' she said swiftly.

He relaxed again. 'Yes, I do. He is a fine child, intelligent, warm and funny. But she cannot see that. She will not even touch him.'

'There is so much sadness in the world,' Penelope said. 'So many children unwanted and unloved. And women who would give everything they possess to have a child. You and I, we have both lost those we loved.'

'Yes, we have,' he said sadly.

In that moment of empathy she brought out her strongest weapon. 'I am with child, Helikaon,' she said.

'After all this time. Seventeen years after little Laertes died. I am pregnant again. I never believed I could give Odysseus another son. Surely the great goddess herself is guarding me.' She watched his face carefully, saw it soften, and knew she was close to winning this battle. 'Trade from the Seven Hills is growing,' she said. 'Odysseus is holding your profits, as he promised he would. And there has been little trouble among the peoples of the settlement. There are walls of stone now, to protect it.'

Helikaon pushed himself to his feet. 'I must leave,' he said, 'but I hope you believe me when I say it was good to see you, Penelope. You once welcomed me into your home, and my memories of Ithaka are fond ones. I pray your child is born safely, and can grow in a world that is not at war.'

Walking away from her he strode to a small thatched hut high on the beach. The Ithakan garrison watched him with suspicion as he reached up and pulled clear a handful of thatch from the roof, and returned to Penelope. Without speaking, he thrust the thatch into the welcome fire until it smouldered, then lit. He held it a few heartbeats, then threw it down on the beach. Drawing his sword, he plunged it through the burning thatch and into the sand. Then, without a word, he walked back down the strand and climbed aboard his warship.

Penelope watched him go with relief and regret. His meaning was clear. It was a message to Odysseus. By sword and flame he could have destoyed Ithaka and butchered her people. He had chosen not to.

This time.

* * *

Helikaon stood on the high stern deck of the *Xanthos* and gazed at the retreating cliffs of Ithaka. He could no longer see the proud figure of Penelope, but could still make out the thin plume of smoke rising from the welcome fire on the beach.

He had not lied to her. The moment he stepped ashore all thoughts of war had seeped away as memories long forgotten had flowed through his mind: Odysseus, drunk and happy, standing on a table in the *megaron*, enchanting his listeners with tales of gods and heroes, Penelope smiling fondly at him, Bias shaking his head and chuckling.

I hope you burn, and your death ship with you. The words of Bias, so unexpected and harsh, had cut through his defences, sharper than any blade.

Yet he and Bias had sailed together, fought pirates together, laughed and joked in each other's company. To see such hatred in the eyes of a friend was hard to take. In his memories Bias was always good-humoured. He had been helpful and supportive when Helikaon had joined the crew of the *Penelope*. Bias was the man the sailors trusted to settle disputes and to arbitrate disagreements. The crew loved him, for his actions were always governed by his genuine affection for the men who served under him.

Now this man of kindness and compassion wanted him dead, and Helikaon's heart was heavy with the burden of the old man's hatred. Surely Bias knew that he had not wanted this war – that it had been forced upon him?

Once the ships were out of sight of Ithaka Helikaon ordered a slight change of direction, heading north along the coast. There was no wind, and the twin banks of oarsmen began pulling to the steady beat called out by his first mate, Oniacus. Once the rhythm was set the stocky, curly-haired sailor approached him. He too had changed since the war began, seeming more distant now. He rarely laughed or sang any more. Long gone were the days when he would sit in the evenings alongside Helikaon and muse about the meaning of life, or the antics of his children.

'Sad to see old Bias so crippled,' he said.

Helikaon glanced at the young sailor. 'There seems no end to sadness these days,' he replied.

'Did you see the *Penelope*? Just rotting away in the sun. Makes the heart sick. Always used to marvel when I saw her dancing upon the waters. And seeing her heading for the beach usually meant a night of great storytelling. I miss those days. They shine like gold in the memory now. I doubt we'll see them again.' He walked away.

Oniacus was right. The days of storytelling and comradeship were long gone now. Along with so many dreams.

Three years ago Helikaon had been simply a merchant trader, sailing the Great Green, enduring its storms, exhilarated by its ageless beauty. Young, and in the full glory of his strength, he had dreamed of finding a wife for love alone. No thoughts of dynastic treaties or alliances with rival nations troubled him. Those were problems his little brother would have to face, for he had been named heir to the throne of Dardania.

Three years.

How the world had changed in that time. Little Diomedes, the happy smiling child of his memories, had been drenched in oil and set ablaze by Mykene raiders. Then they had hurled him, screaming, from a cliff. And Helikaon had become king, and had married for the good of the realm.

Staring out over the sun-dappled sea he fought back the waves of bitterness threatening to engulf him. Such anger, he knew, was unfair to Halysia, who was a good woman, and a good wife. But she was not Andromache. Even now he could summon Andromache's face to his mind, so clear it was as if she stood beside him, the sun glinting on her long red hair. When he pictured her smile he was struck by an almost unbearable sadness. She now had a child, a delightful boy, called Astyanax. Hektor doted on him, and to see them together was both a joy and a dagger to his heart.

Helikaon wandered down to the central deck, where some twenty of the wounded were sitting beneath canvas canopies. The raid on Pylos had been brutal and swift, and though the defenders had been few they had fought hard to save their homes and their families. Helikaon's force had overcome them swiftly and burned the settlement, destroying the dams built to service the flax fields. His men had then stormed through the palace of Nestor, plundering it.

Nestor's youngest son, Antilochos, had fought well. Helikaon would have let him live, but he had refused to surrender, leading a last desperate charge in a vain attempt to reach Helikaon himself. He and his few soldiers had been cut down and hacked to death.

It was the fourth successful raid Helikaon had led during the current season, his troops invading Mykene islands, and then the mainland. A Mykene fleet had come against them off the coast of Athens, but the Fire Hurlers of the *Xanthos* had sunk four of them. Others had been rammed by his war galleys. By the day's end eleven enemy ships had been sunk, for the loss of one Dardanian galley. More than 600 Mykene sailors had died, some in flames, others shot with arrows, or drowned.

But the strategy of raiding settlements had proved less effective than had been hoped. Priam had believed the attacks would force the invaders to pull troops back from the front lines in Thraki and Lykia to defend their own homelands, and at first it had seemed his plan was working. Reports from the front lines suggested that some regiments were being withdrawn in Thraki, but these were replaced by mercenary armies from lands to the north.

Helikaon walked among the wounded men, most of whom were recovering. A young warrior with a bandaged forearm looked up at him, but said nothing, his eyes empty of emotion. Helikaon spoke to the men, who listened attentively, but said little in return. There was a distance now between Helikaon and his warriors that he could not cross. As a merchant he could laugh and joke with them, but as a battle king, with power of life and death over them, he found they drew back from him, wary and careful.

'You all fought well,' he told them. 'I am proud of you.'

The warrior with the wounded forearm looked up at him. 'You think the war will end this season, lord?' he asked. 'You think the enemy will realize they are beaten?'

'That is something to hope for,' Helikaon told him. Then he walked away from them.

The truth was that the enemy, far from being beaten, was growing in strength.

In the first year of the war it had seemed that the plans of Agamemnon were turning to dust. The war against Troy could never be won unless the Mykene controlled the lands of the Thrakians. Seeking to cross the open sea all the way from the western mainland would leave them prey to the Dardanian war fleet. With Thraki under Mykene control there would be no such danger. From there they could mass their ships and bring their armies across the narrow straits into Dardania, and then down to Troy.

Initially the Mykene invasion of Thraki had been repulsed, Hektor and the young Thrakian king, Rhesos, winning a decisive battle close to the capital of Ismaros. But this was followed by a rebellion among the eastern tribes, reinforced by barbarians from the north. Hektor had moved swiftly to crush the rebels, only for a second Mykene army to advance from the west, through Thessaly.

Losses were high, and the following year Priam had reinforced Hektor with 2,000 men. Three major battles had been won, but the fighting still raged. And the news now coming from the war-torn land of Thraki was grim indeed. Rhesos had been defeated and driven back to his capital, and the eastern rebels had declared their own nation state, under a new king. Helikaon had travelled through Thraki, and knew the land well. Towering mountain ranges with narrow passes, vast areas of marshy flatland, and verdant plains flanked by huge forests. It was far from easy to move armies through such terrain, and even harder to find suitable battlegrounds to win decisive victories. Enemy footsoldiers and archers could take refuge in the forests, where cavalry were useless, or escape through marshes and bogs, where infantry could only follow at their peril. Hektor's early victories had all come because the enemy, with the great advantage of superior numbers, had believed they could crush the Trojan Horse. So they had met him on open ground, and seen their arrogance washed away in the blood of their comrades.

They were wiser now, launching lightning raids, or hitting the supply caravans.

On the southern mainland below Troy matters were almost as bad. The Kretan king, Idomeneos, had led an army into Lykia, defeating the Trojan ally, Kygones, in two battles. And Odysseus had led a force of twenty ships and a thousand men, raiding all along the coast, plundering three minor cities, and forcing the surrender of two coastal fortresses, which were now held by Mykene garrisons.

Pushing such pessimistic thoughts from his mind Helikaon moved on to the prow, where Gershom was leaning on the rail and staring out over the sea. The big man had joined the fleet just before the last raid on the mainland. Since then his mood had become increasingly gloomy, and he spoke rarely.

'Where next?' he asked now.

'We'll sail up the coast then head west, and down to the lands of the Siculi.'

'Are they allied to the Mykene?'

'No.'

'That is good. And then we head home?'

'No, first we sail north and west to the lands of the Seven Hills. It is a long journey, but necessary.' He looked hard at Gershom. 'What is troubling you?'

Gershom shrugged. 'I am beginning to hate the word *necessary*,' he muttered. Then he sighed. 'No matter. I will leave you to your thoughts.'

Helikaon stepped forward as Gershom swung to leave the deck. 'Wait! What is happening here? A wall has come between us, and I cannot breach it. I can understand it with the other men, for I am their king and their leader, but you are my friend, Gershom.'

Gershom paused, and when he spoke his voice was cold, his eyes hard. 'What would you have me say?'

'From a friend?' said Helikaon. 'The truth would be good. How can I heal a rift when I do not know what caused it?'

'And there is the problem,' said Gershom. 'The man I met three years ago would have understood in a heartbeat. By the blood of Osiris, I would not be having *this* conversation with *that* man! What is wrong with you,

Helikaon? Did some harpy steal your heart and replace it with a rock?'

'What is wrong with *me*? Has everyone been moonstruck? I am the same man.'

'How can you think that?' snapped Gershom. 'We are sailing the Great Green in order to terrorize the innocent, burn their homes, kill their menfolk. War should be fought between soldiers, on a chosen battlefield. It should not visit peasant homes, where people struggle daily just to fill their bellies.'

Anger swept through Helikaon. 'You think I desire such slaughter?' he said. 'You think I revel in the deaths of innocent villagers?'

Gershom said nothing for a moment, then he drew himself up, and stepped in, his dark eyes gleaming. For a heartbeat only Helikaon thought he was about to be struck. Then Gershom leaned close. Helikaon felt a shiver go through him. It was as if he was staring at a stranger, a man of almost elemental power. 'What difference does your joy or guilt make to the widow?' said Gershom, his voice low, but the intensity of his words plunging home like daggers. 'All that she loved is still dead. All that she built is still ash. You were a hero once. Now you are killing husbands and old men. And children barely old enough to lift a sword. Perhaps Odysseus will spin a tale one day about the yellow-haired child on Pylos, with his little fruit knife, and his gushing blood.'

The ghastly image ripped into Helikaon's mind: the small, golden-haired boy, no more than seven or eight years old, running up behind one of Helikaon's warriors and stabbing him in the leg. Surprised and in pain the soldier had swung round, his sword slashing through the child's neck. As the boy fell the soldier had cried out in anguish. Dropping his blade he had taken the dying child into his arms, and struggled in vain to stem the gouting blood.

Other images flowed then. Women weeping over corpses, while their homes burned. Children shrieking in terror and pain, their clothes ablaze. Anger rose, like a defensive barrier against the memories. 'I did not cause this war,' he said. 'I was content trading on the Great Green. Agamemnon brought this terror upon us all.'

The eyes of power did not waver. 'Agamemnon did not bring death to that child. You did. I *expect* Agamemnon to murder children. I did not expect it from you. When the wolf slaughters the sheep we shrug and say, it is his nature. When the sheepdog turns on the flock it breaks our hearts, for his actions are treacherous. By all that is holy, Helikaon, the crew are not cold to you because you are the king. Can you not understand? You have taken good men and turned them to evil. You have broken their hearts.'

With that Gershom fell silent, and his accusing eyes turned away. In that dreadful moment Helikaon understood the hatred Bias felt for him. In the old man's philosophy heroes stood tall against the darkness, while evil men embraced it. There was no subtlety of shade, simply light and dark. Helikaon had betrayed everything his old shipmate believed in. Heroes did not attack the weak and defenceless. They did not burn the homes of the poor.

He glanced at Gershom, and saw that his friend was staring at him once again. But this time the eyes did not radiate power. They were filled with sadness. Helikaon could find no words. Everything Gershom had said was true. Why had he not been able to see it? He saw again the raids and the slaughter, only this time he viewed the images with different eyes.

'What have I become?' he said, at last, anguish in his voice.

'A reflection of Agamemnon,' said Gershom softly. 'You lost yourself in the grand designs of war, focusing on armies and strategies, calculating losses and gains in the same way you did as a merchant.'

'Why could I not see it? It is as if I was blinded by some spell.'

'No spell,' said Gershom. 'The truth is more prosaic than that. There is a darkness in you. In all of us, probably. Beasts we keep chained. Ordinary men have to keep the chains strong, for if we let the beast loose then society will turn upon us with fiery vengeance. Kings, though . . . well, who is there to turn upon them? So the chains are made of straw. It is the curse of kings, Helikaon, that they can become monsters.' He sighed. 'And they invariably do.'

A cool wind blew over the rear deck and Helikaon shivered. 'We will raid no more villages,' he said.

Gershom smiled and Helikaon saw the tension ease out of him. 'That is good to hear, Golden One.'

'A long time since you called me that.'

'Yes, it is,' replied Gershom.

* * *

Towards dusk a northwesterly wind began to blow, buffeting the fleet, and slowing their progress. Increasing weariness took its toll on the rowers. Some of the older vessels, acquired by Helikaon from allied nations, were not as well cared for as his own galleys. They were heavily barnacled and sluggish, unable to keep up with the swifter ships. Slowly at first, the fleet began to lose formation.

Helikaon was concerned, for if the fleet were to come upon enemy vessels the stragglers could be picked off and sunk. He had hoped to have made better progress. Without the wind against them they might have been able to make the crossing to the neutral coastline of Aia. There was no chance of that now.

As the light began to fail Helikaon signalled for the fleet to follow him into a wide bay. This was enemy territory, and he had no idea what forces were garrisoned in this area. The danger was twofold. There could be a hostile army within striking distance of the bay, or an enemy fleet could come upon them as they were beached.

As they entered the bay Helikaon saw a settlement far to the right, and above it a hilltop fort. It was small, and would hold no more than a hundred fighting men.

Eight trade vessels of shallow draught were beached close to the settlement, and already there were cook-fires lit.

As the sun set the galleys began to beach some 500 paces from the houses. Helikaon was the first ashore, calling his captains to him and instructing them to take no aggressive action, but merely to prepare cookfires and allow the men to rest. No-one, he said, was to approach the settlement.

As more and more men came ashore Helikaon spotted a troop of twenty soldiers leaving the fort and marching down towards them. They were poorly armed, with light spears and leather breastplates and helms. Helikaon saw Gershom looking at him, and guessed the Egyptian was thinking of the promise he had made, to raid no more settlements.

Helikaon strode out to meet the soldiers. Their leader, a tall, thin young man, prematurely bald, touched his fist to his breastplate in the Mykene manner. 'Greetings, traveller,' he said. 'I am Kalos, the watch commander.'

'Greetings to you, Kalos. I am Athenos, a friend to Odysseus.'

'You have a great many ships, Athenos, and a goodly number of men. This is a small settlement. There are only five whores and two eating houses. I fear there could be some unpleasantness if your men were allowed to roam free in the town.'

'Your point is well made, Kalos. I shall instruct my sailors to remain on the beach. Tell me, is there any news of Odysseus? I was to have met him and another allied fleet on Ithaka.'

Kalos shook his head. 'We have not seen the Ugly King this year at all. The fleet of Menados passed through several days ago. There have been rumours of more Trojan raiding to the west.'

'Sadly true, I fear,' said Helikaon. 'Pylos was attacked several days ago, the palace burned.'

The young militia man was shocked. 'No! That is grim news, sir. Is there no end to the vileness of these Trojans?'

'Apparently not. Where was Menados headed?'

'He did not share his plans with me, sir. He merely provisioned his fleet and set sail.'

'I hope his fleet was mighty. The attack on Pylos was said to have involved some fifty galleys.'

'There were at least eighty ships with Menados, though many of them were transports. He is a fine fighting sailor, and has sunk many pirate vessels these last few seasons.' The young man was about to speak on, but Helikaon saw his eyes flicker to the left. Then they widened and his expression changed. Helikaon glanced back. The last rays of the setting sun had illuminated the *Xanthos*. A poorly tied knot had slipped at the centre of the sail brace, and the sail itself had loosened, showing the head of the black horse painted there. There were few around the Great Green who had not heard of the black horse of Helikaon.

Kalos backed away. Helikaon turned towards him and spoke swiftly, keeping his voice calm. 'Now is not the time for rash action,' he said. 'The lives of your men and your settlement are in your hands. You have friends here? Family?'

The young soldier stared at him with open hatred. 'You are the Burner. You are accursed.'

'I am what I am,' admitted Helikaon, 'but that does not change the lives that hang in the balance here. I can see in your eyes that you are a man of courage. You would not hesitate to walk the Dark Road in order to strike down an enemy. But what of the people you are sworn to protect? The old ones, the young ones, the babes in arms? Fight me here and all will die. Allow my men to rest here for the night, and we will sail away and trouble no-one. By taking this wise course you will have honoured your obligation to defend your people. No-one will die, no homes will burn.'

The young man stood blinking in the fading light. Some of Helikaon's men began to gather. The militiamen lifted their spears and grouped close, ready to fight.

'Back!' Helikaon ordered his warriors. 'No blood will be spilt here. I have given my word to this brave young officer.' Returning his attention to Kalos, he looked into the man's dark eyes. 'Your choice, Kalos. Life or death for your people.'

'You will all remain on the beach?' asked the militiaman.

'We will. And you will ensure it, by remaining with us. My cooks will prepare a fine meal, and we will sit and eat, and drink good wine.'

'I have no wish to break bread with you, Helikaon.'

'And I have no wish to see you and your men vanishing over the hillside seeking reinforcements. You will stay with us. No harm will come to you.'

'We will not surrender our weapons.'

'Nor should you. You are not captives, nor have I requested your surrender. We are all, for this night, on this beach, neutrals. We will offer thanks and libations to the same gods before we eat, and we will talk as free men, under a free sky. You can tell me of the vileness of the Trojans, and I can tell you of the day a Mykene raiding force attacked my lands and took a child of my house, set him aflame and hurled him from a cliff. And then, as men of intellect and compassion, we will rail at the horrors of war.'

The tension eased, and cookfires were lit. Helikaon gathered the Mykene militiamen to him, and they sat together in awkward silence as the food was prepared. Wine was brought, though at first the Mykene refused it. As the uncomfortable night wore on Oniacus was called upon to sing, and this time he did. Oniacus had a fine deep voice, and the songs he chose were rich and melancholy. Eventually the Mykene accepted wine and food, and stretched out on the sand.

Helikaon set perimeter guards to patrol the beach, and prevent any incursions into the settlement, then walked to the water's edge. He was troubled, his mind unsettled. Gershom joined him. 'You did well, Golden One,' he said.

'Something is wrong,' said Helikaon. 'Those men are not soldiers, and their cheap armour is new. They are villagers, hastily armed. Why would that be?'

'Troops from this area were needed elsewhere,' offered Gershom.

'So far from the war?' Kalos had spoken of the fleet of Menados and said that many of his ships were transports. Those would be used to carry men and horses. An invasion force.

Yet his own fleet had spied no enemy ships, which meant they had hugged the coastline, moving east and north. This removed any thought of an attack on the lower eastern mainland of Lykia. The fleet of Menados was sailing along the Mykene coastline, bringing an army to where?

Up to Thraki to reinforce the armies facing Hektor? That was a possibility. Yet why would it be necessary? The armies of the Thessalian king, Peleus, could march into Thraki. Why denude the southern lands of soldiers and risk them at sea, when it would be so much simpler for the northern allies to mount a land attack?

Then it came to him, and the impact of realization struck him like a blow to the belly.

Dardania! If Agamemnon could land an army across the Hellespont below Thraki, then Hektor would be truly trapped. The citadel at Dardanos would be isolated, the few troops, under an eighty-year-old general, outnumbered and overcome. All the lands north of Troy would then fall under Mykene domination.

Yet again, he realized with a sinking heart, he had fallen back into thinking of the grand design of falling fortresses, and conquered lands. Halysia was at Dardanos, and the child, Dex. The last time the Mykene raided she had been raped and stabbed, her son murdered before her eyes.

'At first light we head for home,' he said.

XXVII

Sons of sorrow and joy

THE SMALL FAIR-HAIRED BOY RAN DOWN THE DUSTY corridor, his bare feet padding silently on the worn stones. At the end he turned to make sure Grey One had not caught up with him, then he lay quickly down and squirmed into a crevice in a dark corner.

The old fortress of Dardanos was a maze of corridors and tunnels, and small holes only a three-year-old could squeeze into. He crawled through the crevice between the walls and out into the gloom of a waiting chamber, behind a dusty tapestry, then dashed across the empty room to the heavy oak door in the opposite wall. The door was not quite closed, and if he lay with his face pressed to the jamb he could see into the great room beyond. He could not see Sun Woman, but he knew she would come, so he squatted more comfortably on the stone floor, his thin arms wrapped round his knees, and waited. He had learned a lot about waiting in his three short years.

He heard a wailing, screeching sound in the distance, which he knew was Grey One seeking him out. She would search the courtyard first. He chose a different hiding place each day, and Grey One was a slow old thing, always many steps behind him.

Bright dawn light was filtering through the high windows of the chamber, and he could smell cooking smells of corn bread and broth as the royal household broke its fast. His tummy felt empty and the smells made his mouth water, but he held his position, waiting for Sun Woman.

Every day he managed to escape Grey One and seek out Sun Woman. Yet he could not let her see him, for he knew she would be angry. Her cold anger frightened him, though he did not understand the reason for it. In his warm cot at night he would dream that one day Sun Woman would seek *him* out, that she would open her arms and call to him, and he would run to her. She would take him in her arms and hold him close and speak sweet words.

He heard movement in the *megaron*, and eagerly pressed his face to the door, but it was only some soldiers and Old Red Man. Old Red Man waved his hands about, giving the soldiers orders, then they all went away. Servants passed close by the chamber door, an arm's length from where he waited, but he knew they would not come in. It was their busiest time of the day.

His legs were growing cramped by the time people started filling the *megaron*. He lay down again and watched intently. All the old men in their long robes came in, their sandalled feet shuffling on the *megaron* floor. Then there were soldiers in armour, their ceremonial greaves shining in the morning sunlight. Ladies of the court murmured and giggled. The boy could tell who they were by their toe rings and ankle bracelets. One girl wore an ankle chain with tiny green fishes dangling from it. He watched, fascinated. They tinkled as she moved.

Then the hubbub ceased abruptly and the boy strained to press closer to the door.

Sun Woman walked to the throne and stood for a moment looking round her. She was wearing a long sleeveless tunic of shining white, decorated with shiny silver dots. Her golden hair was curled and wound on top of her head and threaded with bright ribbon. As always, the boy was dazzled by her beauty and he felt a pain in his heart that made him want to cry.

Sun Woman said, 'Let us begin. We have much to discuss.' Her voice was like silver bells. She sat down and the business of the day began. She spoke to Old Red Man and the other old men, then people were brought before her one at a time. One of them was a soldier. His hands were tied. He talked to her angrily, his face red. The boy felt a moment's fear for Sun Woman, but she spoke quietly, then other soldiers led the man away.

The day was passing into noon and the boy was half asleep when Sun Woman rose from her throne. Looking round the *megaron*, she asked, 'Where is Dexios? The boy must be here for the ritual. Lila!' She gestured impatiently. Grey One shuffled out from a corner of the *megaron*, wringing her old hands, her face creased with worry.

'I could not find him, lady. I'm sorry. He runs so fast, I can't keep up with him.'

'Have you searched the stable? He hides in the straw, I understand.'

'Yes, lady. He was not there.'

Behind the door Dexios sat frozen for a few heart-beats, scarcely able to believe his ears. Sun Woman was asking for him? She wanted *him*? He jumped to his feet, ready to run to her, but in his excitement and confusion he pushed against the oak door instead of pulling, and it closed silently, the locking bar snicking into place. It was shut fast.

He beat his hands against the oak. 'I'm here. Here I am!' he cried. But they could not hear him.

Panicking now, he pummelled the door with his small fists. 'Here I am! Open the door! Please open the door!'

A soldier, sword in hand, suddenly dragged the door open. Dexios, his face a mask of tears, stood framed in sunlight as everyone in the *megaron* stared at him.

Falling to his knees in front of Halysia, queen of Dardania, he said, 'Here I am, Mama. Don't be angry.'

The black bullock, bright blood gouting from its throat, fell to the courtyard floor. Its windpipe severed, it made no sound apart from a dying wheeze. Its legs thrashed weakly, then it was still. The priest of Apollo, a young man naked save for a loincloth, handed the ritual knife to his assistant and started to recite the words of worship to the Lord of the Silver Bow.

Halysia closed her mind to the sight and stench of blood, and followed the familiar words for mere moments before her thoughts turned once more to her duties.

She noticed the boy was still beside her and a spasm of irritation ran through her. Why was he here? Why had Lila not taken him back to his room? He was looking up at her from time to time, fair hair flopping back from his face. She always avoided looking at his face, his dark eyes.

She wished Helikaon were here. She had been queen in Dardania for fifteen years, first as a frightened child, then a young mother, then a widow, her heart stricken near to death by the murder of her son. Each day she calmly discussed with her counsellors the peril that faced them from the north and from the sea. They listened to her plans and suggestions, and carried out her orders. But even old Pausanius had no idea of the freezing fear that gripped her heart each time she imagined a second Mykene raid. She saw once again the blood-covered warriors entering her bedchamber, killing her lover Garus, dragging her screaming to the cliff top, her son Dio beside her, and the horror that followed. She remembered the dark-eyed brute, a Hittite she was told, who had raped her. She remembered the agonized cries of her child as he died.

She could not look at the small boy beside her, could not hold his hand, could not embrace him. She wished he had never been born. She wished he would go away. When he was older she would send him to Troy on some pretext to be brought up with the royal children there.

She glanced down and saw him looking up at her, an expression on his face she could not interpret. Was he frightened of her? Did he even know who she was? She realized she understood this boy's thoughts less well than she understood those of the horses she loved. The dark eyes bored into her, full of some unexpressed need, and she turned angrily from their gaze. She signalled to Lila and the old nursemaid hurried to take the child away.

The ritual ran slowly to its conclusion, and as the priests set about dismembering the bullock Halysia walked back into the palace, flanked by her senior officers: old Pausanius; his grand-nephew, the red-haired Menon; the annoying Trojan Idaios; and his two young aides.

She had only one more duty today, the daily briefing on the course of the war. In an anteroom off the *megaron*, she sank to a couch while the five officers stood around her. The doors were closed against the ears of servants.

'Well, Pausanius, what have you to report today?'

The old general cleared his throat. He was past eighty now, and had served the rulers of Dardania for more than sixty years. These days there was always a look of concern on his weather-beaten face.

'No news from Thraki, lady. No messengers have arrived for five days.'

She nodded. A Dardanian infantry force had travelled to Thraki with the Trojan Horse. No news was to be expected this soon, yet every day Halysia feared she would hear they had been wiped out and Mykene and Thrakian rebels were galloping for the straits. But her voice was calm when she asked, 'And the horse messengers? My plans have been completed?'

Pausanius hesitated a moment and cleared his throat again. 'Yes, lady. It will be as you order. Within a few days our plans will be complete.'

In Helikaon's absence, Halysia had taken it upon herself to set up a team of king's riders throughout Dardania, modelled on those of the Hittites, with armed staging posts a day's ride apart. Her plan was to have riders carrying messages constantly to and from Troy, sharing intelligence with Priam on the progress of the war. Teams of horsemen would also carry messages to Dardanos' eastern allies in Phrygia and Zeleia.

Pausanius had been doubtful at first, unhappy at taking skilled horsemen from the army and from the defence of the city.

'Communication is everything,' she had told him. 'If the Mykene come we must have as much warning as possible. The king's riders have orders to fall back to the city in advance of any invasion. They will give us the early warning we need.'

The old man had followed her orders, and horsemen had been chosen from among the Dardanian forces. They were mostly very young, hardly more than boys, but brought up among horses, as she had been herself, so that riding came more naturally to them than walking. She had spoken to each one individually, and their pride at their special task shone from them.

'I have one concern, lady,' said the Trojan, Idaios. Halysia's heart sank, though she maintained a look of cool interest.

'And what is that, Idaios?'

The officer stood with his fellow Trojans to one side of the anteroom. The three men had been sent by Priam, in Helikaon's absence, to advise and support the defence of Dardanos. Their only achievement so far, as Halysia saw it, was to hinder and question every decision she made. The speaker, Idaios – a short, stocky man, with a drooping blond moustache to hide his broken front teeth – was believed to be an illegitimate son of Priam.

'Forgive me, lady,' he said, 'but you know my opinion on these messengers. King Priam . . .' he paused to give everyone time to consider his important connections, 'agrees with me that information is priceless and should be closely guarded, not spread around the countryside in the mouths of young men we have no reason to trust.'

Halysia said tiredly, 'Yes, we know your opinion, Idaios. We have been through this before. These young men have been chosen not only because they are good riders, but because they are intelligent and sharp-witted. They are all Dardanians, and loyal to their king. They cannot carry writing, because most of the people they carry messages to cannot read script. We trust them to deliver messages accurately and only to the people they are intended for.'

Pausanius put in irritably, 'One of my grandsons was chosen as a king's rider. Are you suggesting he is a traitor?'

Idaios bowed to the old general. 'No-one questions the loyalty of young Pammon, General. I am merely pointing out that the possibility for treachery exists where information is too freely bandied about.'

Halysia held up her hands. 'This subject is closed for discussion. Let us talk of the five settlements.'

The five settlements were large villages lying along the coast north of Dardanos, crucially positioned to give early warning of an invasion across the straits. They were inhabited by Phrygians and Mysians, and some Thrakians, who had chosen to live on the warm coastal lands rather than in the harsher hinterlands. Many families had lived there for generations. Halysia had taken the controversial step of arming the settlements, believing the people would reward her trust with their loyalty. She knew Idaios strongly disagreed with the plan, and suspected he had sent back to Troy to tell Priam of his feelings.

Menon, a handsome young general who was increasingly taking the burden from Pausanius' shoulders, said the chiefs of the five settlements had been sent both light armour and arms – bows, spears, swords and shields. The local chiefs had been given total freedom regarding the distribution of the weapons to their people.

'If the Mykene come they will be useless,' said Pausanius grumpily. 'A few hundred armed villagers against thousands of fighting men.'

Menon smiled. 'I know this, Uncle, but if you were threatened by a thousand armed men would you rather face them with a sword in your hand, or naked and defenceless?'

474

The old man nodded in reluctant agreement. Halysia heard Idaios breathe in, about to speak, and she held up her hand. 'I don't want to hear it, Idaios. I have no doubt that you and your comrades consider this a flawed plan, that these people should not be armed for fear they will use their arms against us, or against each other. That might well be true in times of peace, when a Phrygian might kill a Thrakian over the ownership of a cow. But with the threat across the Hellespont constantly in their minds, they will be grateful to be armed, and will repay us with their loyalty.'

Idaios took another breath. 'Tell me,' she said, cutting him off again, 'you have been placed in charge of security on the beach. Are all visitors to Dardanos being searched and disarmed, as I ordered?'

A discontented look came over his face. She knew he resented the role she had given him. Confiscating old wooden clubs and blunted swords from visiting sea-farers, then returning them to the right owners when they left, was beneath his dignity.

'Yes, lady,' he said, 'it is being done. Although—'

'Good,' she said. 'This is a vital task. Do not under-estimate it.' She stood up before anyone else could speak. 'General Pausanius, please walk with me.'

They moved out through the sunlit courtyard and beyond to the bustling stables of the royal guard. Halysia raised her face to the sun and breathed in deeply the smells of horses, sun-bleached straw, and leather. She moderated her pace to allow the old soldier to keep up. She was saddened by his increasing infirmity. In the three years since the attack on

Dardanos, his age seemed to have weighed ever more heavily upon him.

From the stables came the sounds of stamping hooves, then angry neighing. Halysia entered the wooden building. With Pausanius behind her she walked to the furthest stall, where a huge black horse was rearing and bucking, his hooves thundering against the walls, causing them to creak and shudder. As she approached the stall the beast caught sight of her and lunged, eyes wild and nostrils flaring. His massive chest hit the stall door, cracking the top timber. Unflinching, Halysia stood her ground and spoke quiet words to the animal, which glared at her, then backed away into the shadows.

'I don't know why you keep that creature around,' grumbled Pausanius. 'We brought him up here because he was causing havoc down in the paddocks. Now he's upsetting the guards' horses instead.'

'I thought being away from the mares would calm him down,' she said. 'He's always so angry. I wonder why.'

'He'd be less angry if we cut his balls off,' offered Pausanius. 'Then he might settle and become a good mount.'

'Helikaon thinks he will make a fine stud animal, and create a new breed of war horse.'

Pausanius shook his head. 'Too much spirit to be allowed to roam free. You know he almost crippled one of my best riders? Threw him, then stamped down on his legs. Broke them both. He's wrong in the head, lady.'

'Open the stall, Pausanius.'

The old man stood his ground. 'Please don't do this, my queen.'

She smiled at him. 'He is merely a horse. Not some savage killer. Do as I order you.'

Pausanius stepped forward and lifted the locking bar, pulling the door open just wide enough for Halysia to enter. She saw him draw his sword, and knew he was ready to cut the beast's throat if it threatened her. 'Put that away,' she said, softly, 'and lock the stall behind me.' Stepping inside, she began to hum a soft, soothing tune, then slowly and smoothly lifted her hand and gently stroked the stallion's neck. It pawed the ground, its ears flat against its skull. 'One day,' she whispered, pressing her face against the horse's cheek, 'you and I will ride out into the meadows. You will be a king among horses, and the mares will flock to you.' Taking a handful of straw, she brushed the stallion's broad back. After a while its ears pricked up and it turned its head to look at her. 'You are so beautiful,' she said. 'So handsome, so strong.'

Dropping the straw, she walked slowly back to the stall door. Pausanius opened it and she stepped out. As the locking bar fell into place the stallion suddenly reared and lashed out. Pausanius stumbled back and almost fell. Halysia laughed.

'He will be a fine, fine horse,' she said.

'I do not know how you do that,' said the old general. 'I'd swear he understands you when you speak to him.'

Outside, Halysia turned to Pausanius. 'Will you ride with me, General?'

'I would be honoured, my queen.' He called out to a stable boy to fetch mounts. The youngster brought out Halysia's old bay gelding, Dancer, and a gentle sway-backed mare Pausanius had recently taken a liking to. They rode through the stable yard and down to the Seagate, overlooking the harbour. Halting their mounts on the steep rocky incline, they stared across the narrow ribbon of sea to the shore of war-torn Thraki.

Pausanius voiced the fear she felt. 'If eastern Thraki falls, both the armies of the west and rebel Thrakians will arrive on that shore in their thousands.'

She turned and looked at the Seagate. Helikaon had ordered the gate towers reinforced, and the stone entrance faced with green marble brought from Sparta. The steep gradient from the harbour would make it near impossible to force the gates. An enemy labouring up the hill would lose many men to bowmen safe on the high walls.

'With enough soldiers we could hold out for months,' she said.

The old man grunted. '*Enough* would be five times what we have.'

Without another word Halysia turned her horse and rode up along the narrow, rocky trail round the outside of the walls, past the highest point of the cliffs, called Aphrodite's Leap. She smiled as she thought of the old general following her. The ground was uneven, and, in places, the trail so narrow that her outside foot hung over an awesome drop to the rocks below.

Pausanius did not fear the dangerous ride, but he feared for her. He could not understand her desire to take such risks. Halysia did not try to explain. Out on the plains of her youth there were many summer fires. They would blaze in the dry grass, the winds fanning them, driving them towards the settlements. The only way to combat them was to set controlled blazes ahead of the inferno, so that when the blaze reached the burnt-out areas it would have nothing to feed upon, and die away.

These perilous rides were, for Halysia, a way of containing the greater fears she suffered, by enduring a lesser fear she could control.

Eventually they reached the wider path leading to Dardanos' second great gate. The Landgate was the oldest part of the city, built by ancient craftsmen whose names were lost to history. It was a massive bastion, facing south towards Troy, the walls deep and solid, the two sets of gates narrow and high. Yet the land outside the gates was wide and flat. An invading army could camp there in safety for a season, and attack at will.

From the Landgate a narrow road crossed the dry plain, then dipped through a long steep defile. The two riders followed the road downwards towards a deep crevass, crossed by a narrow wooden bridge with a permanent guard stationed at each end. The road to Troy flowed from it towards the south. The horses' hooves clattered on the timbers as they rode across. Halysia glanced over and down. The drop was dizzying. On the far side she reined in her mount and glanced back, marvelling at the skill and the courage of the men who had built the bridge. Although it was no more than three spear-lengths across, it would have been no easy feat preparing the ground. Cross timbers and joists had been set deep into the rocks below the bridge. Men would have had to hang from ropes and hack away at the stone to create deep indentations: the kind of work her own brothers were famed for.

Away from the city Halysia breathed in deeply, enjoying the scent of the damp earth and the summer grass, and the feel of a breeze unhindered by walls of stone. The light was beginning to fail when Pausanius said: 'We should be getting back across the Folly. I have no wish to be riding the high roads after dark.'

Halysia reined in her mount. 'The Folly?'

'I meant the bridge, lady.'

'Why do you call it a folly?' she asked. 'It shortens the route to Troy, cutting off a day's travel for merchants.'

'The place had the name long before the bridge was built. Only old men like me use it still. Parnio's Folly.' Pausanius sighed. 'A young rider made a wager with his friends that his horse could leap the crevass at its narrowest point. He was wrong. It took two days to bring up his broken body. A few years later the bridge was constructed above where he died.'

'You knew him?'

'Yes, I knew him. A vain and reckless boy. But there was no malice in him. He thought – as all young men do – that he was immortal. Had he lived he would have been sixty years old now, white-haired and long in the tooth. He would have railed at the recklessness of youngsters, and told us all how it was different in his day.' He glanced at the queen and smiled. 'How strange it is,' he said, 'that I can remember the old days so clearly, and yet I cannot recall what I had for breakfast this morning. I fear I am becoming increasingly useless, my queen.'

'Nonsense, Pausanius. I rely on your wisdom.'

He smiled his thanks. 'And I rely more and more on young Menon. You will too, when I am gone.'

'You are fond of the boy, and it shows,' she said.

Pausanius grinned. 'You won't believe it, but he looks just like me when I was young. He is a good lad. Constantly in debt, though. Loves to gamble. Which was also my curse as a youngster.'

'Will he be as truthful with me as you are?'

Pausanius' face stiffened. 'I am not always as truthful as I would wish to be. It has been bothering me of late. We are alone now, with no-one to overhear. So, if you will allow me, I will speak my mind.'

'I had hoped you would always feel able to do so,' Halysia told him.

'On matters martial I have. But this is not about soldiering.'

'Speak on then, for I am intrigued.'

'You care for that wild horse, and you struggle to understand its pain and its anger. When you stroke it the beast calms, for it senses you have affection for it. Yet there is another little horse, starved of affection, longing to be stroked and loved. And this one you ignore.'

Anger rose in her. 'You of all men should understand my revulsion. The child's father was an evil man, who murdered my son and planted his vile seed in me against my will.'

481

'Yes he was,' said Pausanius. 'And Helikaon nailed him to the gates of his fortress to die a wretched death. But the boy is not his father. He is the son of Halysia, a queen of courage and dignity, loyalty and compassion. He has her blood and her spirit.'

Halysia raised her hand. 'You will speak no more of this. You were quite right, General, to hold those views to yourself. Do so in future.'

Swinging her gelding, she rode back to the citadel.

Andromache awoke from a dream, and lay still, trying to hold on to its fleeting fragments. Kalliope had been with her, and Laodike. The three of them had been sailing together on a great white ship. There were no oars or sails, nor any crew, and yet the vessel had glided on towards a distant island, bathed in the gold of the rising sun. Andromache had been happy, her heart freed by the presence of her friends. In that moment of the dream she had not recalled the fate of the two women.

Then a fourth figure had joined them, a young, dark-haired woman of dazzling beauty. There was something familiar in her cold gaze, but Andromache had not, at first, recognized her.

'And here you are,' the woman told Andromache. 'Sailing with those you have slain.' They were all standing very still now, and staring at her. A red stain began to seep through Laodike's pale gown, and a black-shafted arrow appeared in Kalliope's chest. The dark-haired young woman stood before her, saying nothing. Then her skin began to age, and draw tight over her face, and Andromache saw that she was Hekabe the queen.

'You deserved death,' said Andromache.

'Was I wrong, Andromache? Has not Odysseus proved a deadly enemy?'

Andromache awoke on a couch on the eastern terrace overlooking the barracks stables. The sounds of the horses, their gentle whinnying and the clop of their hooves, came to her ears mixed with the distant shouts and oaths of the soldiers. The dream clung to her with misty fingers, bringing guilt and sorrow.

Beside her couch her servant, Axa, was sitting in a straight chair working on a piece of embroidered linen, squinting from time to time at the tiny stitches. She looked up. 'Oh, you're awake, lady. Can I get you anything?'

Andromache shook her head and closed her eyes again. Was there no escape from such guilt, she wondered? I could not have saved Laodike; the wound was too deep. But then Kalliope's face appeared in her mind, and her heart sank. When she had seen the assassin draw back on his bow she had thought the arrow was aimed at her, and had flung herself to the ground. If only she had called out a warning, Kalliope might have avoided the speeding shaft.

Opening her eyes she sat up and took a deep breath. The truth was that guilt was ever present. And not just for the loss of her friends. It seemed that it was a cloak suited to every occasion. She even felt guilty for the joy in her life. In spite of the war and the fear and deprivation it was bringing to Troy, in spite of the fact that the two men she loved were away fighting, in spite of the fact that her family in Thebe was under threat – in spite of all these things she was happier than she had ever been in her life.

The cause of that happiness slept in the room behind her. Astyanax lay, she knew without looking, on his back with his arms and legs flung out like the starfish they had found together on the beach one day. They had brought it home in some water, but it had died and the child had forgotten about it, but Andromache had hidden it in a box of discarded jewellery and still took it out from time to time as a reminder of that happy day and the toddler's breathless delight at finding the tiny sea creature.

The mere thought of the boy made her chest close up, and she fought down an urge to rush to him and hold his sleeping body, warm and milky, against her own.

The birth had been difficult, as Hekabe had predicted. Andromache's narrow hips had seen to that. The labour had taken most of a night and the following morning, the pain harsh and rending. Yet it was not the moment when they laid the babe in her arms that always brought a lump to her throat when she recalled it. It was the time, some days later, on a bright cool morning, when he had looked up at her. His eyes were a brilliant, sapphire blue.

Helikaon's eyes.

Axa's voice cut through her memories. 'Kassandra was here to see you,' she said.

'Kassandra? Where is she?'

'You needed your sleep. I didn't want to disturb

you. So I sent her away,' Axa said, a little defiantly.

'*You* sent her away?' Andromache almost smiled. The Princess Kassandra, daughter of the king, sent away by a servant. Then a small fear struck her. 'If King Priam hears of such an affront he is likely to order you beaten. Send a servant to ask her to come back. No, better still, go and ask her yourself.'

Axa, looking contrite, gathered up her sewing bag and left the terrace. As she went, Andromache heard her mutter, 'She won't come.'

Andromache thought she was probably right. Kassandra had been difficult as a child. Her feyness and gift of prophecy had always made people shy away from her. Even those who loved her, like Andromache and Helikaon, feared her uncanny ability to predict the future. Now the girl was fourteen, and since the death of her mother she had turned in upon herself, becoming quieter and more reserved. As a child she had always spoken up boldly; now she guarded her words with a care that was almost painful to watch. She stayed in the shadows of the women's quarters and the temple of Athene, and Andromache saw less and less of her.

It was Kassandra who had sparked Andromache's most recent argument with Priam. The king had announced that the girl was to be dedicated to the isle of Thera, as her mother Hekabe and Andromache herself had been. Kassandra had accepted the decision without complaint, but Andromache was furious when she heard.

She had confronted Priam in the *megaron*, scene of

so many of their battles. He had watched her as she walked the length of the great hall to stand before him, his eyes roving over her body. She had heard the king was ailing, but he looked strong, though he wore a wine-stained robe, and his eyes were unnaturally bright.

'Andromache,' he said, 'you are a stranger to my palace these days. But I can guess why you are here. You have not come to pay respects to your king. Interfering, I suppose, as always.'

'I heard Kassandra is to be dedicated to the Blessed Isle,' she said quietly. 'I thought you might seek to consult me, as I spent two years there.'

He laughed. 'And what would you have said, daughter, had I consulted you?'

'I would have said, Father, that the journey to Thera is too dangerous. I had a friend who suffered the horror of rape and the threat of death from pirates. And there are now enemy fleets in those waters.'

'A friend?' he sneered. 'You talk of Kalliope the run-away, whose treachery to her calling created the need for me to send my daughter to replace her. Still, what else could one expect from the daughter of Peleus – a family steeped in treachery and vileness.'

Andromache's response had been instant and icy. 'Had it not been for the *treachery* of Kalliope I would now be mouldering in a tomb, and my son would never have opened his eyes on the world.'

At the mention of Astyanax his expression had softened. 'It was always intended,' he said, 'that Kassandra would serve the Sleeping God. Her mother

Hekabe wished it, and Kassandra herself foretold it.'

'You never believe Kassandra's predictions,' she said angrily.

'No, but *you* do.'

Andromache knew that was unanswerable. She had spoken to Priam in the past about the accuracy of Kassandra's prophecies. She could not now argue that the girl was wrong.

'She will be escorted to Thera by Helikaon's fleet,' Priam had said, 'early next spring. Nothing you can say will alter my decision.'

A slight breeze was blowing through the balcony window, and Andromache rose from her couch, stretching out her arms. She heard a sound on the terrace behind her and turned, expecting to see Kassandra, but saw instead the dark-haired Prince Dios step out from the shade of the palace.

'Dios!' She almost ran to greet him and he held both her hands in his. 'You are back quickly. What news from Thebe?'

'Your father is well, Andromache. And your brothers. They are preparing for war, but they are all safe as yet.'

'Is there news of Hektor?' she asked. 'I enquire every day, but no-one seems to know.'

'The situation in Thraki is confused by the civil war,' he said. 'And it is hard to estimate the truth of any information we receive. Hektor and the Trojan Horse were fighting in the mountains, the last we heard.'

'How can the Thrakians be fighting among themselves when the threat from Mykene is so great?' she said angrily. 'It is so stupid.'

'How much do you know of Thraki's recent history?'

'Very little,' she admitted. 'King Eioneus was a good ruler, and there were no wars. Now the land is beset by rebellion.'

Dios sat down on the couch, and poured himself a goblet of water. 'Shall I tell you of Thraki, or shall we talk of happier matters?'

'Matters more seemly for the ears of women?'

Dios laughed. 'You are not like most women, Andromache, and I will not be drawn into such a pit of scorpions.'

'Then tell me of Thraki.'

'The problem is both tribal and historic,' he replied. 'There are several tribes occupying Thrakian lands, but the two most prominent are the Kikones and the Idonoi. Before you were born, Eioneus – a Kikones king – conquered the eastern tribes of the Idonoi, absorbing their lands into a greater Thrakian federation. To ensure his success he slaughtered thousands. Most of the Idonoi leaders were executed and the royal line was wiped out. Eioneus tempered this savagery with generosity to the captured cities, allowing them some self-rule. And he also established profitable trade routes which brought wealth to the Idonoi, thus securing an uneasy peace for a generation. However, Eioneus' death in Troy, during your wedding games, unleashed old tribal rivalries. The Idonoi are now backed by Agamemnon and, spurred by him, have risen against Rhesos, seeking to win back their ancestral lands, and be free of Kikones domination.'

'To be replaced,' said Andromache, 'by Mykene domination.'

'Indeed, but old hatreds sit deep.'

'Hektor speaks highly of Rhesos,' said Andromache. 'Surely the two of them can conquer?'

Dios considered the question. 'Rhesos is a fine young man, and would be a good king if his people would let him. But even without outside agitators and Mykene reinforcements the civil war would have been hard to win. And with enemy troops pouring in from Thessaly and Makedonia his situation is dire. Already loyal troops are outnumbered five to one. Hektor wants Rhesos to hold the plain of Thraki and the land east of the river Nestos as a buffer between the Mykene and the Hellespont. But it is looking increasingly impossible.'

'Hektor is known for achieving the impossible,' she pointed out.

'Indeed he is. The sad truth, though, is that Hektor could win a score of battles and still not win the war there, whereas he only has to lose one and Thraki falls.' He smiled at her, and once again she saw the resemblance to Helikaon. Their fathers were cousins and the blood of Ilos ran strongly in both. As she thought of Helikaon her mind went back to the sleeping child, and as if he read her thoughts Dios said, '*Now* let us talk of happier matters. How is the boy?'

'Come and see,' she said. They walked together into Astyanax's room, where the red-haired boy was awake and fretting, anxious to go out to play. Naked, he squirmed from the small bed and, dodging round his young nurse, ran out onto the terrace, his chubby arms and legs pumping as he tried to escape.

The nursemaid called out to him in vain, then Dios said firmly, 'Astyanax!'

The child stopped instantly at the deep male voice and turned back to look at his uncle. His mouth open, he stared at Dios in wonder.

Dios picked the boy up and swung him round high in the air. The child gurgled then screamed with delight, his piercing cry echoing in their ears. Dios, with no sons of his own, grinned at the joyous reaction from the boy. As he put him down Astyanax reached up his arms to be spun round again.

'He's a brave one,' said Dios. 'Truly his father's son.'

He swung the boy again, higher and higher. Watching their noisy play Andromache had not seen Kassandra quietly come onto the terrace. When she spotted the girl she turned to her with a smile. Kassandra stood with her hands behind her back, her face half hidden, as usual, by her long black hair. She wore a drab dark robe, unbelted, and her feet were bare.

'Kassandra, I've not seen you for days. You wanted to speak to me?'

Dios put the boy down and went to embrace his sister, but she moved away from him into the shade of the building.

'You tried to stop me going to Thera,' she said to Andromache, ignoring Dios and the child. Her voice was trembling.

'Only immediately, while there is a war on,'

Andromache told her. 'Once the Great Green is safe again you can go to the Blessed Isle if you still wish to. There is plenty of time. You are only fourteen.'

'There is *not* plenty of time,' the girl said angrily. 'I must go there. I have no choice. Father is right, Andromache – you are always trying to interfere in other people's lives. Why don't you leave me alone?'

Andromache said, 'I am only trying to keep you safe, sister.'

Kassandra drew herself up, and when she spoke the shrillness had gone from her voice. 'You cannot keep other people safe, Andromache,' she said gently. 'You should know that by now. Have the last few years taught you nothing? You could not save Laodike or Kalliope. You cannot guard this boy from the world's hurt.' She gestured at the child, who stood silent, staring at the girl with wide eyes. 'You cannot keep his father safe on the Great Green.'

'No, I cannot,' said Andromache, sadly. 'But I will try to save those I love. And I love you, Kassandra.'

The girl's eyes narrowed. 'Mother tells me you loved her too.' Then she swung on her heel and left the room.

XXVIII

The Trojan Horse

A COOL BREEZE WAS BLOWING THROUGH THE RHODOPE mountains, shimmering the long grass of the Thrakian plain, and whispering through the tops of the trees that flanked the high hills beyond.

Hidden beyond the tree line Banokles sat his mount and waited, along with 1,000 other riders of the Trojan Horse. On the plain below 1,500 Trojan soldiers appeared to be preparing for a midday halt, clearing areas for cookfires. Three hundred Thrakian cavalry were with them, and some 200 archers. Banokles had little interest in strategy. Either the enemy would march into the trap or they wouldn't. It didn't matter much to the big warrior. If not today then they would crush the rebels tomorrow. Or the next day.

He glanced at the rider to his left, the slim, yellow-haired Skorpios. The man had removed his helm. He was unnaturally pale, and there was a sheen of sweat on his face. Banokles looked along the line. Everywhere there were signs of nerves and fear. He couldn't understand it. We are the Trojan Horse, he thought. We don't lose battles. And Skorpios was a fine fighter and a superb horseman. So what was he worried about?

It was a mystery, and Banokles did not like mysteries. So he promptly put all thoughts of Skorpios from his mind. There were more important things to think about.

For one, he was hungry. The food supply wagons had not reached them, and there had been no breakfast. This was intolerable to Banokles. No-one should be asked to fight a battle without breakfast. The wagons that had come over the high pass had carried spare swords and a supply of arrows. This, while welcomed by those soldiers whose blades had been ruined by the battles of the last few weeks, had been a disappointment to Banokles. Supplies of cheese and dried meats had run out, and the men had eaten nothing but crushed oats, soaked in water.

An itch began in Banokles' armpit. This was especially irritating, as the armour worn by Trojan Horse riders was intricate: small, overlapping bronze discs, like fish scales, that covered the chest, belly and lower throat. It was impossible to reach inside and scratch.

Banokles' horse shifted under him, then tossed its head. Idly he patted the beast's black neck. 'Steady, Arse Face,' he said.

'By the gods, why don't they come?' said another nervous man to his right, a heavy-set warrior with a carefully trimmed trident beard. Justinos dragged his helm clear, then pulled a cloth from his belt and wiped the sweat from his shaven head. Banokles did not know how to answer him. How in Hades would he know why the enemy hadn't arrived? 'I hate this bastard waiting,' added Justinos.

'We should have had a better breakfast,' said Banokles.

'What?'

'Those oats make a man fart all day. Red meat before a battle. That's how it should be.'

Justinos stared at him for a moment, then donned his helm and turned away.

Glancing along the line of riders Banokles saw Kalliades dismount and walk to a tall tree. He removed his sword belt and helm and climbed up through the branches, seeking a clear view of the northern slopes. It was days since they had spoken, and even then it was only a few words concerning where to picket the horses. Kalliades was an officer now, and spent little time mixing with the men. Even at Banokles' wedding last spring he had seemed distant, withdrawn.

He had never recovered from the death of Piria. That's what Red said. Kalliades had closed himself off. Banokles didn't understand it. He too had been saddened by the girl's death, but in equal measure he had been happy to have survived the fight. Hektor had rewarded them with gifts of gold and appointed them to the Trojan Horse. With the gold Banokles had bought a small house and convinced Red to join him there. It had taken some doing.

'Why would I marry you, idiot? You'll only go and get yourself killed somewhere.'

But he had worn down her resistance, and the wedding had been joyous.

Banokles loosened his sabre in its scabbard. Kalliades climbed down from the tree and spoke to his aide. Word was passed along the line.

'They are coming.'

Banokles leaned forward, trying to see through the trees. He could make out the lower slopes of the Rhodope mountains, but as yet could see no enemy infantry. On the plain the Trojan soldiers were now moving hurriedly to form battle lines, bumping into one another in an appearance of panic. He saw Hektor riding along the front line on a pale horse, his armour of bronze and gold gleaming in the afternoon sunshine.

'You think the supply wagons will have got through by now?' Banokles asked Skorpios.

The blond warrior paused in the act of donning his helm, and turned to gaze at him. 'How would I know? And why would I care?' he answered. 'Any moment now we are going to be surrounded by blood and death.'

Banokles grinned at him. 'But after that we'll need to eat.'

Through a break in the trees Banokles saw the first ranks of the enemy move into sight. There were some heavily armoured warriors, carrying long shields, but the mass of men around them were rebels, in breastplates of leather, or padded linen. Their clothes were brightly coloured, from their cloaks of garish yellow and green to their leggings of plaids and stripes. Many of them had painted their faces, in streaks of crimson or blue. Their weapons were spears and axes, though some carried longswords, with blades the length of a man's leg.

A ululating battle cry began from the enemy ranks, and they broke into a charge towards the Trojan lines. Hektor had dismounted, and now stood, shield ready, at the centre of the front line.

The rebel horde was in full sight now, and Banokles scanned them. They outnumbered the force on the plain by at least ten to one. Twenty thousand men racing across the open ground, screaming their battle cries.

A volley of arrows ripped into the charging men, but it did not slow their advance.

The Trojan front line braced themselves, leaning into their shields, spears drawn back. Just as the enemy were upon them the Trojan veterans surged forward to meet them. The sounds of battle were strangely muted within the forest. Banokles gathered up the reins of his mount in his left hand, the heavy lance sitting comfortably in his right.

'At a walk!' shouted Kalliades.

A thousand riders nudged their horses forward. Banokles ducked beneath an overhanging branch, guiding the black gelding out through the trees. Bright sunshine shone down upon the armoured riders as they moved out onto the hillside.

The rebels had not seen them yet, but they would hear them soon enough.

'Close formation!'

Banokles kicked the gelding into a run, and the thunder of hooves sounded on the hillside.

Hefting his spear Banokles nestled the haft alongside his elbow, the point aiming forward and slightly down. The gelding was at full gallop now. Banokles saw the rebels on the flank turning to meet the charge. He was close enough to see the panic in their painted faces. Then the Trojan Horse slammed into the horde. Banokles rammed his spear through the chest of a powerful warrior. As the man was thrown back the spear was wrenched from Banokles' hand. Drawing his sabre he slashed the blade down, cracking the skull of a rebel. All was chaos now, the air filled with the screams of the wounded and dying. Banokles drove the gelding on, deeper into the ranks of the enemy. An axe blade clove through the gelding's neck and it fell. Banokles jumped clear, launching himself at the axe-man. There was no time to bring up his sabre and he head-butted the warrior, sending him staggering back. Another warrior thrust his sword at Banokles, who parried it, then sent a reverse cut slashing through the man's throat. Justinos charged in, scattering the enemy around Banokles. Then other riders closed around him. Banokles saw a riderless horse and ran across to it. Just as he reached it the beast reared, then galloped away. Two rebels rushed at Banokles. The first swung an axe, which he tried to block with his sabre. The blade shattered. Banokles hurled the hilt at the second man, who ducked. The axeman raised his weapon again. Banokles charged him, grabbing the haft, and ramming his head into the warrior's face. The warrior fell back, losing his grip on the axe. Banokles swept it up, and with a bellowing war cry leapt towards the second warrior. The man's nerve broke and he tried to run. Skorpios came alongside him, his lance plunging through the warrior's back.

Banokles ran to a fallen rider. Dropping the axe he took up the man's sabre and hurled himself back into the fray, hacking, slashing and stabbing. The enemy were hardy and tough, but they had no training. They fought as individuals, seeking space to swing their longswords, or use their spears and axes. But they were being crushed together in a mass by a highly organized army of veterans. Desperate to find room to fight, the warriors began to peel away, running for open ground. The Trojan Horse cut them down as soon as they moved clear. Banokles knew what had to happen next. He had seen it a score of times. The horde began to scatter, the army sundering like a smashed plate. With no organized defensive lines to oppose them the heavily armoured riders surged in among the enemy and the slaughter began.

Panic swept through the Thrakians and all across the battlefield the rebels began to flee. Horsemen rode after them, cutting and killing.

Horseless, Banokles remained where he was. Hektor came striding towards him. His helm and breastplate were smeared with blood sprays, and his sword arm was crimson from the wrist to the elbow.

'Are you hurt?' he asked Banokles.

'No.'

'Then help with the wounded,' said the big man, moving on past him.

'Any sign of the supply wagons?' Banokles called after him. Hektor ignored the question.

Banokles cleaned the sword and slid it back into his scabbard. Then he gazed around the battlefield.

The victory had been complete, but the losses were high. He worked alongside soldiers and stretcher bearers until almost dusk, by which time he had helped to carry at least a hundred corpses. In all more than 400 Trojans had died that day. It mattered little that the enemy dead were in their thousands. There were thousands more waiting to take their place. Armour and weapons were stripped from the Trojan dead, and soldiers gathered round to replace broken swords, smashed helms, and ruined breastplates. Banokles himself acquired a shortsword and an ornate scabbard. The sabre was a fine weapon when hacking down from horseback, but once afoot it was not as deadly as a good stabbing sword.

Off to the right he could see a group of Thrakian prisoners being questioned by Trojan officers, Kalliades among them. Banokles watched, and though he could not hear what was said he could tell by the surly faces of the captured men that they were giving little away. Hektor did not allow torture of prisoners, which seemed to Banokles to be foolish in the extreme. Most men would tell you anything you desired to hear if their hands were being held in a fire. And how could a warrior like Hektor be so squeamish? Banokles had seen him ripping into the enemy like an angry lion. The minds of generals and princes were a mystery to Banokles.

The supply wagons arrived just after dark, and Banokles joined a group of warriors around a cookfire. Bald Justinos was there, and Skorpios, his long blond hair tied in a pony tail that hung between his narrow shoulders. Three of the men were unknown to Banokles, but the last was a slim, round-shouldered rider named Ursos. He and Banokles had trained together back in Troy.

'Another victory,' said Ursos, as Banokles sat beside him. 'Beginning to lose count now.'

'Lost my horse,' grumbled Banokles. 'Old Arse Face was a good mount.'

'Could be him cooking there,' muttered Ursos. 'No meat on the wagons. Just more damn oats.'

As they were talking, a rider came thundering into the camp. Men scattered before him. The man dragged his horse to a halt close to where Hektor was sitting with his officers, and leapt down.

'This looks important,' said Ursos, rising and walking across to listen to the message.

Banokles remained where he was. The night was cool, the fire warm, and the smell of roasting meat intoxicating.

Ursos returned a little while later, and slumped down. 'Well,' he said, 'that robs today's victory of any value.'

'Why?' asked Banokles.

'Achilles has invaded, with the entire Thessalian army, and has taken Xantheia. Rhesos has been driven back to Kalliros in the mountains. Perhaps worse, Odysseus has taken Ismaros, and enemy galleys now block the sea.'

'Doesn't sound good,' agreed Banokles.

Ursos stared at him. 'You don't know where these places are, do you, or why they are important?'

Banokles shrugged. 'Friendly cities or enemy cities. That is all I need to know.'

Ursos shook his head. 'Xantheia guarded the Nestos river. Our supply ships travel that river, up to the old capital at Kalliros. With the city taken we'll get no supplies. And if Kalliros falls we'll have armies on three sides of us. North, south and east.'

'And we'll crush them all,' said Banokles.

'I appreciate your optimism. But we started out with over eight thousand men. We now have around three thousand. The enemy gets stronger every day, Banokles. With Ismaros in enemy hands the seas are clear for Odysseus. His fleet could sail to Carpea and sink our barges. Then there'll be no way home.'

Banokles didn't feel like arguing. He had already forgotten the names of the cities Ursos had so carefully described. As far as he was concerned they had won a battle, had eaten good red meat, and were being led by Hektor, the greatest general on the Great Green. They would fight on and win. Or they would fight on and lose. Either way there was nothing Banokles could do about it, so he pushed himself to his feet and went back to the cookfire for another slab of horse meat.

* * *

The interviews with the prisoners had yielded little Kalliades did not already know. The men were Idonoi tribesmen from the cities of the far west. The defeat would set them back for a while, but do nothing to end the rebellion.

He wandered away from the captives and stood staring up at the Rhodope mountains. There was snow still on the peaks, and dark rain clouds were gathering.

How many more battles could they be expected to win? Four hundred and eleven men had been killed today, with more than 200 suffering wounds that would keep them from fighting for some while. Of the rest there were few men who hadn't suffered some injury, from bruising and sprains to concussions and minor breaks of the toes or fingers.

Western Thraki and the lands of the Idonoi were lost to them now, and would not be retaken. Beyond the line of the Rhodope mountains the land was seething with discontent. To the south only the broad river Nestos, and the citadel at Kalliros, prevented the enemy sweeping into eastern Thraki and cutting off the Trojans' escape route. And now Achilles had taken Xantheia.

A chill wind began blowing down from the snow peaks, fluttering Kalliades' cloak. When Hektor had presented him with the garment a year ago, on the day he became an officer, the cloak had been as bright as a sunlit cloud. Now it was a murky grey, stained with dried blood. An aide brought him a plate of meat. Kalliades thanked the man and walked away to sit on a fallen tree. He had little appetite and ate mechanically.

Some distance away he saw Banokles sitting beside a fire, chatting to the lantern-jawed Ursos.

Kalliades missed the big man's company. He thought then of Piria and sighed. Three years now, and still her face haunted him. The weight of grief at her loss had never abated, and Kalliades knew he could not face another such burden. Better, he decided, never to love, and to avoid comradeship.

The moment of decision had come at Banokles' wedding. He had been standing by the far wall of the garden, watching the dancing and listening to the wine-fuelled laughter. Banokles had been capering around, drunk and happy, Big Red watching him fondly. Kalliades had suddenly felt like a ghost, separate and disembodied. The joy of the occasion floated around him, never touching his senses. He stood quietly for a while, then slipped away, walking back along the broad avenues of Troy. A whore had approached him, a thin woman with yellow hair. Kalliades had allowed her to lead him to a small house, which stank of cheap perfume. As if in a dream he had removed his clothing and climbed with her to the bed. She did not take off her yellow gown, merely hitched it up so that he could enter her. At some point he had whispered: 'Piria!'

'Yes,' answered the whore. 'I am Piria for you.'

But she was not, and Kalliades had shamed himself by bursting into tears and sobbing uncontrollably. He had not cried since he was a small child, sitting beside his dead sister. The whore had moved away from him then, and he had heard her pouring wine. He had struggled to stem the flow of tears, but he did not know how.

In the end the whore had leaned over him. 'You need to go,' she said. The lack of compassion in her voice cut through his sorrow. Reaching into his pouch he pulled out a few copper rings and tossed them onto the bed. Then he had dressed and walked out into the sunlit city.

Now, sitting on the fallen tree, he heard someone approaching. He swung round and saw Hektor. The prince was carrying two cups of watered wine, one of which he passed to Kalliades before sitting down alongside him. 'A cold night,' he said. 'Sometimes I feel summer has no place in these mountains. As if the rocks hold winter deep within them.'

'It always seems cold after a battle,' said Kalliades. 'I don't know why that should be.'

'Nor I. Somehow, though, it seems appropriate. I take it the Idonoi prisoners gave nothing away?'

'They did not. Nor did I expect them to. Once they realized they faced no pain their courage flowed back.'

Hektor gave a weary smile. 'You are not alone in requesting torture, Kalliades. Many of my officers have urged me to harsher treatment.'

'They are right. As I recall, last year we found one of our scouts with his hands cut off and his eyes put out. The rules of behaviour you insist upon are costing us lives.'

'Yes, they are,' agreed Hektor, 'but I will not allow my actions to be swayed by the enemy's malice. It falls to generals to look beyond the events of today, or this season. Why do you think the rebellion has gathered such pace?'

'The death of King Eioneus,' answered Kalliades. 'When he fell from his horse at the wedding games.'

'He did not fall,' said Hektor. 'He was struck by a stone, hurled by a slinger in the pay of Agamemnon. But his death alone is not why we are fighting here. When Eioneus invaded and conquered the Idonoi homelands twenty or more years ago he butchered the royal line, men, women and babes. He slaughtered cities, cutting the right hands from men who fought against him. Others he blinded. He cowed the people with a display of terrible savagery.'

'And he won,' pointed out Kalliades. 'The land was unified.'

'Yes, he won. But he planted the seeds of *this* upheaval. There is not an Idonoi family without a martyr, without a relative who suffered horribly. Idonoi children have grown to manhood nursing deep hatreds for the Kikones tribe. *That* is why Agamemnon found it so easy to inspire rebellion. One day, and I hope it is soon, Troy will need to make treaties with the Idonoi, perhaps future alliances. We will need to become friends. So I will not follow the path trodden by Eioneus. No man will say that the Trojans butchered their children or raped their wives and mothers. No blinded man will say to his sons: "Look what they did to me, those evil men!"'

Kalliades looked at the prince. 'You are wrong, Hektor. This a war with only two possible endings. Either Agamemnon triumphs and Troy is a fire-gutted ruin, or we destroy Agamemnon and his allies. If torturing a prisoner means learning of the enemy's plans we have a greater chance of defeating them. It is that simple.'

'Nothing is that simple,' Hektor told him. 'In a hundred years what will victory or defeat here have meant?'

Kalliades was confused. 'I don't know what you mean. We won't be here in a hundred years.'

'No, we won't. But the Kikones will, and the Idonoi, and the Mykene, and hopefully Trojans. What we do here now will have meaning *then*. Will we all still hate one another and yearn for vengeance for past atrocities? Or will we be at peace as neighbours and friends?'

'I don't care about what might happen in a hundred years,' stormed Kalliades. 'We are here *now*. We are fighting *now*. And we are losing, Hektor.'

Hektor finished his wine, and sighed. 'Yes, we are. You think torturing a few prisoners will change that? With Ismaros fallen the enemy will swarm along the coast, cutting us off. With no reinforcements, no food supplies, and no fresh weapons, we risk being cut to pieces. As a general I know we should pull back to the coast now, get to Carpea and the barges, and cross to Dardania. Thraki is lost, and we should save the army. But as Hektor, son of Priam, I cannot follow my own advice. My father has ordered me to defeat all our enemies and re-establish Rhesos as king of a united Thraki.'

'That is impossible now,' said Kalliades.

'Yes, it probably is. But until defeat becomes inevitable, Kalliades, I must remain. I will ride to

Kalliros, and support the young king. With luck we will crush Achilles and his Thessalians, and gather a new force to retake Xantheia.'

'You know we will not,' said Kalliades. 'At best we will hold them back for a few months.'

'Anything can happen in that few months. The heavy rains of autumn will slow their supplies, and open up the sea to us. A fierce winter will sap the morale of the besiegers. Priam could make peace with Agamemnon.'

Kalliades shook his head. 'That last will not happen. You are right, Hektor, we are soldiers, and we have a duty to obey. The orders, though, are senseless now. They were given when there was some hope of success. Now, if we follow them blindly, we face our doom.'

'Yes, we do,' admitted Hektor. 'So, will you still ride with me, Kalliades?'

'We'll *all* ride with you, Hektor. Whether it be to victory or ruin.'

XXIX

Orphans in the forest

FOR SIX DAYS THE ARMY OF HEKTOR MOVED SOUTH, through the Rhodope mountains. The journey was slow and fraught with danger. Somewhere behind them an Idonoi army was marching hard, seeking them out. Ahead was the broad river Nestos, where Thessalian troops and a second Idonoi army were facing King Rhesos at Kalliros. All the men knew there was likely to be a major battle as soon as they sighted the city.

There were no supplies reaching the Trojan army now. Rations were short, and teams of hunters rode out daily seeking deer and game. Even when they were successful the result was pitifully inadequate to feed 3,000 men.

Banokles, on a new mount, a dappled grey with a mean eye, was riding with Ursos and twenty other men ahead of the main force, scouting for enemy troops. The long lances had been left behind, and the riders now carried Phrygian bows, as well as their sabres.

Their orders were specific. Avoid direct conflict and upon sight of the enemy send a rider back to report.

Ursos had been placed in charge of the troop, and the responsibility had made him surly. His mood was not improved by Banokles' constantly calling him General, a title swiftly taken up by the other riders.

In the course of the afternoon a young horseman named Olganos spotted a wild pig in a thicket. He and Justinos and Skorpios set off in pursuit of it. Ursos ordered a halt while the hunt continued, and the rest of the troop rode into a stand of trees and dismounted. They had seen no sign of enemy forces, though earlier that day they had spotted some woodsmen felling logs above a river. The men had been Kikones tribesmen, and they told Ursos they had hidden from an Idonoi raiding party two days before.

Olganos and the hunters returned triumphant, carrying the dead pig. It was a scrawny, thin beast, but they gutted and quartered it, built a fire and a spit and settled down to wait while the meat cooked.

Banokles walked to the tree line and sat down, scanning the land to the south. It was green and verdant, with rolling hills and wooded valleys. Good farming land, he thought. Not like the parched farm on which he had been born, his family scratching a living, always hungry. He pictured a house on the hillside below. There was a stream close by. Cool water in the summer, a gentle breeze blowing through the trees. A man could raise horses, or pigs or sheep. All three perhaps. He wondered if Red would like to live in the mountains, far from any cities.

Then he saw the smoke on the horizon, huge plumes rising from beyond the distant hills.

Banokles pushed himself to his feet and called out to Ursos. The troop leader walked over and stood next to him, staring silently at the smoke. 'Forest fire, you think?' he asked at last.

Banokles shrugged. 'Could be. I don't know what's beyond those hills.'

The other men gathered round. Olganos, a hawk-nosed young man with black curly hair, voiced the concern they all felt. 'According to the Thrakian scouts we should be reaching Kalliros by tomorrow. What if that smoke is the city burning?'

'Don't say that!' hissed Ursos. 'If Kalliros has fallen we are all dead men.'

'Speak for yourself, General,' snapped Banokles. 'I promised Red I'd be back, and no sheep-shagging Idonoi is going to stop me. Nor any other sheep-shagging bastards from any other sheep-shagging country.'

'The mind of a philosopher, the language of a poet,' said young Olganos, with a smile. 'Is there no end to your talents?'

Banokles did not answer him. The distant smoke had darkened his spirits.

Moving back into the trees, the men ate their fill of roast pork, then mounted their horses and continued south.

They rode warily, in a staggered skirmish line, for the land was broken by sudden dips and gullies, and stands of trees that could hide enemy warriors. Several of the riders had bows in their hands, arrows notched to the strings. Banokles, who was far from a skilled archer, remained alert, ready to charge his horse either at or away from any enemy who came into sight.

It was close to dusk as they rode up the last hill. Ursos called a halt below the crest and they dismounted, moving cautiously up to the rim. Their worst fears were realized. Below them the fortress city of Kalliros was aflame, and they could see enemy warriors outside the walls, carrying plunder. By a huge campfire Banokles saw a group of warriors holding long spears in their hands, with heads impaled on them. Around this grisly scene were cheering crowds, waving their swords in the air. Banokles scanned the open area around the eastern wall. Several thousand fighting men were in sight. Many more would be inside the city, and encamped by the western wall, beyond his line of sight. Out on the river beyond there were scores of ships.

Ursos moved alongside Banokles. 'How many soldiers, do you think?' he asked.

Banokles shrugged. 'Anywhere from ten to fifteen thousand. Many of them are not Idonoi. No paint. No leggings. I'd say they were Thessalian or Makedonian.'

Ursos swore softly. 'Look at the river. More galleys coming in. If they move on to blockade the Hellespont we won't get home even if we reach the barges at Carpea.'

'Well, it's no use sitting here,' said Banokles. 'We should get back.'

Ursos pulled off his helm and ran his fingers through his long black hair. 'Hektor will need to know how swiftly they get on the march again, and in what direction they head. They could move east to block us, or north to meet us in the mountains.'

'Or both,' said Olganos, who had been listening.

'Yes. Or both.'

'And there is another Idonoi army somewhere behind us,' Olganos pointed out.

Ursos turned to Banokles. 'You stay here with five men and watch where the enemy march. I'll take the rest of the troop back to Hektor and stop the advance. Once the enemy are on the move you head north to join us as fast as you can.'

'Why don't *you* stay behind?' asked Banokles.

'Because I'm the bastard general – as you keep pointing out. I am leaving you in charge, Banokles. Don't do anything reckless. Just gather the information and move out when you have it.'

'Oh, you don't want us charging the fortress and taking it back, then?'

'No, I don't.' Ursos sighed. 'Just keep yourself safe.' Then he swung to Olganos. 'You stay here too as second-in-command.'

'Second-in-command of five men? I'm not sure I can handle such responsibility.'

'And I'm sure you can't,' snapped Ursos. 'But you've a quick mind,' he added, his voice softening, 'and you have nerve. I'll leave Ennion, Skorpios, Justinos and Kerio with you. Any problem with that?'

Banokles thought about the question. Kerio was a troublemaker, a sly man who constantly sought to irritate him. But he was a good fighter, and a fine archer. 'No problem, Ursos,' he said.

'You might want to swap Ennion's mount,' put in Olganos. 'He's older and slower than the others, and we might need speed tomorrow.'

'Good thought,' said Banokles. 'I always like to have someone around to do the thinking.'

The moon was high above the forest but Skorpios could not sleep. He'd had enough of battles and war, and wished with all his heart he had not run away from his father's farm to join the army. He still recalled the bright morning two years ago when the recruiting captain had arrived in the settlement, his armour gleaming, sunlight glinting from his helm. He was, Skorpios had decided on that day, the most handsome man he had ever seen. The officer had dismounted in the market square and called out to the men gathered there. 'Your nation is at war, Trojans. Are there heroes among you?'

Skorpios, though only fourteen then, had moved forward with the other men, and listened as the officer spoke of the evil of the Mykene, and how they had sent assassins to murder the wife of Hektor. Skorpios had never been to Troy, but he had heard of the mighty Lord of Battle, and his lady, Andromache, who had shot an assassin with an arrow, just as he was about to slay the king. To Skorpios then the names of the great were synonymous with the names of the gods, and he was lost in wonder as the soldier spoke of the golden city and the need for brave men to take up their swords to defend it.

In that glorious moment such action had seemed to

the youngster to be infinitely more exciting than tending cattle, or shearing sheep, or cutting the heads from chickens. The officer had said that only men over the age of fifteen summers could enlist, but Skorpios was tall for his age, and had walked forward, with some twenty other young men. The officer told them what stalwart warriors they would be, and how proud he was of them. Father had never mentioned pride once in Skorpios' hearing. Mostly the words he heard were lazy, shiftless, careless and good-for-nothing.

Two years later the officer's words seemed less golden. Skorpios had seen four of his friends maimed, and five others killed. The rest were scattered through Trojan regiments still based in Troy. At sixteen Skorpios was a veteran, skilled with bow and sword, who had been wounded twice, and now prayed every day that the great goddess would see him safely back to his father's farm, where he would happily gather cattle turds for the rest of his life.

The sound of gentle snoring came to him, and he sat up, and stared across to where Banokles was sleeping beneath the branches of a tree. The man was utterly fearless. Skorpios felt that the warrior's bravery should inspire his own, but the reverse was true. The calmer Banokles appeared in battle, the more Skorpios would tremble and picture himself lying on a battlefield, his guts in his hands.

He saw Justinos sitting in the moonlight, idly scraping the stubble from his head with a small bronze knife. Skorpios glanced around the campsite. Ennion and Olganos were missing, but the slender, red-headed

Kerio was close by. Skorpios did not like Kerio, who was always complaining, but his dislike was offset by the fact that he was a doughty fighter, and a good man to have alongside you in a skirmish.

Kerio moved smoothly to his feet and walked across to squat down close to Justinos and Skorpios. 'Listen to him snoring,' he whispered, his voice rich with contempt. 'How could Ursos have left him in charge? I have two hounds back home with more brains than him.'

Justinos shrugged and carried on shaving his head. Skorpios looked at Kerio, and his dislike got the better of his intellect. 'I notice you are whispering, and only saying this while he's asleep.'

'Are you saying I'm a coward, you little catamite?'

'He's just making an observation,' said Justinos calmly.

'Oh, now he needs you to speak up for him, does he?'

Skorpios wanted to defend himself, but the truth was he was frightened of Kerio. There was something about the man, a weirdness in his eyes. He remained silent. Justinos finished his shaving, and then replaced his knife in a small sheath in his belt. 'You know, Kerio,' he said, his voice flat, the tone bored, 'I have never liked you. Given a choice between following Banokles or you, it would be Banokles every time. Actually, given a choice between following you or one of those hounds you spoke of, I'd take the hound.'

Now it was Kerio's turn to fall silent. Casting a murderous glance at Skorpios he walked back across the campsite and sat down with his back to a tree.

'Not a good enemy to have,' said Skorpios.

'No enemies are good to have, boy.' Justinos observed him gravely. 'I've seen you fight. You have no reason to be frightened of him.'

Skorpios tried to mask his embarrassment. 'I am not frightened of him.'

Justinos shrugged and stretched. Skorpios sighed. 'Actually I am. Somehow it is different in a battle, charging in with your comrades. But with Kerio . . . I would be fearful of falling asleep and having my throat cut.'

Justinos nodded. 'I know what you mean, but I do not believe Kerio is evil. He is just a hothead. Truth is he is as frightened as everyone else. This whole country is a death trap for us.'

'You are frightened?'

'Oh, yes.'

'What about Banokles? You think he is?'

Justinos grinned. 'You know the stories as well as I. Rescued a princess from pirates, saved the Lady Andromache from assassins. Now that makes him special. But what really takes the breath away is that he married Big Red, the most terrifying whore in Troy. Any man who could do that is frightened of nothing.'

The warrior Ennion came walking back through the trees, dropped his bow and quiver to the earth, and slumped down beside the two men. Dragging off his helm he gave a great yawn. 'I could sleep for a season,' he said. 'There is so much grit in my eyes I feel that if I blink too hard I'll bleed to death.' Scratching at his black chin beard, he stretched out on the ground.

'See anything?' Skorpios asked him.

'A lot of people fleeing towards the east, and the city is still burning. I'll be glad to be heading east myself come morning. Now that Kalliros has fallen we'll be going home. Man, that's good enough for me.'

'You don't think Hektor will try to retake the city?' persisted Skorpios.

Ennion sat up and swore. 'Now why did you put that thought into my head? I'll never sleep now.'

'We don't have the men to take a city,' said Justinos. 'So rest easy. Tomorrow we'll see which way the enemy marches and ride back to the army. Then it's Carpea and home.'

'May Zeus hear those words and make them true,' said Ennion. 'Now which of you is going to relieve Olganos?'

'I'll go,' said Skorpios. 'I can't sleep anyway.'

Just then they heard a child's cry echo through the woods. Banokles came awake instantly and rose, drawing his sword. Justinos grabbed his helm and donned it. Skorpios scrambled to his feet, along with Ennion and Kerio.

Young Olganos came running back through the trees. Banokles moved to meet him, and the others gathered round.

'A war party of Idonoi,' whispered Olganos. 'Ten, maybe a few more.'

'Gather your bows,' Banokles ordered.

'Ursos said to avoid fighting,' Kerio pointed out.

'So he did,' said Banokles. 'I'm glad you pointed that out. Now gather your bastard bows, and let's see what we're facing.'

With that he moved through the trees. Skorpios ran back and took up his bow and quiver of arrows. Then he set off after Banokles.

The stars were bright above the forest clearing as the elderly nurse, Myrine, moved away from the sleeping children. There was a stream close to the abandoned logger's shack in which they hid, and she hitched up her old grey gown and made her way to the bank. Stiffness in her swollen knees made it difficult to kneel and drink, but she had found an old cup in the shack, and dipped it below the surface. The water was cool and refreshing and she drank deeply. A small crack in the cup allowed some of the liquid to seep out over her hand. Pushing her fingers through her grey hair, she rubbed away some of the soot that clung there.

In the bright moonlight she saw that her gown was singed at the hip, and there were cinder burns on the sleeves.

Myrine knew nothing of sieges and battles, but she had heard the soldiers of the palace bragging of how they could hold out for months. She had believed them. Why would she not? They were fighting men and understood the ways of warfare.

Then the fires had swept through the wooden buildings and enemy warriors had poured through the city of Kalliros, shrieking their awful battle cries. Myrine shivered at the recent memory. In the palace there had been panic. The young king – her own sweet Rhesos – had led his royal guards towards the action. His steward, the ancient Polochos, had ordered Myrine to take the two royal children to the west of the city, and the barracks there.

But a fierce blaze was already raging through the lower town, and Myrine had been forced to take the northern streets. She had been carrying the three-year-old Prince Obas and clinging to the hand of his older brother, twelve-year-old Periklos. There was panic everywhere, with soldiers running through the flame-lit streets, and panicked townsfolk streaming towards the eastern gates and the open land beyond. Myrine had steadily worked her way round to the north. Then she had seen the fighting, and had realized there was no way to reach the barracks.

Uncertain of what action to take she had decided to leave the city by the northern postern gate, and make her way into the woods until the battle was over. It had seemed sensible at the time, for surely King Rhesos would destroy these foul invaders, and tomorrow she could return with his children. But from their vantage point in the high forest they had watched the fires spread. Worse, they had seen enemy cavalry galloping past the postern gate, and attacking the fleeing townspeople. The slaughter had been great, and Myrine had taken the children deeper into the forest, so that they would not see the murders.

Little golden-haired Obas had wept. The fires and the battle cries had frightened him, but Periklos had comforted him. He was a strong boy, like his father, dark-haired and dark-eyed, his expression always serious. Obas was more like his mother, the gentle Asiria, who had died in childbirth the previous summer.

'I want to go home,' Obas had wailed. 'I want Papa!'

'Papa is fighting the bad men,' said Periklos. 'We will go home when he has defeated them.'

Even here, high in the forest, Myrine could see the distant flames over the city. She knew in her heart that Rhesos had not defeated the enemy. She also knew that he would not have run while his people were in peril. He was too brave for that. Which meant that her sweet boy was dead. Tears began to fall, but she brushed them away, and tried to think of what to do. Where could they go?

Her stomach tightened with the first flutterings of panic. They had no food, and no wealth, and her swollen knees would not carry her far. Even now the enemy would be scouring the city for the princes, determined to wipe out the royal line.

To *wipe out the royal line.*

The thought of Rhesos once more filled her with heartache. The wind whispered through the trees, and she glanced up at the bright moon, remembering the day she had first been taken to the royal apartments. So long ago now. Little Rhesos, she was told, was a disobedient child, and needed firm discipline. King Eioneus had told her to beat him with a stick if he disobeyed her. Myrine had never done so. From the first moment she saw him she loved him. An ugly, stocky woman, Myrine had never been courted, and had resigned herself to a life of lonely service. With little Rhesos she had discovered all the joys and heartaches of motherhood. She had watched him grow from a skinny boy into a fine youth, and a strong young man.

Even as king, with all the duties of war bearing down upon him, he would smile when he saw her, and hug her to him. When his first son, Periklos, was born he had brought Myrine to his palace to nurse him. And that had been the second great joy of her life, for Periklos was just like his father, and, save for her growing infirmity, it was as if the years had melted away, and she was young, and a mother, again.

Even the war and the fighting had not intruded on her happiness. Inside the palace all was peaceful and safe, as it always had been.

Until today.

Hearing movement behind her she swung round, fear lancing through her. But it was not an enemy soldier. It was young Periklos. The prince squatted down alongside her. Immediately she filled the cracked cup with water and passed it to him.

'What are we to do, sir?' she asked him. Even as the words slipped out she felt ashamed. Yes, he was bright, his mind swift as a striking hawk, but he was still a boy. She saw his face tighten, his dark eyes widening with fear. 'Oh, I am sorry, dear one,' she said. 'I was just thinking aloud. Everything will be well. I know it!'

'My father is dead,' said Periklos. 'Nothing will be well, Myrine. They will come for us now, for Obas and me.'

Myrine did not know what to say to him, and his words filled her with dread. The darkness around them now seemed menacing, the whisper of wind in the branches eerie and threatening. 'We will hide in the forest,' she said. 'It is a big forest. We . . . we will not be found.'

Periklos considered her words. 'They will offer gold to any who catch us. Hunters will come. We cannot stay here. We have no food.'

A child's voice ripped through the silence of the night. 'Periklos! Periklos!' shrieked little Obas, running from the ruined shack. The older boy ran to him, kneeling down beside him.

'You must not make so much noise,' he said sternly. 'Bad men will find us if you do.'

'I want Papa! I want to go home!'

'Bad men are in our house, Obas. We cannot go home.'

'Where is Papa?'

'I don't know.'

Myrine pushed herself painfully to her feet and walked across to the two boys. As she did so she heard movement in the trees behind them. Periklos rose swiftly and looked round.

'It's Papa! It's Papa!' shouted Obas.

Three men stepped from the undergrowth. They were tall, their long, blond hair braided, their faces streaked with paint. Myrine moved to the children, picking up Obas and hugging him to her. Periklos stood his ground, staring at the Idonoi tribesmen, and the longswords in their hands. There was blood on their clothes.

'Now you leave us alone,' shouted Myrine. 'You just go away.'

Another seven warriors emerged from the shadows

of the trees, their expressions hard, their eyes cruel.

Myrine backed away towards the shack. The leader of the Idonoi stared hard at Periklos. 'You look like your father,' he said. 'I'll put your head on a spear next to his.' Obas started to cry, and Myrine patted his back.

'There, there, little one,' she said. 'There, there.'

The warrior stepped towards Periklos and raised his sword. The boy stood still, staring defiantly up at him. 'Do your worst, you coward!' he said.

Then another voice sounded in the clearing.

'It's no wonder you sheep-shaggers paint your faces. Ugliest bastards I've ever seen.' Myrine turned to see a powerful man in shining armour move from the trees behind the shack. He was carrying two swords, one a sabre, the other a short, stabbing blade.

The Idonoi warrior swung towards him, the other men grouping together, weapons poised.

The newcomer halted some fifteen paces from the Idonoi leader. 'Well?' he demanded. 'Why are you just standing there? Balls of Ares, are you gutless as well as ugly?'

With a roar of fury the Idonoi rushed at the warrior, his men surging after him.

To Myrine's surprise the newcomer suddenly dropped to one knee. A volley of arrows hissed through the air, slamming into the charging group. Four men fell, and two others staggered back, black shafts jutting from their upper bodies. The warrior in the shining armour came to his feet and launched himself at the remaining Idonoi. The battle was short and bloody. The newcomer tore into the warriors, swords hacking and slashing. The leader went down, blood gouting from his throat. Two others fell to arrows. The last man spun on his heel and ran.

Moments later two horsemen galloped from the trees, bows in their hands, and set off after the fleeing warrior.

Myrine felt weak and giddy. She tried to put Obas down, but he clung to her. So, still holding the boy, she lowered herself to the ground, grunting as pain seared through her left knee.

The warrior in the shining armour walked past her, to where one of the wounded Idonoi was trying to crawl back into the trees, and plunged his short sword between the man's shoulder blades.

Three other men, similarly armoured, came into view. Myrine watched as a warrior strode across to the man who had saved them.

'The orders were to avoid battle,' said the newcomer, dragging off his helm. He was young, his hair dark and curly.

'Gods, Olganos, that wasn't a battle! That was a . . . a skirmish!'

'Skirmish or not it has increased our danger.'

'You regret saving the children?'

'No, of course not. I am glad they are alive. But I am more glad that we are. You know very well that we should have stayed hidden. If any one of them had got away we'd have been forced to run, and then we wouldn't have been able to complete our mission. And that mission is more important than the lives of two children.'

Banokles saw the old woman staring at him, her eyes fearful. Leaving Olganos he strolled over and squatted down beside her. As he did so the chubby, blond-haired child in her arms began to wail.

'By Ares, boy, you make more noise than a gelded donkey,' said Banokles.

'My brother is very young, and very frightened,' said the dark-haired youngster.

Banokles rose and turned towards the lad. 'And you are not frightened?'

'Yes, I am.'

'Very wise. These are frightening times. I like the way you stood up to those ruffians. You've got nerve, boy. Now comfort your brother and make him stop that damned squealing. It is making my ears ache.'

At that moment there came the sound of a running horse. Banokles rose to his feet as Kerio rode into the clearing, and walked over to him. 'I take it you caught and killed him?'

'Of course we killed him!' answered the wiry rider. 'And I left Justinos at the tree line to keep watch for more of them.' The contempt in his tone rankled with Banokles, but he struggled to hold his temper.

'Did you drag the body back into the forest?' he asked.

'No, you oaf. I nailed it to a tree with a sign pointing this way,' answered Kerio, lifting his leg and jumping to the ground.

'You should do something about that nose bleed,' said Banokles.

'What nose—' Banokles' fist slammed into the man's

face, hurling him from his feet. His helm was knocked clear and clattered against a tree trunk. Kerio hit the ground hard and struggled to rise, but Banokles reached him first, grabbing him by his hair and hauling him upright.

'I'm going to ask you again,' he said. 'Did you drag the sheep-shagging bastard back into the forest?'

'I did,' answered the redhead, blood dribbling from his broken nose.

Banokles released his grip on Kerio, who slumped down to the ground. Then he walked over to face the remaining three men. 'Any one of you drooping cow turds want to call me an oaf? Come on! Speak your minds!'

Ennion stepped forward and stood quietly tugging at his chin beard, as if in deep thought. Finally he spoke. 'In truth, Banokles, I do not need to be included in this debate, since I have already called you an oaf on many occasions. The last time, I recall, was at your wedding, when you decided to dance on the table, fell off and got your foot stuck in a piss pot.' The men all laughed. Banokles' anger ebbed away, and he grinned.

'That was a good day,' he said. 'Or so I'm told. Don't remember much.'

Justinos rode into the camp. 'More men on the road, Banokles,' he said. 'Looks like they are searching for something, or someone. We need to move.'

'Who in Hades are they searching for in the middle of the night?' muttered Banokles. 'They ought to be celebrating their victory.' Olganos tapped him on the shoulder and pointed to the old woman and the two boys. Banokles walked over to where Myrine was sitting. 'They are looking for you?'

'Yes, sir, I fear they are.'

'Why?'

'These boys are the sons of King Rhesos. The Idonoi will want them dead.'

Banokles helped the old woman to her feet. The chubby boy started to cry again. Olganos approached the nurse. 'Let me have him,' he said softly, lifting the boy into his arms. 'We are going for a ride on a magic horse,' he told him. 'Have you ever seen a magic horse?'

'Where's the magic horse?' asked the child, instantly distracted.

'Back in the trees. We'll ride him, and if any bad men come he will sprout wings and we'll fly away from them. What is your name?'

'Obas.'

'A fine name,' said Olganos.

The group moved back beyond the abandoned shack to where the horses were tethered. Banokles lifted the old nurse to the back of his dappled grey, then swung up behind her. Glancing round he saw Kerio staggering towards his horse. 'Hey, Broken Nose, take the other boy with you.'

Kerio hauled himself to his horse, then reached down and swung the dark-haired prince up behind him. In the distance Banokles heard men shouting, and guessed they had found the body of the Idonoi killed by Kerio and Justinos. Touching heels to his mount, he led the group deeper into the forest.

'Will we be safe, sir?' whispered the old woman. Banokles did not answer her.

They pushed on through the night, struggling up steep, rocky hillsides, and through dense stands of trees. The going was slow and hard, and the riders dismounted often, leading the horses, to rest them. Banokles' mount was tiring fast as dawn approached. The old nurse, Myrine, had been too weak to walk the slopes and the grey had carried her constantly.

As the first light showed in the east Banokles called a halt. They had reached a wooded hilltop, high in the mountains, and from its vantage point they could see the drifting smoke still rising over the distant city of Kalliros. Below them lay the woods and slopes they had passed through, still shrouded in the last of the night's gloom. Banokles could see no sign of human movement, but felt in his heart that the enemy were still pursuing them.

While the others rested in a hollow Banokles strolled up to the edge of the trees, and sat down to watch for pursuers. There was no way to escape – not with the old nurse and the children. The only choice was to leave them behind. The thought sat uncomfortably on him. During the ride through the night the old woman had constantly thanked him for his heroism. Truth was, Banokles had been feeling uneasy about his leadership role and had decided to attack the Idonoi to relieve his stress. Fighting always calmed him, made him feel more in control, somehow. He didn't understand it, or question it. But then Banokles was uncomfortable with questions. What he did know was that last night's skirmish had not calmed him. He had broken the nose of one of his men, and had landed himself with three unwelcome burdens.

The nurse had called him a hero. At any other time this would have been pleasant. It was good to be considered a hero – especially in the comfort of a drinking hall, with wine flowing. After the rescue of Andromache he and Kalliades had been lauded through the city. It was months before Banokles had been asked to pay for a drink or a meal.

Banokles didn't know much, but he did know that in times of war heroes were usually idiots. More important, they also died young. Banokles had no intention of dying at any time. No, he decided, the children and their nurse had to be left behind. It would be uncomfortable, though, telling the old woman. Then a bright thought occurred to him. Perhaps the riders could slip away quietly while she and the boys were sleeping.

Banokles swore softly, as the face of Kalliades appeared in his mind. He knew Kalliades would never leave them, but then Kalliades would come up with a brilliant plan to save the children, the nurse, all of his men – and probably the entire Trojan Horse.

Pulling off his helm, Banokles leaned back against the tree. 'May the gods bless you, dear,' the nurse had said. A pox on blessings, he thought. Just give me a fast horse that doesn't stumble and a blade that doesn't break.

Olganos joined him at the tree line. 'Any sign of pursuit?' he asked.

'No.'

'We're being forced northwest,' he added.

'No other way to keep hidden,' Banokles pointed out.

'I know, but we can't keep heading this way.'

Banokles nodded. 'We'll cut back to the north when we've lost our pursuers.'

'We may not have time,' said Olganos. 'Ursos will have reached the army by now, and the chances are they will head east, towards the pass at Kilkanos. You agree?'

Banokles had no idea where they would head. He hadn't even remembered the name of the pass. 'Go on,' he said.

'We know there was an Idonoi army pursuing them. If we don't reach the pass soon the chances are that the Idonoi will be there first. Then we will have an enemy behind us seeking the children, and an army ahead of us pursuing Hektor.'

'You have a plan?'

'Yes, but you won't like it. We need to ride fast. We cannot do that unless we lose our pursuers. We need to move on alone – unencumbered.'

'You want to leave the children?' asked Banokles, his mood lifting.

'No, I don't *want* to. Listen to me, Banokles. I know you have the reputation of a great hero. You fought pirates to rescue a princess, and you fought off twenty men who were trying to kill Hektor's wife. But this situation is different. The truth is Kalliros has fallen, Rhesos is dead, Thraki is lost. It no longer matters that the children are royal. They have no army, no leverage, and no value. All they can do is slow us down.'

'They will indeed—' began Banokles, but Olganos cut him off.

'I know what you are going to say. So let me say it first. Yes, they will slow us, but heroes do not abandon those in need. And, yes, I feel bad about it.' Olganos reddened. 'It is just that I am trying to think like a soldier, Banokles.'

'Nothing wrong with thinking like a soldier,' Banokles told him.

Olganos swore, and turned away. When he spoke again his words were full of regret. 'Now you are just trying to make me feel better about my cowardice,' he said. Then he sighed. 'Heroes shouldn't be frightened of dying for what is right. I couldn't see that last night, when you risked your life for those children. I see it now, and I burn with shame.' The young man looked Banokles in the eye. 'Forget what I said. I'll stand with you.'

Banokles was lost for words. What in Hades was he talking about? Then he saw movement in the far distance, around the city. 'Your eyes are keener than mine, Olganos. Can you see men marching?'

Olganos shaded his eyes with his hand. 'Yes, heading south it looks like. That will take them down towards the coast.'

'Away from us, anyway,' said Banokles.

'For a while. If they turn east they'll cut across Hektor's line of march, and catch the army as it comes down from the mountains. We need to get to Hektor and warn him.'

'I agree,' said Banokles. 'How many would you say are in that army?'

'Hard to judge. They are still leaving. Five, perhaps six thousand.'

'The Trojan Horse can beat that many without breaking sweat,' said Banokles.

'Are you not forgetting Ismaros?'

'What about it?' snapped Banokles, who had indeed forgotten the port city.

'Odysseus has taken it, which means there will be another army on the coast. If they link with this one there could be twice as many foes.'

Banokles fell silent. All these damned places were a mystery to him. Armies marching hither and yon, south, north, east, heading for areas he did not know, and passes he could not remember. Ursos had done this to him on purpose. It was revenge for calling him General.

'Keep watch on those slopes,' he told Olganos, then walked back into the trees and down the short slope into the hollow where the group was camped. The old nurse was sitting apart from the soldiers, the boys close, little Obas in her lap, the taller Periklos beside her, his arm on her shoulder.

Banokles smiled at her, but she gazed at him suspiciously. The men gathered round him, their faces stern. Black-bearded Ennion spoke first. 'Did Olganos speak to you about the . . . the problem?' he asked.

'Yes, he did. You want to add something?'

'We've been talking about it, Banokles. We want you to know we are with you.'

'With me?'

Ennion looked uneasy. 'I know we joke with you, and appear to mock, but we are all proud to fight alongside you. None of us would have rescued those children the way you did. And we all know how you attacked the assassins and saved the Lady Andromache. We are none of us great warriors, but we are soldiers of the Horse. We won't let you down.'

Banokles glanced at the other men. 'You want to keep the children with us?'

Skorpios nodded, but Justinos rubbed his hand across his shaved head and looked doubtful. 'I have to say I think Olganos is right. We'll probably not make it with them. But, yes, I am with you, Banokles. We'll bring the children to Hektor – or die trying.'

It was like a bad dream. Banokles swung towards Kerio. The man's eyes were swollen and black, and there was dried blood on his nostrils. 'What do you say?'

'You don't need to worry about me,' answered Kerio. 'I'll stand.'

Olganos came running down the slope. 'Some twenty warriors,' he said. 'And they are not far behind.' Banokles walked across to where the old nurse was sitting with the boys. Periklos stepped to meet him.

'We will not leave her behind,' said the boy sternly. 'Take Obas with you, and I will stay with Myrine.'

'No-one is being left behind, boy,' said Banokles sourly. 'Stay with the horses. If you see Idonoi coming down that slope, then ride like the wind.' Turning back to his men he called out, 'Fetch your bows!'

Olganos moved alongside him. 'We're going to fight them all?'

Banokles did not answer him, but ran to his horse and grabbed his bow and quiver of arrows. Then the six warriors ran back up the slope and crept through the undergrowth to the edge of the tree line. Carefully Banokles eased back the branches of a thick bush, and peered down the slope.

Some way below he saw a ragged group of Idonoi warriors moving out onto open ground. There were twenty-two of them. In the lead was a thin man, in a cloak of faded yellow. He was following the tracks of the horses.

The slope was steep. Banokles gauged it at around 300 paces. 'You see that little group of boulders on the hillside?' he asked his men. 'We'll hit them when they reach those rocks. If they're gutless they'll break and run, and we'll fade back and ride on. If not, they'll charge, and we'll keep hitting them. When you see me drop my bow and lay into them, you follow hard. Now spread out. Not too far.'

The five warriors eased their way back, then crept to better shooting positions.

Banokles felt calmer now. There were no more decisions to be made. Notching an arrow to his bow, he waited.

The twenty-two Idonoi were approaching the boulders. They were closely bunched and talking to one another, obviously expecting no ambush. They would have seen the tracks and known there were only six horses. Outnumbered more than three to one the Trojans would *have* to be fleeing before them.

The thin man in the yellow cloak moved past the boulders and glanced up. Banokles came to his feet, and sent a shaft at him. It missed – and slammed into the thigh of the warrior behind him. Five other arrows slashed into the advancing men. One warrior took two in the chest. Then a second volley hit the Idonoi. Again Banokles missed his target, the shaft striking a boulder and ricocheting up into the air. Seven of the attackers were down.

Banokles prayed the rest would turn and run.

They charged.

Drawing back on the bowstring Banokles let fly. This time the arrow punched through the skull of a running warrior, who fell back, then rolled down the slope. Two more of the enemy fell to well-aimed shafts. The Idonoi were close now, no more than twenty paces from the tree line. Banokles shot one last arrow, dropped his bow and drew his sabre and short sword.

With a bellowing battle cry he surged out of the undergrowth and raced towards the twelve surviving warriors. A tall Idonoi with a painted face leapt at him, swinging a longsword. Banokles ducked under the blow, plunging his shortsword into the man's chest, then hitting him with a savage head-butt. As the warrior fell back the sword tore clear of his body. Banokles lashed out at a second man, his sabre slicing through the flesh of the warrior's forearm.

Banokles saw Ennion and Kerio charge in, and two more Idonoi fell. Then a blow struck his helm, spinning it clear. Banokles swung round, half dazed, and launched himself at his attacker. The two collided and hit the ground. Banokles scrambled up, then clove his sabre into the man's skull. The blade stuck fast. Letting go of the hilt Banokles spun round – just in time to parry a thrust from a spearman. Grabbing the spear with his left hand he dragged the man towards him, and kicked the warrior's legs from under him. As the man fell Banokles leapt on him, plunging the short-sword into his neck. An Idonoi warrior loomed over him, sword raised. The man suddenly gasped, blood spraying from his throat. As the warrior slumped to the grass Banokles saw blond Skorpios behind him, his blood-smeared sabre in his hand.

And then the remaining five Idonoi fled the battle-field. They were running so fast that two of them fell on the steep slope and lost their swords as they rolled down.

Banokles pushed himself to his feet. Olganos brought him his helm. Justinos called out to him, and Banokles saw that the warrior was kneeling beside the fallen Kerio. Banokles looked round for the other men. Ennion was sitting down. There was a long cut to his head, blood flowing over the left side of his face. Skorpios was moving round the battlefield, despatching wounded Idonoi. Olganos had several cuts to his fore-arms, and was bleeding freely.

Banokles walked over and knelt beside Kerio. The man was dead, his throat torn open.

'Strip his armour,' said Banokles.

Then he walked among the Idonoi dead. Two of them had been carrying packs. Banokles searched the first, and found several loaves and some dried meat. His mood lifted. Tearing off a chunk of bread he took a bite. It was flat-baked salt bread, which had always been a favourite of his. Putting the pack down he opened the second.

Inside was more food – and a small, wax-stoppered amphora. Breaking the wax seal he lifted it to his nostrils. The glorious scent of wine came to him. Banokles sighed. Olganos came alongside.

'Now this,' said Banokles, hefting the amphora and drinking deeply, 'was worth fighting for.'

XXX

The Temple of the Unknown

HELIKAON STOOD AT THE STERN OF THE *XANTHOS*, alongside Oniacus at the port steering oar. The long journey round the western coastline had been largely without incident. They had seen few ships, and those they had were small trading vessels which had hugged the coastline, and sped for land the moment the Dardanian fleet was sighted.

No war galleys, however, had patrolled the seas, and this worried Helikaon.

By now Agamemnon's fleets were huge, and the uneasy question remained: where were they?

The rocky coastline of Argos was close off the port bow, and the fleet sailed on past small villages and ports, cutting towards the east, and the islands south-west of Samothraki.

Towards dusk they spotted a high-prowed trading galley heading east. The ship made no effort to evade them, and Helikaon signalled two of his flanking galleys to intercept her. The trader complied, edging his vessel alongside the *Xanthos*.

Helikaon strode to the starboard rail and gazed down onto the decks of the trader. The rowers were sitting idle now, their oars drawn in. A fat-bellied merchant, wearing voluminous robes of bright purple, looked up at him. The man had long dark hair, and a beard that had been curled with hot irons in the Hittite manner. 'We travel under the protection of the emperor, and have no part in your wars,' he called out.

'Where are you headed?' Helikaon asked him.

'Through the Hellespont and home.'

'Come aboard and share a cup of wine with me,' said Helikaon. A rope was lowered and the chubby merchant heaved his way up to the taller ship, clambering over the rail red-faced and breathing hard. He gazed round with interest.

'I have heard of the *Xanthos*, King Aeneas,' he said. 'A very fine vessel.'

'My friends call me Helikaon, and I have always been a friend to those who serve the emperor.'

The man bowed. 'I am Oniganthas. Last year I could have described myself as a rich merchant. These days poverty beckons. This war of yours is ruinous to trade.'

Helikaon ordered wine brought, and led Oniganthas to the high rear deck. The merchant sipped his wine, murmured appreciative comments concerning its quality, and then stood silently, his large, dark eyes watching Helikaon.

'Where has your voyage taken you?' asked Helikaon.

'From Athens along the coast and up to Thraki. No trade there any longer.'

'So you sailed down to Argos?'

Oniganthas nodded. 'And sold my cargo at a small loss. These are not good days, Helikaon.'

'And what news did you carry to Argos?'

'News? I carried spices and perfumes.'

'Let us not play games, Oniganthas. You are a neutral vessel. Were I one of Agamemnon's generals, or admirals, I would seek to use such a vessel to carry information. Have you been asked to perform such a service?'

'We must be wary here,' said Oniganthas, with a sly smile. 'Many people will talk on beaches or at ports, but as a neutral it would be ill advised of me to offer my services to one side or the other. That would make me an agent of one of the powers, and my neutrality would be forfeit.'

Helikaon considered his words. On the surface the argument seemed reasonable enough, but neither Agamemnon nor his generals would respect the neutrality of a Hittite vessel unless it suited their purpose. The only way Oniganthas could sail safely through the war zone would be if he carried evidence of Mykene safe conduct. With trade so savagely disrupted the Hittite merchant was probably supplementing his income by relaying messages to and from Mykene generals.

'I can see,' said Helikaon, at last, 'that you are a man of subtlety.'

The merchant drained his wine and handed the cup

back to a waiting sailor. 'As all merchants must, I seek profit. There is no profit for me without neutrality. With it I am free to conduct business with any of the city states or nations around the Great Green. Indeed, it has always been my hope to strengthen my dealings with Dardania.'

'And no reason why we should not,' said Helikaon. 'I have been looking for a man of enterprise to hold some gold for me, against such time when I might need that gold.'

Helikaon saw the glint of greed in the man's eyes. 'How much gold are we speaking of, Helikaon?'

'Enough, were it to be used so, to build several trading galleys, and certainly enough to offset a poor trading season.' Helikaon paused, watching the man, and allowing the lure of the suggested bribe to work upon him.

'And this man would merely hold the gold for you?' asked Oniganthas.

Helikaon smiled. 'Or perhaps make it grow to our joint advantage?'

'Ah, you seek a business alliance then?'

'Indeed so. We should talk more of this. Perhaps you would stay with us for the night?'

'I would enjoy that,' said Oniganthas, 'for I have been starved of intelligent company recently. Most of my nights have been spent listening to Mykene sailors and soldiers and . . .' he looked into Helikaon's eyes, 'their endless talk of wars and victories and plans.'

The fleet beached on a barren, uninhabited island, and Helikaon, Oniganthas alongside him, watched as

Oniacus and several of the sailors brought out items they had plundered during their raids. There were cups and goblets of gold, inset with gems, and heavy jewellery of Mykene design. Everything was laid on a blanket on the sand.

Oniganthas knelt to examine the pieces in the fading light. 'Exquisite,' he said.

While the cookfires were being lit Helikaon led Oniganthas away from the men, and they sat and talked until they were called to eat. Later, as the merchant slept, Helikaon walked away from the campsite, and up to the crest of a high hill. What he had heard from Oniganthas was dispiriting.

Gershom and Oniacus joined him. 'Did you learn much from the merchant?' asked Gershom.

'I did – and little of it good. I need time to think. Let us walk awhile.'

The island was rocky and inhospitable. But on a nearby hilltop someone had built a temple. Moonlight shone on its white columns.

'I wonder who it is dedicated to,' said Oniacus.

Helikaon did not care, but he strolled with the others to the deserted building. There were no statues around the perimeter, and none inside. The dust of centuries lay on the stone-slabbed floor. Part of the roof had collapsed, allowing moonlight to shine through. They searched the building, but found no carvings, no implements, no broken cups or lamps.

Helikaon knelt and brushed away the thick dust from a section of the floor. Beneath it was a deep, curved line carved into the stone slabs. Gershom and

Oniacus joined him, and together they scraped back the dust from adjoining slabs. The symbol they revealed covered the entire floor. There were two circles, the larger enclosing the smaller, and a diagonal line cutting through them both.

'What does it mean?' asked Oniacus.

'It is an ancient symbol,' Helikaon told him. 'You can find it on old maps. Merchants once used the symbols to mark areas of trade or military power. The outer circle, if broken, means there are no hostile forces. A broken inner circle means little trade exists in the area. Unbroken circles mean the opposite, strong defences, but good trade.'

'And a line like this, running through two unbroken circles?' asked Oniacus.

'It means the area has not been scouted. It is unknown.'

'So,' said Gershom, staring down at the carving. 'Someone came to this barren rock and built a temple to the unknown?'

'It would appear so,' Helikaon answered. 'How strange. They would have had to transport the marble and timber across the Great Green, then haul it up here. Scores, perhaps hundreds, of workers and stonemasons constructing a building no-one would visit, on an island without a settlement.'

Gershom laughed. 'I think it is a grand jest. We all worship the unknown, and the unknowable. That is the essence of our lives. All we can ever know is what was, not what will be. Yet we yearn to know, to understand the mystery. Whoever built this had a fine sense of humour, and an eye for the future. A temple to the unknown, built by someone unknown, for an unknown purpose. It is delightful.'

'Well, I think it is a nonsense,' complained Oniacus. 'A waste of good marble and labour.'

When they walked back out into the moonlight Helikaon stared out over the starlit sea. Gershom said: 'Are you ready to talk about what you learned?'

Helikaon took a deep breath. 'Ismaros has fallen, as has Xantheia,' he said. 'That only leaves Kalliros. The fortifications there are not strong. So we must assume it will be under siege or lost by now.'

'But Hektor is in Thraki,' said Oniacus. 'He never loses. He will crush the enemy.'

'According to Oniganthas Hektor has won several battles, but more and more enemy forces are pouring in from Thessaly and Mykene lands. The last reports said Hektor was in the Rhodope mountains, facing three enemy armies.'

'He will fight them, and defeat them,' insisted Oniacus.

'Perhaps,' agreed Helikaon, 'but small victories will mean nothing. Thraki is lost. I think Hektor will try to get his army back to Carpea and the barges, then cross to Dardania. It is his only hope of survival.'

'What about the fleet of Menados?' put in Gershom.

'Either they are heading into the Hellespont to intercept Hektor, or they are planning to raid Dardania. If it is the former, and Hektor's barges attempt to cross the channel unprotected, they will be sunk.'

'You will forgive me for pointing out,' said Gershom,

'that there are a number of assumptions here. Hektor may *not* be heading for Carpea. He may have gone to the aid of Kalliros. And, even if you are right, he may already be at Carpea, and preparing to make the crossing. There is no certainty that we will be in time to help him.'

Helikaon walked away from them both, leaving them arguing. He needed time to think.

If he sailed for Carpea, and the Mykene admiral Menados attacked Dardania, the slaughter would be great. If he sailed home to defend his lands and the Mykene destroyed Hektor and the Trojan Horse, the war was lost.

And there was another nagging thought, one which he had no intention of sharing with his lieutenants. The fortress of Dardanos could withstand a siege – unless the enemy were sure that the city gates would be opened to them. Agamemnon was a cunning enemy, and had already used traitors once against Troy, when he bribed Priam's son, Agathon, to rebel against him. What if he had agents within Dardanos?

He thought then of Halysia. The last time the Mykene attacked they had raped and stabbed her, and murdered her son before her eyes. Will you see her put through that again, whispered a voice from his heart?

Not a man given to passionate outbursts, or foul oaths, Helikaon suddenly swore long and colourfully. His two companions fell silent. 'There is no rational way to reach a decision,' he said, at last. 'There are too many imponderables. Menados may already be in the Hellespont, or he may have landed an army in

Dardania. Hektor may be fighting at Kalliros, or battling his way to the coast. Then there are the fleets that Odysseus used to attack Ismaros. Where are they? We know nothing.'

'Then we are starting from the right place,' said Gershom, glancing back at the moonlit temple.

Banokles edged his grey clear of the trees and rode out onto the downward slope. Behind him came Justinos, with the young Prince Periklos sharing his horse. After that came the nurse Myrine and the child Obas, riding Kerio's mount. Skorpios and Ennion followed them. Banokles glanced back. Skorpios was carrying his bow. Ennion, his head wound still seeping blood through the stitches, looked all in, his shoulders hunched, his head bowed.

Some way ahead Banokles saw Olganos dismount just before the crest of a low hill, and creep to the top, peering out over the open land beyond.

The midday sun blazed down from a clear sky, but a cool wind was blowing through the mountains. Banokles was sick of being in command, and a dull headache was throbbing at his temples. He had no idea where they were heading, save that Olganos had talked of a high pass. Banokles recalled travelling through such a place, but would not be able to find it again if his life depended on it.

Which, of course, it did.

The throbbing increased. Banokles pulled off his helmet, allowing the breeze to cool his sweat-drenched fair hair.

Justinos drew alongside. 'Ennion is suffering,' he said. 'That blow may have cracked his skull.'

Banokles donned his helm and heeled the grey into a run up the hillside. Reining in alongside Olganos' mount, he crept up to crouch alongside the young soldier.

'See anything?' he asked. Olganos shook his head.

'I think we are close to the pass,' he said, pointing to the towering, snow-capped mountains forming a massive wall across their path. 'We have to cross that dry valley, and the hills beyond. There are stands of beech and pine along the way that could hide an army.'

Banokles peered down into the valley. There was no sign of horsemen or soldiers. However, as Olganos said, there could be men hidden from view within the trees. Olganos voiced the same concern. 'Once we move into the open,' he said, 'we will be spotted by any enemy scouts within the tree line.'

'You have a plan?' asked Banokles, hopefully.

'We don't have a choice. We must reach the pass.'

Banokles was relieved. He didn't want any more choices. 'Good,' he said. 'Can we make it by dusk?'

'On fresh horses, yes. Ours are tired, and once we come out of the valley the land rises all the way to the pass.'

Rising to his feet Banokles waved the others forward, then mounted his grey and led them over the crest.

As they approached the valley floor the heat began to rise. The horses plodded on, heads down, their hooves raising small plumes of dust, sweat streaking their flanks. The valley was dry and hot, with little vegetation.

The going was slow, and the afternoon wore on. Then Skorpios called out. Banokles looked back to see that Ennion had fallen from his mount. Calling a halt, Banokles swung the grey and rode to where the wounded man was struggling to rise. Banokles dismounted and walked over to him, taking hold of his arm and hauling him to his feet. Ennion's eyes were glazed, his face ashen. Suddenly he doubled over, fell to his knees, and vomited.

Banokles stepped away from him, then looked around at the small group. The horses had little more in them, and the men were exhausted. 'How far to the pass now?' he asked Olganos.

The young man shrugged. 'In the state we are in? Not before nightfall, I'd say.'

Off to the right was a thick stand of beech trees. 'Ride in and see if you can find water.'

'If we don't reach the pass ahead of the Idonoi—'

'I know what *might* happen,' snapped Banokles. 'Now go!'

Olganos rode off. Banokles helped Ennion to his feet and lifted him to his horse. 'Do not fall off again. Hear me?'

'I hear you,' mumbled the warrior.

'Let's get into the trees,' Banokles told the others. 'It will be cooler there.'

Olganos found a hidden glade and led the group to it. There were boulders of white marble, and flowering bushes sprouting between the stones, their crimson blooms trailing down into a wide rock tank full of cool water. The tank was fed by a stream which gushed

down over the boulders in a succession of tiny water-
falls. There was good grass here, and the glade was of
such beauty that Banokles could almost believe that
nymphs and dryads were hidden close by.

The old nurse limped to the waterside, and eased herself down, splashing her face and hair, then drinking
deeply. The two princes went with her. Justinos and
Skorpios helped Ennion from his horse and sat him
down with his back to a tree. Banokles filled his helmet
with water and took it to the injured man. Ennion
drank a little. His face was still grey, but his eyes were
less glazed. Banokles examined the man's head wound.
The long cut to his skull had been stitched, but the flesh
was now swollen and discoloured. Head wounds were
always problematic. Banokles had once known a man
who took an arrow through the temple and survived.
Another soldier, a tough, burly man, had been struck by
a fist in a tavern fight and had died on the spot.

Leaving Ennion to rest, the others saw to the horses,
using dried grass to wipe the foamy sweat from their
flanks. Once they were cooled down the beasts were led
to the pool and allowed to drink their fill.

As the men settled down in the shade of the beech
trees, the horses cropping the rich grass near by,
Banokles stripped off his armour and jumped into the
rock pool. It was deeper than he had thought and he
sank beneath the surface. The water was cold, the feeling as it closed over him exquisite. All sounds faded
away, as did the headache he had endured for most of
the day.

Coming to the surface, he swam back to the bank

and hauled himself clear of the water. He saw
Olganos and the slender, blond-haired Skorpios sitting
quietly together. There was no sign of Justinos.
Banokles dried himself off and walked over to the two
warriors. 'You lads should take a swim,' he said.

'What if the enemy comes?' asked Olganos.

Banokles laughed. 'If they send an army you'll be just
as dead, whether you're hot and stinking like a pig, or
cool and refreshed.'

'Truth in that,' said Skorpios, rising to his feet and
unstrapping the ties of his cuirass.

'Where's Justinos?' asked Banokles.

'I told him to wait back in the trees watching the
valley,' replied Olganos.

'Good. While he's doing that I think I'll take a nap.'

Olganos and Skorpios leapt into the rock pool with
a mighty splash, and Banokles walked over to sit beside
Ennion. 'How are you feeling?' he asked.

'Better. Head feels like there's a horse trapped inside,
trying to kick its way out. Shame about Kerio.
Miserable cowson, but he could fight.'

'The time to think about the dead is when you are
safe back home,' said Banokles.

'You think we'll get safe back home?'

'Why shouldn't we?'

Ennion smiled. 'It doesn't bother you that we're outnumbered and trapped in an enemy land?'

'Never saw the point in worrying about tomorrow,'
Banokles told him. 'At this moment we have water, the
horses are resting and eating, and I'm about to have a
blissful sleep. If the enemy come I'll kill as many of the

cowsons as I can. If they don't, well, we'll ride on, find Hektor and the rest of the lads, and then go home. Get some sleep, man.'

'I think I will,' said Ennion. Suddenly he chuckled. 'All my life I've wanted to do something heroic, something to be remembered for. And now I've rescued two sons of a king, and fought off twenty enemy soldiers. It feels very fine, Banokles. Very fine. Everything I could have hoped for – except for this bastard headache.'

'It'll be gone by morning,' said Banokles, stretching himself out on the grass, and closing his eyes. Sleep came almost immediately.

It was dark when he woke, bright stars shining in the night sky. Sitting up, he glanced at Ennion. The warrior was lying on his back and staring up at the stars.

'How is the head?' asked Banokles.

Ennion made no reply. Banokles passed his hand over the warrior's face. There was no response. Leaning over him, Banokles closed the dead man's eyes, then pushed himself to his feet.

Olganos was swimming, Justinos sitting beside the pool. The old nurse and the boys were asleep. Olganos climbed out of the water. Banokles strolled over to him. 'You put Skorpios on watch?'

'Yes.'

'Good. I'll relieve him in a while.'

'How is Ennion? You think he'll be able to travel tomorrow?'

'He is already travelling,' answered Banokles. 'He's walking the Dark Road. His horse is in better shape than the others. Let the fat old nurse ride him. You should take his sword. Yours is looking battered and like to break the next time you use it.'

'By Ares, you are a cold bastard,' Olganos told him.

'He is dead. We are not. We leave at first light.'

The boulder-strewn road leading up and through the high pass of Kilkanos was littered with the debris of a departed army. Broken swords lay among the stones. A shattered helm glinted in the early morning sunshine. Discarded items that had once been of value now gathered dust. Here and there Kalliades could see splashes of dried blood, where the wounded had been tended. The pass itself was narrow and winding, climbing ever higher into the mountains. Kalliades and his 300 volunteers had taken up a defensive position some eighty paces below the highest point, where the pass narrowed to a mere thirty paces across. Towering rock faces rose on either side. Kalliades placed his hundred archers on the higher ground to left and right, where they could shelter behind rocks. The more heavily armoured infantry were stationed at the centre. The men were all Kikones, with nowhere left to run.

Scouts had warned Hektor that an Idonoi army some 7,000 strong was marching towards them. They were close, and would be in sight before noon.

Kalliades had volunteered to remain with the rear-guard for the two days Hektor had requested the pass be held. Hektor had urged him not to stay. 'I will need you in the days to come, Kalliades. I don't want you dead on some Thrakian rock.'

'If you know of a better man to plan a defence then let him stay,' said Kalliades. 'The Thrakians are good fighters, but there is not a strategist among them. And you need this pass held. We can't afford to have armies coming at us from two sides.'

Reluctantly Hektor had agreed, and they had said their farewells that morning.

The Thrakians were grim men, who had fought well during the long campaign. It irked them that it had all ended so badly. Hektor had offered them the chance to come with him back to Troy, but they had decided to stay and fight on against the invaders.

Kalliades moved among them, giving orders. They responded with instant obedience, but little warmth. Though they trusted his judgement, and respected his skills, he was a foreigner and a stranger to them.

A foreigner and a stranger.

It suddenly occurred to Kalliades that he had always been a stranger, even among his own people. Climbing to a high rock he sat down, and gazed back down the pass. When the enemy came they would be tired from the climb. They would be hit with volley after volley of arrows, and then, when closer, bronze-tipped javelins. The sheer walls of rock would compress their formations, making it difficult to dodge the missiles. Then Kalliades would attack them with his heavily armoured Thrakian infantry, forcing them back. They would retreat and regroup. He had no doubts the defenders could hold for several charges. But they would take losses, their arrows would soon be exhausted, and concerted attacks by an enemy with the advantage of numbers would wear them down. No matter what strategies he concocted the result would be the same. If the enemy were determined and brave they would break through before dusk.

Hektor had understood this. The rearguard was doomed. It was unlikely that any of them would leave the pass alive.

The face of Piria appeared in his mind, sunshine glinting from her shorn blond hair. In his memory she was standing on the beach, laughing as the men of the *Penelope* struggled to catch the errant pigs. It had been a good day, and it had taken on a golden hue these last three years.

Then the image blurred, and he saw again Big Red, standing in the doorway of his small house, wearing robes of scarlet and black. It was the day before the army was due to return to Thraki for the spring campaign. Kalliades had invited her in, but she had stood her ground.

'I will not enter your home, Kalliades. I do not like you, and you have no affection for me.'

'Then what are you doing here?'

'I want Banokles to come home safely. I do not want him drawn into your need for death.'

The words had surprised him. 'I don't want to die, Red. Why would you think that?'

She looked at him, her expression softening. 'I have changed my mind. I will come in. You have wine?'

He had led her through to the small garden at the rear of the house, and they had sat together on a curved bench in the shade of a high wall. The wine was cheap and mildly bitter on the tongue, but Red did not seem to mind. She looked him in the eye, her gaze direct. 'Why did you rescue the priestess?' she asked.

He shrugged. 'She reminded me of my sister, who was killed by violent men.'

'That may be true, but it is not the whole reason. Banokles talks of you with great respect and affection, so I have heard all the stories of your travels. I am not young any more, Kalliades, but my wisdom has grown with the years. I know men. By Hera, I know more about men than I would ever have wished to know. So many of you are quick to notice flaws and weaknesses in others, while being completely blind to your own faults and fears. Why do you have no friends, Kalliades?'

The question had made him uncomfortable, and he had begun to regret inviting her in. 'I have Banokles.'

'Yes, you do. Why no others? And why no wife?'

He had risen then from the seat. 'I do not answer to you,' he said.

'Are you afraid, Kalliades?'

'I fear nothing.'

He could not escape her gaze, and it disconcerted him. 'Now *that* is a lie,' she said, softly.

'You do not know me. No-one does.'

'No-one does,' she repeated. 'And you are wrong again. I know you, Kalliades. I don't know *why* you are the way you are. Perhaps a favourite pony died when you were young, or you were buggered by a friendly uncle. Perhaps your father fell off a cliff and drowned. It doesn't matter. I know you.'

Anger had surged through him. 'Just go!' he said. 'When I need the wisdom of a fat whore I'll send for you.'

'Ah,' she said, no trace of anger in her voice, 'and now I see that deep down you also know. You are just too frightened to hear it.'

In that moment he had wanted to strike her, to wipe that smug look from her face. Instead he had stepped back away from her, feeling trapped in his own home. 'Tell me, then,' he demanded. 'Speak this dreadful truth. I do not fear it.'

'The dreadful truth is that, deep down, you have one great fear. You fear life.'

'What is this nonsense? Have you been chewing *meas* root?'

'You saved a woman who meant nothing to you, and faced almost certain death as a result.'

'She was worth saving.'

'I'll not disagree with that. On its own it was a fine deed. Heroic. The stuff of legends. When Odysseus walked down to face the pirates you went with him. You told Banokles you wanted to see what would happen. You are an intelligent man. You *know* what should have happened. They should have cut you to pieces. Banokles thinks you are a man of enormous courage. But I am not Banokles. There is a part of you, Kalliades, that yearns for death. An empty part, with nothing to fill it. No love, no intimacy, no dreams, no ambition. That is why you have no friends. You have nothing to give them, and you fear what they could give to you.'

Her words cut through his defences like an icy blade. 'I have known love,' he argued. 'I loved Piria. That is no lie.'

'I believe you. And that is how I came to know you. You are close to thirty years old, and you have had *one* great love. How curious then that it should have been for a woman who could never return that love. A woman you *knew* could never return it. Shall I tell you what you saw in that frightened, abused and doomed girl? A reflection of yourself. Lost and alone, friendless and deserted.' She had stood then, and brushed the creases from her robes.

'Banokles is my friend,' he said, hearing just how defensive those words were.

She shook her head, dismissing even this small attempt to stand his ground. 'My Banokles is not a thinker, or he would have understood you better. He is a friend to you, yes, but in your mind, whether you know it or not, he is no more than a big hound, whose adoration allows you to deceive yourself, to let you believe you are like other people. He saved your life, Kalliades, and you have dragged him into every dangerous folly. Friends do not do that. The day you finally decide to die, do not allow Banokles to be beside you.'

She had walked away then, but he called out to her, 'I am sorry that you despise me, Red.'

'If I despise you,' she had told him, sadness in her voice, 'it is only that I despise myself. We are so alike, Kalliades. Closed off from life, no friends, no loved ones. That is why we need Banokles. He *is* life, rich and raw, in all its glory. No subtlety, no guile. He is the fire we gather round, and his light pushes back the shadows we fear.' She had fallen silent for a moment. Then she looked at him. 'Think of a childhood memory,' she said.

He had blinked, as an image flared to life.

'What was it?' she asked him.

'I was a child, hiding from raiders in a flax field.'

'The day your sister died?'

'Yes.'

She had sighed. 'And that is your tragedy, Kalliades. You never came out of that flax field. You are still there, small and frightened and hiding from the world.'

High in the rocks Kalliades pushed thoughts of Red from his mind. The men had lit cookfires and he was about to stroll down and eat with them when he saw riders in the distance.

At first they were little more than specks, but as they came closer he recognized the glint of Trojan armour.

On the far side of the pass he saw that his archers had also spotted the group, and were notching arrows to their bows. Calling out to them not to shoot, he climbed down and walked out to meet the small group.

Banokles came riding up towards him, then lifted his leg and jumped clear of the weary grey horse he was riding. 'Good to see you,' he said. 'We've rescued the sons of Rhesos, and now you can take charge. I'm sick of command.' He gazed round. 'Where's the army?'

'Heading for Carpea. I am in charge of the rear-guard.'

'You've not enough men. We caught sight of the Idonoi horde. They're close. Thousands of the cowsons.'

'We only have to hold them for two days.'

'Ah well, I expect we can do that.'

'There is no *we*, Banokles. This is my duty. You must take the sons of Rhesos on to Carpea. Hektor will be glad to see them.'

Banokles pulled off his helm and scratched his short blond hair. 'You are not thinking clearly, Kalliades. You'll need me and my boys here. These Thrakian sheep-shaggers will probably run at the first sight of a painted face.'

'No, they won't.' Kalliades sighed, and thought back to his conversation with Red. 'Listen to me,' he said. 'This is your troop. Ursos told Hektor he had placed you in command. So I am now ordering you to ride on with them. I'll see you at Carpea, or over in Dardania if you have already crossed the Hellespont.'

'Have you forgotten we are sword brothers?'

Kalliades ignored the question. 'Stay wary as you head east. There are other, smaller passes through the mountains and there may be enemy riders out there.'

'I take it you won't object if we rest the horses for a while,' said Banokles, coldly. 'The climb has taken it out of them.'

'Of course. Get yourself some food, too.'

Without another word Banokles led his horse up the pass. Kalliades watched his riders follow him.

It was close to midday when they rode away. Banokles did not say goodbye, or even look back.

Kalliades watched as they cleared the crest of the pass. 'Farewell, Banokles, my friend,' he whispered.

'I see them!' shouted an archer, pointing down the pass. Kalliades drew his sword and called his infantrymen to him. Far below he saw sunlight glinting from thousands of spears and helms.

XXXI

The reluctant general

BANOKLES WAS STILL ANGRY AS HE LED HIS SMALL TROOP over the crest of the pass and down towards the wide flatlands below. After all they had been through together why would Kalliades have treated him so curtly? It was hurtful and it confused him.

The old nurse, Myrine, urged her horse alongside his. Untrained as a rider she looked uncomfortable on Ennion's bay mare, clinging with one hand to the reins, the other to its mane. Her face was red with the effort of maintaining her balance. 'Is it far to Carpea?' she asked.

'Yes,' Banokles told her.

'I don't know if I can sit this horse for much longer. I have bad knees, you know. They pain me.'

Banokles didn't know what to tell her. She was too old to walk to Carpea. 'It'll get easier,' he said, though he didn't know if it was true. Wheeling his horse away, he rode back to where Justinos and Skorpios were bringing up the rear. 'You know how far it is to Carpea?' he asked Justinos. The big warrior shrugged.

'A few days, I guess. Perhaps four. I didn't count the travelling days when we set out.'

'Me neither.'

Skorpios spoke up. 'Olganos says it will take us around three days.'

'I vote we put Olganos in charge,' said Banokles. 'He seems to know what he's doing.'

Justinos shook his head. 'Too young. We'll stick with you. The old woman looks ready to fall off the mare.'

'Bad knees,' said Banokles.

Skorpios touched heels to his mount and rode over to her. Banokles and Justinos followed. The youngster dismounted and held the reins of the mare while Myrine eased her right leg over the beast's back until she was sitting side on. 'Ennion's horse is a gentle creature,' Skorpios told her. 'She will not be startled, or throw you. Is that easier on the knees?'

'Yes,' the old nurse told him, settling Obas more comfortably on her lap. 'Thank you. You are a sweet boy.'

The afternoon sun was strong, but a cool wind was blowing through the mountains as they rode on. The land was wide and open, rising and falling through gentle, wooded hills and gullies. High above Banokles saw a flight of geese, heading north towards a distant lake. He had always liked geese – especially roasted in their own fat. His stomach churned.

The dark-haired young prince, Periklos, brought Kerio's mount alongside him as they approached a small wood. Banokles glanced at the lad. His pale tunic was edged with gold thread, and there was more gold in his belt than Banokles would earn in a season.

'We should find you a sword,' said Banokles, 'or perhaps a long dagger.'

'Why? I could not defeat an armoured foe.'

'Perhaps not,' said Banokles, 'but you could slash off his balls as he killed you.'

Periklos grinned. It made him look even younger and more vulnerable. 'I'm sorry about your father,' said Banokles. 'People say he was a great man.'

The boy's smile faded. 'What will we do in Troy?' he asked.

'I don't know what you mean.'

'Will I even be welcome there? I have no lands, no army, no fortune.'

Banokles shrugged. 'Neither have I. Maybe you could train to be a metalsmith. I always wanted to do that, when I was young. Melt metal and bash it.'

'Not me,' said the prince. 'They all become crippled. My father said that heating the ore makes the air bad. All the smiths lose feeling in their fingers, and then their toes.'

'You are right,' said Banokles. 'Never really thought of it before. Bad air, eh? Never heard of that.'

Periklos leaned in. 'We have deep caves in the mountains where the air is really bad sometimes. People go into them to sleep and then just die. When I was small some travellers took refuge in just such a cave. Five men and several women. A passer-by found them all dead, and ran to a nearby village to alert the headman.

They returned to the cave, but it was night, and they were carrying torches. The headman went into the cave and there was a sound like thunder, and a great brightness. The headman was hurled from the cave, his eyebrows and beard singed off.'

'Was he dead?' asked Banokles.

'I don't think so. After that no-one went near the caves. They say a fire-breathing monster lived there.'

'Maybe he liked the bad air,' offered Banokles.

Periklos sighed. 'What is Troy like?'

'Big.'

'Do you live in a palace?'

'No. I did once. For a while anyway. I have a house, with my wife, Red.'

'You have children?'

'No.'

'Maybe Obas and I could stay with you. Myrine could cook.'

'The cooking sounds good,' said Banokles. 'Red is a wonderful woman, but the food she prepares tastes like goat droppings. Except for the cakes – but then she gets them from a baker she knows. Anyway, I expect Hektor will give you rooms in his palace. Have you met him?'

Periklos nodded. 'My father likes him a lot.' His head bowed. '*Liked* him, I should say.' His expression hardened. 'One day I will come back with an army, and I will kill every Idonoi. There will be nothing left of them. Not even memories.'

'Always good to have a plan,' said Banokles.

'What is your plan?'

Banokles grinned. 'To get home and snuggle up to Red, put my head on the pillow and sleep for several days. After getting drunk, of course.'

Periklos smiled. 'I was drunk once. I crept into father's rooms and drank a cup of wine, without any water. It was horrible. The room spun and I fell. Then I puked. I felt sick for days.'

'You need to work at it,' Banokles told him. 'After a while you find the golden moment. That's what my father called it. All worries cease, all problems shrink, and the world just seems . . . seems happy.'

'What then?'

'Then the room spins, you puke, and you feel sick for days.'

Periklos laughed. 'I shall never drink wine again. Even the thought of it makes my stomach tremble.' They rode in silence for a while, then Periklos said: 'You seemed angry when you spoke to the officer in the pass. Why was that?'

'He used to be my sword brother. But when I offered to help him hold the pass he refused.'

'Perhaps he didn't want you to die with him. I spoke to some of the Kikones. One of them was an officer at the palace. He said they were there to fight to the death.'

Banokles shook his head. 'Kalliades will have a plan. He'll outwit the enemy. He always does.'

'If you say so,' said Periklos.

Banokles heeled his horse forward and headed it up towards the top of a low hill. Periklos was just a boy, and knew nothing of the skills of Kalliades. Even so, the lad's pessimism nagged at him. Banokles had seen the Idonoi horde. No way could a few defenders hold them for long.

Lost in thought he rode over the crest of the hill – straight into a large group of some fifty cavalrymen, their faces smeared with paint.

Banokles swore and drew both his swords.

Kalliades was once more back on the *Penelope*, a fresh wind filling the sail. Piria was beside him, staring back at a black pig struggling in the sea. Her expression was one of concern.

'Can he make it?' she asked.

'He will outlive us both,' Kalliades told her.

She tried to speak to him again, but a great wall of noise shrouded her words, the clash of swords, the screams of men. Her face faded.

Kalliades opened his eyes. He was lying in a group of boulders, his head pounding, his vision blurred. Struggling to rise, he felt a lancing pain in his chest. The Sword of Argurios lay on the ground beside him, the blade smeared with blood. Kalliades looked down at his arms. They too were blood-covered. Rolling to his knees he tried to straighten his legs beneath him, but fell again, and rolled onto his back. Blood dripped into his right eye and he brushed it away. Dragging himself further back from the battle he sat against a rock. His right eye was swollen, and closing fast. He remembered then the bronze axe that had hammered against his helm, shattering it, and hurling him from his feet.

Five attacks they had survived. In the first the enemy had not even reached the infantry, forced back by the deadly rain of shafts coming from the rising ground. Then they had regrouped, bringing shieldmen to the front, and advancing again. Still the arrows had found targets, thudding into legs, arms, and shoulders. Kalliades had led a charge which splintered their front rank, and again they had fallen back.

The third attack had come swiftly, showing Kalliades that the enemy general was a man of stern discipline. His troops would not crack. They would pound on the Thrakian lines like an angry sea.

For a while then the strategy changed. Enemy archers creeping forward, shooting up at the Thrakian bowmen, pinning them down.

Then came a charge of horsemen. Kalliades had ordered his men to stand firm, locking shields. No horse would willingly ride into a wall. Instead the Idonoi riders leapt them up and into the massed ranks, scattering the defenders. The fight was short and bloody, the riders lightly armoured. Even so, the losses among the Thrakians were high: broken bones from the kicking horses, and wounds from lances that had driven through helms and breastplates.

By the fifth attack the Thrakian bowmen had been running out of shafts, and the enemy advanced with great confidence.

More than half of the Thrakians were dead, and now there were barely enough to hold the narrow pass.

Kalliades gazed at the hundred or so fighting men. He wanted to join them, but there was no strength left in his limbs. A great tiredness settled on him, and he found himself leaning back and staring up at the sky. The clouds above the mountains were streaked with gold from the dying sun. He saw a flock of birds flying there. It was a beautiful sight. How fine it must be, he thought, to spread your arms and take to the skies, soaring and dipping high above the worries of the world.

The pain in his chest flared again. Glancing down, he saw that his breastplate was torn, and blood was seeping over the scales. He couldn't remember the wound at first. Then he recalled the leaping horse, and the lance that had struck him, knocking him back.

From where he sat he could see the complete fighting line. It was becoming more concave, almost ready to burst inward. At that point the battle would be over. The line would fragment into groups of skirmishers, the warriors surrounded.

Instinctively Kalliades looked around for somewhere to hide. What are you doing, he asked himself? There is no escape.

And he saw again the child he had been, hiding in the flax field.

Red was right. There was a part of him that had never left it. His sister had been the sun and the stars to him; her love a constant on which he could rely. Her death, so sudden and violent, had scarred him more than he could have known. The little boy in the flax field had decided never to allow love into his life again, with its terrible pain, its awful anguish.

Do you want to live, he asked himself?

In that moment, with the last of the sunlight bathing the pass, he knew that he did.

Then get out of the flax field!

With a cry of rage and pain Kalliades took up the Sword of Argurios and forced himself to his feet. Then he staggered forward into the fray.

As he did so he heard the thunder of hooves on stone. Turning, he saw a force of some fifty horsemen galloping down the pass.

At the centre, swords raised, rode Banokles.

The Thrakian defenders cut away to left and right, allowing the cavalry through. The lancers tore into the Idonoi warriors, cutting them down. Panic swept through the enemy ranks and they turned and ran back down the pass, pursued by the cavalry.

Kalliades tried to sheathe his sword, but his arm was too weary, and the blade clanged to the ground. He sank down to sit on a boulder. Curiously, he could hear the sounds of the sea in his ears.

Then he slid from the boulder.

When he finally awoke he found he had been stripped of his armour, and the wound in his chest stitched tight. There were fires lit. Banokles was beside him.

'Good to see you,' said Kalliades.

'A pox on you, dung brain,' Banokles told him. 'You might have said you were waiting to die.'

'Would you have gone if I had?'

'Of course I wouldn't. That's what I'm saying. Sword brothers stand together.'

Taking hold of Banokles' arm, Kaliades drew himself

up to a sitting position. 'Where did you find the cavalry?'

'Down on the plain. They fled the fall of the city. I thought they were enemies at first and charged them. But they rode away from me, laughing. Bastards. Anyway, once they'd had their fun I told them there was a battle coming, and led them here. Just as well, eh? Who's the thinker now?'

'That would be you, Banokles, my friend. My good, dear friend.'

Banokles peered at him suspiciously. 'I think that crack to your skull has loosened your wits. So, how much longer do we have to hold this place?'

'No longer,' said Kalliades. 'To stay now would be foolish and achieve nothing. Leave the fires burning brightly, and then lead the horses out as quietly as you can. Bind their hooves with cloth. We'll slip away in the darkness and make a run for the sea at Carpea. With luck the Idonoi will not mount an attack until morning, and we should be far away from here by then.'

'That's more like it,' said Banokles happily. 'You rest here. I'll get Olganos to organize the withdrawal. He's good at organizing. Did they leave you any wine?'

'No,' said Kalliades. Banokles swore and moved away.

Kalliades dozed a little, and dreamed once more of Piria. She was on the deck of a dark ship, sailing towards a sunset. He was standing upon a golden beach. Kalliades lifted his arm and waved to her, but she was facing towards the setting sun and did not see him.

* * *

The journey east was slow, much of the flatlands marshy and impassable, and thick with midges and flies. The allied force of 142 men, led by the reluctant Banokles, was forced to take a meandering route, seeking firmer ground. On the first morning they had come across six deserted supply wagons. They had been looted, the horses gone. Banokles, on the advice of young Olganos, had horses hitched to them. Some of the more seriously wounded, Kalliades among them, were transferred to the wagons.

Towards mid-afternoon they came across more fleeing Thrakian soldiers. There were 43 infantrymen, well armoured, and 20 light horsemen. They were heading from the northwest, where a garrison fort had been taken by an Idonoi force.

Banokles had hoped Kalliades would be well enough to take charge of the journey, but his condition had worsened during the night. He was now sleeping in the lead wagon, and even when he occasionally regained consciousness his mind wandered. A fever had begun, and he was sweating heavily. Banokles had stitched the wound to his chest, but there was no way of knowing how deep it was, and whether it had pierced any vital organs.

Olganos sent out scouts to the north, south, east and west, to watch for signs of enemy movement. As the slow journey progressed the scouts came across more refugee Kikones warriors, and sent them on to the main force. By dusk there were more than 300 soldiers under Banokles' command.

'We are attracting them like flies to shit,' he complained to Olganos.

The young man shrugged. 'It makes us stronger if we come under attack.'

The first good news came in as they were making camp for the night. One of the scouts from the west reported that the Idonoi army at the pass had made no move to march east, and were now almost a day behind them.

As the men rested Banokles sought out Kalliades. He was awake now, but weak. Banokles brought him some water. 'There's no food,' he said.

Kalliades said nothing for a moment. His face was ashen, and glistening with sweat. 'There will be farms and settlements to the north and east,' he said. 'Send out riders tomorrow morning. Gather some cattle or sheep.'

'Good plan,' said Banokles.

'And walk among the men, Banokles. Make your presence felt. The Thrakians are proud men, but they are volatile, swift to anger or despair. You need to hold them steady.'

Kalliades stretched out and began to shiver. Banokles covered him with his cloak. 'You'll be fine,' he said. 'You're tough. You'll be fine.' Still trembling, Kalliades fell asleep. Banokles sat with him for a while, then stood. All around him men were sitting in small groups. Mostly there was no conversation among them, and an air of dejection hung over the camp. Banokles strolled over to where Periklos was sitting with the old nurse, and the sleeping Obas. 'We'll find food tomorrow,' he said. 'Farms and suchlike to the east.'

Periklos nodded, but he too looked dejected.

Banokles moved on. A group of the riders he had brought to the pass were sitting together. They looked up as he approached.

'Any of you know this area?' he asked. They shook their heads.

'We are Kalliros men,' said one, a tall man, with blue streaks on his brow. Banokles recalled that his name was Hillas.

'Good fighters, you Kalliros men,' he told him.

'Not good enough,' grunted Hillas.

'You gave those Idonoi at the pass a good arse-kicking. And you are still alive. By Hades, lads, I've been in worse situations than this. And I'm still here.'

Hillas hawked and spat on the ground. 'What could be worse than this? Our families are either dead or enslaved. All our cities have fallen and we are running for the sea.'

Banokles had no answer. Then Periklos appeared. 'My grandfather took all the Idonoi cities,' he said. 'They also were a conquered people. Now look at them. Today is not for ever. Serve me faithfully and one day we will return and take back our homeland.'

The warriors fell silent, then the blue-streaked soldier rose to his feet. 'We pledged our allegiance to King Rhesos. It may be that one day you will be a great man like him. But now you are just a boy. I am Hillas, Lord of the Western Mountain. I will not pledge allegiance to a boy.'

Periklos appeared undaunted by the insult. 'You need to look beyond my years, Hillas. My father has an alliance with Troy. As his son, and heir, I *am* that alliance. In Troy we will regroup, and gather to us a new army. It will take time. In that time I will grow into a man.'

'And in that time,' asked Hillas, 'who will be our war leader? Whoever it is will seek to establish his own claims to the crown. I see Vollin over there.' He pointed to another group of warriors nearby. 'He would not follow me, and I certainly would never ride under his inept leadership.'

The man, Vollin, barrel-chested and bald, surged to his feet, along with his men. Swords hissed from scabbards, and knives were drawn.

'No-one move!' bellowed Banokles angrily. 'By the gods, you are a bunch of stupid cowsons. You,' he said, glaring at Hillas. 'I don't care if you are the High pigging Lord of the Western Sheep-shaggers. You rule nothing now. Understand? Nothing. And you,' he snarled at the bald warrior, 'you don't draw your sword on any of my men. At any time and for any reason. What is wrong with you people? Not enough bastard enemies for you? You need to kill each other?'

'We are not *your* men, Trojan,' snapped Hillas. Banokles was about to step forward and punch the man from his feet when the young prince spoke again.

'He is *my* general,' said Periklos. 'And he is right. It is stupid to fight amongst ourselves. Yesterday,' he went on, turning towards Vollin, 'you were preparing to die at the pass, like a Kikones hero. Today you are alive. And why? Because another Kikones hero – Hillas, Lord of the Western Mountain – rode to your defence. *That* is how we will survive, and return to conquer. By standing together and putting aside petty differences.'

Hillas took a deep breath, then sheathed his sword. He glared at Banokles. 'How can this man be our general? He is a Trojan.'

Banokles was about to point out that he was not a Trojan, but the bald Vollin spoke first. 'I think it is a good idea,' he said.

'You would! Because I am against it,' retorted Hillas.

'That may be true, but what the lad says has merit. There has always been discord between the nobles. Likely there always will be. This is why we need a strong king. If I was twenty years younger I might try for the crown myself, and cut your throat in the bargain. But I am not, and my sons are all dead. With a foreigner as the war chief there should be no jealousy, no vying for position. We can unite behind Periklos.'

'We are three hundred men,' said Hillas, his anger fading. 'We are not going to retake Thraki.'

'We are three hundred *now*,' said Periklos. 'Yesterday we had less than half that number. Others will have escaped, and with the blessing of the gods make their way to Troy. When we return we will gather men from the northern mountain tribes, and others who will have tired of Mykene and Idonoi domination.'

'Sounds like his father, doesn't he?' said Vollin.

'Yes, he does,' agreed Hillas. 'I am still unsure about being led by a Trojan.'

'He has already led you into battle,' said Periklos. 'And to a victory. More than this, though, when I stood alone in a forest, surrounded by Idonoi warriors who were ready to kill me, this man walked out and risked his life for me. I have seen him now in three fights. Each one should have been lost, but Banokles is a great warrior and a fine leader.'

Hillas suddenly laughed. 'When he first saw my fifty men he drew his swords and charged us.' Banokles felt the mood change, like a fresh breeze after a storm. 'Very well. I will accept him as general.'

Banokles walked away, hungry and confused. No-one had bothered to ask *him* whether he wanted to be a general, and no-one had mentioned payment of any kind. Not that it mattered, since when they reached Carpea he would happily pass on the problem to real officers.

A cool breeze was blowing and Banokles found a spot where a thick bush acted as a windbreak. Stretching himself out, he prepared for a dreamless sleep. He was just floating off when he heard someone approach. Opening his eyes, he saw the youngster Periklos. The boy squatted down beside him.

'I thank you for your actions back there,' said Periklos. 'I fear there would have been bloodshed.'

'How old are you?' asked Banokles.

'Almost thirteen. Why?'

'You don't talk like any thirteen-year-old boy I've ever known.'

'I don't know how else to talk,' said Periklos.

'I meant you don't sound like a boy. You sound like an old teacher. *I fear there would have been bloodshed,*' he mimicked. 'Boys don't talk like that where I come from. They talk about games and girls, and they brag about all the great deeds they will do when they are grown.'

'All my teachers were old men,' said Periklos. 'Father did not believe in games – unless they served a purpose, like running to make me stronger, or manoeuvring formations of toy soldiers to better understand strategies. Mostly I spent my days with old men, who talked of old wars, and old histories, and the deeds of the great. I know how deep to build foundations for a house, and how to fit dowels into timbers. He was preparing me to be a king.'

'Did he not play with you when you were young?'

'Play? No. We spent little time together. Last year, on my birthday, he took me aside and told me he had a special gift for me. Then he took me to the palace dungeons, where a traitor was kneeling on the floor, his hands tied behind his back. Father let me cut his throat, and watch him die.'

'Not exactly what I meant,' said Banokles.

'I shall spend time with my sons – if I live long enough to have any.' He glanced at Banokles. 'Do you mind if I sleep here with you?'

'I don't mind,' lied Banokles, not relishing the prospect of sleeping alongside a weird youngster trained to slit throats. Periklos stretched himself out, his head pillowed on his arm. Banokles decided to wait until the boy was asleep, then find somewhere else to rest.

XXXII

The Battle of Carpea

PELEUS OF THESSALY HAD NEVER BELIEVED IN THE principles of heroic leadership, where the king fought in the first rank among his men. It was simply stupid, for a stray arrow, or a lucky javelin, could then alter the whole course of the battle. It had nothing to do with cowardice, he told himself. The king must keep himself in a position close enough to the battle to make decisions based on events, but out of harm's way at all times.

So it was that he sat back on his tall white horse, surrounded by his elite bodyguard of 300 heavily armoured footsoldiers, while his Thessalian warriors and their Idonoi allies charged at the Trojans on the plain of Carpea. It was the perfect battleground, wide and flat, no high hills for the enemy to hold, no woods for them to escape into. Only grassland and the sea beyond. Even the small settlement offered no secure hiding places. Carpea was not even a stockaded town.

In most circumstances, Peleus knew, Hektor would have withdrawn to more suitable ground against an army well nigh four times his strength. But he could not on this occasion, for drawn up on the beach were the barges he needed to escape Thraki.

A lesser commander would have withdrawn anyway, knowing his cause was lost against 12,000 enemy soldiers. But Peleus had guessed correctly that Hektor's arrogance would lead him to risk all on one last, great battle. Only now he had no woods to hide his cavalry, no time to plan elaborate traps. His force, less than 3,000 men, were fighting for their lives.

Peleus began to feel gleeful as the battle progressed. From his vantage point he could see the Trojan line being forced back. The enemy were fighting mostly on foot, though a small force of Trojan cavalry was riding on the right, holding back the Idonoi horsemen who sought to cut in and attack the enemy flanks.

Hektor had adopted a phalanx formation, three blocks of some 900 men each, armed with long spears and tall shields. It was a fine defensive manoeuvre for an outnumbered army. Peleus knew it might even have succeeded against a foe with only twice the advantage of numbers. But the Thessalian force was far greater than that. At any moment now one of the three Trojan lines would crack and his soldiers stream round the enemy, forcing them in on themselves, limiting their ability to move and fight. *That* was when the slaughter would begin. And that time was not far off.

How wonderful it would be to see Hektor's head upon a spike. The bliss of the moment would wash away the gall he had tasted these last few years.

Peleus had always been proud of his son Achilles, and gloried in his achievements. For he was renowned as the son of Peleus the king, and the triumphs of the son had shone upon the father. Then had come a change, unwelcome and bitter. The brilliant Achilles, master of war, began to radiate his own light. And somewhere along the way the fame of Peleus dimmed, save that he was father to the hero.

The words should have meant the same. Son of Peleus or father to Achilles. But the emphasis had changed. This had nagged at Peleus. With each new victory Achilles was growing more famous. The conqueror now of Xantheia and Kalliros, the liberator of Thraki.

In a bid to wrest back his rightful share of fame Peleus had led his own army against the city of Ismaros. Odysseus had been given the task of blockading the port. Then the Ithakan king had led a night raid, his men scaling the walls, and opening the gates for Peleus and his Thessalians. The city had been taken. And whom did men acclaim?

Odysseus, the Sacker of Cities. Cunning Odysseus. Clever Odysseus.

But not today. This triumph would be for Peleus the king – the Battle King, the conqueror of the mighty Hektor.

Some way ahead the Trojan phalanx on the left looked about to break. Peleus watched the scene with eager eyes. His triumph was coming, and the taste of it was strong.

Then he saw Hektor, in his armour of bronze and silver, surge to the front of the faltering line. His men gathered round him, their courage renewed.

A little longer, then, to wait. All the better, thought Peleus. The anticipation will make the victory more sweet.

His breastplate was tight, and chafing at the neck. In the last few years his weight had been steadily growing. It was good for him to come to war, he realized. He could become strong again, and lean as he once was. Like his children.

He thought then of Kalliope. She was slim, and he had so loved to hold her to him when she was a child. So like her mother.

But, just like her mother, she had turned on him. Treacherous, deceitful girl. Had she not been raised in privilege, wanting for nothing? And how did she repay him? By flaunting herself naked, and seducing him. Yes, that's what she had done. Turned him into a Gyppto, lusting after his own flesh.

It should have come as no surprise. All women were sluts. Some could disguise it better than others, but they were all the same.

Now she was dead. Which proved that the gods were just.

Kovos, the general of his bodyguard, approached him. The man was a veteran of many battles, and a good soldier, but he had little imagination. 'We should move forward, lord. They are ready to crack.'

'Not yet, Kovos,' Peleus told him.

'If we hurl ourselves at the centre we will break through. The Trojans are exhausted.'

Yes, and I would have to move in with you, thought Peleus, close to the slashing swords and plunging spears.

'We move when I say,' he told the general. Kovos moved back to stand with his men.

He should be grateful to me, thought Peleus. He does not have to face death. But then he is a stupid man, without the brain to appreciate his good fortune.

Beyond the battle Peleus could see the huts and shacks of the fishing village, and the barges pulled up on the beach behind. The barges which would now allow his army to cross the narrow straits into Dardania. Peleus had feared he would be forced to ride those ghastly, low-lying boats. But now, basking in the glory of the defeat of Hektor, he would be able to return to Thessaly in triumph, and let Achilles lead his men across the sea.

Returning his gaze to the battle he saw that the losses endured by his men were heavy. Apart from his body-guard the Thessalian force was armoured lightly, in padded leather breastplates. They offered little pro-tection against the heavy spears of the Trojan Horse. But then breastplates of bronze were expensive, and men were cheap. The Idonoi were also being cut down at a rate of three to every one Trojan. The tribesmen were less well protected even than his own men. Many of them had no armour at all.

It mattered not. The battle was almost over.

Then he saw the men of his bodyguard swinging round to stare back towards the west. Peleus turned.

A line of horsemen had appeared, lance points glinting in the sunlight.

Peleus called out to Kovos, 'Send a messenger to them. Tell them to attack on the flank.'

'They are not our men,' said Kovos grimly.

'Of course they are our men. There are no enemy forces behind us.'

'Look at the man at the centre,' said Kovos, 'on the grey horse. He is wearing Trojan armour.'

'Plundered from the dead,' said Peleus, but a small worm of doubt gnawed at him.

The man on the grey horse drew two swords and held them high.

Then the horsemen began to move, slowly at first. The thunder of hooves sounded and they swept towards the Thessalian rear.

'Form up!' bellowed Kovos. 'Turn, you dogs! Death is upon you!'

The 300 men of the king's bodyguard carried no spears, only shortswords and long shields. Hastily they tried to re-form, facing west. Peleus backed his horse through them, terrified.

He could see the man on the grey horse clearly now. He was broad-shouldered and blond-bearded. He carried no shield. In his right hand was a cavalry sabre, in his left a stabbing sword.

He must turn, thought Peleus. No horse will charge into a wall of shields.

But the shield wall had not completely formed.

The rider found a gap and powered into it, his sabre slashing down and opening the throat of a guardsman.

All was suddenly chaos. Peleus did not even draw his sword. Panic swept through him as he watched his battle line sundered. All he could think of was flight. Heeling his horse he forced his way through his men, scattering them, and further widening the gaps in their ranks. Then, on open ground, he kicked the stallion into a gallop. The guardsmen close by, seeing the king in flight, followed him. Within moments the battle became a rout.

Peleus did not care. His mind was no longer functioning, save for the need to run and run, and never stop. To find some hiding place. Anywhere! Behind him he heard the screams of dying men.

The stallion was at full gallop now, heading west, along the line of the sea.

A spear hurtled past Peleus. Then another. Glancing back he saw that four of the enemy riders were closing on him. Then a spear went between the legs of his mount. The white stallion stumbled, pitching Peleus over its head. He landed hard, rolled and came to his knees, the breath all but knocked out of him. The horsemen rode up, surrounding him.

He struggled to his feet. 'I am Peleus the king,' he managed to say. 'There will be a mighty ransom paid for me.'

One of the riders touched heels to his mount and rode forward, his lance extended. He was fair-haired and lean, and there were blue streaks on his face. 'I am

Hillas, Lord of the Western Mountain,' he said. 'How big a ransom?'

Relief swept through Peleus. He would be taken to Hektor, who was a man of honour and understanding. Achilles could pay the ransom, from the plunder of Xantheia and Kalliros.

Then the rider on the grey horse appeared. 'What's going on?' he asked.

'The king here is talking of a golden ransom,' said Hillas.

'Just kill the cowson. The battle's not over yet.'

Hillas grinned. 'As you say, General, so let it be.'

Peleus heard the words, but could not believe them. 'I am Peleus!' he shouted. 'Father to Achilles!' The blue-streaked rider heeled his horse forward, his lance levelled. Peleus threw up his arms, but the lance plunged between them, ripping into his throat.

Choking on his own blood, the king fell to his knees. Then his face struck the ground, and he could smell the scent of summer grass.

'Come on, you sheep-shaggers!' he heard someone cry. 'Kill them all!'

XXXIII

Death upon the water

OVERCOME BY A BLISSFUL WEARINESS, KALLIADES SAT down in the shade of a rock wall close to the beach. The wound was still troublesome, though it was healing well. The real damage seemed to have been the tear in the chest muscle, which restricted the movement of his left arm. The blow to the head still caused him occasional dizziness, but the injuries he had suffered could not dampen the euphoria he had experienced since surviving the attack on the pass.

It seemed to Kalliades that a new world awaited him, one filled with light and colour and scent that had somehow been lost to him. It was not that he had never appreciated the brilliance of a summer sky, or the magnificence of a crimson sunset. That appreciation, however, had been cool and rational. The glory of the world had not touched his emotions as deeply as now.

Even the barges on the beach, flat-bottomed and ungainly, had a sturdy beauty, the sunlight causing their oiled timbers to gleam like pale gold. Everywhere there was noise and confusion, but this spoke of life and movement, bringing with it a sense of joy.

Banokles came to him there, and slumped down. 'Apparently I shouldn't have killed the king yesterday,' he grumbled, pulling off his helm and laying it on the sand.

'I did not know it was you who killed him.'

'Well, it wasn't me – but I ordered it. Hektor's generals said we could have used him to force the Thessalians from Thraki.'

Kalliades shook his head. 'Achilles would not have agreed.'

'That's what Hektor said. His generals don't like me. Cowsons!'

Kalliades smiled. 'You won the battle, Banokles. One crazy charge.'

'What was crazy about it?'

'It should not have succeeded. You attacked the strongest force – the Thessalian royal guard. If they'd had a braver king they would have withstood the onslaught and then cut your riders to pieces.'

'Didn't, though, did they?' observed Banokles.

'No, my friend, they didn't. You were the hero of the day. Banokles and his Thrakians. What a story that will make.'

Banokles chuckled. 'Yes, it will. In some ways I am going to miss them.'

'Miss them?'

'They are being left behind.'

'Why?'

'Only around forty barges. Not enough to take everyone in a single crossing. Hektor is taking the Trojan Horse across, and leaving the wounded and the Thrakians. Says he'll send the barges back tomorrow. By then it's likely there'll be an enemy fleet in the straits, or another cowson army on the horizon.'

'Where does that leave you?' asked Kalliades.

'Me? What do you mean? I go with the Horse.'

'You and I have fought in many battles. How would you have felt if one of our generals had decided to cut and run, and leave us behind on some enemy shore?'

'Oh, don't you start on me. I knew I shouldn't have come to see you. Cut and run? I'm not running. I am a soldier of the Horse. Not a cowson general.'

'You are a general to them, Banokles. They trusted you enough to follow you into battle.'

Banokles stared angrily at Kalliades. 'You always take the simple and make it complicated.'

'That's because nothing is ever as simple as you would like it to be. Anyway, I'll be staying with the wounded. And, as you pointed out, we are sword brothers. We should stick together.'

'Pah! Sword brothers when it suits *you*. Didn't suit you back at the pass, did it?'

'I didn't want you dead, my friend. This is different. Those Thrakians revere you. They are pure warriors, Banokles. They've suffered defeats and seen their pride ground into the dust. You've given it back to them. At the pass, when they routed their enemies, and yesterday, when they killed one of the kings who brought ruin to their land. You are like a talisman for them. You've rescued the sons of their king and made them feel like men again. Don't you see? You can't leave them now.'

'I did all that?'

'Yes.'

'I suppose I did.' Banokles paused. 'I guess I could stay with them at least until Troy.'

'That would be good.'

'I have to admit I was wrong about them. They can fight, those boys.'

Kalliades laughed. 'They fought for you, General.'

'Don't you start calling me that! I'm warning you, Kalliades. I'm sick of it. And Red will chew my ear off when she hears. You see if she doesn't.'

Kalliades grinned and gazed round the deserted settlement. There were some twenty shacks, and several tall huts for the smoking of fish. 'Where have all the people gone?' he asked.

'They took their fishing boats and travelled across the straits,' said Banokles. 'Didn't want to be here when the enemy arrived. Don't blame them. I don't want to be here when they come again. How is the chest wound?'

'Healing well. Beginning to itch.'

'That's a good sign,' said Banokles. He sighed. 'I hate being a general, Kalliades. I just want somewhere to sleep, some good food in my belly, and a jug of wine by my side.'

'I know, my friend. Once we get back to Troy it will all seem simpler. The Thrakians can choose their own general, and you can return to whoring and drinking, and a life without responsibility.'

'No whoring,' said Banokles. 'Big Red would break my face. But the rest of it sounds good.'

Smoke from the funeral pyres out on the plain began to drift over the settlement. 'How many did we lose yesterday?' asked Kalliades.

'I didn't ask,' said Banokles. 'Judging by the size of the pyres it must have been a few hundred. The enemy lost thousands. That's the trouble when you break and run. My lads kept killing them until their arms got too tired to lift their spears. Even so, I reckon a few thousand of them escaped. They could re-form and come back.'

Two men approached them. Kalliades glanced up to see a tall warrior, with fair hair and blue streaks on his face, and the stocky, bald Vollin, who had served with him at the pass. Both looked angry.

'We are to be left behind?' asked the tall man.

'Until tomorrow,' said Banokles, 'when they send the barges back.'

'They are leaving us here to die,' said Vollin. 'This is betrayal.'

Banokles pushed himself to his feet. Kalliades levered himself up alongside him. 'Hektor is not a betrayer,' said Kalliades. 'The barges will return.'

'If that is so,' Blue Face asked Banokles, 'why are you leaving with them today?'

'I am not leaving. What sheep-shagging cowson said I was leaving?'

Kalliades saw the two Thrakians glance at one

another. Then Vollin spoke. 'Your three men, Olganos and the others. They have already boarded the barges. We thought you would be going with them.'

'And leave you lads behind? How could you think that? After all we've been through.' The men both looked shamefaced. Then the tall one spoke.

'If you are staying,' he said, 'then I will believe the barges will return for us. They would not leave you behind otherwise.'

'Good,' said Banokles. 'Then that's settled.'

'I'll send scouts out,' said Vollin. 'At least then we'll have some warning if the Idonoi come back.'

Most of the barges had been launched and Kalliades watched the oarsmen struggle in the strong currents. Although the coastline of Dardania could be clearly seen across the straits the currents would sweep the barges southwest to land further along the coast. Out on the straits three Dardanian galleys waited to escort the fleet.

The last of the forty-one barges, packed with troops and their mounts, was hauled off the sand, the fleet strung out in the narrow straits. The sky was clear, and there was little wind, which was a blessing, Kalliades knew. Overladen as they were, and wallowing in the blue water, it would not take much to cause a disaster. A brisk wind, or a storm, or even panic among the horses. The distance between the upper timbers of the hulls and the water below was less than a man's forearm in length. If a barge tipped even a fraction the water would flow in, and it would sink like a rock. The heavily armoured men aboard would have no chance of survival.

'May Poseidon grant calm seas,' he said.

Banokles suddenly swore. 'Never mind Poseidon,' he said, and pointed up the straits towards the northeast. 'Worry about those cowsons!' Rounding the headland, behind which they had been hiding, a fleet of black galleys was heaving into view. Kalliades counted twenty ships.

Kalliades felt suddenly cold. The packed barges were defenceless against war galleys. They would be rammed and sunk long before they could reach the safety of the shore.

Olganos had never been a good sailor. It was a source of embarrassment to his family, who were Scamander fishermen. Even on balmy seas his stomach would rebel. His father promised him the sickness would be shortlived, that his body would acclimatize to the motion of the sea. It never did, which is why he was the first of his family to join the army.

The moment he had boarded the flat-bottomed barge that morning the nausea had begun. Justinos had clapped him on the back and chuckled.

'Hades' balls, boy, we are still on the beach, and already your face is grey.'

Olganos had not replied. Instead he had gritted his teeth and prepared for the ghastly ritual of giddiness, surging heat through his belly, and the inevitable retching. The rope at the front of the barge tightened as the Dardanian galley hauled the vessel off the beach. Olganos gripped the deck rail and stared down at the sea. The barge lurched, then floated clear.

Olganos stared now round the flat-bottomed vessel. Eighty men and twenty horses were crowded on its deck. The warriors around him were carefree and happy, for they were leaving behind the benighted realm of Thraki, and heading home to loved ones and the security of Troy. Olganos belched, and tasted hot acid in his throat. In that moment he hated the sea.

The eight bargemen on either side had little room to work their long oars, and they swore at the soldiers jostling around them. At the rear of the craft the two steering oarsmen laughed at the chaos.

Olganos gazed gloomily back at the beach. He would have preferred to remain there with Banokles and the Thrakians, but it would only have delayed the crossing.

The last barge was being launched and Olganos watched it bobbing and wallowing. He closed his eyes as a fresh ripple of sickness caused his belly to lurch.

'Perhaps they'll take us all the way back to Troy,' said Skorpios.

Olganos felt panic overwhelm him at the prospect. Then common sense asserted itself. The barges had to return for the Thrakians and Banokles. He glared at Skorpios, who was grinning at him.

'Very funny,' he managed to say.

'Doesn't the swell of a boat make your heart leap?' Justinos asked Skorpios. 'As it bobs and sways and bobs and sways.'

Olganos swore at them, leaned over the side, and emptied his belly into the sea.

It did not help. The nausea remained and now his head was pounding.

As he straightened, he saw a fleet of black ships rounding the headland to the northeast. For a moment he thought they were Dardanian. Then reality struck him.

Alongside him Justinos muttered an oath.

The three Dardanian galleys had seen the enemy fleet, and were turning to face them. The current was swift, and the Mykene galleys bore down on the slow-moving barges with murderous speed.

A Dardanian warship managed to block the first of the galleys. Three more swept past. Olganos watched horrified as the last barge was rammed amidships. The timbers cracked, and the barge tilted sharply. The Mykene galley backed oars, leaving a gaping hole in the stricken vessel. The sea rushed in, and it suddenly tipped. Horses and men were hurled into the blue sea. The horses began to swim, but the heavily armoured Trojan soldiers struggled desperately to stay afloat. They began crying out for help. Olganos watched their heart-wrenching battle for life. One by one they sank below the surface. Eighty men dead in a matter of heartbeats.

'Get out of your armour!' Olganos shouted at the men around him, as he tore at the leather straps holding his cuirass in place.

'Not me,' said Justinos. 'I can't swim.'

'I'll keep you afloat, my friend.'

Justinos shook his head. 'The moment the bastards ram us I'll climb aboard their ship.'

Olganos dumped his cuirass to the deck. 'You won't have the chance. They'll ram and then pull back. Trust me.'

Skorpios had also stripped off his armour. Most of the other men were doing the same, and the barge rocked ominously.

A Mykene galley closed on them, but was itself rammed by a Dardanian warship. The men on the barge cheered – but the sound died away swiftly. Another Mykene vessel slammed into the Dardanian ship, splintering its hull.

The rowers on the barge were powering their oars furiously, but in their panic the rhythm was lost. Slowly the vessel swung, the current hitting the port side of the stern. The overladen barge was now broadside on, presenting a wide target. Olganos crouched down and removed his bronze greaves, tossing them to the deck. He straightened – just in time to see the looming prow of a war galley. Its ram thundered against the timbers of the barge. Men were hurled from their feet. The horses panicked as the deck tilted, rearing and kicking out. Then they lunged through the mass of warriors, and leapt or tumbled into the sea. The barge lurched dramatically as the galley backed oars and pulled away. Water gushed up through the deck timbers.

Then the barge tipped forward. Olganos was hurled against the deck rail, and cartwheeled into the water.

As he surfaced an arrow slashed past his head, slicing into the water and bobbing up alongside him. Sucking in a deep breath he dived down. When he came up for air the black galley was moving away, in search of fresh kills.

He heard someone cry out, and saw Skorpios holding on to Justinos, whose heavy armour was dragging them both down. Swimming swiftly across to them he helped support the powerful warrior, while struggling to untie the straps of his cuirass.

More arrows slashed by them. One glanced from Skorpios' arm, ripping the skin. Olganos had managed to loosen Justinos' cuirass, but there was no way to remove it.

'You will have to duck out of your armour,' he told his friend. 'Sink below the surface and push it away.'

Justinos' eyes were wide and frightened. 'No,' he said.

'You must! Or you'll kill us all. I won't let you drown. I swear it!'

Justinos sucked in a great breath, then lifted his arms – and sank.

As Skorpios dragged at the armour Olganos dived below the surface. The heavy cuirass came free, but Justinos suddenly panicked, and began to thrash out madly, bubbles of air whooshing from his mouth. Olganos dived deeper, grabbing hold of Justinos' shirt, and kicking out for the surface. But the weight was too much, and they both began to sink. Then Skorpios dived down alongside him, and together they pulled Justinos' head clear of the water.

'Calm yourself and breathe!' Olganos shouted. Justinos took in great gulps of air.

Just below the surface the body of a soldier floated past them, an arrow through his neck. Another Mykene galley was closing in on them, and Olganos could see a line of archers on the port bow. Some of them were grinning as they notched arrows to their weapons. The only way to survive was to dive deep. Yet the moment they let go of Justinos he would drown.

Justinos understood this and said grimly, 'Save yourselves! Go!'

Then Olganos saw something dark flying through the air towards the galley. It was a skull-sized ball of dried clay. It struck a bowman and shattered, spraying what appeared to be water over the man and those around him. Then another hit the deck.

Olganos twisted round – and saw a massive golden ship, with a black horse sail, bearing down on the Mykene. Archers were massed along its deck, and they sent a hail of fire arrows at the enemy.

What happened then made Olganos gasp. He expected the arrows to smoulder, perhaps even setting fire to the Mykene sail. Instead the entire deck burst into flame. The archer who had been struck by the pottery ball was ablaze from head to toe. Olganos saw him leap from the ship. When he surfaced his body was still burning, his screams awful to hear.

The golden ship thundered into the Mykene galley, splintering its hull. From the upper deck Olganos saw more pottery balls sail out towards other enemy vessels.

Black smoke was pouring now from the stricken galley, and the bowmen, who only moments before had been preparing to use Olganos and his friends for target practice, were leaping into the sea. Elsewhere Olganos could see the Mykene fleet desperately swinging away from the pursuit of the barges, as more and more Dardanian galleys bore down on them.

A Dardanian ship drew alongside the men in the water. Someone called down: 'Who are you?'

'Three Trojan Horse,' called back Olganos.

Ropes were lowered. Justinos grabbed the first and hauled himself up to the deck. Skorpios followed, and finally Olganos. A stocky sailor approached them, offering Skorpios a cloth to bind his wounded arm.

Olganos walked to the rail, and watched the sea battle unfold. There were six Mykene ships ablaze, four others rammed and sinking. The golden *Xanthos* continued to rain fire down upon the surviving vessels. The strong current that had swept the Mykene towards the barges was now their most powerful enemy. Their rowers, tired after maintaining ramming speed to intercept the Trojan fleet, had little strength left to escape the avenging Dardanians. A group of archers pushed past Olganos, then leaned over the rail. In the sea below Mykene sailors were shouting for help. They received only death.

By late afternoon the battle was over. Five Mykene vessels managed to escape to the north, and one had slipped past the Dardanians, heading out towards open sea.

Dusk was approaching as the Dardanian ship carrying Olganos and his friends crossed the straits and beached close to the barges.

Once ashore Olganos, Skorpios and Justinos made their way to where the Trojan army was gathering. Despite their escape the mood was sombre among the survivors. Almost 200 men and 60 horses had been lost in the crossing.

Food fires were lit and the soldiers gathered round them. There was little conversation. Olganos stretched out on the ground, enjoying the warmth of the blaze, and slept for a while.

When Justinos nudged him awake it was dark. Olganos sat up, rubbing sleep from his eyes. All around him men were hastily putting on their armour, and gathering horses. Olganos climbed wearily to his feet.

'What is going on?' he asked.

'Fires to the south. Dardanos is burning,' said Justinos.

XXXIV

Traitor's Gate

EARLIER THAT AFTERNOON THE MYKENE ADMIRAL Menados had sat on a hillside, gazing down at his army, camped on the beach below. But he was not thinking of his mission, or the capricious nature of war. He was thinking instead of his grandchildren. During forty years of warfare Menados had learned that often, when faced with a particularly complex problem, it helped to close one's mind to it for a time, and summon other, happier thoughts. And so he relived his last visit to his son's farm, and the chase through the woods, the children squealing with mock fear as he pretended to be the monster pursuing them. Menados smiled at the memory. When he had caught little Kenos, hiding in a bush, the boy had suddenly burst into tears, and cried out: 'Don't be a monster any more!'

Menados had swept him into his arms and kissed his cheeks. 'It is only a game, Kenos. It is me. Grandpapa.'

Now in the afternoon sunshine, his army and fleet

hidden in a secluded bay, only a short march from the fortress city of Dardanos, the old admiral allowed the happy memories to fade back into the scriptorium of his mind. He sighed and focused once more on the bleak prospects facing him.

Every martial instinct now told him he would be best advised to get his men back on the ships and transports, and sail for safer waters. Unfortunately, as a long-time follower of Agamemnon, he also understood that matters martial were inextricably linked with politics.

Agamemnon had ordered him to take the fortress of Dardanos and kill Helikaon's wife and child – retribution for the savage attacks on the Mykene homeland. This raid was to be combined with an invasion led by the victorious Peleus. What a fine plan it had sounded. With an army rampaging across the Dardanian countryside, and the fortress held by loyal Mykene troops, Dardania would fall. This would give Agamemnon a good land route to Troy.

Menados scratched at his black and silver beard. A fine plan, he thought again, save that Peleus had not followed it. The last he had heard, before today, was that the Thessalian king was leading an army in pursuit of the fleeing Hektor. Now, according to the traitor within the fortress, Peleus was dead, and the war fleet of Helikaon had been sighted heading into the Hellespont. Menados had no way of knowing how many of the Trojan Horse had survived the battle with Peleus, but, based on the numbers of barges the traitor claimed were being used, he assumed there would be at least 2,000. Helikaon himself was known to have around fifty ships. Another 2,000 fighting men, at the very least.

Soon the Mykene would be facing a battle on two fronts, against the Trojan Horse on land, and Helikaon's war galleys out beyond the bay. Taking the fortress was not a problem. They could hold Dardanos for a while, but with no food, and no means of supply, they would be starved out by the autumn.

Yet, if he slipped away, and returned to Agamemnon, his decision would be made to seem cowardly rather than practical. The vile Kleitos would say: 'Let me understand this, Admiral. You had a man inside the city ready to open the gates to a fortress containing no more than two hundred Dardanians. Yet you, with your three thousand men, decided to run?'

Agamemnon would be furious. Menados would not survive his anger.

So, sadly, withdrawal was not an option. The message from the traitor had been specific. Attack tonight! The Seagate will be open!

But what then?

With the queen and her son dead he could try to hold the fortress, and send his fleet to Ismaros, requesting more men and supplies. Menados dismissed the thought. In order for reinforcements to reach him the fleet would have to battle its way past the dread Helikaon. It would not survive. Most of his sailors were recruits, the ships newly launched, the crews untried. The Dardanians would destroy them.

Equally, the men of his army were not the finest. Agamemnon had scoured the mainland for troops, and the soldiers under Menados' command were of mixed quality: mercenaries from the high country, former pirates from the islands, robbers and brigands. All of them served for gold alone. Menados had no way of knowing if they would hold when the battle turned grim. What he did know was that they were hard, cruel men, pitiless and violent.

The officers were little better, save perhaps for Katheos and Areion. Katheos was young and ambitious, determined to seek the favour of Agamemnon, and to rise through the ranks. He had shown himself to be skilful and resourceful. It went some way to offset the fact that he had been selected for this mission to spy on Menados. Areion was an older man, who had served with him for close to twenty years. Unimaginative yet solid, he could be relied upon to obey any order, and see it through.

Menados ran through all the possible outcomes of an attack on Dardanos. There was no doubt they would take the fortress, but was there any way to hold it? Peleus was dead, but there would still be forces at Ismaros. Perhaps by now Achilles was there. Would he gather men swiftly enough to make the crossing and attack the Trojans? Unlikely. His father slain, Achilles would now be the king of Thessaly. Custom and honour would dictate he took his father's remains home for proper entombment.

At last Menados was forced to the only decision that made sense. He would take the fortress tonight, torch the gates and the warehouses, and all the buildings of timber. This would render Dardanos useless for months. Then he would withdraw and sail for Ismaros having at least completed the main part of his mission, the murder of Halysia and the boy.

Walking down the hillside, he called his officers to him. From his tunic he took the drawings the traitor had supplied of the defences inside the city, and where the queen and the child were likely to be found.

'It is imperative,' he said, 'that the traitor is not accidentally slain when we attack. He is a senior officer. We want him to survive, and rejoin Helikaon. He will be wearing a white tunic, no armour. He will have two swords belted to his waist. Make sure that every man knows this description.' Swinging to a gaunt young officer, with deep-set blue eyes and a forked chin beard, he said: 'You, Katheos, will lead the attack through the Seagate. Hold the gatehouse until reinforcements, led by Areion, arrive. Once they are with you, send a swift force into the palace to seek the queen and the boy. The rest will close in on the defenders and burn every building they can.'

'Are we not to hold the fortress?' asked the grey-bearded Areion.

Menados shook his head. 'It seems that our Thessalian ally, Peleus, got himself killed. No reinforcements are coming from Thraki, and the Trojan Horse is likely to be here soon. So now it becomes a punitive raid, and then we get out, and sail for Ismaros. We need to cause as much damage as possible. It is possible we could return this season. If so, we want Dardanos crippled when next we face it. Douse the gates with oil, pile them high with bracken and dried wood. There is also a bridge close to the fortress, that cuts the journey to and from Troy. We will burn this also. The success of this raid,' he went on, 'depends on discipline and speed. Make it clear to the men that there is to be no rape and plunder.'

'I am not sure we can stop them, Admiral,' said Katheos. 'They have little loyalty to the king. They are ruled entirely by lust and greed.'

Menados considered this. 'You are correct, Katheos. Tell them that a portion of Helikaon's treasury will be shared among them. That will take the edge from their greed. Tell them also that any man found on a personal raid will have his guts ripped out and tied round his throat.'

Katheos nodded, and gave a grim smile. 'That will help a little, Admiral. But some of them, like wild dogs, will follow their murderous natures. Speaking of which, we none of us know what the queen looks like, nor her brat.'

'Our man inside has told us where they are likely to be found. The queen should pose no problems as to identity. She is young, golden-haired and beautiful, and will be dressed in clothes befitting her rank.'

'That may well be true, Admiral,' put in Areion. 'But once she knows we are coming she could change clothes, and flee with the other women. Surely Agamemnon King will desire proof of her death?'

'The traitor will identify her body, and that of her son,' said Menados, at last. 'But you make a good point. We will not have long in the fortress, and cannot risk their escape. Every woman with pale hair, and every small child, must be put to the sword.'

The forked-bearded Katheos looked uncomfortable with the order. 'A problem, General?' asked Menados.

'Only with the timing, Admiral. We have one night to kill the Dardanians, take the fortress, burn the gates, the buildings and the bridge, and then board our ships. Scouring the area for every child and pale-haired woman will divert us.'

'Organize three death squads, ten men in each. Give them the order to hunt through the fortress buildings. Now, dusk is approaching. So let us move.'

The old general stepped from his dark apartments and squinted into the low light of evening. Storm clouds lay heavy above the high fortress, but the westering sun shone like a golden shield on the horizon. Pausanius paused for a moment before firmly grasping his black wooden staff and setting off for the Seagate.

The pain which nagged at him constantly had eased a little. It had troubled him for more than a year now, eating deep into his back and groin. The physician had given him a series of increasingly disgusting potions.

'And these will heal me?' Pausanius had asked him.

'Only the gods could heal you, General,' answered the man. 'My potions will take away much of the pain. Though not all.'

In the past few days the pain had increased, making it hard for him to think of anything else, and forcing him to stay in his rooms. To piss was almost impossibly painful and difficult, and when urine finally dribbled out it was dark red with blood. A shiver of fear went through him each time he saw it. However, a little while earlier, he had stood bent over the piss pot, and had finally managed to empty his bladder. The relief was immense.

Pausanius saw it would be a moonless night. Looking down from his chamber balcony a few moments earlier, he had seen two new ships arriving. They are cutting it fine, he had thought, wondering where they came from. He had decided to find out.

It would annoy young Menon, he knew. The boy had become increasingly concerned for his uncle's health. 'You need rest,' he had said earlier that day.

'I have a feeling I will be resting more than I would like soon enough,' grunted Pausanius. 'Fetch me some wine, would you, boy?'

Menon had laughed. 'If you feel like wine you must be improving.' They had sat together then, and talked for a while of the problems they faced. Pausanius gazed affectionately at the young man, the sunlight glinting on his red-gold hair. So like me, he thought.

'What are you thinking, Uncle?'

'I am proud of you, Menon. I know it has not been easy to walk in my footsteps. But you have it in you to be a great man, and to help save this kingdom. I hope the gods bless you, as they have me.'

Menon had blushed. Like Pausanius he was obviously uncomfortable with compliments. The old general had chuckled. 'Am I sounding maudlin?'

'Not at all, Uncle. Rest here today and gather your strength. Tomorrow, if you are feeling better, we will ride together.'

But Pausanius no longer felt like resting. For nearly

sixty years he had been charged with the safety of the fortress, and few visitors arrived of whom he was unaware. So he plodded on towards the Seagate.

The fool Idaios worried him. Did Priam have so little faith in the army at Dardanos that he thought a moron like Idaios could be of any help? Idaios had been given the Seagate to guard. A simple task – let no-one pass this gate bearing a weapon. But Pausanius doubted he was up to it.

As he walked his mind drifted back to his conversation with the queen four days before. He regretted criticizing her treatment of the boy Dexios. She has enough problems to contend with, he thought. Adversity was a harsh tutor, but a good one. Perhaps the boy was too sensitive and needed to find some backbone. Pausanius dismissed the thought almost instantly. Dex was only three years old, unloved by his mother, and raised by servants. On the rare occasions when Helikaon was home he would talk to the boy, and take him riding, or fishing in the sheltered lake. There were few such opportunities when the king was absent.

It had heartened Pausanius to see young Menon playing with the child a few days back. The young soldier had perched Dex on his shoulders and run around the courtyard, making neighing sounds like a horse. The child's laughter had been joyous to hear.

Pausanius thought of his own son, dead these thirty years. When he had first heard the gorge called Parnio's Folly he had been offended, as if a joke had been made out of his private tragedy. But over the long years his grief had been washed clean by the relentless waves of time.

He pressed on. Crossing the busy stable yard, he walked with care down the sloping stone roadway to the Seagate. When he arrived there, Pausanius was surprised to see the gates open. They were always closed tightly before sunset. Who had opened them? He looked for the guards but could not see them. A maggot of fear wormed into his heart.

As he stood there, unnoticed, an old man with a staff, a troop of soldiers came running up through the gateway and past him. Pausanius peered at them, his vision blurred by his eighty years and the light of the low sun. By Ares, they are Mykene, he thought! Mykene soldiers in the fortress? For a moment he thought the pain was making him hallucinate, and recall the invasion three years earlier.

Another troop of Mykene in their distinctive, bronze-disced armour charged unchallenged through the Seagate and up into the fortress. From far away Pausanius heard the sounds of combat beginning, screams and shouts, and clashing metal.

Confused and uncertain, he stumbled forward, leaning heavily on his staff. Through the open gate he saw Mykene troops still pouring off the two ships and climbing the hill to the fortress. More ships were beaching, soldiers leaping to the sand. A group of Mykene officers stood outside the gates, a few paces away, talking casually. They glanced at the old man but ignored him.

The gate guards lay dead. On a sagging wooden table beyond the two bodies Pausanius saw a sad pile of old swords, knives and battered clubs confiscated from visitors during the day. As Pausanius had feared, the fool Idaios had no system for dealing with the weaponry. It was just dumped in a heap, and guarded by two bored soldiers. Two dead soldiers now.

The body of Idaios lay with them, a great wound in his throat.

Traitor! Pausanius thought with rage. I believed him to be just a fool, but he was a traitor too. He opened the gates for them, then was slain by his new masters. A fool and a traitor both.

One of the group of Mykene officers noticed him, and said something to the others. They all turned to look at the old general struggling towards them. Some of them smiled. One man dressed all in white stepped forward, two swords belted at his side.

Flame-haired Menon spoke. 'I am sorry to see you here, Uncle.'

The shock was almost too great to bear, and Pausanius groaned as if in pain. Dead Idaios was not the traitor. The man who had delivered the fortress to the enemy was his own flesh and blood.

'How could you do this?' he said. 'Why, Menon?'

'For the kingdom, Uncle,' Menon said calmly. 'You said I could help it to be great. And I will. As king. You think Dardania and Troy can withstand the might of all the western kings? If we continue to resist Agamemnon the land will be laid waste, the people slaughtered or enslaved.'

Pausanius stared at him, then at the Mykene officers close by. In the distance the sounds of battle echoed through the fortress. 'People who trusted you are being slaughtered now,' he said. 'You have broken my heart, Menon. Better for me to have died than to see you as a traitor and a cur.'

Menon flushed and stepped back. 'You never did understand the nature of power, Uncle. When Anchises died *you* could have seized the throne. *That* is how dynasties are born. Instead, you pledged allegiance to a simpering woman and her get. And look where it led. To a war we cannot win. Go back to your apartment, Uncle. You do not have to die here.'

'Of course he has to die,' said a Mykene officer with a forked beard. 'He knows you, and once we have left he will tell Helikaon of your deeds.'

'Best listen to your master, little dog,' said Pausanius contemptuously. 'When he says bark you bark!'

Menon's face turned crimson. Drawing one of his swords he stepped in. 'I did not wish to kill you,' he said, 'for you have always been good to me. But you have lived too long, old man.'

The general's body was ancient, but it remembered sixty years of battles. As the sword swung down at his neck, wielded with casual arrogance, he lunged and head-butted the younger man. Grabbing the front of Menon's white tunic he dragged him forward, then curled his hand around the hilt of Menon's second sword. Blood streaming from his broken nose, Menon wrenched himself clear of the old man's grip. As he stepped back he failed to notice Pausanius pull the sword clear. The old general stepped in with a straight thrust that stabbed through Menon's jugular. Blood sprayed over the white tunic. Menon gave a gurgling cry and staggered back, his hands clamped round his throat, seeking to stem the gouting flow.

Pausanius fell to his knees, his strength suddenly gone. He heard the sound of running feet and felt a blow, two blows, to his back. All pain ceased. Menon collapsed before him, his head drooping onto Pausanius' shoulder. The old general looked at the dying Menon, as his own vision blurred and darkened.

'I . . . so loved you . . . boy, ' he said.

XXXV

The rider in the sky

THE LITTLE BOY AWOKE WITH A START. RUBBING HIS SMALL fists in his gummy eyes, Dex sat up and looked around him. It was dark in the bedchamber. A single candle guttered low in the corner, and by its dim light he could see Grey One was not in her bed. He was alone.

He remembered leaving his own bedroom, after a nightmare, and coming crying to Grey One's room, tapping lightly on her door. She had opened it, and, as she always did, had chided him gently for his fears. She always relented, though, and last night as usual had carried him to her own bed, laying him down beside her. 'Sleep safely, little Dex,' she had whispered. 'I am with you.'

But she wasn't with him.

Muffled sounds came from outside the room, both in the courtyard below and on the stairs outside the door. There were harsh shouts and hard clanging noises.

Unused to being alone in the dark, the three-year-old

was frightened. Grey One was always there when he woke up. She took him to the kitchens for breakfast.

Pushing his feet out from under the warm sheet, he slid to the edge of the bed and climbed down. Padding across the cold stone and the soft rugs, he dragged a wooden stool to the open window, then climbed up to peer down into the courtyard. It was dark outside as well, but he could see fires, and the smell of smoke drifted up to him, tickling his throat and making him sneeze. He could see the shapes of men and women running about and hear their cries.

The sight of the fires made him think of breakfast again. Grey One would toast yesterday's bread and smear it with honey. He climbed carefully down from the stool, pushed open the heavy door and slipped out into the corridor.

Outside he saw someone lying on the floor. By the light of a flickering torch on the wall he could see it was Grey One. She was lying huddled, knees drawn up. Her eyes were closed. He squatted down beside her for a while, but she didn't wake up. Wondering what to do he patted her hand uncertainly.

'I'm hungry,' he said, leaning close to her ear.

Just then he heard the sound of running feet coming towards him. Had Sun Woman discovered he had left his room? Would she be angry with him? On an impulse he ran into a dark corner and hid behind a heavy curtain masking a window.

The curtain did not quite reach the timbered floor and he lay flat, staring out through the gap. A group of soldiers ran into sight. He liked soldiers, but he didn't recognize any of these men and decided to stay where he was.

They ran past him, their hard metal greaves glinting in the torchlight, their heavily sandalled feet noisy on the timbers. He could smell their sweat and leather.

'Find the boy!' one shouted, his voice bouncing off the corridor walls. 'He wasn't in his room. He must be with the queen.'

When the soldiers had passed, their footsteps echoing down the staircase, he made his way out into the small courtyard. Staying in the gloom of the courtyard walls, he edged towards the stables. Dex liked the stables. It was never quiet there. He liked the sound of the horses' heavy breathing, and the shuffling of their hooves on the stone floor.

Dex didn't know why, but he knew he was in trouble. Grey One had gone to sleep in the corridor, and Sun Woman had sent angry soldiers to find him. Keeping to the shadows, he saw more soldiers with swords race past him towards the tower. Then someone he knew, the man who put him on the pony sometimes, ran out into the courtyard. He was limping and Dex was about to go to him when the man fell down. Two soldiers came up behind him and stuck their swords into him as he lay on the ground. He screamed and screamed, and then was still.

Terrified now, Dex cringed into the shadow of the wall. He heard a woman cry out and could see flames coming from the kitchens, leaping high into the night, bathing the courtyard in an orange glow. Two women ran from the kitchen doors, pursued by more soldiers.

The soldiers were laughing and waving their swords.

Dex closed his eyes. He could feel the heat of the flames.

'Dex!'

He opened his eyes to see a soldier he knew. He had a red beard and he made Dex laugh when he carried him on his back. The man snatched him up and held him close to his chest. Dex felt a surge of pleasure and relief, although the man's armour was hard against him. He tried to tell the red-bearded soldier about Grey One lying down.

'Hush, boy, I'll see you safe,' the man said.

He sprinted across the courtyard towards the stables. There were bodies everywhere, servants and soldiers. As they passed the kitchens Dex could feel the heat against his bare legs and smell cooking meat. He pushed his face into the soldier's chest.

The soldier ran into the stable, then put him down. Kneeling down, he took hold of Dex's shoulders. 'Listen to me, boy. You must hide. Like you always do. You know? Find a place in the straw and burrow deep.'

'Is it a game?' asked Dex.

'Yes, a game. And you must not come out until I come for you. Understand?'

'Yes. But I am hungry.'

'Go now and hide. Do not make a sound, Dex. Just stay hidden.'

He pushed Dex away, and the boy ran to the last stall and ducked inside. The stall was empty and straw had been piled here. Dropping to his belly Dex eased himself into the centre of it, and sat, hugging his knees.

From within the straw Dex could just make out the image of the soldier. He had drawn his sword and was standing quietly. Then more men came, and there were angry shouts and the terrible clanging he had heard earlier. He saw one soldier fall down. Then another. But then the friendly soldier also tumbled to the ground. Other soldiers jumped on him, hitting him again and again with their swords.

Then they began running through the stable, looking in all the stalls.

Dex stayed very quiet.

Halysia had always been told she had courage. By the time she was five she had tumbled from her old pony many times. Her father would tend her bumps and scrapes, and once a broken arm, and as she suffered his rough care he would look into her eyes and tell her how brave she was. Her brothers would laugh at her and put her on the mare again, and she would laugh with them and forget her injuries.

When, at seventeen, she had been sent to wed Anchises she had been terrified at first – of the old man himself, and the dark foreign fortress where she must live, and of the perils of childbirth which had claimed her mother and her beloved sister. But when she was frightened, she would remember her father's dark eyes on her, and his words, 'Have courage, little squirrel. Without courage your life is nothing. With courage you need nothing else.'

Now, some way past her thirtieth year, she no longer believed in her courage. Whatever strength she possessed had been ripped from her during the attack on Dardanos three years before. No night had passed since when she had not been ravaged by fears. Her sleep was broken by terrifying visions in which her son Diomedes fell in flames from the cliff, his screams terrible to hear, and she felt the pain and humiliation as the invaders held her down and brutally raped her, a knife at her throat. She would awake sobbing and Helikaon would reach for her in the darkness and hold her in the fortress of his arms. He told her time and time again she was a brave woman sorely tested, that the fears and nightmares she suffered were natural, but would be overcome.

But he was wrong.

She had known the invaders would come back, known with a certainty which was bone-deep and had nothing to do with her fear. She had always received visions, even as a child among the horse herds of Zeleia. Her simple predictions about the foaling prospects of a young mare, or the illnesses which struck down the wild horses in the wet season, always came true, and her father would smile at her and say she was blessed by Poseidon, who loved horses.

Now, as she sat on the great carved chair of Anchises in the *megaron*, her hands gripping the wide wooden arms in a death-grip, she knew that once again her visions were true. Mykene soldiers were inside the fortress.

Thoughts swarmed like bats through her mind, images flaring. Helikaon had sent word to beware of traitors, to watch for strangers. But it was no stranger who had opened the Seagate. One of her soldiers had seen Menon walking with Mykene officers.

Menon! It was almost inconceivable that he could have committed such a dark and terrible act. He was always charming and thoughtful, and Halysia had believed he was genuinely fond of her. To sell her for rape and slaughter was beyond understanding.

More than 300 Mykene soldiers had entered the citadel, scarcely hindered by Dardanos' depleted garrison. The Mykene had known exactly when to come – they had slipped in on unguarded seas on the one day she had sent – on Menon's advice – Dardania's small remaining fleet to Carpea to escort the fleeing Trojan Horse.

Surrounded by her personal bodyguard of twenty, she sat silent as a stone statue in the *megaron* as they all listened to the sounds of battle outside. Through the high windows she could see the flickering light of flames. She could hear screams and shouts and battle cries. She trembled so badly that her teeth chattered, and she clamped her jaw tightly so the men would not hear.

The bodyguard, handpicked by Helikaon, waited grimly round her, swords in hand. She shook her head, trying to shake free the terror paralysing her mind.

A young blood-covered soldier ran into the *megaron*. 'They have taken the north tower, lady,' he said between laboured breaths. 'The kitchens have been set afire. The eastern barracks have also fallen. There are more Mykene outside the Landgate, but they cannot get in. We are stopping the invaders inside from reaching it.'

'How many more outside?'

'Hundreds.'

'Where is Pausanius?' she managed to ask, surprised that her voice sounded firm.

The soldier shook his head. 'I have not seen him. Rhygmos commands the defence of the *megaron*. Protheos is holding the invaders from the Landgate.'

'What of the boy?'

'I saw him with Gradion, at the stable, but there were Mykene soldiers closing in on them. Gradion took the boy inside. I had to run then. I did not see what followed.'

She stood on leaden legs and turned to the captain of her guard, clasping her hands in front of her to stop them shaking. 'Menesthes, we always knew the *megaron* could not be held. We cannot waste life defending it. We must pull back to the eastern tower.'

Just then the double doors to the *megaron* crashed open, and Mykene soldiers streamed inside. Menesthes drew his sword and rushed at them, followed by his men. Halysia knew they could not hold for long. Then Menesthes shouted back to her, 'Flee, lady! Flee now!'

Halysia gathered up her gown and ran across the great room, pushing open the door to the antechamber, which she barred behind her. It would not stop determined men, armed with axes and swords, but it would delay them.

She paused for a moment, fearing she would black out from the terror in her heart. Forcing her legs to move, she ran up the narrow stone staircase to her bedchamber. Its door was heavy and cross-grained. It would take them a while to batter it down. She closed it behind her and placed the solid wood locking bar across it.

The room was lit by low candles. There were soft rugs on the floor and jewel-coloured tapestries on the walls. She paused for a heartbeat, breathing in the light perfume of roses on the night air, then walked out onto the balcony.

Helikaon had planned for this moment for three years. He respected her visions, and the warrior within him believed even more in Agamemnon's desire for vengeance. Shortly after the last invasion, Halysia's bedchamber had been moved from its old place in the north wing to these rooms high above the sea behind the *megaron*. It boasted a wide stone balcony overlooking the west.

The queen walked to the end of the balcony and thrust aside a hanging curtain of creeping plants. Looking down, she could see the first of the short wooden bars set into the stone of the outside wall.

Under cover of renovations to her new apartments, lengths of seasoned oak had been set deep into the stone, descending to an overgrown garden overlooking the sea. No guards or palace servants were permitted to enter the garden, and it had been allowed to grow wild with roses and vines. The work had been skilfully done, and it was hard to discern the handholds from the ground, even if you knew what to look for.

The craftsmen responsible for the work had returned to her brother's tribe in Zeleia, heaped with honour and silver, and sworn to secrecy.

With Helikaon absent, only two people in the fortress knew of the escape route beside herself: Pausanius, of course, and his aide Menon.

Menon, the betrayer!

She hesitated in an agony of indecision, looking at the escape route into darkness. What choice do I have, she thought? I cannot stay here and wait for them.

She bent over the balcony wall and listened, trying to calm the thumping of her heart. She could hear nothing in the undergrowth below. All was still.

She hurried back to the door of her room and listened there. She heard the distant pounding of metal on wood as they battered down the antechamber door.

Moving to a great carved wooden chest, she heaved open the heavy lid. It thumped against the wall. Pushing aside embroidered shawls and gem-encrusted gowns, she pulled clear an old servant's tunic of dull blue, and a hooded cloak in dirty brown. Rummaging deeper she found the scabbarded dagger her father had given her on her fifteenth birthday. It had a handle of deerhorn, and a curved blade of shining bronze. She slipped off her dress of white linen and donned the drab tunic. Then, taking a deep breath, she unbarred the door to her room and opened it a crack. From below the sound of splintering wood was loud in her ears. She could hear the grunts and shouts of men struggling with broken timbers.

She stood calmly and thought her plan through one more time. Then she carefully placed the locking bar against the wall and opened the door wide.

* * *

Pelopidas the Spartan ran up the narrow stairs, his bloody sword in his hand. He knew what he would find. One more locked door, which the axemen following him would splinter in a few heartbeats. The queen would not be inside. She would have taken the secret climb to the garden below, where more of his men were waiting for her. Or, he thought, with quickening desire, she would see the men below and climb, in panic, back to the bedchamber. Pelopidas hoped this was true. Far more comfortable to rape her on a bed. Easier on his ageing knees.

A veteran with greying hair and beard in long braids, Pelopidas reached the top of the stairs, and saw the door wide open. Stupid bitch, he thought. In her terror she had made it all the more easy for them. He was followed by three other men, all sweating and cursing the splinters in their hands from breaking down the lower door. They went straight out onto the narrow balcony. Pelopidas thrust aside the tattered curtain of plants, tearing them down.

'You two,' he said, gesturing at his men. 'Follow her down. When you catch her bring her back here. I want her first.'

The two soldiers looked doubtfully at the narrow handholds and the drop into darkness beyond, but they followed his orders, as he knew they would, climbing swiftly over the stone wall and lowering themselves down.

Pelopidas grunted and returned to the bedchamber. The last soldier was standing by the bedside, rummaging in a jewellery box decorated with ivory.

'Leave that, you scumbag,' said Pelopidas. 'You know what the general said about looting. Get below and find that damned child. There's twenty gold rings for the team that brings his head to Katheos.'

'How are we going to find him?' answered the man. 'The stable was empty. He could be anywhere.'

'He's three years old – and alone. He'll be huddled somewhere weeping and shitting himself. Now go!'

The soldier lingered for a moment, looking round the bedchamber, at the soft gleam of gold and jewels all around. Then he ran from the room.

Pelopidas sat down on the soft bed, and rubbed at his left knee. There was swelling there, and the joint was stiff. Stretching out on the bed he caught the scent of perfume from the pillow. Arousal swept through him. It was said the queen was slim and beautiful, though past thirty now, golden-haired and sweet of face. He chuckled. It wasn't her face that interested him.

The bitch had to die, and die slowly, so the Burner would hear of it and know it was vengeance for his raids on the mainland. Pelopidas felt his anger rising at the thought of the villages burned and sailors drowned by the vile Helikaon and his crew. Those crew would lose many of their loved ones before this night was over.

The Spartan took off his helm, and dropped it to the floor. Rising from the bed he stepped over to a flagon of water on a small table and took a great swig. Then he poured some over his head, shaking his braids.

He looked round assessingly at the bedchamber, its soft draperies and the gleam of bronze, copper and gold in every corner. He breathed in the scent of flowers. Lifting the carved ivory box that the soldier had been searching he saw the dark sparkle of jewellery. Reaching in, he pulled out a handful of gold and gems, scarcely glancing at them before thrusting them into the leather pouch at his side. There was a heavy gold bracelet, worth a year's pay, and he slid that into the pouch too.

His eyes alighted on the huge wooden chest, its lid flung open as if left in haste. Inside among folds of embroidered cloth he could see the gleam of gems. Dragging out the top garment, he found it was decorated with gold wire, amber and carnelian. He hesitated, wondering what to do with it, then snorted with laughter at himself. He could hardly carry a woman's dress on campaign.

Filled with good humour, he bent down to delve deeper into the chest, searching for hidden jewellery. Suddenly he detected a movement deep in its depths and, in the heartbeat it took him to react, a face, white and ghost-like, surged up towards him. He felt an agonizing pain in his throat, and fell back, blood gouting out in front of him. Panic-stricken, he clutched at his throat, trying to stop the fountain of blood. A small, golden-haired woman climbed from the chest, a gory dagger in her hand.

Pelopidas struggled to his knees and tried to call out for help, but pain seared through his severed vocal cords, and blood gouted between his fingers. The woman was staring at him with wide eyes. He felt his limbs weakening, his life draining away.

His head struck the floor, and he found himself staring at the pattern of deep red swirls on the rug. It seemed then that the rug was melting, crimson fluid spreading across it. A great calm settled on him. Something warm flowed across his leg, and he realized his bladder was emptying.

Have to get up, he thought. Have to find . . .

Halysia stood very still, watching the dying man thrash upon the floor, his blood pumping over the ornate rug. Her thoughts fluttered like moths round the flame of reality. His throat was severed. She had killed him. But all she could think of was that the rug had been a gift from her father on her wedding to Anchises, embroidered with eastern silk. The blood will not come out, she thought.

Forget the blood, came the harsh voice of reason. Halysia blinked, and took a deep breath. The warrior's leg twitched. Then he was still. Stepping back from the body she sheathed the dagger.

You must get out! They will return!

Donning the brown hooded cloak she ran down the steps and through the shattered remains of the ante-room door. Pausing at the entrance to the *megaron* she peered inside. All was silent. Her bodyguards lay slain, more than thirty enemy dead around them. The stone floor was awash with blood, the room thick with the smell of death.

Fear struck her anew, knotting her stomach. She wanted to run as fast as she could, and put this scene of nightmare behind her. Failing that she needed a place to hide, some dark and gloomy hole the enemy would not find.

Then the face of her son appeared in her mind. She was shaken by the image. Instead of seeing, as she usually did, the living proof of her rape, and the constant reminder of the murder of her beloved Diomedes, she saw now his large, imploring eyes, and the sweetness of his mouth, so much like hers. Halysia gave a soft groan. At least Dio had known the love of a mother. He had been held and nurtured, caressed, and told many times how much she loved him. Little Dex – as Pausanius had so accurately pointed out – had been starved of her affection.

And now cruel men were seeking to kill him.

Instinct urged her to run out of the *megaron* to the stables, in the hope that Dex was still there. Reason told her she would never make it. A running figure would be spotted. Halysia decided to make her way through the side entrance of the *megaron*, pass by the kitchens, and reach the stables from the back.

Determination fuelling her courage, she made her way to the side door. She could hear shouting from beyond it, and saw movement as a shadow crossed the doorway. Crouching down behind a column she waited, not even daring to breathe. Then there was silence. Carefully she rose, and peered round the column. Whoever had paused in the doorway had moved on.

The kitchens beyond had been destroyed by fire. The wooden buildings must have gone up like tinder, she thought, but now the fire was largely over. A pall of thick choking smoke lay over the vegetable gardens in front of the building. Halysia slipped into the smoke, disappearing like a wraith in sunlight.

She could hardly breathe and dropped down to her hands and knees, hugging the stones, where a carpet of fresh air flowed gently beneath the smoke. Carefully she crawled along the path to the stables, her knees snagging in the drapes of her tunic and cloak. Along the way she passed many bodies, some dead, some mortally wounded.

Ahead she glimpsed movement and lay still. Mykene soldiers, some coughing and spluttering, came striding towards her. Pressing her face to the earth she lay as one dead, eyes closed. Feet pounded close by, then came a sharp command to halt.

A foot slammed into the back of her thigh. The soldier stumbled and swore. The pain made her bite her lip, but she made no sound.

'Damned smoke all over the place,' came a voice. 'Can't see a thing.'

'It's no use running around in this,' said another. 'Let's get to the Landgate, kill the bastard defenders and let the Atreans in. Then we can loot the place and get out.'

'Shut your mouth,' said a third voice irritably. 'That boy's head is worth twenty gold rings. Now keep looking.'

The men hurried off. Halysia remained where she was until the creak of leather and their grunting breaths passed from earshot. Then she came to her feet and ran for the stables.

It was pitch dark inside and she could hear the horses moving anxiously, smelling the fires. She walked among them confidently, speaking quietly to them, patting the solid warm horseflesh that bumped gently against her as she felt her way through the stable.

'Dex,' she whispered into the gloom. 'Are you here? Dex.'

She could hear nothing but the sounds of horses and the far shouts of men. Then she heard a command that caused her heart to beat wildly. 'Fetch fire. If he's hiding in the stables we'll smoke him out.'

The horses shifted and whinnied around her, but soon calmed as she walked among them. Only the great black horse carried on clattering in his box, banging his flanks against the wooden sides, and kicking out against the barred stall door.

'Dex! Dexios. Are you here?' she whispered urgently.

Suddenly she stopped. Standing motionless in the dim rays filtering in from the entrance to the barn, she saw a small figure, hands to his face. Motes of straw whirled in the heavy light around him. He was quite still, quite silent. For a heartbeat mother and son stood looking at one another.

Then a small voice asked, 'Are you angry with me, Mama?'

She knelt down and opened her arms. 'I'm not angry with you, Dex. Now we must go. We must run away.'

He ran to her then, and his small body hit hers with the force of a battering ram, almost knocking her over. She felt his arms round her neck, his wet, grubby face against hers.

Picking the child up she ran to the front of the stable. If she could just make it down to the outer wall, and the hidden postern gate, she could carry Dex out into the countryside, and hide in one of the many caves.

Looking out she saw a group of enemy soldiers running towards the building, flaming torches in their hands. Hugging the boy to her, she fled back to the rear entrance, and peered though a crack in the door. Just paces away she saw a burly Mykene warrior. In one hand he grasped the hair of a young horse boy. In the other he held a blood-covered sword which he slashed across the lad's throat. The tow-headed boy twitched as his lifeblood ran out. The soldier dropped him to the earth and turned towards the stable door.

Quelling her panic, Halysia carried Dex back through the stable and stood holding the boy, eyeing both entrances. Hefting the child into one arm, she backed up against the stall where the black horse was fidgeting and clattering.

There was no way out now, and within a few heart-beats the enemy would find her and her son.

'Not this time!' she whispered. 'Not again!'

Reaching behind her she opened the door of the stall and slipped inside. The huge black horse regarded her with a wild eye but made no move. Putting Dex down she moved to the horse and took his head in her hands, resting her cheek against his dark face, feeling the hot breath.

'I need you now, greatest of horses,' she whispered. 'I need your strength and your courage.'

Patting the horse for reassurance, she picked Dex up

and set him on the beast's back. The horse shifted about but then was still. Levering herself against the side of the stall, she climbed up behind the child. Putting her face close to his ear she said, 'Courage, little squirrel. Be brave!'

'I will, Mama!'

The main doorway to the barn burst open and torch-bearing Mykene warriors swarmed in. Taking a deep breath, she leaned over and flung wide the stall door, then grabbed the horse's mane and kicked at his sides. With all the breath in her body Halysia screamed the war cry of the Zeleians.

The horse bunched its great muscles and took off at a run, its huge hooves clattering on the stone floor.

The Mykene warriors shouted out as the horse surged towards them, waving burning brands to frighten it. Instead it thundered into them. One man was hurled from his feet, his head smashing against a timber column. A second went down under the stallion, and Halysia heard the sickening crack of a hoof striking bone. The other warriors leapt aside.

Outside the stable Halysia made for the Landgate. If it was open now she could ride straight through and down the defile to the bridge at Parnio's Folly.

They sped through the great courtyard, hearing the shouts of the enemy as they realized who rode the horse. An arrow hissed by her. Then another. Drawing Dex more tightly to her, she urged the stallion into a full gallop.

The Landgate was just ahead, beyond the next

corner. The horse's hooves skidded on the stones as she turned him.

Ahead she saw that a battle was still being fought. And the gate was closed.

A group of Dardanian soldiers, engaged in a desperate last stand, had formed a shield wall in the gateway. They were close to being overwhelmed.

Halysia dragged her mount to a halt, and there was an eerie pause as the fighting came to a slow stop. Her soldiers looked at her with sudden recognition and wonder, and she looked down with pride at their doomed faces. Some of the Mykene turned and saw her, and she heard a voice snarl, 'That's her! That's the queen! Get the bitch!'

With the enemy's attention distracted the Dardanians clove into them with renewed effort and she saw many Mykene go down. She knew she had bought her soldiers more time. But now some of the Mykene were racing towards her.

Swinging the great horse she dug her heels into his flanks. Half rearing, he came down running. Halysia headed him down the stone streets and cobbled alleys leading to the Seagate and the high cliff. She felt a painful blow to her thigh. Glancing down she saw an arrow there, buried deep in her leg. A dull ache began, then flared into sharp pain.

The Seagate came into view, its huge stone towers looming up in the darkness. The few soldiers around it scattered as the stallion bore down on them. Then the great horse galloped on, under the stone and marble gateway, and out into the night.

Halysia knew she could not keep to the road. It would carry them down to the beach and more Mykene soldiers. Dragging back on the horse's mane she shifted her body weight, causing the beast to turn. Its hooves clattered on stone, then slipped as the precipice loomed. For a moment Halysia thought it would fall from the cliff, but it righted itself and ran on, up the narrow path alongside the walls.

In daylight this ride was perilous, but at night, she knew, only luck and the blessings of many gods would see them to safety.

The stallion climbed on, moving slowly over the broken ground. At the highest point, where Halysia knew the path narrowed, she halted him. The walls towered up on her left, and to her right she could see the star-spattered sea, and the Mykene galleys gathered all along the beach.

Then she saw another fleet beating towards Dardanos across the Hellespont. For a moment she thought they were more Mykene vessels, then she recognized the great bulk of the *Xanthos*. Exhilaration swept through her.

Her husband was coming home, and now the Mykene would know the meaning of fear. His vengeance upon the enemy would be both terrifying to behold, and good to savour.

The Mykene crews on the beach had also seen the Dardanian fleet, and were racing to launch their vessels. Halysia smiled. Whether they sought to run or to fight the result would be the same. They were all dead men.

Relief washed over her. All she had to do was wait quietly beneath the walls until Helikaon came ashore.

Then something hissed by her, striking the stones and ricocheting off. She heard shouts from above, and gazed up to see men leaning over the battlements.

Hugging Dex tightly to her, she patted the horse on the shoulder, speaking firmly and calmly to him. Gently she urged him on. Arrows flashed by her, startling the horse. 'Be calm, great one,' she whispered soothingly. Dressed in a dark cloak, and sitting a black horse, she made a poor target for night shooting. Even so, if they stayed where they were, a shaft would eventually strike home. Halysia decided to circle the fortress, outrun the enemy soldiers beyond the Landgate, then make her way to Parnio's Folly and safety.

The land dropped away sharply to her right into darkness. On her left the walls of the citadel rose like a cliff. The big horse dropped his head and carefully picked his way along the narrow path. At times his hooves slipped on the crumbling rock. Arrows continued to slash by them, but few came close.

When the Landgate came into view she saw it was still holding. Hundreds of Mykene troops were milling around uselessly outside, waiting for their comrades inside to open the gates. There were cries and curses of frustration, but they were all staring at the walls, at the gates, and had no attention to pay to a woman and a horse quietly emerging from the darkness.

Halysia saw movement in the distance, and a line of brightly armoured horsemen appeared there. The Trojan Horse had arrived! The Mykene saw them too, and began to form a defensive shield wall.

Then someone shouted from the battlements, 'The queen is escaping! Kill her!'

There were only a few horsemen beyond the gates, but they immediately kicked their horses into a run.

Halysia heeled the black stallion and he took off again, racing past the rear of the Mykene forces, and straight for the defile. Glancing round she saw four Mykene riders falling back. The stallion was pounding now at full gallop, and his speed was colossal. Halysia had ridden many horses in her life, but none had the strength and the speed of this huge beast.

She felt the wind in her hair, and allowed her heart to lift. Helikaon would sink the enemy fleet, and the Trojan Horse would slaughter the enemy soldiers left on land. All she needed to do was outrun the Mykene riders, and she would be safe.

The stallion galloped on, and she saw the defile widen just before the bridge. Only now there was no bridge – merely a smoking ruin. Its remains hung blackened and charred, dangling from the edge of the chasm. There was no way out.

A group of Mykene soldiers came running out of the darkness beside the defile, sprinting towards her, shining blades in their hands. Swinging her mount Halysia rode back along the defile, then turned again. The Mykene horsemen were close now, and she heard their shouts of triumph.

'Whatever happens, little Dex, we will be together,' she promised. Then she slapped the stallion's rump. Startled, he set off down the defile towards the chasm.

His speed increased as he thundered on. Halysia held his mane in a death grip. She saw soldiers just a blur in the corner of her eye. She felt a blow in her side, but the spear point ripped through her flesh, and did not bring her down. Pain seared through her. Ignoring it, she focused on the horse moving beneath her, the small warm body huddled against her, and the chasm yawning just ahead.

Could even this great horse make such a jump? Halysia did not know. What she did know was that the horse might baulk at the edge, and throw her and her son to the rocks below.

As they closed towards the chasm she dug her heels into the horse's side for the last time and screamed her tribal yell, the sound high-pitched and ululating. The horse bunched his great muscles and leapt.

Time came to an end. The only sound was the beating of her heart. There was stillness all around. She could not feel the horse's back. She could not feel the boy at her breast. She wondered if her life had ended there and the gods were carrying her away. She even had time to glance down, at the jagged black rocks so far below.

Then the stallion's hooves hit the ground on the other side of the chasm. The horse stumbled a moment, his rear hooves scrabbling on the lip of the cliff. Then they were over and running free.

Halysia halted the stallion and looked back at the Mykene. Not one of them had the nerve to follow her, and they screamed insults at her. Then they rode back along the defile. Weariness flowed over her.

'Have the bad men gone, Mama?' asked Dex.

'Yes, they have gone, little squirrel.' Halysia lifted her leg and jumped down from the horse. She cried out as the arrow in her thigh twisted, ripping her flesh. Sitting down on a rock she released the boy. He did not move away, but clung to her. Halysia kissed his brow.

'You are my son, little Dex. And I am so proud of you. Soon your father will be home, and he will be proud of you too. We will sit here quietly and wait for him.' The child looked up at her and smiled. Such a sweet smile, she thought, like sunshine spearing through cloud.

The left side of her tunic was drenched with blood from the spear wound. She thought to stem the bleeding with her cloak. But then the cloth slipped from her fingers. It seemed to her that the night was growing brighter. Someone was close by. Halysia turned her head with a great effort. The light was almost blinding now. A small, golden-haired figure came into sight. Halysia squinted against the brightness – then cried out with joy. It was Diomedes, her son. He was smiling at her, and holding out his arms.

Tears filled Halysia's eyes. Both her sons were with her now, and the world was in harmony again. In that one, blissful moment, as the light faded, Halysia realized she had never been happier.

EPILOGUE

WHITE LONG-HAIRED GOATS WERE GRAZING ON THE CLIFFS beneath the high walls of the palace of King's Joy. The animals darted away as Kassandra made her way to the cliff top, and she paused to watch them. So sure footed, she thought, as they leapt from rock to rock. No fear of heights, or the sharp rocks so far below. Was it confidence or stupidity, she wondered, or a mixture of both?

Kassandra moved past them, climbing to the highest point above the shore. Hitching up her ankle-length tunic of glistening white she sat upon a rock and gazed out to sea. There were no ships in sight, and only five vessels were drawn up on the once busy beaches below. A score of small fishing boats were out in the bay, casting their nets.

Up here, high above the world, all seemed peaceful and serene. Kassandra glanced towards the south. Beyond the line of the Ida mountains armies were moving, preparing for war and death, rape and murder. A brief and ghastly vision of fire and horror swept into her mind, but she ruthlessly suppressed it. Turning her gaze towards the north she saw again the images of last night's dream, the fortress of Dardanos engulfed in flames.

Thraki was lost, and soon the Mykene would be crossing the straits into Dardania. From north and south the enemy would come, their armies closing like a great fist around the golden city.

Then the peaceful beaches below would play host to a fleet of ships so large that not a speck of sand would be seen between their hulls. Kassandra shivered in the bright sunshine.

A moment of brilliant doubt touched her then. All these visions might not be true.

Slowly she pushed herself to her feet, and edged her way to stand above the awesome drop. To test the truth of them all she had to do was take a single step forward. If she fell to her death on the jagged rocks, then they were false, for there would be no winter journey to Thera, no flight into the midday sky, no roaring thunder and the end of worlds. Troy might survive, and Hektor live to be a great king.

Just one step . . .

Taking a deep breath she closed her eyes and stepped forward.

Rough hands grabbed her, hauling her back from the precipice.

'What are you doing?' asked a young shepherd boy, holding tight to her arms.

Kassandra did not answer him.

The journey to Thera would be long – and full of perils.

THE END